the last hun†ress

Published by SparkPress, a BookSparks imprint,
A division of SparkPoint Studio, LLC
Phoenix, Arizona, USA, 85007
www.gosparkpress.com

Published 2022
Printed in the United States of America
Print ISBN: 978-1-68463-173-5
E-ISBN: 978-1-68463-174-2

Library of Congress Control Number: 2022910136

Interior design by Tabitha Lahr

MIRROR REALM SERIES BOOK I

the last huntress

LENORE BORJA

SPARKPRESS

ALICE WATCHED THE BLOOD POOL *into a dip in the asphalt.
It was darker than she'd imagined—thicker. It began to spill over,
creeping toward the toe of her sneaker. She stepped back.*

*The headlights from Hadley's car pierced through the blackness
like a neon sign, its message a blatant warning: Keep moving. Way
too much to see here.*

"Alice, honey, we need to hurry."

*Someone killed the engine. She knelt down, her eyes adjusting
to the dark. Three flashlights flicked on in quick succession, their
beams crossing back and forth as the word "hurry" hung in the air.
She watched one of them pause on a wrist. Two fingers with black nail
polish took center stage, searching for a pulse they would never find.*

*Olivia's voice broke the silence. "He's gone. Alice, you still
with us?"*

"Relax. Just give her a minute."

"I can't believe it came to this."

"He didn't give us much of a choice," she heard herself say.

"No," Soxie agreed. "No, he didn't."

*There was no turning back. It was done. She felt a hand on her
shoulder.*

"It's okay if you need to sit the rest of this out."

Alice stood and looked around. The desert was dark and quiet. Cold. It was the last place she expected to be, in the end.

She looked into her friend's eyes, barely visible in the moonless night.

"No. Let's finish this."

part
one

chapter 1

One year earlier

"Sweetheart, can you get that?"

Alice set down the glass she was unwrapping and peeled herself off the kitchen floor.

"Coming!" she called, weaving her way through stacks of boxes. Something furry and black darted in front of her. She tripped.

"Dammit, Boop!"

He meowed like his tail had just been caught in a mousetrap.

"Oh, like it's my fault?"

Yellow eyes regarded her with scorn. The doorbell rang again.

"Alice! Can you please get the door?"

"COMING!"

She hopped to the foyer as Boop ran figure eights between her legs. Exasperated, she scooped him up and held him tight to her chest as she pulled the door open with her free hand.

"Yes?" she said, with maybe a bit too much bite.

"Hi, I'm David."

He was as handsome as they come, and she was suddenly very aware of her ratty appearance. She attempted to smooth her hair back but was interrupted by claws digging into her neck. The stranger on her doorstep stepped forward.

"Aw, hi, kitty," he said, reaching toward the squirming feline.

Boop flattened his ears and hissed. Then a razor-sharp claw sliced into Alice's arm.

"Ow!" she cried, releasing her hold. Boop leapt over her shoulder and disappeared back into the house, leaving her disheveled and more than a little embarrassed.

"Nice cat."

"Sorry," she said, licking her finger to dab at the fresh wound. "He's not usually like that. I think he's just stressed from the move."

"Colorado, right?"

She looked up. His green eyes sparkled in the afternoon sun. "How did you know that?"

He smiled. A devilish sort of smile. The kind tall, dark, and swoon-worthy guys like him perfected. The kind girls like her needed to be leery of.

"License plate," he said, gesturing casually behind him to the Volvo in the driveway.

"Oh. Right. Sorry, who are you again?"

"David Martin. I live down the block. Saw the moving truck and thought I'd stop by, welcome you to the neighborhood."

"Oh, okay. Thanks." He seemed nice enough, but something about him was unsettling.

"So . . . Do you have a name? Or should I just call you 'girl with the psycho cat'?"

She laughed and extended her hand. "Sorry. I'm Alice. Alice Daniels."

He took her hand in his. The unsettling feeling increased tenfold.

"Alice," he repeated, leaning forward until his face was inches from hers. "It's nice to meet you."

Smiling uneasily, she pulled hard until she wrenched free from his grasp.

"Hello. Can we help you?"

His eyes darted over her shoulder, and he didn't miss a beat.

"You must be Ms. Daniels."

Alice turned as her mother paused at the doorway. She could tell from her face she was already smitten; it took everything in her power not to roll her eyes.

"Mom, this is David. He lives down the street and stopped by to welcome us to the neighborhood."

"Well, isn't that nice," her mom said as she reached out to shake his hand. "Good to meet you, David. And call me Judy. Do you go to Remington?"

"I do," he said, glancing at Alice. "You too? Senior?"

Something told her he already knew that. Her eyes wanted to narrow, but it would be too obvious. So she just said yes instead.

He slapped his palm on his thigh. "Then you have to come to the real party tonight!"

"As opposed to a fake one?"

"Alice," Judy tsked. "Don't be rude."

He chuckled. "Sorry, that was confusing. *The Remington Reel.* It's kind of a newsletter-slash-blog. They're having a back-to-school party tonight."

"Well, that sounds like fun. She'd love to come."

"Mom . . ." Alice said, grabbing hold of her mom's arm and squeezing tight. "I thought we were unpacking tonight."

Judy ignored her. "David, just tell us when she should be ready."

He dug his hands in his pockets and slid his gaze back to Alice. "Pick you up at eight."

"You realize he could be a serial killer."

Judy shook her head as she cut into a box of books. "You're so dramatic. He seemed perfectly nice."

"So did Ted Bundy."

"Alice, would a serial killer stop by just to welcome you to the neighborhood?"

"Are you kidding? Yes. One hundred percent, yes."

Judy tossed the box cutter on the floor and pinched the bridge of her nose. "I'm sorry, honey. You're right. I was just trying to help."

"It's okay, Mom. But you don't have to worry about me. I'm fine. I promise."

Judy closed her eyes and nodded. They spent the rest of the afternoon unpacking in silence.

Alice was in the tub reading when the doorbell rang at eight.

It had been a long day. The last thing she wanted to do was to go to a not-fake party with a guy who might be planning to chop her into little pieces. She heard the front door open and craned her neck to listen. The sound of muffled voices carried up the stairs. She waited, silently urging her mom to get rid of him faster. Normally she'd feel guilty for bailing, but in this case she just felt relieved when the front door finally closed. Even the house seemed to shudder and settle back into its eighty-year-old foundation, as if breathing a sigh of relief on her behalf.

She tossed her damp Austen paperback aside, leaned back, and sank further into the warm water. The drip-drip of the old faucet echoed in the cavernous bathroom, putting her in a trancelike state. She counted the seconds between each drop, wondering how long before it would need to be fixed. Her grandparents' house may have once been the nicest on the street, but now, after sitting empty and neglected for longer than most HOAs allow, it was the neighborhood eyesore.

She stared at the peeling wallpaper with the faded yellow daisies. All she could do was imagine them when they were new and vibrant. When two little girls shared this same clawfoot tub, covered in bubbles and giggling.

It had to be strange for her mom. Coming back here after all this time, dusting off old furniture full of memories. She thought about how angry her aunt Molly had been when she found out—the vitriol in her voice as she shouted through the phone. Alice had been ten feet away and had still heard both sides of the conversation, loud and clear.

You know how I feel about that place!

I'm sorry, Molly. But this isn't about you.

Fine. At least let Alice come live with me. Don't drag her down with you.

She's my daughter. Not yours. And it's her choice.

I'll never forgive you for this! Do you hear me?

Alice closed her eyes, held her breath, and pulled herself under. She stayed like that for several seconds, relishing the calm beneath the surface. The quiet. Her life for the past year had been too chaotic. The affair. The divorce. It sucked leaving the only real home she'd ever known, but it was getting too hard watching Judy struggle to cope—seeing her break apart bit by bit with each passing day. They'd had to leave. And Phoenix had been the only option.

Her lungs began to burn. She opened her eyes, imagining what it must have been like for Molly, lying here under ten inches of water that slowly turned red.

Her mom was pounding on the door. "Alice?"

She broke through the surface, inhaling and squeezing her eyes shut from the sting of the soap. "Yes?"

"That boy David left the address to the party, in case you change your mind. It's only a few blocks away."

"Not interested."

"Honey, he had friends with him. Even a couple of girls. Are you sure?"

Alice put her head in her hands. If she didn't go, Judy would pester her for days, her guilt somehow threatening to suffocate them both.

"Fine. But I'm not staying long."

Attention all Senior Sharks! One final reminder about tonight's back-to-school party at Chez Carver. It's your last weekend of freedom before senior year officially begins, so don't waste it at home binge-watching your favorite serial. It'll still be there tomorrow, so get off your lazy butt and live a little. Your forty-year-old self will thank you. Link to directions here.

See you there!
Your friends at The Reel

There was still enough light left in the sky, so she decided to walk. Even with her hair wet, it was still hot. She pulled at her shirt, wondering if a sundress would have been a better idea. But as usual, she'd gone with comfortable and safe: a plain T-shirt, jeans, and sneakers. If Chloe and Rachel were with her now, they'd probably scoff. Chloe would say something like, "It's a party, Alice, not a baseball game." Rachel would laugh and tell Chloe to back off while secretly agreeing with her, then gently convince Alice to at least put on some makeup.

As pushy as they could be, they were still her two closest friends. Her only friends, if she was being honest. And of course she was going to miss them, but part of her had always felt like an outsider to their dynamic duo—the new girl they adopted in second grade when it just so happened three was more fun than two. They'd always be her friends, but the truth was she'd never felt easy in their spotlight and they had to be tired of dragging her, kicking and screaming, into it.

She looked down, watching each boring sneaker as it stepped in front of the other, as she slowly walked through the stifling heat toward her new life. She may have been born here, but this place had never been home, and after her grandparents' passing ten years ago, it had become even less so. There had never been a reason for them to come back.

Until now.

She teased her wet hair with her hands and looked up at the smattering of stars competing with the fading light. At least it was just one year. It was just high school. She'd get through it—maybe even learn to like it here.

She slowed her pace and closed her eyes, listening for the sounds of the desert. Aunt Molly had made her do this once when they were hiking near Estes Park. "Close your eyes and listen," she said. "Maybe the forest will sing for you." To her dismay, Alice never heard a thing, but Molly swore up and down that it *was* singing. She just wasn't listening hard enough.

She smiled as she thought of her strange and beautiful aunt. If anyone could make listening to trees seem de rigueur, it was Molly.

Well, it wasn't like she was in a hurry. She slowed her pace even more, extending her awareness, trying to make her aunt proud.

She listened. Distant traffic hummed. Palm leaves rustled. Otherwise, nothing that could be construed as "song." The desert was not obliging. She frowned, straining to listen harder. She worked on parsing out and identifying each new noise before moving on to the next. A car horn. A faraway siren. A lawn mower that could be a leaf blower—she wasn't sure.

And then, suddenly, there it was. Cicadas. How had she missed them? Once she noticed them, they were impossible to ignore. The sound was strong and determined, mocking her for the oversight. It filled the air, ebbing and flowing like the constant rolling of ocean waves. The rhythm was subtle, but it was there. Molly was right. The desert was singing.

She would have laughed out loud, but a strange tickle in her stomach pulled her from the insect aria. She stopped and looked down, wondering if one of the little buggers had somehow flown down her shirt. But it wasn't that kind of tickle. No . . . it was more of a tingle. A tingle *inside* her stomach, like the kind she felt when she was nervous or excited. Only this was much stronger. So strong it felt like there really could be a bug in there, buzzing around and maybe even helping itself to the pepperoni pizza she'd eaten for dinner.

Something was definitely happening. She looked back up, peering into the dim light of dusk and the long sidewalk that stretched ahead. Nothing seemed out of place. Most of the houses around her were lit from within, their occupants settling in for post-dinner television or putting young children to bed. Vehicles were already tucked into garages, and with the exception of her cicadas, the neighborhood was quiet.

Her stomach moved again, this time with more force. It was nudging her like an invisible hand, all but pulling her backward. Whatever was happening, it was happening behind her. Her breath held and her hands shaking, she slowly turned around.

A blue car was idling in the middle of the street, two houses down, sitting there like it was waiting for a row of geese to cross the road. Only there were no geese. Or turtles, or lizards, or whatever else might cross a road in Phoenix. There was nothing but empty blacktop and an unexplainable feeling that the driver of the car was stopped because of *her*. She stared at the dark figure behind the wheel, convinced with every fiber of her being that the figure was staring back. Her heart began to race and the tingling in her stomach turned to a flutter, like a butterfly flapping its wings for the first time.

The car began slowly accelerating toward her.

At that moment a tsunami of feelings slammed into her all at once, nearly sucking the air from her lungs. Confusion. Excitement. Anxiety. Euphoria. Before she could even take a breath, the flutter in her stomach turned into a frenzy—this time like a thousand butterflies taking flight. Or maybe even locusts. It was so intense she clutched her midsection, lest the swarm of locusts exit her belly button and bring with it the end of days.

It frightened her. Not because she was scared of whoever was in that car. Because in fact she had an irrational urge to throw herself in front of it. To stop it from driving away, stop it from ever, ever leaving.

It made no sense, and that's what scared her. That's what made her turn and run.

It felt wrong, somehow. Like she was running from something she should be running to. Yet her feet barely touched the ground as she sprinted into the night. She ran and ran, ignoring the stitch in her side and the pepperoni threatening to come back up. Whether her actions were rational or not, she didn't care. She was spooked.

She was in decent shape but not a typical runner in the athletic sense—yoga was more her thing—so it was only a matter of time before she lost steam and had to stop to catch her breath. After a couple minutes bent over and wheezing, she almost forgot why she had been running in the first place.

When she finally stood and turned around, the street behind her was empty, and her butterflies were gone. She couldn't help but wonder if they'd ever been there at all.

She had to backtrack ten blocks to get to the address David had left her. She considered heading home, but when she saw all the cars parked on the street, curiosity got the better of her. She needed a distraction. A dose of normal to drown out the abnormal.

Whoever ran *The Remington Reel* had gone all out for a back-to-school party. A banner displaying their class year hung from the roof, and the trees out front were covered in purple-and-white lights. Her new school colors.

She twisted her hair into a top knot and ascended the steps to the front porch. A few kids were leaning against the railing, vaping. She noticed one of them pass eyes over her, then quickly lose interest. It surprised her at first, until she remembered she was alone. Chloe and Rachel were the head-turners. She'd always been more filler.

Attempting not to look as self-conscious as she felt, she ignored the vapers and made her way to the front door, which was ajar. She squared her shoulders and pushed through.

The outside made her expect more, but on the inside, it was just a typical party. Loud music. Red solo cups. Random bits of pretzels and popcorn littering the floor. People huddled in their respective groups, chatting about whatever amazing show was streaming or debating the latest hot-button topic trending on social media.

She gave a group of dancing girls a wide berth, eyeing the amber liquid as it spilled from their cups, and paused to watch a trio of guys in the corner playing with VR glasses. Even with life happening five feet away, they seemed perfectly content with the virtual over the real.

With no obvious icebreaker at the ready, she slowly navigated her way through the house and did her best to blend in. She made eye contact with a few people, and even smiled once or twice. But nobody seemed interested in starting a conversation, so she kept moving.

Eventually she made it to the backyard, which was clearly the hub of the party. It was landscaped and well adorned, full of twinkling white lights and purple balloons. Partygoers mingled around tables of food while others sat on the edge of a bean-shaped pool, cooling their feet in the lukewarm water.

"Welcome back, Sharks!" shouted a voice through a megaphone.

Alice automatically looked up. Someone in a shark costume was standing on the second-floor balcony with a water cannon. And he wasn't alone.

"Suck it, Tapper!" a guy by the pool yelled.

There was no time to react. Four heavy streams of water began pummeling the backyard, one of them hitting her square in the sternum before she realized what was happening. She sputtered as water ricocheted up her nose, then stumbled backward as another stream made contact with her stomach. Within seconds a joyful sort of chaos erupted—everyone running, screaming, and laughing at the same time. Alice ducked and ran toward the house, soaked to the bone by the time she was out of the line of fire.

She couldn't help but laugh along with everybody else. She was a drowned rat, but the cool water felt nice just the same.

A girl with wet hair plastered to her face stopped next to her, giggling like a maniac. Together they laughed, almost hugging each other over the absurdity of their situation.

"Come on," the girl said. "Let's get inside and dry off."

Alice stopped to wring out her shirt before following her toward the sliding glass doors.

"Wet T-shirt contest. Nice."

Her back stiffened. His voice was easy to recognize; it was full of confidence, with a heavy dose of rude. Watching with disappointment as her new friend disappeared into the house, she pulled her shirt away from her body and kept it there before turning around.

"Hi, David."

"Glad you made it."

The wicked gleam in his eye confirmed her earlier suspicions. Okay, maybe he wasn't a serial killer, but he was definitely not a nice guy. She could feel it.

"Yeah, well. Thanks for the invitation. It was nice seeing you." She turned to go.

He stepped in front of her. "Whoa, where do you think you're going?"

She gave him a hard look. "Home. Not that it's any of your business."

"After I went through all that trouble to get you here? I don't think so."

Inexplicable goose bumps rose on her arms. "You're kind of a jerk, aren't you?"

He put his hand to his heart. "That hurts."

"You'll live."

His pupils grew in size, turning his green eyes black in an instant. Her breath caught and she stepped back. What was that? She'd never seen anything like it, except when someone had a flashlight pointed directly into their eyes. Except in that case, the pupils got smaller, not bigger.

He seemed surprised by her reaction; he stared at her like she was a puzzle he was trying to solve. Then he shook his head to clear it, as if he'd simply forgotten what he was talking about. His gaze moved up and down her body in a revolting once-over.

"On second thought, why am I wasting my time?" he said, posturing for anyone within earshot. "You look like a crappy lay."

Her mouth dropped open. She couldn't believe her ears. "Excuse me?"

"And let's face it, you're not exactly a stunner in the looks department."

Someone snickered. He might be right, but she still saw red. At times like these, she liked to channel Aunt Molly. "Don't ever undervalue your worth, Bunny," she used to say. "And when you have to, don't be afraid to fight back. Your strength will always save you." This probably wasn't the situation she had in mind, but practice made perfect.

"Let me guess," Alice said, raising her voice. "You drive some kind of tiny, douchey sports car, right?"

"Porsche!" someone coughed.

She crossed her arms and smirked, happy she'd guessed right. "Well, you know what they say. Small car. Small brain. Small . . ." She paused to lower her gaze, then gestured to the people listening nearby. "I don't need to say it, right? They know."

His eyes blazed, but at least this time they stayed green. "You're a little bitch."

She shook her head and laughed. This guy was as basic as they get. He wasn't worth her time, or her fight. "Goodbye, David."

She turned and marched into the house, ignoring the whispers. Coming here had been a mistake. School hadn't even started yet, and she already had an enemy. Sure, he deserved it, but she knew better than to lock horns with a guy just because his eyes turned black and he said something mean.

"Wait, what?"

She jumped in surprise and lifted her hand to her heart, like a startled countess in a period film. A girl with black hair and kohl-rimmed eyes was standing in the doorway of the kitchen staring daggers at her. She had exotic features and the kind of style that screamed goth. She reminded Alice of a modern-day Cleopatra. Beautiful, intimidating, and a little bit scary.

"Are you talking to me?" Alice asked.

"Yes," the girl hissed, stepping closer. "Whose eyes turned black?"

"I never said . . ." Hang on. Now she really *was* imagining things. Had David put something in her drink? No. She didn't have a drink.

"David . . . David Martin? Are you sure?"

Alice nodded, too stunned to speak.

The girl muttered something and walked away, her black dress and combat boots a stark contrast to the sea of trendy around her. If Alice didn't know any better, she'd think scary goth girl had just read her mind.

Goth Girl stopped and shot her a scathing look. Alice felt her heart leap into her throat. It was definitely time to go.

She took a shortcut through the kitchen and into the dining room, a room that boasted an aquarium wall with tropical fish and an enormous light fixture made of antlers. A raucous card game was taking place around a black lacquer table. A guy with an Ace of Clubs stuck to his forehead sprang from his chair.

"You must be the new girl," he said, slightly out of breath. "Alice, right?"

"Yes," she said, shaking his hand and searching for the exit.

"I'm Remington Carver. This is my party."

She paused. "Remington?"

"Yeah, I know. Came in handy, though, when the school tried to shut down *The Reel*. Can't stop me from using my own name, can they?"

"I guess not. Listen, it was nice meeting you. I have to go."

"Wait!" he said, and looked back over his shoulder. "Aaron, get over here. You gotta meet the new minnow."

She blinked. "What's that supposed to mean?"

A paunchy kid in a bow tie and starchy vest sidled up to Remington. A lollipop was stuck in his mouth. He pushed it to the side, forming a lump in an already chubby cheek, and extended his hand. "Aaron Tapper. No relation to the CNN guy."

She shook his hand, then turned back to Remington. "What do you mean, minnow?"

"Oh . . . I figured someone told you by now."

"Told me what?"

He and Aaron exchanged looks. Aaron pulled the lollipop out of his mouth with a loud pop.

"Sharks and minnows," he said. "You know, the pool game. You're the new minnow, and all the Sharks want a bite."

She stormed home in a rage. So that's what David was up to? Hoping to get the first bite out of Remington's new minnow? It was so degrading and wrong. But it also made sense. A guy like David wouldn't normally spit in her direction, let alone go out of his way to "welcome her to the neighborhood." What a joke.

At least she didn't fall for it. She smiled as she remembered the look on his face when he realized he'd lost. But then, his eyes—

The sound of a car slowing behind her put her on alert. She twisted around and lifted her hand to block the harsh beams. When it pulled up next to her, a figure popped through the sunroof.

If she hadn't been so distracted, she might have had time to dodge what was coming. Unfortunately, she didn't.

"Fish out of water!" yelled a familiar voice just as a bucket of something foul-smelling was thrown in her face.

The little black Porsche peeled away, vicious laughter echoing in the empty street behind it. Alice watched it go in utter shock as she stood there, her arms lifted and her mouth hanging open, covered in slimy water and fish guts.

It was 2:00 a.m. by the time she decided to take action. After showering and shampooing her hair three times, she flipped and flopped for hours, reliving the night's events. Jerks aside, it was just plain weird. Eyes turning black. Girls who read minds. Strange cars idling in the road.

She brought her hand to her belly as she stared at the ceiling. Her stomach was quiet. No fluttering or buzzing wings. Just . . . emptiness. Longing. She felt like her heart was being squeezed by the longing. But longing for what?

Ants were crawling all over her body; she could not sit still. So she threw on some leggings and a hoodie, grabbed a carton of eggs, and snuck out the back door.

It didn't take long to find his house. His douchey little car was parked at the top of the driveway.

She waited on the other side of the street to ensure the coast was clear. It gave her time to study his house, an Italian villa–type mansion that could have been plucked straight from the hills of Tuscany. It was hard not to admire its beauty. Too bad it was wasted on a guy like David.

The house was dark, nothing but dim solar lights lining the drive. After waiting another few minutes for signs of movement, she pulled her hood down as far as it would go and darted across the road.

It was too much to hope that he'd have left it unlocked—not his precious, elitist Porsche. But when she squatted down next to it, she discovered something even better. *The dummy left the sunroof open.*

Oh, this was good. She only hoped he slept in late so the sun had ample time to bake her gifts into the upholstery. *Minnow, my ass*, she thought. *I'M the shark.*

She started out slow, quietly cracking eggs and leaning over the top to deposit their contents inside. But it wasn't long before she was smashing them on the roof and letting their goo pool on the edge before pouring down in yolky streams. She saved a few for the shiny black paint, pitching them at the car like baseballs, not at all concerned with the noise she was making. She was having too much fun to care.

"Enjoy your Porsche omelet, asshole," she sang with a laugh.

Without warning a light flicked on, blazing through a window by the garage and nearly sending her into cardiac arrest. She fell flat to the ground like a starfish, blood pounding in her ears. Crap. She'd never considered what would happen if she got caught. What if they called the police? She'd be humiliated, not to mention possibly charged with vandalism. Maybe this wasn't such a good idea after all.

Seconds ticked by in agonizing silence. She might not be visible from the house, but the longer she stayed in this position, the more vulnerable she became. Psyching herself up, she pressed her palms into the concrete and prepared to make a break for it.

Then she heard it. It wasn't a scream; it was more like a strangled yelp. Muffled, but definitely a sound of distress. She froze in a half push-up and lifted her head to listen.

There it was again.

Part of her wanted to ignore it. What business was it of hers, anyway? She shouldn't even be here. But even as she tried to talk herself out of it, she knew she was going to investigate. Curiosity didn't just kill cats, apparently.

With a resigned (silent) sigh, she pushed herself off the ground and crept toward the lit window, tiptoeing like a burglar in an old-timey film. God, she hoped they didn't have security cameras; how embarrassing would *that* be.

At the sound of glass breaking, she threw herself flat against the exterior wall. Even through her hoodie, she could feel the rough stucco as she pressed her back against it. It was warmer than she expected, still trapping heat from a sun that had set hours earlier.

Despite the warmth, the sound of someone's voice sent immediate chills through her body. Thankfully, it was coming from inside the house, which meant whoever was in there probably didn't know she was here. Eager to get this investigation over with, she sidestepped closer to the window to listen.

"This is annoying. Why is it taking so long?"

"Colin wants it done tonight."

They were female voices. David must have sisters. She wondered if they hated him as much as she did.

"Still can't believe we missed it."

"Hadley, get real. David's always been an asshole. Why would we ever think he was infected?"

"Maybe because it's our job?"

"Please. We hunt demons. We're not psychics."

What did she just say? Alice shimmied closer to the window and slowly peered around the edge.

It took a moment to process what she was seeing. It was a large bedroom, full of sleek and expensive furniture. The bland colors and minimalist design screamed David; they were cold and uninviting, just like him. A white leather chair sat in the middle of the room. David was perched on it, blindfolded. His hands were tied behind his back, and directly in front of him was a freestanding full-length mirror. A tall girl with blond hair stood behind him, holding his head in some kind of choke hold.

Alice sucked in a breath. David was clearly in some sort of trouble. As much as she loathed him, she couldn't just stand here and do nothing. The blond might look like a supermodel, but she had the physique of an Amazon warrior.

Alice reached for her phone to dial 911, but her hand patted nothing but legging. She glanced down in surprise, then mouthed a curse word at her own stupidity. Of all the times not to bring her phone! Crap on crap. Now what?

Her eyes darted back to David and the bizarre scene unfolding in front of her.

Wonder Woman was struggling to keep his head still. He kicked at the floor, scraping the hardwood with slivers of broken glass from an overturned lamp. A redhead with a mop of curls stood across from them, her arms folded, her stiletto heels stabbing the floor. Her outfit looked like something straight off a Paris runway. For a burglary or kidnapping (or whatever this was), she looked painfully overdressed.

"It should be working by now. Olivia, how much did you give him?"

"Enough," a voice answered from the other side of the room. "Try again."

The redhead seemed to take a second to decide. If Alice were to guess, she'd say Miss Devil Wears Prada was the leader of the operation. She carried herself like someone in charge, and the fancy getup only made her more intimidating. Alice stared at her shoes, wondering how on earth she walked in those things, but was interrupted when they suddenly click-clacked across the floor.

She gripped the window ledge as Red stopped next to David, ordered the Amazon to stand down, and pulled the blindfold off his head.

His eyes shot open. From her vantage point, Alice could see them perfectly in the mirror's reflection—although she wished she couldn't. Because they were black—not just his pupils but the *whole* of his eyes, as if they had been injected with ink. She'd seen similar images in movies, but to see it in person . . . it was beyond disturbing. They weren't just black; they were true black—that color that wasn't a color. The one that absorbed instead of reflected light. That was what his eyes had become: little black holes of horror.

As soon as he caught sight of himself, his entire body froze. He stopped struggling and instead focused on his reflection. Gone was the cocky jerk who'd insulted her just a few hours earlier. In his place was someone who looked scared—scared of his own image.

If Alice wasn't so scared herself, she might have chosen that moment to go and get help. But then something went wrong with the mirror. The surface started moving. It rippled like water in a pond on a windy day. For a moment she thought maybe it wasn't even a mirror. But then the surface stopped moving, and darkened—from silver, to gray, to black, and then some. It didn't stop until it was the same color as David's eyes, so black and so dark that it was no longer a mirror but a tunnel to nowhere.

Her body began to quake. This was bad. She shouldn't be here. Yet her feet might as well have grown roots. Whatever twisted and messed-up thing she was witnessing, she couldn't turn away.

David's mouth opened in a silent scream, the tendons in his neck standing out so sharply they nearly cut through his skin. Alice wanted to scream too, especially when *something* began oozing out of his eyes—tears of black blood that didn't fall but instead floated off his face and sliced through the air like exploring tentacles. They moved in jerky, twisting motions, as if the tendrils themselves were afraid. The closer they got to the dark tunnel, the more they seemed to struggle, splitting and branching erratically, trying to avoid the inevitable. But they were no match for the mirror. It was literally inhaling them, like gravity to an imploding star.

Alice's eyes watered, held open by invisible toothpicks. This couldn't be real. It had to be a nightmare. Why was she still standing here? Living black licorice had just danced out of David's eyes. If there was a good time for her to haul ass out of here, it was five minutes ago. *Move*, she told herself. *MOVE.*

She didn't, though, because suddenly everything was normal. Well, normal-ish. One second David's eyes were being stretched and pulled like sooty rubber bands. The next they were closed, his body was slack, and the surface of the mirror was nothing but a silver piece of glass.

Alice blinked a few times, doubting both her vision and her brain. What did she miss? Where did the black hole go?

"Finally!"

"Okay, it's gone. Let's get him back to bed."

She watched them untie him and start dragging his unconscious body toward the bed. He was already snoring. Well, it was better than dead.

"Olivia, a little help, please?"

Alice gasped. Goth Girl, from the party, walked into her line of sight and then stopped in the middle of the room.

"Wait! Someone's listening." Goth Girl turned to the window.

Oh, shit.

There was no need to talk herself into moving this time. Alice's feet sprang into action before her mind did, slipping and sliding through the damp lawn in a fevered attempt to get away. Far away. That was all that mattered. Aunt Molly was right. Something was wrong with this place.

She darted straight into the street, unaware of the car until it was almost on top of her. Tires screeched, and the smell of burning rubber wafted through the still night air. The shock made her trip over her own feet. She stumbled and fell, landing feet away and seconds shy of being roadkill.

When she lifted her head, she found herself staring into the headlights of a familiar car. Her stomach started swirling out of control, the butterflies and locusts back with a vengeance. She scrambled to her feet, but there was no reason to keep running. Not anymore.

The car door opened. A figure emerged and paused behind it, masked in shadow.

"Who are you?" he asked quietly.

She closed her eyes. That voice. It destroyed her.

"Alice," she whispered.

The car door closed. Footsteps. Closer. Closer. He was right in front of her. She could sense the energy radiating from his body, feel the slightest breeze from his labored breath. Her pulse quickened.

"Alice," he repeated.

She opened her eyes.

He was a stranger. An achingly familiar stranger. An impossible, beautiful stranger she would lie down and die for, right this second. She stared into his pale blue eyes, wondering how she'd ever existed without them. It made no sense, yet nothing before had ever made more.

"Where have you been?" he asked.

"I'm here now," was all she could say.

He slowly reached a hand toward her face, as if confirming she was real. She closed her eyes again.

His touch was fire. Hot, crucial, life-saving fire. Nothing else mattered. Nothing existed before this moment. She was suddenly, and for the first time, *awake*.

Which was unfortunate, really. Because a second later, she passed out.

chapter 2

The room was dark. Alice waited for her eyes to adjust, rubbing them a couple of times to make sure they were still working. Once satisfied, she pushed herself onto her elbows and looked around.

It was a large bedroom, even larger than David's, yet somehow cozier. A gaslit fire burned in the corner, and heavy damask drapes covered the windows. Antique furniture and crystal lamps littered the space. It was the kind of room that begged for a cup of hot cocoa and a good book.

Or rather, it would be, if her first instinct wasn't to get the hell out of it.

She sat up and swung her legs off the bed, pausing for a moment as the blood rushed from her head. She looked down. Her shoes were missing, but at least she was still dressed. She slid off the bed, carefully padded over to a window, and pulled the heavy fabric aside. It was too dark to see much, but when she pressed her nose against the glass, she was able to make out two additional stories beneath her. Unless she planned on tying sheets together and rappelling down, there was no escaping from here.

She turned around and made her way across the room toward the door. She stopped when she noticed her sneakers by the bed. After quickly slipping them on, she tiptoed over to the door and pressed her ear against it. An old grandfather clock chimed somewhere deep inside the house. She waited and counted: four chimes. 4:00 a.m. She really needed to get out of here.

Holding her breath, she slowly turned the knob. The door opened with an almost inaudible click. She gripped the crystal handle and waited, listening. Besides her own heartbeat, she heard nothing. It was probably silly to be acting like the victim of a kidnapping; the door wasn't locked, and she hadn't woken up tied to the bed. But still. Her instincts were to get home first and put the puzzle pieces together later. So she entered the hall in search of a quick exit.

The house was a maze of corridors, wide and narrow, each one full of oil paintings, random window seats, and way too many doors. Was she in a hotel? The elevator she came across made her seriously consider the possibility. But it was too quiet and dark to be a hotel, and it had the general *feel* of a home. A really freaking big one, but still a home.

By the time she made it to the first floor, a clock in the foyer was announcing the quarter hour.

" . . . last time, I don't want any of you going near her."

She froze like a prisoner caught in a guard tower spotlight. It was that voice again. *His* voice. A set of blue eyes flashed through her mind, bringing with it the now-familiar flutter in her belly. She glanced down. Light was shining through the bottom of the door to her right. She leaned in to listen.

". . . kind of hard considering she's currently sleeping in my bed."

It was the redhead from David's house. She recognized the scratchy, raspy voice.

"I said I'll handle it, Soxie."

"But something's not right."

"What do you mean?"

"It's just . . . I'm getting a weird feeling."

"Me too."

It was the Amazonian blond. Her voice was airy and sweet, almost like it was dipped in powdered sugar. So did that mean . . .

"Same here."

Yep, the girl in black. The gang was all there.

"What kind of feeling?"

"I know this sounds crazy . . . but do you think she could be one of us?"

"No."

"Are you sure? 'Cause it's starting to feel like—"

"I said NO. Enough!"

Alice jumped at the anger in his voice, which reached her even through the door. Maybe she should be offended, but all things considered, his denial was a relief. What did they mean by "one of us," anyway? Someone who practiced black magic on privileged white boys? Um, no thanks.

She eyed the front door, ready to make a dash for it. Until something behind her whined.

She spun around. Two very serious-looking Dobermans had snuck up behind her and were now well within biting distance. They had to be eighty pounds each, and they were just standing there, staring at her like she was a giant milk bone. Had they been stalking her through the entire house? The idea made her shudder. If only she weren't a cat person.

"Nice puppies," she whispered, putting her hands up and smiling, as if being nice and cordial was the key to their canine hearts. One of them cocked its head to the side. The other one barked. The sound echoed off the marble floor and cathedral ceilings, announcing her presence like a bullhorn.

She closed her eyes. So much for a stealthy exit.

"How long has she been out there?"

"Couple minutes."

"Dammit, Olivia."

Before she could even think of moving (not that the Dobies would allow it), the door she'd been eavesdropping through flew open. She cringed before opening her eyes, weirdly embarrassed.

"Alice."

Even though she was expecting it to be him, her initial response was to go weak in the knees. Levity was the only weapon she had.

"Sorry," she said. "I think I'm lost. Which way to yesterday?"

Someone behind him snorted. He frowned, stepped forward, and closed the door behind him. The dogs forgot all about her and started bouncing around his feet and howling. In the span of a moment, they'd gone from murderous intruder hunters to frenetic balls of needy fur. All they wanted was attention. They were kind of cute, actually—if you took away the massive, flesh-ripping fangs.

"Are you okay?" he asked, ignoring the dogs. The concern on his face was surprising. It made everything else fade away.

"I am now."

He smiled. A heart-stopping, megawatt smile. Her locusts and butterflies passed out.

"Come on," he said, taking her hand in his. "I'll get you home."

She again felt a jolt of electricity from his touch. When she looked down at their clasped hands, she no longer cared where she was or what was going on. Because this moment—right now—this was where she'd always been meant to be.

She smiled and let him lead the way.

He was quiet for the first part of the drive, giving her the opportunity to imagine things she wasn't sure she should be imagining. Like what his hair would feel like if she reached over and ran her fingers through it, or how comfortable it would be to nestle her head in the crook of his neck. She leaned a few inches left, inhaling his scent—clean and masculine. What was wrong with her? This man was nobody to her. And yet. If Nobody asked her to marry him right now, she'd say yes. She wouldn't hesitate.

"Where do you live?" he asked instead.

"Um, it's a couple blocks from Remington High School. Do you know where that is?"

His body seemed to tense. "Yes."

She nodded, at a loss for what to say next.

"My name's Colin, by the way."

She turned to look at his perfect profile. "Colin," she repeated. "That doesn't sound right."

He glanced at her. "Why do you say that?"

"I don't know. I don't know what's happening. Do you?"

He slowed down and pulled over. The sky was that pale gray color it gets just before dawn breaks, when the air is cool and the birds are still. A car blasted its horn as it flew by, making her jump. But Colin didn't move. He just sat there, staring into the coming morning.

"I need you to forget everything you saw tonight," he said. "Can you do that?"

She laughed, because crying would be inappropriate. "You can't be serious."

"Please. Just promise me you'll try." He shot her a look and another smile. This time she spotted a dimple on his right cheek. It was all she could do not to reach out and touch it.

"And if I can't?"

He stared at her, his eyes lingering for a split second on her mouth. She felt herself lean in, with no conscious decision to do so. All she cared about was the two feet of space between them. It was two too many.

"You have to," he said, snapping her out of whatever trance she'd just fallen into.

It took a moment for his words to sink in. When they did, they felt heavy—like a threat.

"Wait a second," she said, leaning back to reclaim her power. "You want me to forget *you* too, don't you?"

"Everything. It's for your own good." He turned away, as if looking at her was some kind of punishment. It made her . . . angry.

"Look at me," she demanded.

He wouldn't.

"I said, look at me!"

When he did, his eyes were vacant. Haunted, almost.

"I don't know what I saw tonight, and I don't care," she said evenly. "All I know is I saw *you*. And I'll never forget that. Ever."

His breathing turned shallow. "Then I'm sorry, Alice. I really am. But I need you to go. I need you to go now."

"What?"

He turned away again. "Get out."

She felt herself begin to panic. He didn't mean it. He couldn't. "Colin, can we just—"

"I said, GET OUT!"

It came out of nowhere, and she wasn't prepared. Up to this point he'd been so gentle and kind. For him to turn on her like this felt wrong—like a betrayal. But his voice was so commanding, even her butterflies and locusts retreated into their cocoons. She had no choice but to retreat with them, exiting the car and slamming the door behind her.

When he drove away, all she could do was stand there on the side of the road, watching helplessly as he took her confused heart with him.

She barely registered the walk home. The sun was just breaking across the horizon as she shuffled through the back door and made her way blindly to her bedroom. Without even bothering to take off her shoes, she fell on the bed and rolled over, pulling the duvet over her head to block out the light.

Monday came too soon. She'd have preferred to sleep until graduation, but Judy would have noticed. So she made her way to school in the blazing morning sun, sweat forming under the strap of her backpack and dread forming in the pit of her stomach.

She'd spent the rest of the weekend going over what had happened, bouncing between denial and fear. At one point she'd almost convinced herself she'd been drugged. But then her rational brain kept circling back to the one thing she couldn't let go of.

Demons.

She hadn't been drugged. She'd felt it the second she opened the door that day. Even Boop had felt it. There was something off about David. She'd seen his eyes turn black. Twice. Then she'd watched three girls perform what she could only assume was some kind of exorcism. But they hadn't spouted religious texts or donned crucifixes. All they'd used was a mirror. A mirror that turned black . . .

Despite the heat, she shivered. Colin had asked her to forget everything she saw. But that was before he left her on the side of the road, blindsided, with a heart smashed to pieces. She hated him for that. And hate was easier to handle than the other thing.

It came down to a simple choice, really: forget and move on, or dig deeper, regardless of what might lie beneath.

It was a short debate.

She'd start with David.

She didn't spot him until she was on her way to fifth period. He was crossing the triangular patch of green by the cafeteria aptly named the Triangle, according to the school map she'd received at orientation.

She paused for a moment to watch him. He carried himself with such confidence and entitlement. She could almost see the privilege he took for granted seeping from his pores.

She gripped her books to her chest like a shield and made her way across the grass, waiting until she was almost on top of him before calling his name.

He gave her a bored glance, then a double take. "Yeah, I'm David . . . Oh, you're that new girl from Colorado. Alice, right?"

"Ha ha. Very funny. You know who I am."

He stepped back and gave her a quick once-over. It was so crude and so David. If only she could slap him. That would make everything she'd been through in the past seventy-two hours worth it.

"Sorry, Alice from Colorado," he said, his tone anything but apologetic. "If we hooked up or something, consider it a one-time thing. And you're welcome."

Her stomach turned. "Jesus! No. No, we did NOT hook up."

"Fine, whatever," he said, his eyes wandering as his attention waned. "You want an autograph or something?"

She did her best to stay calm. It wouldn't surprise her if David was a pathological liar. But right now, he seemed genuinely clueless.

"You . . . really don't remember?" she asked.

"Oh my god," he said to the sky. "You're already boring me, new girl. What do you want?"

She couldn't help but let her mouth fall open. This was not what she was expecting.

"Nothing, I guess," she finally managed. "My mistake."

He made a *pfft* sound and then walked away, making sure she heard him whisper, "Pathetic," before he was out of earshot.

It was hard to say who was more confused at this point—David, or her. She hadn't gotten the same unsettling feeling she had the day he'd shown up at her door, but he didn't seem all that different either. He was still an—

"Asshole," finished a voice behind her.

She whirled around—almost dropping her books in the process, like a proper dingbat. *Goth Girl*—

"Please," Goth Girl said, putting her hand up in a stop gesture. "My name's Olivia. If you call me Goth Girl one more time, I'll lose it. And you're right: David is an asshole. Demon or no demon."

Alice just stared at her. She didn't know what to say. Or think.

Olivia folded her arms in front of her. "For the record, we're not witches."

"Witches?" Alice said. Her mind started to spin. *Who said anything about witches?*

Olivia gestured randomly to students rushing past. "Them, usually. But I know you're smart enough to make up your own mind."

Alice spared her peers a quick glance. Some of them seemed agitated by Olivia's presence, quickening their pace as they walked by.

"But how . . . You don't know me. You don't know anything about me." She'd meant to sound brave, but it came out like a question. Olivia rolled her eyes.

"Okay, maybe you're not that smart."

Alice gripped her books tighter, annoyed at her own stupidity. The girl could read minds for God's sake. Of course she knew who she was. She probably knew what she had for breakfast.

"Fine, I'll admit that was dumb," she said, slightly embarrassed. "Can you please just tell me what is going on? Who *are* you?"

Olivia smiled. "You're asking the wrong question, Alice."

The late bell rang, and the energy around them faded as people disappeared into buildings and classrooms. Within seconds, she and Olivia were alone on the Triangle.

"I don't know what you mean."

Olivia stepped forward. She placed her hands on Alice's shoulders and leaned her forehead into hers. It was strange and awkward, yet one of the most pleasantly intimate moments of her life. She didn't want it to end.

"I hope one day you do," Olivia whispered.

Alice felt her mouth go dry. She had a sinking feeling Olivia was saying goodbye, and it nearly shattered her.

"It's only goodbye if you let it be," Olivia said. "It's up to you, Alice."

Then she let go and walked away without another word.

Alice felt colder as the space between them grew. She ached to stop her, but her heart and her head were no longer in alignment. So she just stood there like an idiot as Olivia turned the corner into the glass walkway and vanished into thin air.

According to Merriam-Webster, the definition of "Occam's razor" is as follows:

> *A scientific and philosophical rule that entities should not be multiplied unnecessarily, which is interpreted as requiring that the simplest of competing theories be preferred to the more complex or that explanations of unknown phenomena be sought first in terms of known quantities.*

It took a few days, but Alice eventually narrowed it down to two theories. One, supernatural forces were at work. Two, she was imagining things. It was clear which was the simplest of the two, but it did little to ease her mind.

And then there were the mirrors.

They stopped working properly. There was no other way to put it. At first it was subtle: She'd be brushing her teeth or washing her face and could swear her reflection's movements were just a second too slow. She'd blink, watch herself blink back, and then get out of the room as fast as possible, the heebie-jeebies taking over her body in waves.

After a while, these "malfunctions" became more pronounced. Her reflection stopped moving a second behind and instead started moving seconds *ahead*. Sometimes she had to scramble to catch up with it, which made her wonder if she was living in an alternate universe stuck on fast-forward.

It wasn't until she was getting ready for bed one night, flossing with her back to the mirror, that she came to terms with what was going on.

It was the light tap on her shoulder that did it. She nearly jumped out of her skin, wondering if her reflection had graduated to physical contact. The fact that she was referring to it as a separate entity confirmed just how bad things were getting.

It felt like ages before she was brave enough to turn around. When she finally did, all she found was plain old Alice staring back at her, a string of floss dangling from her teeth.

Then something happened.

Her brown eyes, always a smidge too far apart, were suddenly in the right place. And green. Emerald green. They widened as her lifeless brown hair pulled itself into tight, bouncy red curls. With a gasp she slammed her eyes shut and gripped the sides of the sink, ignoring the urge to run. Running was pointless. Besides, she had to see. She had to know. When she opened her eyes again, they had turned a vibrant, cornflower blue. Wavy blond locks cascaded down her back, and the floss hanging from her perfect lips was somehow charming. She felt a lump form in her throat, already knowing what was coming next. Rather than delay the inevitable, she focused on the image and, slowly but deliberately, blinked.

Olivia stared back at her, her dark eyes full of sadness and longing.

At that point, she simply turned around and went to bed. When she awoke the next morning, the string of dental floss was still stuck in her teeth, and she was still 99 percent sure she was losing her mind.

In a way, she was relieved. Psychosis she understood. It wasn't ideal, but at least it was real.

It was also in her blood.

No one ever talked about it. All she knew was that it had happened. But if she had any chance of beating this thing, she needed to know more. So, one night in late October—over a typical dinner of chicken and vegetables—she bit the bullet and asked.

"Mom, will you tell me about Aunt Molly?"

Judy speared a piece of broccoli with her fork. The prongs scraped the plate harder than usual. "What about her?"

"You know what I mean."

"Honey, it's in the past."

Of course. That was always her mom's go-to whenever she didn't want to talk about something. *It's in the past.* Well, past or no, Alice needed to know. She deserved to know.

They argued this point for some time, until Alice finally admitted that she already knew what Molly had done. She'd known since she was eight.

"How?" Judy asked.

"Because I have ears, that's how!"

It was amazing what parents thought children didn't pick up on when they were literally one room away.

"Okay. Did you know it wasn't the first time?" Judy snapped.

Alice nearly coughed up her water on that one. "What? She tried it before?"

"Yes," Judy said, waving her napkin like a white flag before tossing it on her plate. "Your grandparents were at their wit's end. The inpatient program was their last hope."

Alice glanced down, wondering if that was where she was headed. "But it helped, right? She was better after that?"

"I guess. I mean, yes. Better, but different."

"Different how?"

Her mom's gaze turned distant, as if she was mining deep within her memories for the right one. She took a sip of wine before responding, "Her priorities changed."

It was an answer, but Alice had been hoping for more. A lot more. She prodded Judy to elaborate.

"Oh, honey, I don't know. She was suddenly just so . . . happy."

"Gee. How awful that must have been."

Judy gave her a look. "Don't be smart. You didn't know her like I knew her. Molly was never your typically happy kid. She was anxious and worried, all the time. Making a simple decision like what color sweater to wear could send her into a two-day tailspin. We tried, but we didn't know how to help her. If things weren't exactly the way she pictured them in her mind, she'd fall apart. And then after she . . ." Judy took another sip of wine, looking overwhelmed.

Alice placed a hand on her arm. "It's okay, Mom. Just tell me."

Judy smiled weakly, the moisture in her eyes reflecting the light of the old chandelier. "It was awful. It was the closest she ever came; the doctors said we almost lost her. We were relieved when she pulled through, but we never expected her to get better overnight. These things take time. Therapy. Medications. God knows she'd tried them all. But then . . . two weeks later, she's out of the hospital and she's a completely different person. The first thing she wanted to do was go *shopping,* of all things."

Alice laughed. "Definitely sounds like Molly."

"You don't understand. Your aunt had severe social anxiety. To her, before, going shopping was like standing in front of a firing squad. We always did it for her. And then bam—all of a sudden she wanted to be a part of everything; she wanted to *do* everything. Not just shopping. Every weekend she was out dancing, or taking off on a whim to go white water rafting. For God's sake, she even went hang gliding. Forget about college and bills; she didn't care. She just wanted to have fun and be fabulous. It was impossible to keep up with her. Don't get me wrong, we were thrilled she was better, but . . . it was a lot to take in. *She* was a lot to take in."

Alice couldn't help but sense some jealousy on her mom's part. Did she resent Molly for getting better? Seemed harsh. Then again, so was cutting your own wrists and leaving yourself to drown in a pool of crimson water. Alice had no business judging either of them.

"And then you were born," her mom said.

Alice's head shot up. "Me? What did I have to do with anything?"

The look on Judy's face was incredulous. "Are you kidding? It had everything to do with you. You're the only reason she stuck around. If it weren't for you, she would have taken off on some crazy adventure and we never would have seen her again. You know she slept by your crib for a week straight after we brought you home from the hospital—I told you that, right?"

Alice couldn't help but smirk. To this day, whenever Molly stayed over she'd wake up to find her sleeping on the bed next to her, Boop purring happily between them. It was nice to know she had something to do with her aunt's recovery, but the pressure sometimes got to her. Seeing Molly always made her a tad nervous—like she was about to be graded on a test she'd never taken.

Judy pressed her fingers into her temples and closed her eyes. Alice knew that meant a migraine was coming on, and dinner was almost over. But she had one more question to ask.

"Why was she so angry about us moving back here?"

Judy kept her eyes closed. "Because she hated this place. She hated who she used to be, and she never wanted to be reminded of that person again. But honestly, honey, sometimes I miss her. I miss the old Molly—how close we used to be. I'm happy she's well, but I never really got to know her again. Isn't that strange?"

Alice appreciated the question, but she'd never had a sister. She didn't know what that kind of bond was like. Her mind drifted to the moment Olivia pressed her forehead against hers. She'd felt something then. Something . . . more.

"Yes," she answered. "That is strange."

Judy nodded once, then stood to clear the table.

Weeks went by, the days blurring together into a kaleidoscope of fear and doubt. Alice avoided mirrors like the plague, and her mom commented once or twice that maybe she should run a comb through her hair. But the last time she'd caught her reflection, the Alice on the other side hadn't even attempted to mimic her—she'd been too busy pressing her hands against the glass, her mouth open in a frozen scream.

Terrifying didn't begin to describe it.

Upon seeing this, Alice had smacked her palms against the glass and let out her own bloodcurdling scream. Her reflection had screamed back at her, then done something even worse: dropped to the floor, beneath the mirror and out of sight.

Alice had pushed away and stumbled backward, staring at a mirror that no longer held her reflection. Then she'd crumbled to the bathroom floor and covered her eyes, resigned to the fact that whatever was happening to her was only getting worse.

She needed professional help. But every therapist's office she called required parental consent, and Judy had been through enough for one year. She tried to reason with them. Couldn't they make an exception? Her birthday was right around the corner. "Why don't you give us a call then," they said. "Thanks for nothing," she replied.

There was a girl at school named Kara who kind of looked like her. A teacher even got them mixed up once. Alice didn't know her personally, but she knew she was eighteen. She remembered her carrying around a large display of balloons one day advertising it.

Kara was elated when Alice returned her bag. It was weird that it had turned up in the gym, because she could have sworn she'd had it in statistics. But no matter—after a quick search of the contents, she was delighted to find everything—her iPhone, keys, lip balm, and wallet—accounted for. She was too busy counting the cash inside to notice the missing driver's license.

"So Kara, tell me what brings you here."

"I'm seeing things."

"What kind of things?"

"Every time I look in a mirror, my reflection does something different."

Dr. Williams looked intrigued. "Can you give me an example?"

Alice didn't hold back. She unloaded her full bucket of crazy.

He scribbled a few notes, then leaned back and gestured to the wall behind her.

"Can you look into that mirror and tell me what you see right now?"

It was the last thing she wanted to do, but maybe this was the only way. The only way to know if she was truly headed for the loony bin.

"It's okay, Kara. This is a safe space."

Alice wasn't sure about that. As spaces went, this one felt cold and sterile. It wasn't at all what she'd expected based on the movies she'd seen. There were no mahogany shelves or leather-bound books, or an inviting sofa to lie down on. Instead, it was a boxy room with white walls, beige carpet, and a padded bench for a chair.

Dr. Williams stared at her over his marble slab desk, patiently waiting for her to do as he asked. Well, she'd gone to all this trouble. Might as well see it through. Wiping her sweaty palms on her jeans, she slowly stood and turned around.

The Alice in the mirror wasn't doing anything out of the ordinary. She was just standing there, waiting for answers that might never come.

"She looks so sad."

"She? Don't you mean you?"

She shook her head, watching her reflection do the same. "No, I don't. I don't know who that is anymore."

"Well, perhaps that's the problem."

She ran her fingers through her stringy hair. "What do you mean?"

"Get to know her. Maybe she can tell you something you don't know."

A few days later, Kara discovered her driver's license in her locker. A Good Samaritan must have found it and returned it through the vent.

chapter 3

The Remington Reel—Tuesday, February 26th
News, Weather, & Sports
By Aaron Tapper (no relation)

Well, Sharks, bundle up, 'cause it's a chilly one this week. Highs expected in the upper 50s, lows in the 40s. Enjoy it while it lasts, 'cause we all know come March, those thermostats will start climbing and that Lacoste sweater you got for Christmas will become obsolete. I, for one, will miss it.

In other news, the Astronomy Club would like to remind all Sharks that they will be hosting their first open viewing of Bolle-Marin this Thursday evening on the Triangle. For the non–Stephen Hawkings among us, Bolle-Marin is a comet that hasn't done a flyby in almost 2,500 years. The good news is it will be visible for sixteen months, so you'll have plenty of chances to see this celestial wonder in action. However, the Twitterverse is already speculating that July will be the telescopic equivalent to a cosmic orgy: a total lunar eclipse and Bolle-Marin passing at its midway point, the closest this sucker will ever get. So be on the lookout for tickets to the Reel Red Moon & Comet Party, details TBA.

Now, on to sports.

Word has it David Martin is stepping down as captain of the Shark lacrosse team, due to an undisclosed illness. With the loss of midfielder and former co-captain Colin Tinsley, this leaves a severe vacuum in leadership as we head into the season. We can only hope Coach LaPorte has a backup in mind. As for you, Mr. Martin, we wish you a speedy recovery . . .

Alice almost choked on her cereal. Below the article was a picture of last year's lacrosse team. Smack dab in the center was David, handsome and smug as ever. But it wasn't his face that got her attention. It was the one next to it. The one with pale blue eyes.

Her stomach tingled. *Colin Tinsley.*

It still didn't sound right. But why would it? After all this time, she still knew nothing about him, except that he was a stranger who'd broken her heart. A stranger who continued to haunt her dreams.

At least now she had a last name. She opened up the browser on her phone and typed "Colin Tinsley." But she couldn't bring herself to hit GO. What if she found him on social media? Could she stop herself from following him? And when he denied her request, would she die a little inside? Or worse, what if he accepted and she was granted access to photos of him and some beautiful girl, with captions like "True love" and "Together forever"? The thought made the lone butterfly in her stomach sick.

Her phone rang, interrupting her spiraling thoughts. She looked at the name. Her thumb hovered over Decline but moved to Accept, like she knew it would.

"Hi, Dad."

"Hi, Peanut. How are you?"

She bit the inside of her cheek. *Peanut.* She used to feel special when he called her that, as if the term itself confirmed their unwavering relationship. Now it just felt forced and contrived.

"I have an actual name. It's Alice, in case you forgot."

His sigh was nearly loud enough to blow her hair sideways. "Funny. Glad to see you're keeping that blade on your sarcasm nice and sharp."

"Only for you. *Daddy.*" If he wanted to resort to juvenile nicknames, so would she.

"Okay, okay. Point made. So, tell me. How's everything? How's school?"

She almost laughed out loud. *How's school?* Here she was, teetering on the precipice of insanity, and her dad wanted to know how school was going.

"School's great, Dad. I'm great. Mom's great. Everyone's great. So you can check this call off your monthly to-do list. Anything else?"

"Jesus, Alice. Can't you give me a break, just once? What is wrong with you?"

A snort escaped through her nose. "I don't know. Maybe we should ask Karen. She's the expert, right?"

"Honey, don't."

"Oh, I'm sorry. Did she dump you already? That's too bad." She hated hearing the nastiness in her own voice. It slithered out of her, like the black tendrils from David's eyes. She didn't want to be like David. She didn't want to be unforgiving and cruel. But when it came to her dad, it was hard to resist.

"That's enough," he snapped. "I'm not going to keep having this conversation with you. My relationship with Dr. Kline—with Karen—is my business. Furthermore, whatever lies your mother has been feeding you, I'm sick of it. I'm sick of being treated like the bad guy here."

She felt her hand shake as she gripped the phone. "The only liar in this family is you."

Silence.

"Grow up, Alice."

"You first."

"You know what? I think it would be best if you didn't come out next month."

She laughed, even as the kitchen in front of her began to blur. "Oh, you'd love that."

"What do you want from me? More money? Well, guess what. That well is dry. Your mother made sure of that."

As usual, the gloves had come off fast. Alice knew part of it (okay, a big part) was her fault, but she couldn't help it. She might one day forgive him for leaving, but she'd never forgive him for breaking her mom's heart.

"I don't want anything from you, Gavin," she said finally.

"Honey, c'mon. I'm trying here, but you don't make it easy. Not everything is about you."

"You're right. I'm not the one who cheated."

"For Christ's sake, Alice. You win! Are you happy? Because I'm done. I can't do this anymore."

"Then don't!" she screamed, before throwing her phone across the room. It slammed into the antique mirror over the buffet, sending shards of glass flying. She saw a flash of fur as Boop darted out of sight.

She stared at the empty frame and slivers of mirror littering the floor. Why did she do this every time? Yes, she wanted to punish him, but what good was it doing her? At the end of the day, he was still her dad. She would always love him. But the anger . . . she was having a tough time letting it go. Gavin had moved on. Even Judy—to some degree—was putting the past behind her; she had a new job, and she was making friends at work. (Unlike Alice, whose only friend at the moment was a spoiled and disinterested cat.)

Honestly, her dad was right to ask the question. What *was* wrong with her? Not only had she just made a damaged relationship worse, she'd also destroyed a family heirloom. Her mom was going to be furious. She sniffled and wiped her eyes as she retrieved the broom from the laundry room.

As she swept up the glass, tears began to flow freely down her face. She couldn't stop them. An all-consuming sadness was enveloping her, entombing her in its cold, debilitating embrace. It wasn't just her dad. It was everything. Her life since she moved here. The feeling of constant fear and confusion. Therapy wasn't helping. Nothing was helping.

She dropped the trash can and sank to the floor, letting the broom fall with a smack on the broken glass. She clutched her stomach as sobs racked her body. She didn't know what to do anymore. She had no one to talk to. And it wasn't because people hadn't tried. The girl she'd shared a laugh with at the party, Kelly, had invited her to the movies once. But she'd declined. She'd declined every invitation extended to her. She spent her lunch hour alone on a park bench behind school, and her weekends either on the couch or hiking to a secluded spot overlooking the city. She didn't want friends.

She wanted . . . Olivia. And the redhead with the raspy voice. Soxie. And the blond with cornflower-blue eyes. Hadley. She more than wanted them. She *needed* them. It hurt how much she needed them. Where were they? Who were they? *What* were they?

The loneliness and despair were bordering on dangerous. Something had to give.

She was standing in front of her bathroom mirror with a razor in her hand. She watched her reflection give her a curious look as she moved the blade toward her wrist.

"What are you doing?" asked Alice.

"I'm just so tired," said Alice.

"Tired of what?"

"Tired of feeling this way. It worked for Molly. Maybe it'll work for us."

"You're wrong."

"Well," she said as she lowered the razor to her wrist, "only one way to find out."

A hand shot through the mirror, grabbing her arm. "Grow up, Alice."

She smiled. "You first." Then she sliced her wrist open. Blood splattered the mirror in an arc of angry red.

Her reflection screamed.

"Alice, what are you doing?"

She was in the bathtub, drowning in red water. Olivia, Soxie, and Hadley were standing over her.

"Jesus," Soxie said, shaking her head of curls slowly back and forth. "This is messed up."

"Alice, honey. It's going to get better." Hadley reached through the water to caress her face. "Do you know the question yet?"

"Hadley," Olivia said. "Don't push her."

"Olivia, look around. Maybe she needs a little push." The bathroom was covered in blood; it looked like something from a Wes Craven film.

Alice blinked through the water, wondering why her lungs weren't burning.

"Because you're not really drowning, dope," Olivia said. "But this is bad, Alice."

Soxie stepped into the tub, designer boots and all, and sat on the edge. "Yeah, Daniels. Get your shit together."

Alice broke through the water's surface and pulled her knees to her chest. "I'm trying!"

"You call this trying?"

"Alice," Hadley said, shooting Soxie a dirty look. "You're not crazy. You don't need a therapist, and you don't need this morbid guilt thing you've got going on. All you need to do is trust and let go."

Alice slapped the water with both hands. "I don't know what that means!"

"Yes, you do," Olivia said. They were back on the Triangle, and Olivia's forehead was pressed against hers.

Alice grabbed her by the shoulders. "Don't leave me!"

But Olivia was gone and Alice was back in the bathroom, her hands gripping her own arms through the mirror. Only this time, she was the reflection, begging herself not to leave.

"She's right, Alice. You have work to do."

She turned around. A long, dark hallway loomed in front of her. Thousands of empty frames hung on its walls, floor, and ceiling. She watched as each of them filled black in an instant, consuming all the light around them. A lone figure stood not far away, shrouded in darkness.

"The answer is *we*."

She awoke with a start, her hair plastered to her forehead with sweat. She leaned over to turn on her bedside lamp and was instantly comforted by its light.

Boop groggily lifted his head in question. She gave him a quick scratch behind the ear, then covered her face with her shaky hands.

Now even her dreams were going off the rails.

She scanned the crowded restaurant, smiling when she spotted her aunt Molly's auburn head. She was sitting at a corner table—her dark sunglasses, elegant chignon, and tailored dress giving her the look of a mysterious heiress. Probably exactly what she was going for.

"Sorry I'm late."

Molly took off her sunglasses. "You look tired."

"Thanks."

"And you're too thin."

"Anything else?"

Molly laughed—her signature high-pitched, nasally laugh. Then she leaned over to wrap Alice in a crushing hug of silk and Chanel. It wasn't the typical wardrobe for a flight attendant, but Molly's talent for living beyond her means was legendary.

"How's your mother?" she asked the second she pulled away.

"She's good. Maybe you'd know that if you called her once in a while."

Molly ignored her, motioning to the waiter for another glass of wine. "And your father?"

"Who knows."

"Hmph."

Alice pulled her napkin off the plate and set it in her lap. "So, what about you? How's work?"

"WELL, just wait 'til you hear about our emergency landing in Milan . . ."

And so it went. Three courses and almost two bottles of wine later—none of which Alice partook in—she learned of a sleepwalking passenger who peed in the galley, a nervous flier who thought the comet would bring down the plane, and, of course, the emergency landing in Milan, due to an armrest battle that ended in blows. Thirteen years with the airline and Molly had seen it all. Her life was one big adventure, and Alice was her favorite audience.

It wasn't until the waiter brought a slice of chocolate cake with a lit candle that Alice remembered this was supposed to be her birthday brunch. She put her head down, embarrassed, as Molly, the waiter, and two nearby tables sang "Happy Birthday" to her.

"Eighteen, Bunny. How does it feel?"

Alice pulled out the candle and licked the frosting off the bottom. "It feels like I'm too old for you to keep calling me Bunny. It's bad enough Dad still calls me Peanut. Also, it's tomorrow. You know that, right?"

"Of course," Molly said, flicking her hand like she was shooing a fly. "But I'm on a red-eye back to New York tonight."

"So you're not even going to try and see Mom?"

"Next time."

It was always "next time." In fact, she couldn't remember the last time her mom and Molly had spent more than five minutes in the same room. It made her sad, and she vowed to one day get to the bottom of it. But for now, she had more important things to discuss. She picked up her fork and began making crisscross patterns in the thick frosting. All the while she could feel Molly's eyes boring into her head, as if she was attempting to read her mind like Olivia.

Approaching the subject delicately was the only smart move.

"Can I ask you something?" she asked, her eyes still on her cake.

"You can ask me anything. You know that."

Alice set the fork down and braced herself. "When you were . . . sick, did you ever have strange dreams? Or, I don't know, sometimes feel like you were dreaming when you were awake?"

"Meaning . . ."

"Meaning, did you ever see anything sort of . . . impossible? That only you could see?"

Molly's eyes flashed with what looked like alarm, but her body remained still. "No."

Alice wasn't expecting such a curt reply, and she suddenly felt very small. She stammered a quick "okay" and "never mind, then" before forking a generous section of cake and stuffing it in her mouth.

"Are you going to tell me what this is about?" Molly prodded.

With a mouth full of cake, Alice waved her off, reiterating that it was nothing and to forget she ever brought it up.

But Molly wasn't stupid. Flighty sometimes, but definitely not stupid. She grabbed Alice's wrist and leaned in, her voice loud and threatening. "Listen to me very carefully, Alice. You are perfect. All you need in this life is you. Do you hear me?"

Heat rose in Alice's cheeks. "I think the whole restaurant heard you."

Molly let go of her wrist, grabbed her by the chin, and forced her to look in her eyes. "I'm only going to say this once." Then she hesitated, as if debating whether she should say it at all.

Alice frowned. "Well?"

"He'll destroy you if you let him. Don't let him."

Alice inhaled and coughed on a stray crumb. "What are you talking about? Who?"

But Molly didn't answer her. She looked like she was about to, but then the waiter appeared with the check, and she seemed to remember where they were. By the time he cleared their dessert plates, the Molly of thirty seconds ago was gone. This one was all smiles and no talk. When Alice tried to bring it up again, Molly shot her down in a polite, breezy way—"Oh, Bunny, it was nothing. Just the jet lag talking."

That night Alice sat alone in the dark on her bed, facing her dresser mirror. It was no use trying to rationalize what was happening to her. She might be crazy. Molly might be crazy. Hell, maybe none of this was real and she was in a padded room somewhere, being observed by a panel of lab coats. Did it really matter? Regardless of whether it was real or not, she still had to live through it. So maybe dream Hadley was right. Maybe the only thing left to do was trust and let go.

She leaned over and switched on the light. Her hands clasped in her lap, she sat as still as possible and stared into her own eyes. It was time to face her fear—to look herself in the eyes and let whatever was going to happen, happen. No more hiding. No more waiting.

Her breaths in the mirror began to slow down, causing her own to speed up. *Calm down, Alice. Let go. TRUST.*

She lifted her chin in an attempt to look brave. For months her reflection had been trying to tell her something, but she'd been too freaked out and stubborn to listen. *Well, I'm here*, she thought. *I'm listening. Tell me something I don't know.*

Her reflection smiled. "Tomorrow, Alice. Tomorrow it begins."

Her eyes started to water, but she couldn't blink. Somehow she knew if she blinked, the connection would be lost.

"Who are you?" she whispered.

"I'm you. You're me. Don't you see?"

A tear spilled down her cheek as she realized that yes, finally, she did. She nodded, too overcome with joy to speak.

Her reflection nodded back a second later. "Happy Birthday, Alice."

They both blinked.

The next morning, she sprang out of bed like she was five and it was Christmas. For the first time in months, she wasn't scared of her own reflection. She even took extra time to blow-dry her hair and apply a little makeup. It was almost disappointing that the image in the glass behaved the way it was supposed to. Although she had no idea what the day would bring, she knew it was the start of something big. *Today it begins.*

When she got to school, she waited in the parking lot for Remington to arrive. The second his Hummer pulled in, she was at his driver's side window, pounding on the glass.

He jumped.

"Do you know where Olivia lives?"

He pressed the button to lower his window. "What?"

"Olivia. Black hair, goth—I mean, wears a lot of black . . . she was at your back-to-school party. You know her, right?"

He turned off the ignition. "Oh, you mean Olivia Diaz."

"Okay . . . Olivia Diaz. Where does she live?"

"What do I look like, Google Maps?"

"You're editor of *The Reel*. Isn't it your job to know everything about everything?"

He leaned back, as if appraising her for the first time. "What's your deal, Alice? You walk around here like a zombie all year, and now you want to go messing with the Waywards?"

"The what?"

He leaned over to grab his bag. She stepped back as he opened the car door.

"Pick up some Shakespeare once in a while. The Wayward Sisters. The witches in *Macbeth*."

She had a sudden urge to punch him. "They're not witches."

He shook his head like she was a lost cause. "Look, I don't know what they are, but I know they tend to keep to themselves and do not like people snooping around in their business."

He started to walk away, but she stepped in front of him. "Wait. Please. Do you have any idea where I can find them? I've only seen Olivia on campus once, and I don't even know Soxie's or Hadley's last name."

"It's Sharon. Sharon Roxland and Hadley Caldwell. They're not officially enrolled; they sort of come and go as they please. Some kind of arrangement with the school. I think they have private tutors."

"And . . ."

He looked to the sky. "All I know is Soxie lives with her uncle in some mega-mansion by the mountains—guardhouse, guard dogs, the works. You're not gonna get anywhere near it if you're not expected."

She crossed her arms and smiled. "Don't worry. I'm expected."

Remington laughed and slung his messenger bag over his shoulder as he backed away. "Okay then. Guess you're headed to Wayward Palms. Good luck!"

———— 🦋 ————

"Wayward Palms is pretty vague. You got an address?" asked her taxi driver.

"No, but I'll know it when I see it." Her attempts to locate an address online had proven fruitless, but she wasn't going to let that deter her.

"Okay, hon. Meter's running, though."

Wayward Palms was more than vague. It was enormous. The closer they got to the mountains, the farther apart the houses, and the higher the walls separating them from the road.

The meter was nearing sixty-five dollars by the time Alice spotted something familiar. It wasn't the tall stucco wall or the black iron gates with curlicue Rs. It was the blue car pulling out of the driveway.

She felt him before she saw him. It had been so long, like her butterflies and locusts were awakening from a long nap. She hated to admit it, but she had missed them.

He turned and stared at her as the two cars slowly rolled past each other. She couldn't see his eyes behind his mirrored glasses, but she felt their iciness. Well, she wasn't here for him. She turned to face front.

"Can you pull up to the gate, please?"

The driver whistled. "Nice place, missy."

"We'll see."

An older gentleman stepped out of the gatehouse, motioning for them to stop. He bent down and tapped on her window. "Ms. Daniels?"

"Yes."

"Ms. Roxland is expecting you." Then, to the driver, "Just follow this road to the main house."

Alice could barely contain her excitement as the gates swung open. The drive was lined with palm trees, their massive fronds barely moving in the warm desert breeze.

She remembered the house being big—but in the light of day, it was bigger. Sprawling, like a collection of hotel villas combined into one grand residence. She craned her neck to see over the front seat. Between the house and the mountains sat a magnificent stone barn, complete with paddock and grazing horses. Forget hotel. This was more like a resort.

Her taxi pulled up to the front entrance, loose gravel crunching beneath its tires. A giant fountain bubbled and frothed in the center of the drive, and leafy vines lined the walls of the main wing. Gazing out the window, she felt like Elizabeth Bennet seeing Pemberley for the first time: awed and nervous, and wholly unsure of her place.

She paid the fare and stepped out of the car.

Just as she shut the cab door, two heavy doors burst open and Olivia flew down the steps in a blur of black clothing. After all but tackling Alice in a fierce embrace, she whispered, "Thank God you're finally here."

Alice hugged her back with equal ferocity, relieved and moved by the enthusiastic welcome.

Stiletto heels slowly descended the granite steps behind them. "It's about damn time."

Alice looked over Olivia's shoulder. Soxie stood on the bottom step, smiling. She was dressed in a sleek green jumpsuit that was tailored to within an inch of its life. Bright red hair danced around her face in the wind, and her chunky gold jewelry looked serious enough to warrant a bodyguard. And then there was Hadley. In her white tank, leather pants, and motorcycle boots, she was a *Maxim* magazine cover: beautiful, blond, and a little badass. Considering Olivia's exotic features and gothic-style wardrobe, these three couldn't be more different. And yet.

Soxie and Hadley exchanged looks, then laughed.

Olivia pulled away, wiping her eyes. "Don't worry, they're laughing at me, not you."

"*With* you, O, with you," Soxie corrected her.

Olivia ignored her, her eyes still fixed on Alice. "You ready?"

She looked from Olivia to Hadley to Soxie. Finally, she was where she was supposed to be. This place. This time. These girls.

"I'm ready."

chapter 4

Alice stood in Soxie's immense closet, surrounded by red soles and designer labels. As she ran her fingers over a butter-soft leather bag, she couldn't help but wonder where the money came from. She felt rude even thinking it.

"We asked the same question," Olivia said. "It's really boring. Inherited."

Alice turned around. Olivia and Hadley were busy digging through a jewelry box, arguing over who was going to borrow a black-and-gold cuff bracelet. "Am I going to be able to read minds too?" she asked.

"No, honey," Hadley said. "It's just Olivia. And trust me, that's enough."

Olivia smacked her on the arm. "Came in handy when you wanted to know if Tom was cheating, didn't it?"

"Like the whole world didn't already know. Here, take it." She pushed the cuff onto Olivia's arm. "Looks better on you anyway."

"It really does," Olivia said, turning her wrist to admire her prize.

Alice felt like she should be doing something. Like grilling them for information, or demanding they take her to the secret underground lair that surely must exist. But she found their banter fascinating. It was just so *normal*.

Olivia laughed. "Alice, we're not mutants."

"Sorry. I'm just feeling a little confused. I thought something was supposed to happen."

"Technically, it already did. But we still need to complete your fusion."

"My what?"

Hadley's head popped up. "Ooh, can we hit up Choney's after? I'm starving."

"We literally just ate."

"So?"

"You have the metabolism of a cheetah."

They argued about whether they should in fact go get food for five minutes, then whether it would be Choney's or pizza. Alice felt like a spectator at a tennis match, her head moving back and forth with every innocuous volley.

Soxie turned the corner, her heels sinking into the soft carpet. "Okay, Tinsley said to go ahead without him. He'll catch up with us later."

"Really?" Hadley cocked her head. "That's weird."

Alice's chest had already seized at the sound of his name. "Why is that weird?"

They all looked at each other.

"Uh, well, maybe it's not," Olivia said. "Just because he was there for ours doesn't mean . . ."

"Doesn't mean what? You guys do realize I have no clue what's going on. Can you stop speaking in code?"

Soxie walked over, grabbed her by the shoulders, and spun her around so they were both facing her full-length mirror.

"Don't worry, Daniels. It'll all make sense. But first things first. What's the question?"

"The question?"

"Alice," Olivia said. "You know this."

All three of them were now standing behind her, staring at her reflection in the glass. She met each pair of eyes before answering. She did know this.

"Who are *we*?"

She barely had time to take a breath before her brain was assaulted with a barrage of images. It was like a dream she was having—and recalling—at the same time. Three girls waking up one day at age thirteen with an overwhelming need. A need to find each other. A boy with pale blue eyes telling them a story. Lecturing them. Protecting them. An impossibly long hallway. Mirrors. So many mirrors. Another dimension. Another realm. A place where demons roamed . . .

She grabbed her head to stop the room from spinning. It wasn't painful. But it wasn't pleasant.

"What is happening?"

Three sets of arms wrapped around her.

"It's okay, Alice. It's just our souls connecting."

"What?"

"You're a part of us now, and we're a part of you. She links us. She makes us we."

"Who?"

"The Huntress."

Alice watched Hadley devour a double cheeseburger like it was a cucumber finger sandwich. Too wired to eat, she pushed her plate of fries away. It was like watching a supermodel take down 5,000 calories. On the one hand, you were impressed she actually ate. On the other, you were jealous she actually ate.

Olivia agreed out loud that yes, it really was unfair. Assuming (correctly) that the comment was about her, Hadley took offense. So rather than get answers about demons and huntresses, Alice found herself refereeing an argument about hyperthyroidism and metabolic rates. Meanwhile, Soxie sat in silence, barely touching her salad and instead scanning the restaurant in judgment. Alice imagined she found most of it wanting, from the tchotchkes on the wall to the waiter who was most certainly high as a kite.

It was comfortable sitting there with them, eating lunch like regular teenagers. They might hunt demons and be forever connected by some supernatural being, but they were also just friends. Really good friends. And she was one of them now. The thought made her giddy.

"Hello, ladies. Hello, Alice."

And then there was *him.*

The mood turned on a dime. She could feel them joining forces, like children whose lame dad just showed up to ruin all the fun.

"So how'd it go?" he asked the table. "Everything good?"

Hadley shoved her plate aside and leaned back. "Well, the fries were a little soggy and my burger was overcooked. I think this place is overrated."

Colin looked at her like he'd been down this road a thousand times, and the masked chuckles from Soxie and Olivia didn't help. His lips thinned.

"Fine. Alice, we need to have a talk. Come with me."

Her stomach started swirling. "Where are we going?"

"For a drive."

She turned to the girls for help. Hadley was already on her phone, and the other two looked bored.

Olivia nudged her under the table. "Just go, Alice. We'll see you tomorrow."

She should have said no. After the way he treated her, she wanted to. But in the end she did what she was always going to do. What her butterflies were begging her to do. She went.

"It really is a beautiful spot. No wonder you spend so much time here."

They were on her favorite rock overlooking the city, a sacred, quiet place far above the noise and din. Getting there took time—the trail was steep and the undergrowth was prickly—but it was worth the effort. The air was clear, and the sunsets were so intense she burned calories just looking at them.

Colin eased himself down onto the warm rock, dangling his legs off the edge like she had done so many times before.

"Sit," he said, motioning to the spot next to him. He said it so casually, as if they did this all the time. As if this wasn't *her* rock, where she'd spent countless hours staring at the city, hoping for answers and praying for guidance. Those were private, personal moments she'd thought were her own. Until now.

"I'll stand. How did you know about this place?"

"It doesn't matter."

Her blood began to boil. "Doesn't matter? You kick me out of your car, disappear for months, leave me to think I'm losing my mind, and the whole time you were spying on me?"

"Alice, it's . . . complicated. There's more going on here than you can possibly understand."

"So now I'm an idiot?"

He groaned and ran a hand over his face. "This isn't going to get us anywhere. Can you maybe table the tantrum until after we've talked?"

"You're a jerk."

"So I've been told."

"Then why do I feel this way?"

His head snapped up. "What way?"

"You know what way." She heard the words come out of her mouth, yet she couldn't believe she was saying them. She might as well rip her heart out and toss it on the ground next to him so he could stomp all over it again.

"You're confused. It's been a long day."

She laughed. "Confused? Yes. I'm confused about a lot of things right now. But not that."

"Well, you're wrong."

Stomp. It hurt just as much as she knew it would. She'd spent months building a thick wall around her heart, only to have it crumble in the span of an afternoon. David had been right that day on the Triangle. She *was* pathetic.

"I want a different handler."

"Excuse me?"

"Or protector. Or whatever you are. I want another one."

His scowl turned into a smile—so radiant it almost blinded her. "What do you think this is? The FBI?"

Now he was laughing at her. She might be suffering from the mother of all crushes, but it didn't mean she was going to let him make fun of her. Last she checked, she still had her dignity.

With an audible huff, she turned and started marching back down the trail. Did she really need him? Maybe she could figure out this Huntress thing by herself.

Before she had a chance to think it through, a hand grabbed her by the elbow and spun her around.

"Dammit, Alice—"

"What the—"

Everything stopped. The desert song. The blowing wind. The rotation of the earth, maybe. They were standing too close. The heat from his body made her dizzy. When he released her, she didn't push away. She just stood there, staring at the hollow of his throat, struggling not to press her lips against it. They stayed locked in a frozen dance for as many beats as a heart takes to surrender. Because there was no denying it. The sun was setting, night was falling, and so was she.

It was Colin who finally broke the silence, his eyes glowing in the red light of dusk.

"I see a lot, Alice. She makes sure I do. But not you. I didn't see you coming."

She lay in bed awake that night for hours, Boop curled into a ball beside her, his breathing a metronome ticking steadily along with her repeating thoughts. Colin. *Colin.* His voice lingered in her ears, like a song she would never forget.

I'm not going to stop you. If you want to go, go. But I'm asking you . . . please stay and hear me out.

She couldn't have refused if she wanted to. Once given the choice, there was only one to make. Stay.

So they sat perched on her rock until the temperature dropped and the sun disappeared beneath a distant horizon of pink and gold. It was going to take some time to wrap her mind around everything she learned. She almost wished she'd brought a pen and paper to take notes.

"I know you have a lot of questions, but I need to tell you a story first."

"What kind of story?" she asked.

"The kind that helps if you keep an open mind. How familiar are you with ancient Greek mythology?"

"Like Zeus and Mount Olympus?"

"Yes. Have you ever heard of the Furies, sometimes referred to as the Erinyes?"

"The what?"

"Tisiphone, Alecto, and Megaera. They were the goddesses of vengeance, sisters. Commonly known as the Furies," Colin explained. "They punished mankind for crimes against the natural order."

"Okay . . ."

"Tisiphone was murder, Alecto was morality, and Megaera was jealousy and envy. Are you following?"

"No."

"Funny. Legend has it—"

"Legend. Really?"

"Touché," Colin said. "As the story goes, Tisiphone was to punish a man named Cithaeron for murdering his rival. So she possessed the body of a beautiful woman to get close and seduce him. You see, the Furies were not gifted with much in the looks department. Snakes for hair, bat wings—pretty hideous stuff. Anyway, instead of punishing him, she falls in love with him."

"Lemme guess. They get married and have lots of bat-winged babies."

"Yes to the baby part. No to the bat wings. Either way, this does not go over well with her sisters. They rip away her mortal disguise and force Cithaeron to see her true form. He takes one look at the real Tisiphone and basically tells her to drop dead. Now, if the name Furies tells you anything—"

"She kills him."

"This is not a test, Alice. But yes. With a poisonous snake from her head."

"Sounds like he deserved it."

"You're right. He did. Now stop interrupting, please. Goddesses aren't built for broken hearts. They tend to lash out, and since Cithaeron was already dead, the only one left to suffer was the offspring. A baby girl. So Tisiphone gifted her with a curse. The curse of never feeling love for another being, god or mortal. Then she took a dagger, slit her own throat, and forced the baby to drink her blood, thereby giving her one last gift: her immortality. Before Tisiphone faded to nothing, she named the girl Philautia, which in ancient Greek means self-love. The kind she never knew. The only kind Philautia would ever know.

"Imagine living forever without the ability to love others, your only companion the image you see in the mirror. After centuries of loneliness, Philautia couldn't take it anymore. She took her mother's dagger and stabbed her own reflection, shattering both mirror and soul into a thousand shards, trapping her in the realm behind the mirror for eternity."

"That's so sad," Alice said.

"Yes and no. The curse was broken. She was free to love the mortals she observed on the other side. They were the companions she'd never had before. She watched over them, even through their subconscious reflections, their dreams.

"But when she entered the mirror, she created another realm—a doorway to mankind that did not exist before. And the universe requires balance. Where there is good, there must also be evil."

"Demons?"

"Demons. Evil spirits. Whatever you want to call them. They gained access to her realm and started infecting humans through their reflections, infiltrating both their bodies and their dreams.

"To make it right, Philautia began gifting pieces of her soul to worthy mortals—those strong enough to enter her realm and do what must be done to protect mankind. Through her human vessels, she has been hunting this evil—these demons—for centuries."

"You're saying Philautia gave a piece of her soul to Soxie, Olivia, and Hadley? They're her human vessels?"

"Not just them, Alice," Colin replied. "Philautia is the Huntress, and as of this morning, so are you. It's no longer just her fight. It's yours too."

"But. It's my birthday." (She still didn't know why she said that.)

"I know. Happy birthday, Alice."

She didn't get a chance to learn more. When her teeth started chattering, he demanded they stop. The path was difficult to navigate in the fading light, so he kept her hand firmly clasped in his the entire way down. She had tried to mind.

As she drifted off to sleep, it wasn't goddesses, broken curses, or mystical realms full of mirrors that filled her head. It was three words.

Tomorrow it begins.

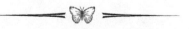

She stood in front of a warped mirror, a golden dagger gripped in her hand. Even though she knew she was dreaming, she pleaded with her reflection not to ask the question.

"Please, Alice. Don't."

"I'm sorry, Alice. We have to."

"Let's say it together, then."

"*What happens when it ends?*"

chapter 5

"So Daniels, how was the history lesson? Tinsley bore you to death, or what?"

Alice stopped in the middle of the hallway as a well-dressed redhead sidled up next to her. A subtle whiff of coconut and jasmine tickled her nose.

She lifted her eyebrows. "What are you doing here?"

"It's a school, right?" said Soxie, giving her surroundings a bored look. "I guess I'm here to learn."

"But—"

"Sox, Alice, wait up!"

Alice twisted around to see Hadley and Olivia jogging down the hall toward them. A few people stopped to stare, and whispers began floating through the air like dandelion fuzz. It wasn't just any old Tuesday.

The Waywards had returned to Remington High.

Once Hadley and Olivia caught up, Alice shook her head. "Guys . . . I don't understand. Why are you here?"

Soxie twirled around and began click-clacking her way backward down the hall. The rest of them kept pace, as if linked together by invisible string.

"Why do you think?" she said. "You're here, so we're here."

Alice smiled as warmth radiated through her body. It didn't bother her that students were nearly nose-diving to get out of their way. Let them talk. Their judgment meant nothing. These girls—they already meant everything.

"Nice to see you, Ms. Roxland," a teacher called from his class doorway.

Soxie glanced in his direction and gave him a quick salute.

Hadley stopped to study a trophy case that was filled not with trophies but a series of collages, compliments of *The Reel*. The rest of them followed her lead.

"This place hasn't changed," she said, trailing a slender finger along the glass.

Olivia looked over her shoulder. "Wow. I can't believe they still have that picture."

Alice squeezed in between them. It was a picture of the three of them from freshman year. They looked so young. How had she never thought to look in here? Or in past yearbooks, for that matter?

"Probably for the best," Olivia said. "You found us when you were ready. That's all that matters."

Alice stared at the photograph. They weren't exactly smiling, but they didn't look unhappy. They looked like three friends posing for a picture. Yet she couldn't help but feel like something was missing.

The early bell rang and the bodies around them started moving en masse, parting for them like the Red Sea.

Soxie clapped her hands together. "Okay, enough reminiscing, girls. We need to get our schedules."

"Thank you for being here," Alice said. "It means a lot." She didn't realize how much until she said it out loud.

Hadley gave her a wink and a smile as the other two girls pulled her away. "We're sisters, honey. We stick together."

Alice felt her heart soar at the thought. *Sisters.*

"Ali, Barry's picking us up at noon for lunch," Soxie called over her shoulder, fluffing her unruly curls. "Faculty parking lot. Don't be late."

"Who's Barry?"

But the bell rang again, and Soxie's red head disappeared in the crowd.

Alice could sense dozens of eyes trained on her, could feel their fear and anxiety, even without Olivia confirming it. All she could do was smile, though. Gods and demons aside, it felt good to belong again. Maybe truly for the first time. She turned around and headed to class.

Barry, it turned out, was the Roxlands' driver, among other things. He was Scottish, compulsively punctual, and preferred driving his '57 Corvette to the Roxlands' Bentley, a car that, he was quick to proclaim, "handled like a whale."

He was there waiting for them without fail every day at 12:00 noon. If one of them had the audacity to be late, she got an earful upon arrival. He was intense but fair, and his heavily accented points were hard to dispute. Alice adored him from the start, and being on time soon became its own reward.

It was nice not sitting alone on her crappy park bench anymore. But if she thought lunch was going to be a bunch of laughs over Sonic burgers, she was woefully mistaken. The next two weeks were a crash course in Greek mythology, held in the Roxlands' kitchen. Despite the impressive layout—granite countertops, double islands, and restaurant-grade appliances—it was fast becoming her least favorite place.

"What was the War of the Titans?"

"A really good movie?"

Olivia shot her a look. "That's *Clash of the Titans*."

"Fine," Alice said, disappointed that her joke fell flat. "It was the war that decided which generation of gods would rule the universe. The Olympians won."

Hadley leaned against the refrigerator, scraping the bottom of a yogurt cup. "And who were the Olympian gods?"

Alice swiveled back and forth on her stool as she tried to recall the names. "Aphrodite, Apollo, Ares, Demeter, Dionysus, Hestia, Hera, Hermes . . ." She paused to think, looking at the ceiling, before continuing, "Oh, Poseidon and Hades. Athena, Hestia. Tyche. And . . . crap. Why do I always forget the name of that ugly one?"

"Hephaestus," Soxie said. "And you said Hestia twice."

"You also forgot my favorite, Artemis," Hadley added, pointing her spoon at Alice. "She kicked ass."

"Okay then, Hephaestus and Artemis."

"And?" Olivia prompted.

Alice recounted them on her fingers. "Wait, who else?"

"Zeus, dummy. Only the most important one."

She threw her hands in the air. "Give me a break. Everybody knows that one."

Soxie pushed her pasta bowl aside. "Ali, this is the world Philautia came from. She's part of us now. You need to understand it and respect it."

"I know, I know," Alice said, waving a hand in surrender. "It's just . . . it's hard to think of them as real. I always thought they were made-up stories to explain things like the seasons or the sun moving across the sky."

"Actually, while we're on that subject"—Olivia picked up a book from the pile next to her—"tell me who the goddess of the harvest is, and explain the origins of the seasons."

Alice sought for patience deep within. "Demeter is the goddess of the harvest. Her daughter, Persephone, was abducted by Hades, and—"

"Wait. Tell us first who Hades and Persephone are."

Alice crossed her arms and stared Olivia down. "Hades is the god of The Underworld, and Persephone is the saucy minx who seduced him."

Hadley stifled a laugh, but Olivia slammed the book shut and hopped off the counter.

"Alice, I get it. This stuff is boring. But it wasn't always myth. It was real. Demons are real too, and they can be dangerous. Colin's not letting you anywhere near the Realm until you start taking this seriously."

"Okay, okay. I'm sorry," Alice said. "What exactly is this 'Realm,' anyway?" She used air quotes because it was hard to say the word "Realm" otherwise.

"It's the world Philautia created behind the mirror. It's where we hunt demons. It's a big deal, Alice. A huge responsibility. You have to know that."

"But . . . what's it like?"

"It's . . . intense," Olivia said slowly, as if trying hard to find the right words. "Magical. Impossible to explain, really. You'll just have to wait and see."

Alice pressed her head in her hands, staring at the remnants of her pasta. "What if I can't handle it?"

Hadley moved to sit on the stool next to her. "Honey, you'll be fine. It's okay to feel a little anxious. Imagine how freaked out we were. We were only thirteen, and Colin wasn't exactly what you'd call patient."

"How did that work, anyway? He just showed up one day and started giving orders?"

Soxie chuckled. "Pretty much. Scrawny, pimply-faced kid then too."

Alice had a hard time picturing it. "But why? I still don't understand his role in all of this."

"Wait a second." Olivia leaned forward. "I can't believe he didn't tell you."

"Tell me what?"

"Alice, the Huntress only exists because one of the Furies fell for a mortal. A mortal man who was killed right after she was born."

"Yeah, he told me that part." Alice frowned. "So, what are you telling me? Colin's a descendant of that man?"

They all looked at each other.

"No," Olivia said. "Colin *is* that man. He's Cithaeron."

She didn't sleep a wink that night. She couldn't get it out of her head. Colin was Cithaeron. The man who'd rejected a goddess thousands of years earlier. The man who'd *died* rejecting a goddess. What was her name? *Tisiphone.* Even thinking it gave her the willies, as if her snake-headed ghost was standing behind her, ready to sink a serpent into her neck.

Granted, she'd seen some impossible things in the past few months. Reflections that talked back. Demons getting sucked into mirrors. But this new information was an even tougher pill to swallow. She didn't want it to be true. It changed everything. Colin wasn't just a guy she had an Everest-size crush on. He was something else entirely.

These thoughts were still raging in her head when her alarm went off at seven thirty. Rather than yawning her way through the day, she decided to skip school and take a "mental health day." Something she'd never needed more before than she did now.

She vegged on the couch with Boop for a while, catching up on morning talk shows and general news. It was all just noise, though. She could barely focus. Everything was happening so fast, yet somehow not fast enough. If she was supposed to be hunting demons, then maybe she should be hunting demons already. She was tired of waiting. It was like the dangling live wires in the Tough Mudder Rachel had made her run the previous year. The zap wasn't the worst part. It was the anticipation of the zap.

She was ready to get zapped again.

When she got out of the shower, she paused before wiping the condensation from the mirror, her hand hovering. The Realm behind the mirror. That was what this was all about. Was Philautia watching her right now? Could she see her through the foggy glass? Strangely, the thought didn't bother her. She should probably feel violated in some way, yet instead she felt . . . curious. Connected. Enchanted.

"Mirror, mirror on the wall," she whispered, laughing at herself. She placed her palm flat on the wet surface and imagined the Huntress on the other side, doing the same. Not that she knew what she looked like, but in her mind's eye she envisioned Helen of Troy. It seemed appropriate. Draped white robe, golden leaf crown, sandals laced to the knee. And, of course, beautiful. A face that could launch a thousand ships. She wondered what that would be like. To look in the mirror every day and see something like that.

She swiped her hand in an arc across the glass, dispersing the moisture and revealing her own, average face. Nope. Definitely not the fairest of them all. With a resigned sigh, she wiped away the rest of the steam.

If she couldn't sleep and she couldn't sit still, she needed to move. So she headed to the one place she knew would ground her.

It was 11:00 a.m. on a weekday, and the parking lot was almost empty. She stopped at the base of the trailhead to stretch, preparing to run all the way to her rock. Maybe by running her body into the ground, her mind could take some time off.

It always felt so easy at first. As if her feet were spring-loaded—or wing-tipped, like Hermes's feet. Hermes, the messenger god. It was crazy that she knew that now. Not as myth (or a luxury handbag line), but as part of the past. Unreal in its realness.

A lot of good it did her after a couple of minutes, though, when her feet started to feel like cinder blocks. She could use Hermes's little wings right about now.

By the time she made it to her rock, she was close to vomiting. She fell onto her hands and knees, gasping for air. Without the energy to stand back up, she crawled forward and collapsed on her back, the sun warming her face and the rock warming her body.

She lay like that for several minutes, staring into the blue expanse.

Then she felt him. Part of her wondered if she was expecting him. She quickly dashed the thought aside and sat up. She stuffed her hair into her Broncos cap, used the end of her T-shirt to wipe her sweaty face, and drained the water bottle in her pack dry. By the time he sat down beside her, she was as composed as she was going to get.

She kept her eyes straight ahead. They sat in companionable silence, staring at the vast metropolis below. She had so many questions—so many things she wanted to know but was afraid to learn. So she said nothing and instead closed her eyes and waited, focusing on the muted sounds of distant traffic.

"It was another age—a different world," he began. "I barely recognize who I was back then."

She held her breath, listening.

"I was shallow and weak," he continued. "Morally corrupt. Born into wealth and power not even imaginable by today's standards. I wanted for nothing. I only knew how to take. I took people's pride. Their hearts. I took their lives. For sport."

Her throat tightened.

"The truth is, Tisiphone did me a favor when she killed me with her snake. It was only through death that I was able to see what I truly was."

She opened her eyes, keeping them fixed on the horizon. "You died."

"Yes, Alice. The mortal body of Cithaeron Augustus Karalis Remes ceased to live a long, long time ago. His soul was sent to Hades."

She turned to look at him. Her stomach moved as their eyes met, but she willed the butterflies back to sleep. She needed to hear this. All of it.

"Are you immortal?"

He laughed. "No."

"How old are you?"

He smiled, his eyes glittering in the sun.

Flutter.

"Despite what you think, I'm eighteen. I *am* Colin Tinsley. But I'm also—"

"Cithaeron," she finished for him.

His blue eyes clouded a deep, dark brown. She gasped.

"Sorry," he said, shutting them and signaling for her to wait. After a few seconds, he opened them again, revealing their crystal-like blue.

She stared at him in disbelief.

"It's been a while since I've heard anyone say it out loud."

"Define 'a while.'"

He ran his fingers through his hair. "I don't know for sure. I have no recollection of my time in The Underworld with Hades. My first memory after my life as Cithaeron is waking up in the body of a thirteen-year-old boy sometime in the fifth century."

"Fifth century? As in sixteen hundred years ago?"

"Yes. My daughter made a deal with Hades for my soul, and I first awoke in the year 432 AD."

"Your . . . your daughter?" she repeated, a little louder than expected.

He took a moment before responding. "Tisiphone's baby, the daughter we left behind. Her name was Philautia."

She felt herself getting light-headed, both from the subject matter and from the heat. She shook her head to clear it, then ran her hands over her face to reset.

"When you 'first awoke' . . . What does that mean?"

He tiredly rubbed his forehead. "You know, this is a lot easier with thirteen-year-olds."

"Oh, I'm sorry. Would you rather I throw a snake at you?"

He let out a short, masculine laugh. "The girls were right about you. Those demons don't know what's in store for them."

She gave him a stony look.

"Okay," he said, putting his hands up in a "you got me" gesture. "And please, no more snakes. A viper got me in the eighth. It was right after I turned thirteen too. Never even got a chance to find my girls. What a waste."

He shook his head in disappointment, as if discussing the loss of a good suitcase or vacuum cleaner. Not a life.

She pulled her knees up and hugged them to her chest. "So you can die." It was difficult to get the words out. The thought alone sent her to a dark place.

"I'm human, Alice. I assure you, I can die. But when this life is over, I'll wake up in another. Maybe two years later, or twenty. It's up to her."

"I don't understand. You just wake up in some random thirteen-year-old's body? What happens to them?"

He scratched his head, thinking. "Actually, 'wake up' is probably the wrong way to put it. I become aware."

"Aware . . ."

"Nothing happens to them, because I am them. I am Colin Tinsley. On the day of my thirteenth birthday, at the exact time I was born thirteen years earlier, I was flooded with the memories of my past lives, and given the knowledge of my current mission."

Alice fidgeted with the brim of her hat, as if the action might help her see more clearly. "And what's your mission?"

"To find the girls Philautia has chosen and prepare them. In this life it's Soxie, Olivia, and Hadley. They're my responsibility; it's my job to ensure they're able to do theirs."

"Why only girls?"

The corner of his mouth lifted. "Good question. I have my theories, but I think it comes down to 'best persons for the job.' After early adolescence, it's harder for her soul to fuse. You were an . . . exception."

She let a few moments pass, trying to make sense of it all. One thing in particular was sticking.

"So in each lifetime since you were Cithaeron, you become aware at age thirteen of all the lives you've lived before."

At the sound of his name, his eyes turned dark again. She watched with fascination as they slowly lightened to match the sky above.

He blinked. "Yes."

She turned her gaze toward the valley below, unable to register what she was seeing. Because all she saw was him. Over, and over, and over.

"That sounds lonely."

"Wha . . . Why do you say that?"

She hugged her knees tighter. "I think it would be sad to remember my family and friends, all the people I've loved in every life. To know I'll keep on living without them. I don't know that I would want to get close to anyone ever again."

"Alice . . ."

She closed her eyes. It hurt to hear him say her name, to know he would be having this same conversation again and again. Maybe next time with a Jennifer, or an Elizabeth. Did it matter? A hundred years from now, when he was someone else, would he even remember her name? She took in a lungful of desert air and opened her eyes.

"You said I'm the exception. What does that mean?"

"I don't know yet. But I promise I'll do whatever I can to keep you safe."

She turned to look at him again, the warm breeze tickling her neck and pain squeezing her heart. "Because it's your job."

"Yes."

She was going to say it. She knew better, yet she couldn't keep the words in.

"What if I want more?"

He closed his eyes and turned away. "Alice, don't."

"Why won't you just admit it? You feel it too."

He quickly rose to his feet, refusing to make eye contact. "I'm sorry. I don't know what you're talking about."

She leapt up, eager for a fight. "You're a liar."

He placed his hands on his hips and kept his eyes on the city as he said, his tone all business, "The girls are bringing you into the Realm tomorrow. Make sure you listen to them, and do exactly as they say. I don't want to hear about you pulling any stupid stunts."

God, she hated him right now. She hated how easy it was for him to turn it off. For him to not feel. Was this what came of living countless lives? It wasn't fair. She wanted to unfeel too.

"Don't worry," she said, fighting to keep her voice steady. "I absolve you of any responsibility. If I do anything stupid, it's on me."

With her head held high, she marched past him and began her walk down the mountain.

This time, he didn't stop her.

chapter 6

The next day was Saturday, and Barry showed up at five o'clock. She'd been so preoccupied trying to catch up on homework that she didn't even hear the doorbell ring. But she did hear her mom's laughter.

She walked down the stairs and paused before entering the foyer to listen to the conversation taking place.

". . . lovely girl. I see she takes after her mother."

Judy laughed. "Oh now, stop. You Scottish men are all alike."

"How's that? Devilishly handsome and charming?"

Her mom laughed again. Alice leaned her head against the wall, relishing the sound. It had been so long since she'd heard Judy laugh in a way that sounded sincere, not forced. Boop, curious to see who was at the door, started to wander past.

"No, buddy," she whispered, bending over to pick him up. "Don't interrupt." Her mom needed this. Maybe some good old-fashioned flirting was just what the doctor ordered.

". . . perhaps we can discuss it over dinner sometime?"

"I'd love that."

Alice's mouth fell open. Okay, maybe it was more than just flirting. Boop chose that moment to let out a high-pitched mewl, squirm from her grasp, and dart around the corner.

"Boop, no!" Judy chided. "Sorry, this is Alice's cat. He loves new people."

"Ah. Well, to be honest with ye, I'm more of a dog person. We have a coupla sweet li'l girls back at the house. Would love ye to meet them sometime."

Alice covered her mouth. If those Dobermans were little, she was King Kong.

". . . will see if she's ready. Alice! Alice, honey, your ride is here!"

She backed up to the bottom of the staircase before answering, "Coming!"

Doing her best to keep a straight face, she turned the corner to see that Boop was working overtime to turn Barry into a cat person. The little traitor was in his arms, purring up a storm.

"Hi, Barry. I see you've found a new friend." She gestured to the cat but gave her mom a sideways glance. Judy pretended not to notice.

After a few more minutes feeling like a third wheel, Alice couldn't hide her grin as she joined Barry in the front seat. At least somebody's love life was looking up. He seemed a little old for her mom, but who was she to talk? She was crushing on a 1,600-year-old.

By the time they pulled into the circular drive, Alice knew a great deal about Barry, the Roxlands' driver (among other things). He was born and raised in Edinburgh. Moved to the States in his late twenties. Was married for two years before he lost his wife to leukemia. Started working for the Roxlands shortly after and considered them family. No kids, unless you counted Soxie and her uncle Mayron, and he trained guard dogs in his "spare time." Oh, and he was also a whiz in the kitchen, if he did say so himself.

Okay, Barry, she thought. *You've got my vote.*

True to his word, Barry whipped up a delicious grilled salmon dinner, which Alice and the girls enjoyed on the back terrace. Afterward, they adjourned to the library: a cozy room with floor-to-ceiling bookshelves and what she assumed was a fortune's worth of first editions.

"A few ground rules, Daniels," Soxie began, falling into one of the two leather couches in the middle of the room.

"I know. Do exactly as you say. And don't pull any stupid stunts."

"He's such an ass." Soxie rolled her eyes. "What else did he tell you?"

"Oh, the usual," Alice said, dropping into the seat opposite her. "How he's been reincarnated for centuries to help his daughter and her huntresses fight evil. That sort of thing. By the way, is he in school, or does he spend all his time stalking people?"

"He graduated early. I guess when you're a thousand years old you get impatient with high school." Soxie shrugged. "But he's deferring a year to start college with us. He's just really protective. You'll get used to it."

She doubted that. "Is that why you were being homeschooled? Because he didn't want you at Remington without him?"

"Ugh," Hadley said from her seat by the fire. "I hate the term 'homeschooled.' It sounds so provincial."

"Easy with your word of the day, Hadz," Soxie said. "And no. We made the switch sophomore year because of the whole Wayward Sisters thing."

"Remington mentioned something about that. Who—"

"Exactly," Hadley interrupted. "Because he's the one who started it."

"But why?"

"Because he's an idiot."

"Agreed. But it still doesn't answer my question."

Soxie shrugged. "We stick to ourselves, there's three of us, we have different-colored hair, and I live in Wayward Palms. You do the math."

"What does the color of your hair have to do with anything?"

"*The Witches of Eastwick*. Some eighties movie. The actresses had black, blond, and red hair."

"That is so dumb."

"We are talking about a guy who drives a Hummer."

"Good point."

"Anyway," Soxie said, "once it made it on *The Reel*, it never went away. Not that we care what people think, but O was the one who had to actually hear it."

Alice turned to look behind her. Olivia was leaning against the wall by the window, quietly observing. She seemed to do that sometimes: fade into the background while others took the spotlight. As extraordinary as her mind reading was, Alice had never considered what an awful burden it must be as well until now.

"I'm sorry," she said. "That's rough. Have you always been able to do it?"

Olivia blew her hair out of her face. "No. Not until I fused. The Huntress gifts it to one in every triad. Lucky me, I guess."

"Triad," Alice repeated. She turned back around and stared at Soxie. "The three of you have been doing this for five years. How many demons have you exorcised?"

"One thousand, four hundred and twenty-three," Hadley recited without looking up from her phone.

"Okay . . . is there any reason to think Philautia isn't happy with that number?"

Hadley raised her head, and Soxie gave Alice a pointed look. "She doesn't hold performance reviews, but it hasn't exactly been easy. What are you trying to say?"

Alice looked down. "Sorry. I didn't mean it like that. It's just . . . why me? Why now?"

As expected, no one was quick to answer. The more she thought about it, the less it made sense. They'd been together for years, knew everything there was to know about each other, shared countless memories, and had made a difference in at least 1,423 lives. Maybe that wasn't a lot when compared to the population of the earth, but history had proven that one man could change the world. Fourteen hundred could potentially end it. Looking at it that way, they were clearly doing just fine without her. So the question remained: What was she doing here?

"Only the Huntress can answer that," Olivia said, walking around to sit on the couch next to her. "But if it's any consolation, we're glad you're here."

Alice felt her eyes sting. Olivia was more than just a mind reader.

Soxie swung her legs off the table and leaned forward. "Listen to me, Ali. You may have come late to the game, but it doesn't make you any less a part of us. Who knows why she chose you now. Hell, maybe she's planning on firing Hadley for always being on her phone."

"Hey!"

"The thing is," she continued, "it doesn't matter why. We still have a job to do, and like it or not, so do you. You're stuck with us, Daniels."

Alice smiled. Those might have been the best five words she'd ever heard.

"Lucky me, I guess."

They took the stairs to the second floor. Alice counted seven doors before they reached the one they were looking for. Soxie pushed it open and flipped a switch to her right, revealing a large room full of mirrors.

"Used to be a ballroom, but Uncle May converted it to a ballet studio when I moved in. He can be pretty clueless sometimes, but he meant well."

Alice walked to the center of the room and stood beneath a crystal chandelier. A grand piano sat diagonally in the corner. She turned in a slow circle, her reflection greeting her at every turn, even from the wall of windows as darkness fell outside.

The three other girls joined her.

"Here," Hadley said as she reached out to offer Alice her hand. "You'll need to be physically connected to one of us when we enter. Make sure you don't let go until we're on the other side, okay?"

"Wait—we're going now? The Realm's in here?" Alice turned in another circle, searching for a secret panel or trapdoor she may have missed.

"It doesn't work like that. The Realm doesn't exist *here*. It exists there." Hadley pointed to her own reflection in the glass.

Alice shook her head. "I don't understand."

"You will," Soxie said. "Now shut up and pay attention."

Alice was about to take offense, but then all three of them pulled shiny silver discs from their pockets and her attention shifted. "What are those?"

"Here." Hadley handed hers over.

The metal object felt heavy in her palm, but not weight-wise. It was hard to explain; Alice could feel its energy pulsing through her hand. She turned it over and noticed tiny writing etched on the back. She squinted to read it: *Sterling—Tiffany & Co.*

She looked up. "Is this a joke?"

Hadley laughed. "No, silly. It's just a compact. It's what's inside that counts."

She tried to open it, but it wouldn't budge. "Why won't it open? What's in it?"

"It won't open for you because it's not yours," Olivia said. "These are our gifts from Philautia. They're fragments of the mirror she shattered to create the Realm."

Alice stared at the object in her hand, in awe of what it represented: thousands of years and a broken curse. "What do they do?"

"They're our keys to the Realm. Our compasses—not in the literal sense, but they guide us, so that's what we call them."

She reluctantly handed Hadley's back. "When do I get mine?"

"Easy, huntress," Soxie said. "That's up to Colin. Besides, let's try walking before we run." She paused to find her eyes in the mirror. "You ready?"

"Yes?" Alice said, not at all sure she was.

Hadley grabbed her hand and squeezed. "Don't worry, entering the Realm from here is *way* better than jumping directly in. Trust me. You'll be fine. Now keep your eyes on the mirror, and don't forget to breathe."

Alice nodded and inhaled sharply, because she had indeed forgotten to breathe. Then she gripped Hadley's hand hard, determined not to let go. Maybe ever.

Soxie counted down from three, and a second later she popped open her compact. Olivia and Hadley did the same. If Alice had blinked, she'd have missed it. One second their reflections were there, and the next they were gone. Like a special effect in a movie. She could still see the reflection of the chandelier, the windows, the grand piano, but their own images had vanished. She waved her free hand in front of her to be sure, but there was nothing. Now she knew how a vampire must feel.

She turned to see the other girls smiling at her.

"Welcome to the other side," Soxie said with an exaggerated bow.

Alice looked around. They were still in the dance studio. It didn't look like anything had changed—and yet it had. The piano seemed off, somehow.

Hadley pried her hand free of Alice's grip. "Go ahead," she said, "look around. Just don't leave the room yet."

Alice began slowly pacing the studio. *Not* seeing herself in the mirrored walls was bizarre, to say the least. But as she drew closer to the piano, she noticed something even more bizarre: the lettering on the gold plate above the keys was wrong. It read: *reztilruW*. She turned to the girls to confirm her discovery.

The three of them were standing under the chandelier, watching her with something akin to pride. She felt like a giddy schoolgirl having passed her first exam. That's why the piano seemed off. It wasn't just the wording on the gold plaque. The whole room was flipped; everything was backward.

"You guys, this is amazing!"

A soft whimper and the sound of clicking paws interrupted her mini-celebration. She turned toward the door just as one of Barry's "little Dobermans" trotted into the room.

The dog stopped, sniffed the air, and then made a beeline for Olivia. Alice tensed, fully expecting her friend to get knocked flat on her goth-clad rear end. Instead, eighty pounds of Doberman ran straight through her. *Through* her.

Alice doubted her own eyes for a second. The dog, clearly agitated, skidded to a halt and let out a long, mournful howl.

"It's okay, girl," Olivia cooed. "I know. It's so frustrating."

Alice turned to the mirror to see an empty room with a manic dog now running in circles, yelping and scratching up the floor.

"We'd better move before Schlemmer gets here," Soxie said.

"She knows we're here?"

"Dogs sense things we can't," Olivia explained. "Hammacher always knows when we cross over."

As the animal ran by, Alice reached out to touch its dark fur, only to have her hand slice through nothing but air. She would have commented on how creepy that felt if it weren't for the sound of another upset canine. The distant howl put them all on alert. Hadley motioned for her to come close, and the four of them formed a tight circle in the center of the room.

"By the way, Daniels," Soxie said with a mischievous gleam in her eye, "we may hunt demons, but it's not all work and no play. Just you wait. You ain't seen nothing yet."

Alice was pretty sure being invisible and intangible was already a lot to "see," so she was happy to learn they weren't melting into the mirrors or disappearing into the floor. All they had to do was leave the room through the same door they'd entered. Easy enough.

But as they were about to pass through, the other dog (Schlemmer, she presumed) careened around the corner. Her paws failing to find purchase on the polished wood floor, she slid right through Soxie and Olivia and banged into the wall of windows with a loud thump. Then she scrambled up and quickly joined Hammacher in an ear-piercing howling contest.

"Schlemmy girl, it's okay!" Olivia yelled.

"Can they hear her?" Alice asked Hadley.

"I don't think so, but you can't blame her for trying. Look at those poor things." She nodded toward the far wall of mirrors. Alice now saw a room containing just a piano and two dogs, each competing to see which could out-crazy the other. She wasn't a dog person, but right now she empathized with their plight. If it was socially acceptable, she would have been screaming and running in circles for the past six months.

"Enough with the damn dogs," Soxie said. "Let's hustle before Barry shows up."

That lit a fire under both Hadley's and Olivia's butts, and the next thing Alice knew she was being hastily herded out of the room.

The wall opposite the door looked exactly how they'd left it: a narrow table with flowers sitting below a Degas-like painting (or perhaps even an actual Degas?). Priceless painting aside, Alice didn't see anything strange or noteworthy—until, that is, she caught a glimpse around the corner. Instead of a long corridor with seven-something doors, there was nothing but blackness; it was a big, empty void. She instinctively jumped back, nearly yanking Hadley's arm off in the process.

"Honey, relax." Hadley patted her hand. "It just looks scary from here. You'll understand once we pass through."

"Pass through?" Alice said, her chest thumping. "I thought we already did."

"We're entering through a mirror. We're on the other side, but that room"—Hadley gestured toward the dance studio—"is not the Realm. Think of it as an antechamber. It'll be like this anytime you enter through a mirror. But like I said, it's way better than jumping straight in."

Alice indicated she understood, even if that couldn't be further from the truth. "Fake it 'til you make it," Aunt Molly used to say. Right now, it was the best advice she could hope for—especially as she watched Olivia and Soxie walk directly into the wall of nothing.

Could a wall of nothing be deemed a wall? It felt wrong to call it that. It was just . . . blank. Empty space, without the space. Almost like static on an old-fashioned television, but black instead of gray. Apparently, this was the entrance to the infamous Realm. At least Soxie was true to her word: Alice clearly *hadn't* seen anything yet.

Hadley kept a firm grip on her hand as the two of them moved toward the void. Alice wanted to keep her eyes open, but right before they stepped through she lost her nerve and slammed them shut. If they were about to plummet feetfirst into nothingness, she'd rather not retain the visual.

To her surprise, the floor never wavered. It remained solid under her feet, as if the Roxlands' hall was still there after all.

She took a few awkward steps, then opened her eyes.

And her jaw nearly hit the still-solid floor.

She'd seen this place before. Or something like it. She was at the end of a long hallway, but it was nothing like the one she'd just left. This one was so long she couldn't see the end. And instead of doors, there were mirrors. More mirrors than she'd ever seen—probably more than anyone on earth had ever seen. They covered every surface, including the ceiling and floor. Some were round or oval with beveled edges and antique-looking glass; others were square or rectangular and very modern. Some were as big as a truck, others so small she could barely see them. They didn't hang; they floated in a blackish-gray space, haphazardly arranged. There must have been thousands of them. Millions.

"Oh my god," she couldn't help but whisper.

As the girls walked on, the mirrors did not reflect them. They reflected only the images of the mirrors across from them, each casting its own dim glow on the space, creating a dizzying spectacle of color and light. Everywhere she looked, Alice saw endless glass and frames, mirrors reflecting mirrors. It was something from a dream, yet somehow even more unbelievable.

"What do you think?"

Alice looked up, and there Olivia was—standing on the wall above her, *sideways*. Before she had a chance to yelp in shock, her friend pushed off the wall and, floating in midair, flipped her body like a circus performer before landing gracefully on another mirror twenty feet away—on the ceiling. Alice had to remind herself to breathe, because unless she was mistaken, Olivia had just *flown through the air* and was now hanging upside down like a vampire bat. Her all-black clothing did nothing to erase the image from her mind.

"How are you doing?" Hadley asked, giving Alice's hand a tiny squeeze.

It was a difficult question to answer. She'd just walked into a world that shouldn't exist. It was beautiful—there was no question about that—but it was overwhelming too.

Hadley nudged her gently, and the only thing she could think to say was what she was feeling: "I had no idea."

"I know," Hadley said. "And this is just one passage."

"There are more of these?"

Hadley nodded. "Oh, yeah. There's more."

"Guys, c'mon!"

Alice looked up. Soxie's red head was poking through the wall above them. Her heavily bangled arm waved at them, beckoning them to hurry.

"Coming!" Olivia called, skipping along the surfaces of mirrors like lily pads, easily turning from ceiling to wall, then wall to floor. With one last leap, she landed next to Alice as if she weighed no more than a paper airplane.

"Isn't it something?" she asked, her face flushed from her weightless acrobatics.

Alice answered with a vehement yes. It was something, alright. It was beyond something.

"Want to demonstrate how we mark it, O?" Hadley asked.

"Mark what?" Alice asked.

Olivia took her by the arm and turned her around. They were now facing a large set of windows that looked into the dance studio. There was the piano, the chandelier, and the wall of mirrors on the other side.

Then it dawned on Alice: These weren't windows. She was looking into the room from *behind* the wall of mirrors. This was what it was like to see human beings from behind their reflections; this must be what the Huntress had seen for centuries. The world as viewed from an endless hall full of supernatural, two-way mirrors.

Olivia flipped open her compass like a police badge and pointed it at the studio. "We don't need to mark this because we've entered through it before. But this is how you'd mark a new one. You're sort of giving the compass the coordinates so it can find it again."

Alice stared at the wall of see-through mirrors. Schlemmer was gone but Hammacher was still there, curled up in a ball, softly whimpering. She turned to look down the long hallway behind her. "Couldn't you just retrace your steps?"

"To what?" Olivia asked.

Alice swiveled back around, only to find another never-ending hall of mirrors. The studio was gone.

"It's constantly changing," said Olivia. "Nothing here is static. Think about what it must've looked like a thousand years ago, before modern mirrors were invented. Just a bunch of polished copper, volcanic glass, and maybe even reflective pools. We tried once to map it. Took about three hours before we realized everything we'd recorded was different when we tried to follow it again. It was a huge waste of time."

"That's why you can't be here without a compass," Hadley added. "Not only would you never be able to find your way back, you can't open any of the mirrors without it."

"Hello-ooooo," came Soxie's voice behind them.

Alice turned around. Wasn't she just above them?

Olivia laughed. "Come on, let's have some fun!" She took off toward Soxie's voice, hopping from mirror to mirror before disappearing into the floor.

Alice gaped. "Wh—where did she go?"

"You'll see," Hadley said. "Don't worry, we'll go slow."

"Do we have to stay on the mirrors?" Alice asked. "What happens if you step between them?"

"Try it," Hadley said, nodding toward the gap of blackish-gray space.

Alice dipped her toe like she was testing the temperature of water in a pool. Instead of sinking through, her foot met something solid. Solid-ish. It was spongy but without the suction, like the ground in a dream. It was there, but it wasn't. She understood why Olivia stuck to the mirrors. She pulled her foot back and scooted away from the edge.

"Yeah, I'm not a fan of the squish either," Hadley said. "For now, just follow my footsteps until you feel comfortable. And keep me in your sight at all times."

Alice did just that, stepping and hopping only on the same mirrors Hadley did. Soon they came to a sharp drop in the floor. She didn't realize it was there until they were right on top of it. The thousands of illuminated reflections created the illusion of one long hallway, but they were now at the edge of what looked like a bottomless elevator shaft, its vertical walls also covered in mirrors. Alice peered down to check if she could see the bottom. She couldn't.

"Here." Hadley offered her hand again. "You might want to hang on for this first drop."

Alice hesitated. They were dropping into that?

"Let's do it together. On the count of three, step forward." Hadley lifted her foot to hover over the chasm.

Alice did the same.

"One, two . . ."

It wasn't lost on Alice that she was literally putting her life in Hadley's hands. There was no reason to think that stepping into what was essentially a hole in the ground would lead to anything other than certain death. But she trusted these girls. Putting her life in their hands was the easiest thing she could ever choose to do.

So on "three," she transferred her weight to her dangling foot and stepped forward into empty space—and as she moved, everything moved with her. Or rotated, was more like it. It was as if gravity was adhering to her rules, and not the other way around. She was now standing on what she thought was a vertical wall, and her other foot was the one dangling. The elevator shaft had become another impossibly long hallway, and the hallway she'd just exited was now an elevator shaft. The switch made her woozy. She quickly pulled her dangling leg in, swayed, and closed her eyes.

"It'll get easier, I promise," Hadley said. "Remember: breathe."

Alice gave herself a couple more seconds before opening her eyes.

This was a new corridor, but it didn't look any different than the last one—just mirrors, mirrors, and more mirrors. But as she examined her surroundings, she did notice something: every few yards or so, there were more "elevator shafts." And not just on the floor, they were in the walls and ceiling, diverting in every direction to God knows where. Endless passages with endless walls of mirrors. The sheer magnitude of it all was impossible to comprehend.

Soxie was lounging on a large gold-framed mirror to their left, hanging on the wall like a coat on a hook. Olivia was kneeling next to her, silently watching and waiting.

"Alice," Hadley said, nudging her to get her attention. "Turning the wall is a little different than dropping into it. You want to try this one alone?" She released her hand and gestured to where Olivia and Soxie were waiting.

Alice took a breath and nodded, then carefully lily-padded over to the base of the wall. From here she could see Soxie's red-soled feet and Olivia smiling down at her, her body jutting out above Alice like a massive nail.

She placed her foot on the wall, as if stretching her hamstring. Once it was flush with the surface of a mirror, she leaned into it and lifted her back foot. Everything rotated again, and suddenly wall was floor and floor was wall. It was like that old Lionel Richie video from the eighties her dad had made her watch once—"Dancing on the Ceiling." Only here, they actually could.

When she twisted around, Hadley was the one now standing sideways—but not for long. She pushed off as if diving into a pool and turned in midair before landing next to Alice.

Forget huntress. They were Spider-Man here.

Alice grinned. "Can I try?"

The three of them looked at each other, all toothy smiles and beaming faces.

"Let's Conga," Soxie said.

Conga, it turned out, was Soxie's term for moving within the Realm in a version of copycat. The basic premise was to move fast and be daring. The more flips and cartwheels and creative ways of turning or hopping walls, the better. Whoever was in the lead set the pace, and the rest were expected to mimic her.

The first few "hops" Alice tried had her stomach landing in her throat. The rotation feeling was one thing when she had her feet on the ground; at least there was a reference point when the world turned.

It was quite another when she was in midair. For a split second it felt like she was falling—as if the phenomenon of personal gravity began to fail. But at the last second, everything rotated to accommodate her new position, and she'd land gracefully on temporary mirror firma. It was a little scary at first, but she quickly acclimated to the constant rotations and let her inner Spider-Man loose.

She'd never had so much fun. They were literally flying at times—leaping and flipping and soaring and laughing.

At the peak of their antics, the surfaces of the mirrors they passed by began to change. Soon, every single one was displaying part of a vast blue sky, complete with fluffy white clouds and even flocks of birds traversing from one mirror to the next. The result was transcendent; it was as if they really were flying through the heavens.

"It's the Huntress!" Olivia yelled, her dark hair flying behind her, as she leapt past Alice.

Eventually, they slowed down. Even in this all-gravity/zero-gravity environment, running and leaping took its toll. Soxie stopped to rest at the lip of an elevator shaft, and Hadley dropped into it. When they each sat down at the edge, their calves were next to each other's thighs. It was an Escher painting.

Alice took a seat next to Soxie, and Olivia hopped down to join Hadley. As the four of them caught their breath, sitting above and below each other, the blue sky faded and a radiant, starlit sky replaced it—thousands of mirrors working in concert to display the Big Dipper. The Seven Sisters. Orion. It was magical. The transition from glass to glass was seamless. If not for the frames and small gaps between the mirrors, Alice would think they were sitting deep in the countryside on a cloudless summer night.

"Beautiful," she whispered.

"She hasn't done this for a long time."

Alice turned to Soxie, whose face was illuminated by the twinkling starlight. "Done what?"

Olivia answered from below. "The Huntress hasn't projected images for us in years. And she's never shown us anything like this." Her combat boots slid back and disappeared. A moment later, her face popped up, her elbows resting on the edge.

"It's you, Alice. She's happy you're here."

Alice lifted her head toward the night sky and smiled. She was happy too.

chapter 7

"So these mirrors . . . where do they come from?" Alice asked as they walked single file through another endless hall. The starlit sky eventually faded, and the glass around them was now back to reflecting itself in a dim light.

Hadley answered over her shoulder. "As far as we know, they're all the mirrors in the world."

"Seriously?"

Hadley stopped and turned around. "Yes. Every single one of these leads to someplace on earth."

"How is that possible?"

"Think about it, Daniels," Soxie said. "How do you think she found us? Found you?"

Alice looked at a mirror on the wall next to her. It was a basic, full-length mirror with a cheap black frame. One you'd find at a superstore like Target or Walmart.

Olivia hopped over. "What do you think is on the other side?" she said, pointing to the superstore mirror.

Alice thought for a moment. She pictured a dorm room and a college student studying for finals. A dingy bathroom in an old gas station. Clothes hanging in a dark closet. It could be anything. It could be the inside of a Walmart where the mirror was waiting to be purchased.

"How do you see in?"

"Ah," Soxie said with a smirk. "Therein lies the rub."

"Huh?"

"The Huntress doesn't give us access to every mirror in the world. I'm guessing only she has that privilege. The compass tells us which ones we can open."

"What's she like? Have you ever seen her?"

"I don't think she exists in that sense anymore," Olivia said. "She exists in us, in all of this."

"She could probably appear to you in a dream," Hadley added. "But it's just a theory. We don't know if that's ever happened."

"Then how would you even know it's her? Couldn't it just be your idea of her?"

"Maybe they're one and the same."

"Maybe," Alice said. "Or maybe all of this is a dream."

Soxie clicked-clacked over and pinched her arm. Hard.

"Ow!"

"So, now that we've got that covered, shall we move on?" she asked.

Alice glared.

Soxie grabbed her chin, lightly this time. "You're doing great, by the way. You've gone a lot longer and a lot farther than any of us did our first time."

"Really?"

"Don't let it get to your head," she said with a sideways grin.

They continued walking, occasionally dropping into an elevator shaft or hopping up to turn a wall. Alice took the opportunity to study some of the mirrors they were passing. Some had cracks, some were fogged up, and others had writing on them. She knelt down to look at a large beveled mirror in the floor. In cursive writing, with what looked like lipstick, was written "uoy evol I," encased in the shape of a heart. She imagined it was the bathroom mirror of a newly engaged couple, one of them leaving a note for the other to find. It made her smile.

She stood up and turned in a slow circle, awed by the miracle of it all. These were literally windows to the world. It made her all the more curious as to how, and why, the Huntress had chosen her. Millions of mirrors, millions of options.

As she glanced back at the backward love note, a crack appeared in the center of the heart. Within seconds, dozens of cracks fanned out like a web until fragments of glass began to "fall" into black-gray space. Soon, there was nothing left but the spongy/not spongy "squish."

"Alice," Hadley called. "You need to stay close."

She looked up. "This mirror just disappeared."

Hadley turned around and hopped over to investigate, but by the time she got there, another mirror had already taken its place. It was similar in size but had a thick wooden frame and unicorn stickers plastered all over it.

Alice paused to make sure she was looking at the right spot. "Crap, it's gone."

"What was it?" Hadley asked. Olivia and Soxie doubled back to join them.

"There was a different mirror here a second ago, and then it cracked and fell into the floor."

"Seven years," Soxie said, shaking her head and tutting.

"Seven years of bad luck?" Alice's eyes widened. "You don't really believe that, do you?"

"I wouldn't do it. I think it pisses her off."

"Why?"

"Because someone's taking away her ability to see. Wouldn't it piss you off?"

Alice looked down at the mirror with the stickers, picturing a six-year-old girl playing with Barbies on the other side. Then she pictured the couple and the now-shattered mirror. Perhaps one of them had been unfaithful, and the other wasn't interested in a reconciliation. The love note too little, too late, a heavy bottle of perfume launched at the glass. Maybe the bad luck preceded the breaking of the mirror, and not the other way around.

She thought of her last conversation with her dad. "I broke my grandmother's mirror recently. Do you think Philautia's mad at me?"

Olivia chimed in. "We don't have any proof she punishes people for broken mirrors. Soxie's just superstitious."

Alice laughed. "Then you better be careful at my house. You'll be crossing a black cat's path every five seconds."

"Oh, I love cats," Hadley said. "But I'm allergic. Wish he was in your dream that night."

"My dream?"

"Hadz," Olivia groaned.

Hadley cringed. "Sorry, I forgot."

Alice took a step back. "Hang on. Are you telling me that night . . . when I was . . ." She closed her eyes, mortified. "You were really there?"

"Honey, you were in bad shape." Hadley stepped forward and placed a hand on her shoulder. "We could feel it. It was making Olivia ill. We had to check on you. And . . . well, we're glad we did."

"But do not," Soxie said, her voice rising, "and I repeat, do *not* tell Tinsley we dream-hopped you. He'd lose it if he knew."

"Dream whatted? And trust me. I have no desire to tell him anything." Least of all that she might be head over heels in love with him.

"WHAT?" Olivia blurted out.

"Um . . ." Alice gave her a pleading look.

"No wonder," she murmured.

"Olivia, what are—"

Before Hadley could finish, Alice heard a sudden loud ringing in her ears. From the look on their faces, they were all hearing it.

"Hadz, keep her close," Soxie said. Then she pulled out her compass and popped it open.

It lifted a few inches off her hand and spun like a top, so fast it looked like a tiny silver tornado. Olivia's and Hadley's did the same. Within seconds, the three tiny tornadoes merged into one silver, whirling ball of light.

"Okay, just one d-bag," Soxie said. "Alice, stick with Hadley."

Alice bobbed her head yes, unable to respond.

The silver ball of light shot forward, then stopped to hover above an elevator shaft a few yards down. Soxie and Olivia took off after it, with Hadley and Alice one leap behind.

By the time they reached the drop in the floor, the spinning light was moving again. Alice was glad they'd played Conga before, otherwise she wasn't sure she would have been able to keep up.

The compasses led them on an intense chase. They were flying again, leaping and flipping through the Realm, only this time there was a sense of urgency. The ringing in her ears subsided, but there was still a soft, static hum—a small vibration that made the glass surfaces of the mirrors pulsate and shimmer.

They caught up to the light when it came to a sudden halt at the lip of a corridor. Soxie turned the wall and stopped just short of it. The hum faded, and it became eerily quiet as the mirrors around them dimmed. They were soon shrouded in darkness, the only light coming from the illuminated shaft in the floor.

The spinning ball split back into three mini-tornadoes, each finding its way back to its charge. Hadley lifted her hand, palm up, and her tornado hovered above it, its spin slowing until it resumed the shape of an open compact. She grabbed it, quietly closed it, and stuffed it back in her pocket.

After securing her own compass, Soxie dropped to her knees and crawled toward the edge of the shaft. Olivia did the same, and Hadley motioned for Alice to follow. Willing her body to stop shaking, she dropped down on all fours and inched toward the square of light.

By the time she reached them, Soxie and Olivia were lying flat on their stomachs, peering down into the chasm. She slowly lowered herself down next to them, curled her fingers over the edge, and pulled herself up until her eyes met the light.

What she saw made no sense. A few feet from where they were hiding stood a little girl in a fancy, pale yellow dress. She couldn't have been more than five years old. She was admiring herself in front of a large oval mirror, but unlike the others around it, this one reflected her image.

A child playing dress-up was the last thing Alice had expected to see. The juxtaposition of her frilly innocence against the dark, empty hall was unsettling.

The girl in the reflection giggled, then grabbed the sides of her dress for a regal curtsy. The *other* little girl—the one on their side of the glass—watched the moving image curiously, then attempted to mimic it. But her giggle was far less sweet. It echoed through the infinite hall, lifting the hairs on the back of Alice's neck.

She knew what she was looking at now. She wanted to scream at the child in the mirror, *Run! Run!* But it was all she could do not to run herself.

Hadley crawled up next to her and the four of them lay side by side on their stomachs, peeking over the edge at the nightmarish spectacle. The girl in the mirror had just noticed something on her skirt. She studied it like a detective, lifting the material this way and that, horrified by what she was seeing. Chocolate. A sticky brown stain on her otherwise perfect Sunday dress.

Alice had heard little girls cry and throw tantrums; it was happening in every toy store and candy emporium across the country at this very moment. But when the demon tried to mimic it . . . that was a sound so disturbing she thought her eardrums might shrivel up and die. It was a cross between a slaughterhouse and a dying whale. She gasped, because sometimes that's the only reaction you can have to witnessing something so undeniably *wicked*.

Her gasp was loud, though—loud enough to be heard over the sound of evil. The demon child's head snapped in her direction. Her eyes were black, and her smile was wrong; there was no joy. Only bitterness. Her pudgy hand slammed into the mirror, and both she and her reflection disappeared.

A second later, the mirrors around them lit up to display their normal, dim light.

"Shit!" Soxie yelled, pulling herself into the hall. Olivia dropped in behind her.

Alice felt simultaneously petrified and rotten. As scary as that thing was, it was her fault it had gotten away.

Hadley, seeing the look on her face, shook her head. "Don't worry about it," she said, before dragging her into the hall to join the others.

Soxie was standing in front of the oval mirror with her compass already out.

"Alice, we have to go after it," she said. "You and Hadley hang back; Olivia and I will handle this one."

Alice nodded but couldn't help but feel slighted at being excluded from this next part. Shouldn't she learn how to "go after it" too? But she'd caused enough trouble already, so she bit her tongue and stayed silent as the pair pointed their compasses at the mirror and disappeared.

"Don't worry," Hadley said once they were gone. "It won't be able to put up much of a fight. It chose a child's mind."

Alice held herself for comfort. "Where did they go?"

"Wherever that little girl is."

"Are you saying they could be in Australia right now?"

Hadley snort-giggled. "Sure. Or Ireland. Patagonia. Madagascar. Who knows."

Alice stared at the mirror, thinking of the very first time she laid eyes on Hadley. "So they'll just make her look at her reflection, like you did to David?"

Hadley sat down, leaned back on her hands, and stretched her long legs out in front of her, getting comfortable. "Yes, but with David it was more complicated. We think he might have been infected for a while. If Olivia hadn't overheard your thoughts that night, we might never have known."

"How would you normally know?"

"It's hard, even with a mind reader. That's why we try to get them while they're still in the Realm."

"What makes you think David was infected for so long?"

Hadley leaned forward and rested her elbows on her knees. "Well, number one we had to drug him to force it out. Two, he lost time."

"That day on the Triangle," Alice said, more to herself than to Hadley. "He didn't remember me . . ."

"Exactly. That shouldn't happen. Demons influence behavior—sort of a devil-on-your-shoulder kind of thing. They don't take over. As far as we know, that's pretty rare."

Alice remembered the story in *The Reel*. David's undisclosed illness. "Is that why he's sick?"

Hadley stared at her. "I heard he was in rehab. But maybe you're on to something . . ."

While the wheels were turning in Hadley's pretty head, Alice thought of the thousands of times in her life she'd stood in front of a mirror. What if she had been infected? Would she have even known? She put the question to Hadley.

"You're a huntress, silly. You can't be infected."

"I meant before."

"Oh, honey. I doubt demons ever had an interest in you."

"Why not?"

"Because they choose what they know. They can shape-shift here, and if they start mimicking a reflection, it means they're interested. They see something in it they recognize."

"What?"

Hadley shrugged. "Evil."

"But that was a little girl!"

"I'm not saying that girl is 'evil,'" she said, miming air quotes on the offensive word. "I'm just saying something about her was giving off that vibe. We all have the ability to make good and bad choices. Some people are prone to the bad ones. Like David. It makes them more susceptible."

"But they can still help her?"

"Yes. She's too young. It can't hide in her subconscious. They'll send it back to where it came from. We call it the Dark Place."

Alice held herself tighter. "And if I hadn't accidentally tipped it off, what would you have—"

Her ears started ringing, and Hadley's body jerked to attention.

"I guess you're about to find out." Hadley hopped to her feet and pulled out her compass. It lifted off her hand and started spinning in the air, this time a smaller ball of light, then shot forward at an alarming speed.

"Stay close!" Hadley yelled, before taking off after it.

There was no time to argue. Alice immediately ran after her, trying her best to keep up.

This compass had them on a chase to end all chases. There were so many twists and turns and long stretches of sprinting that within minutes they had to be at least a mile from where they'd started. Alice didn't let herself think about how tired she was getting. If she lost Hadley, well, that would be it.

When the spinning orb finally came to rest, it was at the mouth of another never-ending corridor. Hadley turned the wall and crawled toward the lip of the shaft, securing her compass on the way. She waved for Alice to follow.

The mirrors around them dimmed as they slunk silently toward the light.

What Alice saw when she peered over the edge made her miss the sight of the creepy little girl.

Something was standing on the opposite wall—from their perspective, upside down. It wasn't human; it was humanoid, with milky, translucent skin and no facial features she could discern. No front or back side. If it weren't a contradiction in terms, she'd label it a fully grown fetus. A monstrous and repulsive thing that was dripping in malevolence. Evil incarnate.

She blinked as it moved. One second it was studying a round mirror. The next it was two mirrors down. Its movements were quick and jerky, skipping space and time. As if the thing itself wasn't scary enough, it was moving in stop motion. She dug her fingernails into her palms to distract herself from the fear.

Hadley nudged her and pointed to a mirror on the wall that was catty-corner to the thing. It was a large, square mirror with a gilded silver frame. Except it wasn't a mirror. It was a framed hole in the wall, a black tunnel to nowhere. The Dark Place.

With hand gestures, Hadley conveyed that their job was to get the demon into that hole.

What? Alice was shaking her head no before she could stop herself.

Hadley grabbed her by the shoulders and nodded a slow but deliberate yes. They had a job to do. This is what they were here for.

After taking a moment to pull herself together, Alice smiled and gave a weak thumbs-up.

Hadley stood and crept around the perimeter until she was standing above the wall with the black hole. As the thing moved to study another mirror, she dropped into the shaft and quietly made her way toward the Dark Place.

When she got there, she knelt and positioned her body across the black surface. For a heart-stopping second, Alice thought she might get sucked into the void, but whatever substance the Dark Place was made of, it held.

Hadley made brief eye contact with her, then settled her attention back on her target. "Yoo-hoo!" she sang.

The demon thing launched off the mirror it had been inspecting and flung itself to the nearest wall, crouching like a spider. It was impossible to tell what was arm or leg; they switched and flopped like double-jointed appendages. It homed in on Hadley immediately.

"Over here, you disgusting piece of garbage," she called, adding in one of her airy giggles to taunt it.

The spider humanoid creature took the bait. It hopped onto the same wall and, with choppy, freakish motions, made its way toward Hadley.

As it got closer, it lengthened and changed. Within a few short steps it was tall and slender, sporting long, golden locks. It giggled—a harsh, shrill chortle that Alice hoped never to hear again as long as she lived.

There were now two Hadleys in the hall below her, one of them skipping toward the other with a fiendish grin and pitch-black eyes. Real Hadley waited until the last second, then rolled off the surface of the black mirror. It almost worked; Alice could see the Dark Place starting to pull at demon Hadley's skin, lifting it off her bones. But then her head turned backward, her body fell flat to the floor, and she crawled away like an inverted crab. Once out of harm's way, she unfolded herself back into full Hadley form and started skipping along the opposite wall.

"*Disgusting piece of garbage, disgusting piece of garbage . . .*" it sang over and over, its vocals ranging from bass to soprano and everything in between.

Real Hadley started walking the walls in predator mode, but she couldn't seem to get close enough. Her twin kept pace with her every move. If she sped up, it sped up. If she changed direction, it changed direction. There was no stopping the scary-go-round. Alice had to do something.

On the next pass she dropped into the hall, taking care to stay behind the demon. With each turn she inched closer and closer to its back. The only weapon she had was distraction, and she hoped it was enough. When she was within arm's reach, she leaned in.

"Hi," she whispered.

Demon Hadley's head spun around; its body swiveled to meet it a second later. Then she cocked her head to the side, as if curious about this new creature that had just joined the game.

"*Hiiiiiiiiiii,*" she whispered, like a hissing kettle right before it screams.

It took every ounce of courage Alice had not to take off in the other direction. Especially when it was no longer Hadley's doppelgänger she was facing but her own.

Demon Alice smiled and blinked her jet-black eyes.

"*Hi,*" she whispered again. "*Hi-hi-hi-hi-hi-hi-hi-hi-hi-hi-hi-hi-hi-hi-hi—*"

"STOP!" Alice yelled, covering her ears.

"*STOOPPP!*" demon Alice yelled, covering her ears.

Alice dropped to her knees. Demon Alice dropped to her knees. Alice slapped herself in the face. Demon Alice slapped herself in the face. They stared at each other, breathing heavily. This thing was an evil shadow. There was no escaping it. Short of strangling herself, Alice was out of ideas.

They heard a faint noise above, and their identical heads jerked up at the same moment. Hadley was crouched on the side wall, ready to pounce.

She would never know what made her do it. Maybe she didn't trust Hadley would get there in time. Or maybe she was just tired of playing evil copycat. But whatever her reason for making it, her decision to lean forward and grab it—grab herself—in a tight, firm hug was . . . peculiar. And bad.

It was a pain that almost defied description. Like every cell in her body, every atom and molecule, was being savagely ripped apart. She felt sick—an ugly, wrenching sickness that twisted her insides into pretzels. She had to be dying. There was no other explanation. The pain was so absolute, the sick feeling so potent, that death would be a welcome respite. Even if she wanted to let go, she couldn't. She wasn't the one holding on anymore. *It* was.

Then her vision went black, and the pain turned to numbness. *Oh, thank God*, she thought, right before her body went slack and oblivion took over.

chapter 8

"I'm telling you, it wouldn't let go."

"What do you mean?"

"I mean it went nuts when I tried to pull it off. I think if it'd had the chance, it would have taken her with it."

"Into the Dark Place? Is that even possible?"

"I don't know, but I've never seen one act like that before. It seemed almost . . . happy."

"Well, that's not terrifying or anything."

"Guys, what the hell is going on?"

"No idea. We need to talk to Colin."

Alice had eavesdropped long enough. Plus, Olivia probably knew she was awake anyway.

"Must we?" she mumbled, blinking as she attempted to focus.

"Damn, Daniels. You've had a day."

The three of them were kneeling over her, their heads silhouetted by the overhead light. A wet nose pushed its way through, and a warm tongue slid across her face.

"Blech," she spat, trying to sit up. The dog placed her paws on Alice's chest and forced her back down, attempting to lick her back to life.

"Hammy, no!" Olivia said, pulling on her collar.

Hammacher whimpered.

Alice managed to pull herself up onto her elbows. They were back in the dance studio. She shaded her eyes from the light of the chandelier.

"How did we get back here?"

"We footballed you," Olivia said.

"Excuse me?"

"Sorry. It would have taken too long to carry you, so we passed you back and forth."

She pushed herself all the way up and pressed the heels of her hands against her eyes, picturing her unconscious body being launched like a football through the Realm.

"I hope you didn't drop me."

Hadley giggled. It gave Alice goose bumps as she thought of the other Hadley uttering a similar sound.

"Of course not, silly. You were light as a feather!"

"Stiff as a corpse?"

"That's not funny."

"Sorry." Alice yawned. "Too soon?"

"Alright. C'mon, killer," Soxie said, grabbing her by the elbow and helping her up. "It's after two. You should rest; we can debrief tomorrow."

Alice was too tired to protest. After texting her mom she'd be spending the night, she was led through sconce-lit hallways to a deliciously soft bed. She was out before she hit the down pillow and thousand-thread-count sheets.

She awoke with a start, images of little girls with black eyes and translucent, spiderlike creatures fresh in her head. If only it were just a dream. But she had been there—had literally embraced evil. And it had almost killed her. She wondered if that qualified as a stupid stunt.

On cue, someone snored beside her.

She turned her head toward the sound. A chair was pulled up next to the bed. In it, Colin slept, his head resting awkwardly to the side. Despite the uncomfortable position, he looked peaceful, his long eyelashes fluttering slightly with every soft snore.

She watched him sleep, wondering what he was dreaming about. Did he dream about past lives? Past loves? The thought was like an anvil on her chest: suffocating and highly inconvenient. Being jealous of hypothetical women who probably died centuries ago was not the best use of her energy right now. She had enough on her plate at the moment.

Irritated with herself, she let out a puff of air. His sky-blue eyes shot open.

They stared at each other for a long moment, neither one breathing or making a sound. She licked her dry lips and his gaze lowered. Then the bedroom door burst open.

He flew out of his chair like his seat was made of nails, and she sat up so fast her pillow could have been on fire. It felt like they'd just been caught in the act, even though there was no action to catch them in. But it was in the air—an undeniable *something* that made even Olivia hesitate as she stood in the doorway, holding a tray of food.

Breakfast, if the smell of bacon and eggs was any indication. Alice's stomach growled in response.

"Good," Colin said, recovering so fast one might think he'd had hundreds of years of practice. He moved his chair next to its twin by the fireplace, then addressed Alice without looking at her. "Eat. We'll talk later."

Without another word, he strode out of the room.

Olivia gave him a strange look as he shoved past her, then shook her head and made her way to the bed. She set the tray in front of Alice and climbed up to kneel next to her.

"Thank you." Alice grabbed the glass of orange juice on the tray and downed the whole thing in three gulps. She wiped her mouth with the back of her hand, then tore off a chunk of waffle and stuffed it in her mouth.

Olivia sat back. "Well, you look better. And you clearly have an appetite."

Alice nodded, grabbed a slice of bacon, and snapped it in half. "What was Colin doing here?"

"We called him after we put you to bed."

"But why was he *here*?" She motioned to the side of the bed.

"I don't know, Alice. Why don't you tell me."

She coughed, nearly choking. "You're the mind reader."

"Yeah, well, Colin's a closed book."

"You can't read him?"

"Nope. Can't dream-hop him either." Olivia grabbed a mini-muffin and popped it in her mouth. "Learned that the hard way."

Alice took a sip of tea, picturing his sleeping face. Well, wasn't that too bad. She'd love to know what was going on in that beautiful head.

Olivia leaned back, studying her. "Just be careful, Alice."

She set the cup down, her face hot with embarrassment. "Oh my god. What is wrong with me?"

"Listen, I respect your feelings. But remember, his job is to protect us. He's been doing this for centuries. I just don't want to see you get hurt."

Alice fell back onto the bed, folding her arms over her face. "Don't worry. It's unrequited. You might as well call me Tisiphone."

Olivia mumbled something Alice couldn't make out.

She peered out at her from beneath her arms. "What?"

"Not important right now." Olivia moved the tray aside. "Colin wants to know what happened in the Realm. We told him what we could, but we need you to fill in the blanks."

Alice sat up. "Blanks?"

"Yes. How did you do it?"

"Do what?"

Olivia looked confused. "Alice, you destroyed it."

She pushed herself back against the headboard. "Are you kidding? That thing almost destroyed *me*." She recalled the searing pain and sickness she'd felt holding the demon. "How did you find us?"

"When we finished with the little girl—she was a biter, by the way"—Olivia held up her arm to show Alice the bandage on it—"we came back through, and our compasses shot out of our hands. We moved as fast as we could, but by the time we got there you were comatose and Hadley was a basket case."

Poor Hadley. Not only had she gotten stuck babysitting, but Alice had also let her down when it mattered most. She didn't even manage to stay conscious.

"You don't understand. You've done something none of us has ever done. Even Colin is confused."

"But . . . I thought you've done this a thousand times."

"Not the same. We've sent them back to the Dark Place, where they come from. What you did . . ."

Alice sat still, waiting to hear what it was she had done.

Olivia placed a hand on her shoulder. "I saw it through Hadley. It turned to ash in your arms. Not only did you destroy it, I think it wanted you to."

After showering, Alice found a gift on her bed from Soxie, accompanied by a note: *Meeting in the library at 10. Poolside for the rest of the day—no argument!*

Inside she found a navy one-piece and matching cover-up. She smiled as she pulled the brand-new swimsuit, tags and all, from the box. Either Soxie had a department store on retainer or she kept extra swimsuits on hand like toothbrushes. Either way, Alice was glad she did. After the night she'd had, lounging by the pool all day sounded like a dream.

By the time she walked into the library, the whole gang was assembled. Hadley was sitting by the fireplace in a red bikini top and board shorts, and Olivia and Soxie were playing chess by the window, Soxie in some fabulous green-and-gold number and Olivia in an honest-to-god yellow polka-dot bikini. She was even sporting a matching sarong and headband. Not what Alice would have expected from a girl whose wardrobe consisted of black and black.

Olivia gave her the side-eye but kept her focus on the game.

"Is that really fair?" Alice asked, throwing a nod at the chessboard.

Soxie kept her eyes on Olivia as she said, "I call it improv chess. I don't think ahead; I just play in the moment. It throws her off like you wouldn't believe. I won once."

Olivia's hand hovered over a pawn. Alice chuckled at the thought of losing a game of chess when you can literally read your opponent's mind.

"It's not as easy as you would think, Alice. She's got a lot of noise going on in there."

Soxie leaned back and smiled.

"Alice," came Colin's sharp voice. She had clocked him the second she walked in, her butterflies and locusts like divining rods. He was sitting on one of the leather couches, staring at her.

"Yes?"

He motioned to the couch opposite him. "Sit down and walk me through it."

She'd never been great at following orders, especially when they were given rudely. But in an effort to avoid a scene, she did as she was told. Once seated, however, she made a show of dusting imaginary lint off a cushion. Impatience wafted off Colin like a heavy cologne.

"What would you like to know?" she finally asked.

He sat forward, aged leather creaking beneath him. "Are we going to play games, or are you going to tell me?"

"I guess that depends. What games did you have in mind?"

"Dammit, Alice, what the hell is wrong with you?"

She flinched. Okay, maybe she was taking it too far, but she wasn't expecting a reaction like that. Hadley's head perked up from her phone, and the chatter by the chessboard died down. Heat began to rise in her face.

"Nothing's wrong with me. I did my job, didn't I?"

"You almost got yourself killed."

"Are you kidding me? How was I supposed to know what was going to happen?"

He took a deep breath, exhaled. "That's my point, Alice. You didn't, yet you did it anyway."

"So what was I supposed to do? Just let it go?"

"Yes!" he yelled, springing to his feet. "That's exactly what you should have done! What the hell were you thinking? How could you be so stupid!"

She found herself recoiling. Normally she would fight back, but the contempt and animosity in his eyes was too much—more than she could bear.

"Colin, c'mon. That's not fair." Hadley was now sitting on the edge of her chair.

"Hadley, stay out of it."

"Seriously, Tinsley," Soxie said. "Back off. Hasn't she been through enough?"

"Alice," Olivia said, "he doesn't mean it."

Her eyes welled with tears, but she laughed through them. "You know, Olivia, normally I'd believe you. But given Colin's the one person you can't read, I'm going to have to call your bluff."

He averted his eyes, seemingly irritated by her tears. "Listen. It's just . . . I'm trying to keep you safe. I need you to be smart, Alice. I need you to use your head."

It was bad enough she was being berated in front of the girls, but now he was treating her like a petulant child.

"Well, guess what," she said with a sob and a laugh, wiping her cheeks. "You don't need to worry about me and my stupid head anymore. I quit."

He sank back onto the couch, as if the sound of her voice was exhausting. "It doesn't work like that. You can't quit."

"Oh no? Watch me." She stood, marched directly into the hall, and slammed the library door shut behind her. The bang reverberated throughout the immense house.

"Nice going, jerk," she heard Soxie say.

She appreciated the support, but a lot of good it had done her in there.

Why was he so angry with her? A little sympathy for almost dying would have been nice. But this . . . it was so unfair. It was so *mean*.

Instead of turning right and leaving, she turned left and ventured deeper into the house. Obviously, she wasn't going to quit. Her soul was tied to the girls; it'd be agony without them. But it felt good to say it. To him, anyway.

She caught her reflection in a hall mirror and stopped to smooth her hair back and pull herself together. Why was she letting him get under her skin? She was smarter than that. And stronger. Usually. But when it came to him . . . she found herself in uncharted territory. Navigating him was like finding her way through a beautiful forest littered with unexploded mines—both his and hers.

She ran her hands down her face—and noticed something near her right temple. *What the . . . ?*

She leaned in for a better look. She had a white streak in her hair. Not gray. *White*. About half an inch thick. Great. Just great. Now her hair was turning white. It wasn't the end of the world, but it was still upsetting. She pressed her lips together to keep from screaming and throwing a tantrum like the demon girl from the Realm.

The sound of movement in the library pulled her from her reflection. Without thinking, she sprinted down the hall and opened the first door she came across.

A closet. A hundred doors in the place, and she chose a closet.

The library door began to swing open.

Closet it is.

She ducked in, closed the door, and sat on the floor in the dark. Musty coats and Wellington boots surrounded her as she hugged her knees to her chest, fuming at her own cowardice. She heard footsteps down the hall, then Colin's voice, muffled through the door.

"Olivia, where is she?"

Please don't tell him, please don't tell him . . .

"Umm," Olivia stalled. "I'm not getting anything. She must've caught a ride with Barry."

Thank you, thank you.

Colin muttered something unintelligible. Alice leaned closer to the door, straining to hear. There was a jangle of keys, and then a slamming door. But it wasn't until she heard his car kicking up gravel in the circular drive that she felt herself relax. She was too close to the edge right now. Another confrontation would do her in.

A few moments later, the closet door opened.

Soxie placed a hand on her hip and shook her head. "You know, I've spent some time in there. I don't recommend it."

Alice looked up, smiled, and burst into tears.

Soxie did not approve. "Oh, for Christ's sake." She pulled Alice roughly to her feet. "This is ridiculous."

"I . . . I . . . I'm sorry," Alice stammered, unable to stop sobbing.

"Oh, Alice . . ." Olivia sniffed, empathetic tears rolling down her face. "It's okay." She grabbed her heaving shoulders and pulled her in for a hug.

"Honey, shhhhh," Hadley said, rubbing her back.

It was embarrassing to fall apart like this, but her emotions were all over the place. It was a miracle she'd lasted as long as she had. The girls seemed to recognize that, and they gave her a full minute or two to wallow. But even they had their limits.

"Alice."

Soxie's stern voice brought her sniveling to a halt. She hiccupped and looked up.

"You are a huntress. A badass demon killer. So cry it out, nothing wrong with that. Just save some for when it really matters. Because right now, that prick?" She stuck her thumb in the direction of the front door. "He doesn't deserve your tears."

Alice stepped back and wiped her nose with her sleeve, nodding to at least appear strong. Then, as if they'd been eavesdropping, the two Dobermans rounded the corner, their paws clicking on hardwood as they trotted up to the foursome. One of them whined. The other sank to the floor and put her nose between her paws, staring at them with big, sad eyes.

"And now look," Soxie said. "You've upset the dogs."

Alice laughed. Hammacher lifted her head and barked. Then all four girls laughed, and both dogs started barking and howling.

"C'mon." Soxie ushered them back toward the library. "Let's get out of here before these two pee in the hall and Jerkwad Tinsley figures out he's been played."

"Where are we going?"

Soxie stopped and looked at Olivia and Hadley. "What do you say, girls? Shall we consult the map?"

"Oh my god, are you serious? Sox, he'll kill us," Hadley said, even as her face took on an excited look.

Olivia's eyes were round, but the corners of her mouth turned up as she turned to Alice. "If you could go anywhere in the world right now, where would it be?"

Something was up. Alice felt hesitant to answer, like she might say the wrong thing.

Olivia shook her head. "No wrong answer. Anywhere. And I really mean that. Anywhere."

Okay, this was a lot of pressure, but she'd play along. She thought for a moment. They were already in bathing suits, so how about someplace warm? And tropical?

"Bora Bora."

"Yay!" Hadley squeaked, clapping her hands together and beaming.

chapter 9

The Remington Reel—Sunday, March 24th

Comet Watch

By Aaron Tapper (no relation)

Okay, kids, tickets are now on sale for the Reel Red Moon & Comet Party, Saturday, July 27th. Doors open at 7:00 p.m. Not only is it an opportunity to witness a super blood moon AND one of the brightest comets in history, it will also be the very last Reel-sponsored party. That's right. Mr. Carver and I will be handing in our press credentials in pursuit of that noble endeavor called higher education. But we can't think of a better send-off than this. Link to details <u>here</u>. We hope to see you there!

———— ✦ ————

"Who wants another daquiri?"

"Me."

"Me."

"Alice?"

"Sure, why not." She picked up her nearly empty glass and slurped the last of the contents through a straw. She scanned the rest of *The Reel* out of habit. As usual, it was boring and predictable. Nothing but inane gossip, game results, and weather updates she could get anywhere. She wondered why she bothered.

"Ali, you better not be posting this to Instagram," Soxie said.

Alice laughed and tossed her phone aside. "Can you imagine? My mom's head would explode."

Hadley picked up the phone to dial room service. "*Bonjour.* Can we have four more frozen daquiris, *s'il vous plaît? Oui.* Roxland. *Merci beaucoup.*"

Thanks to Soxie's platinum card, they were lounging in a private bungalow on stilts surrounded by water. The pictures Alice had seen of this resort didn't do it justice. The ocean wasn't just blue, it was cerulean—that vibrant, almost turquoise blue that screams tropical island paradise.

A warm breeze blew in from the Pacific, and water slapped lazily against their wooden deck. The sound was soothing, and the daquiri was strong and sweet. This was a calm she wanted to snuggle up to and live in for a while.

"You know, I'm digging that white stripe on you," Soxie said, sitting up and leaning in to take another look at Alice's hair. "It works."

"That makes one of us. I should probably dye it before my mom sees it."

Hadley walked toward the edge of the deck. "No way. It's badass. Keep it." She dove into the pool-like water below, her form so perfect she barely created a splash.

"Do you feel okay otherwise?" Olivia asked.

Alice leaned up on her elbows, shielding her eyes to see her friend in the shade. "Actually, I feel great. I mean, look where we are. This is insane."

Olivia smiled. "Good. And don't worry about Colin. I think he's just stressed about *that*." She pointed to Alice's hair. "He's not used to being in the dark. About anything."

Alice felt her stomach flutter ever so slightly. Thousands of miles removed, yet the mere mention of his name still nudged her butterflies. Clearly they didn't have ears to hear how horrible he'd been to her that morning.

"Hey, no Colin or demon talk," Soxie barked. "We're here to relax, remember?"

Alice made eye contact with Olivia. "Yes, ma'am," they said in unison.

To get there, they had entered the Realm through the Backwards Place again. Once inside, Olivia had flipped open her compass and asked it to "find the hidden map." Until that moment, Alice had no idea they could talk to those things. Despite last night's episode, she still wanted hers.

The compass had obediently spun into its little silver ball of light and led them to a plain round mirror no bigger than a dinner plate. At the touch of Olivia's hand, what had appeared to be flat glass ballooned outwards and formed a giant silver sphere that hovered in front of them.

Olivia had given it a spin with the palm of her hand, and silver had quickly bled to greens and blues. Seconds later, a replica of the earth was floating before them. It wasn't a labeled, conventional globe you'd find in a classroom, however, so even with the help of Hadley's iPhone, it had taken them a few minutes to identify the islands of Bora Bora. Once they did, Olivia had gently placed the tip of her finger on the spot. Then the sphere had turned translucent and expanded around them until they were standing in something like a giant soap bubble. After that it had just been a matter of pinpointing where they wanted to enter.

They'd sifted through hundreds of viewpoints displayed on the interior of the sphere until Hadley spotted one that looked right. It was a bathroom mirror, and in its reflection was a window overlooking a sandy white beach. They'd just been able to make out stilted bunga-lows scattered offshore. Olivia had pointed her compass at the image and their soap bubble had vanished, sucked back into the silver dinner plate on the wall.

"Find last reflection," she'd instructed her compass. After a few twists and turns, the dutiful little spinner had led them to the correct mirror. When they were sure the coast was clear, they'd crawled through, stepping over the sink and onto the floor as quietly as possible.

The entry point had turned out to be an empty beachfront villa—lucky them. And now here they were, half a world away in a tropical island paradise, and they'd even be home for dinner. Alice could get used to this.

Well into her second drink and feeling warm and fuzzy, she asked the obvious question: "Why don't you do this all the time?"

Soxie answered with her eyes closed. "Tinsley doesn't allow it. We had a little incident when we were fourteen."

"That's an understatement," Hadley said as she towel-dried her hair.

Alice turned to Olivia. "Translate, please?"

Olivia took a long sip of daquiri and smacked her lips before answering. "We think the Huntress created the map as a reward. It's the only way we can enter mirrors we haven't marked or aren't chasing a demon through. Most of the time, it's hidden. The compass can only find it if she's opened it."

"How do you know when it's open?"

Soxie let out a stilted laugh. "We don't. We ask for the map, and the compass either brings us to it or just sits there like a toad on a road."

Alice chewed on her straw. "So we lucked out today."

"I don't think so," Olivia said. "We can't say for sure, but we think she opens it when we do well. When we've sent demons back."

Alice thought about that for a moment. "So like a mileage points program. Hunt down some demons, earn points to paradise?"

"Ha. Basically. There was a time we were spending every free second in the Realm, hoping for demons to enter so we could earn more map visits. But we started to get sloppy. You saw how long it took to sift through those images."

"Uh-oh," Alice said, sitting up. "Where did you end up?"

"A psych ward in Italy."

"What?"

"We thought it was reflecting a window, but it was one of those backlit pictures—like an HD screen saver. It looked real enough."

"What was the picture? Where were you trying to go?"

"Florence." Hadley moved her chair into the shade next to Olivia's. She sat down with her towel covering her like a blanket. "It was kind of a tight squeeze and we weren't sure how high up it was, so I went through feetfirst. After I drop to the floor, this guy starts screaming his head off in Italian. He was sitting in the corner beneath the mirror. We had no idea he was there."

Alice covered her mouth with her hand. "What did you do?"

Hadley pulled the towel tighter around her shoulders. "I dropped my compass."

"So . . ."

"It was still open."

Alice gave her a blank look.

"It was still connected to the Realm," Olivia said. "If anyone besides a huntress tries to use it . . . Well, long story short, it put him in a coma."

"Oh my god."

"He's fine now," she quickly added. "Came out of it two weeks later. But Colin confiscated our compasses for a month."

Hadley looked down. "I felt really bad."

"Hadz, accidents happen," Soxie said. "Could have been any of us."

"And at least he's okay now," Alice offered.

"Yeah, but that put an end to our global day trips. And it was my fault."

Alice frowned. "But we did it today; clearly he can't stop you. It's not like you're going to tell him."

The phone in their room rang. The three of them looked at each other.

Alice turned to Soxie. "Do you know who's calling?"

"Who do you think?"

Soxie informed the hotel they would be leaving early, and they returned to the Realm through a mirror in their bungalow.

When they arrived at the dance studio mirrors, Alice heard music. With all three compasses still hovering and spinning, Hadley took her by the hand and they stepped through into the Backwards Place.

The four of them walked slowly to the center of the room, ghosts whose images weren't being reflected in the glass around them. Colin sat at the piano, the soft light of dusk casting shadows through the room, partly obscuring his face. He wasn't reading music in this light; his playing was from memory, and it was exquisite. Dazzling.

Olivia sat down cross-legged, closing her eyes. "He never plays anymore."

Soxie and Hadley sat down next to her and leaned into each other's backs, their eyes closed, sailing away on the enchanting sound.

Alice walked to the piano, feeling like an invisible spy. As she got closer, she saw that his eyes were closed and his fingers were flying over the keys. She wasn't a classical music aficionado, but she was sure whatever he was playing had probably been composed by someone long dead. Maybe him. Couldn't Mozart or Bach have been reincarnations of Cithaeron? It was a fun thought.

She bent down until she was kneeling at his feet. With the free-dom to study him undetected, she found herself hypnotized by the sharp curve of his jaw. The subtle movement of his throat. The way his muscles flexed as he played the complex, beautiful arrangement.

It was more than his skin and bones. It was the life force contained within them. Was it his soul? Was she attached to it because of the Huntress? And even so, did it matter? She was still furious with him. But she might as well face it: she was also in love. It was a problem.

You didn't hear that, Olivia.

She glanced over but Olivia's eyes were still closed, her body swaying to the music.

A loud bark came from down the hall. Colin's eyes popped open and he immediately stopped playing. He looked toward the door, right over her head. Still safe in the Backwards Place, she was sure he couldn't see her, but she jumped up and backed away, just in case.

Two hyper Dobermans slid around the corner, all scraping paws and high-pitched whines. They ran straight toward the center of the room.

Colin slammed the cover over the keys and stood. Alice quickly moved to join the girls, who were now being circled by howling, traitorous canines.

"Crap," Soxie said, slowly rising to her feet. "He was just getting to the good part."

"Do these dogs actually guard anything?" Hadley wondered aloud, dusting off her damp board shorts.

Colin marched past them to flip on the lights and then leaned against the wall by the door, his arms crossed and his eyes focused on the center of the room—on them.

"Does he know we're here?" Alice asked.

"Yes," Olivia said. "He knows."

He yelled at them for ten minutes, containing his rage just enough to avoid appearing crazed. Takeaway words: irresponsible, danger-ous, unacceptable, and—Alice's favorite—stupid. They took it rather well, considering. Actually, too well. The drinks had been stronger than they thought. Hadley and Soxie were trying not to laugh and Olivia was turning red, most likely from the effort to drown out their thoughts.

"You think this is funny?"

They shook their heads, but the laughter was bubbling just below the surface. Colin stared at them for a beat, then turned around and walked back to the piano. There was a heaviness to his gait, as if he was walking through molasses. When he sank back onto the piano bench, he did it with the tiredness of an old man. He kept his eyes on the floor and flicked a hand toward the entrance.

"Just go," he said.

It was hard to see him like this, but considering his unpredictable moods, Alice figured it was best not to wait for a second invitation. The girls must have felt the same, because they turned on their heels and headed for the door right alongside her.

"Not you, Alice."

Her back went stiff and her legs stopped moving. She wasn't sure if she willed them to stop or if the sound of his voice scared them still. Regardless, she was frozen at the entrance to the studio, watching helplessly as Soxie, Olivia, and Hadley made apologetic dashes to freedom. Even the dogs were gone; they'd bolted at the first sign of Colin's anger. She was on her own.

Releasing a slow and even breath, she turned around.

Apparently satisfied that she wasn't going to make a run for it, Colin returned his focus to the piano. He lifted the cover and idly fingered the keys with one hand—a simple, maudlin melody. Alice waited, hesitant to move or speak.

"Do you know when I first saw you?" he asked.

The question surprised her. It seemed irrelevant—an unimportant detail of an already complicated story. The image of a car idling in the road flickered through her mind's eye.

"On a street by my house," she said.

"No. It was in a dream when I was twelve. Before I knew who I really was."

"But . . . that's impossible." She knew better than to use that word these days, but sometimes it was the only one that fit.

"Impossible," he repeated, his fingers still dancing softly on the keys.

She took a step forward. "Okay, fine. So you had a dream six years ago about someone you think was me."

He stopped playing and looked at her. "Try sixteen hundred years."

"What . . ." She shook her head. "What are you saying?"

"I'm saying you've plagued my dreams in every life I've lived since Philautia brought me back. Only now, here you are. Living and breathing."

A wing flapped in her stomach, taking some of her oxygen with it. "But I . . . I don't understand."

He took a shallow breath. "You said you thought I lived a lonely existence. You were right. I thought you were just a symptom of that loneliness—something I created to keep me company in each lifetime. You always appeared before I knew I was Cithaeron, so you were my little secret. I clung to the idea of you. It kept me going."

She remained silent.

"And then that night, I saw you." He paused as his voice faltered. "You were just walking. Walking down the street in the fading light, like you'd always been there. I thought I was hallucinating. You weren't real. You couldn't be. Not after all this time."

She saw herself through his eyes, walking down that shadowy street. But it wasn't just him, was it? She'd felt something that night too.

"After you ran away," he continued, "I convinced myself I was wrong. But when you showed up at David's, there was no more pretending. You were real. I knew it the moment I touched you."

"Then why did you push me away?"

He closed his eyes. "Because that was the moment Philautia chose to gift you a piece of her soul."

More oxygen escaped from her lungs. "What? All that time, you knew? How could you not tell me!"

His eyes shot open, blazing in the light of the chandelier. "You were mine. You'd been mine for sixteen hundred years. I thought if you became a huntress, I'd lose you. I was afraid to take that chance. So I kept the girls away. I tried to stop it from happening."

She felt cold all of a sudden. "Well, it happened."

"I know."

"And still you pushed me away."

"I was scared."

"Scared of what?"

He gripped the edge of the piano. "Scared of spending the rest of this life with you only to wake up a hundred years from now alone. I can't . . . I couldn't handle it. It almost broke me. I thought by turning you away I was saving myself centuries of grief."

Her nose started to tingle. Even as her heart ached to comfort him, she was mad as hell. How could he be so selfish?

"But none of that matters anymore."

She was about to scream at him, but those last words stopped her. "Why? What's changed?"

"While you were gone, Philautia sent me a vision. Her last."

"What do you mean, last?"

"Alice, she's gifted you the final piece of her soul. You're the last huntress."

His lifeless blue eyes stared into the starry sky. The same starry sky they'd once stared at together. She quickly turned away.

"Can somebody please close his eyes?"

Olivia put an arm around her shoulders, pulling her close. "It's okay, Alice. It's just his body. It's not him anymore."

She nodded and took in a controlled breath. Now was not the time to fall apart.

"You did good, Daniels. You did what you had to do."

"I hope you're right."

It took almost three hours to dig the hole, each of them taking turns to keep the pace quick. No one spoke, each mourning the loss in her own way. Alice did her best to focus on the job at hand. Spear the shovel into the ground, step on the edge, scoop, and repeat. She would have kept shoveling until she dropped; the physical exertion was a welcome distraction from the mountain of feelings threatening to take over. But Hadley's light touch on her arm told her to stop and rest.

She looked toward the dark sky and the fuzzy white tail of Bolle-Marin, already beginning its long journey back to wherever it had come from. In a few months' time, it would be too far away *to see with the naked eye. In a few years, too far away to see with a telescope. In a few centuries, too far away to care.*

When the comet was gone, she'd never see it again.

He was already gone.

She closed her eyes and pictured his face. She'd loved the man behind it. She'd love him forever.

part
two

chapter 10

Alice started to walk in circles. Somehow moving helped lessen the blow. "What does this mean? Do the girls know?"

"No. I wanted to tell you first."

She stopped and turned around. "Why me? Why now?"

"It's never worked like this before. She's only communicated to me through visions. Sometimes cryptic, sometimes not. With you, it was both."

She knew from his tone it was bad.

"Tell me."

His eyes locked on hers. "She's giving up her existence, which means the Realm ends with you."

It was the kind of news to take sitting down, but the piano bench was her only option. Asking him to scoot and make room felt . . . dangerous.

"But isn't that a good thing?" she said, her voice one octave higher. "If there's no more Realm, then there are no more demons to hunt, right?"

He half smiled. "Right. No more demons."

"Then what aren't you telling me?"

Eons of time passed. The earth made at least three rotations around the sun before something happened. At least, that's what it felt like. Because when he finally stood and walked toward her, she couldn't remember how long she'd been standing there, staring into his tortured eyes. When he was right in front of her, he lifted his hand and brushed the hair from her face, letting the tip of his finger lightly graze her forehead.

"I've imagined this so many times," he said. "Standing this close to you. Breathing you in." He closed his eyes and inhaled.

Her heart rate tripled, locusts and butterflies taking flight. She didn't dare speak or move. She couldn't have if she'd wanted to.

His eyes found hers again. "This moment is worth a thousand lifetimes."

She closed her eyes, unable to handle the potency of his stare. His knuckles slid down her cheek and along her chin; his thumb gently glided over her bottom lip. She'd never been so afraid in her life—afraid that what was about to happen, wouldn't.

She felt him lean in, his breath hot on her mouth.

"An eternity for a kiss," he whispered.

When his lips found hers, it was with the slightest of pressure. A question. A promise. He was waiting. Waiting for her to yield. She let out the tiniest of sighs as her lips parted.

He breathed out her name. "*Alice.*"

She opened her eyes and pulled away. "Cithaeron."

His eyes clouded dark. Then he took her face in his hands and crushed his lips to hers.

Her knees buckled, and every nerve pathway in her body lit up like the Fourth of July. It was too much, and not enough.

His kiss was relentless. Urgent. Almost primitive in its haste. Yet she clung to him, unable to get close enough. Unable to imagine how she'd ever existed without him. Without his perfect lips on hers. The feeling of being in his arms. She closed her eyes and surrendered. She was his. She'd always been his.

"Alice."

Both of them jumped, their heads snapping to attention at the sound of Soxie's voice. She was standing in the doorway, looking like she'd seen . . . well, Alice and Colin in a lover's embrace. A ghost would have probably been less shocking.

Colin quickly stepped back to give Alice room to compose herself. She smoothed her hair and straightened her cover-up, a feeble attempt to mask her embarrassment.

Soxie just stared at them.

"Soxie, I—"

"What is it, Sox?" Colin cut in.

Her green eyes darted in his direction. "Sorry to interrupt your . . . talk. But I thought Alice should know her dad's downstairs."

Alice blinked. "My dad? Here?"

Soxie's eyes slid back over to her. "Yes. He's waiting in the parlor."

"Is something wrong? Is it my mom?"

"He didn't say."

Alice balked, floored by her coldness.

"You okay?" Colin asked, studying her face. "Do you want me to come with you?"

"No, no . . . I'm just surprised. I'm sure it's nothing."

She was well equipped to handle her dad on her own. Besides, how was she supposed to introduce them, anyway? *Hi, Dad, this is Colin. The man I plan to spend the rest of my life with.* She knew it was true—knew it to the marrow of her bones—but she wasn't daft enough to say it out loud. Not when things were *just* getting started.

Colin nodded. "Okay." Aware of a third and watchful presence in the room, he planted a chaste kiss on her forehead. "I should go anyway. But I'll call you later."

On his way out, he nodded casually to Soxie. Even with sixteen hundred years under his belt, he still didn't appear to know female tension when he walked right through it.

"Good talk?" Soxie asked once he was gone.

"Soxie—"

"Save it. I knew something strange was going on between you two, but this?" She paused to wave her hand in a vague circle. "I can't."

Alice stood up straight. Clearly she'd done something wrong—crossed a line of some kind or broken some unspoken rule. Whatever it was, it hurt to see the judgment in her friend's eyes. But her dad was downstairs, so whatever argument they were about to have would have to wait.

"I better go see what my dad wants. Thank you for letting me know he's here."

When she left the room, Soxie didn't make a move to follow her.

The house manager, Morgan, found her on the first-floor landing and escorted her to the parlor. After instructing her to dial 7 if she needed anything, he pulled the heavy doors closed behind her.

The parlor was exactly what its name suggested. It sat right off the foyer, its large windows overlooking the front lawn and circular drive. It was the interior of an old English manor: light-blue-and-gold settees, chaise lounges, and even a table set for tea.

On the other side of the room, in front of a gas fireplace, stood her dad. His back was to her as he stared into the flames. Something had to be wrong; there was no other reason for him to be here.

She quickly crossed the room.

"Dad?"

He turned around.

"Alice. How wonderful it is to see you."

Her breath caught. He looked the same—same receding hairline, same hazel eyes and lanky frame. But something was off.

"Is everything okay? What are you doing here?"

He didn't move; his body remained still, his hands stuffed in the pockets of his coat. "I came to see my little girl."

Alarm bells began ringing in her head. Something was *definitely* not right. She couldn't recall him ever once having referred to her as his "little girl."

She took a small step back. As she did, his brow creased.

"Is this how you would honor me? Is it not customary to embrace the one without which you would not have been born?"

She froze. *What?*

He pulled something shiny from his pocket. "It seems the charade has become unnecessary."

Her eyes moved to the object in his hand, the firelight behind him glinting off its razor-sharp blade. She took another step back, an iron fist of fear punching her in the gut.

He smiled. "It is extraordinary. This body sired you, yet it lacks the proper paternal bond it should possess with its offspring. But do not fret, child. There is little doubt it will mourn your death."

This was not her father. This was something else.

She turned and made a mad dash for the door, knocking over a table and lamp on the way. If she didn't get out of this room now, she was sure she never would.

The double doors might as well have been a brick wall. Instead of flying open, they held firm, and her body ricocheted off them like a bullet. A body slammed into her from behind, sending them both back into the door. As an arm wrapped around her waist, she desperately fumbled with the handle, but she never got a chance to turn and pull. Her feet had already left the floor.

She sailed through the air and landed on her back, *hard*. She tried to scream, but her lungs were empty from the fall. When he pulled her up by the hair, it was all she could do to stay conscious.

"Pathetic mortal," he hissed, nearly ripping the hair from her scalp. She yelped in pain, still struggling for air as something cold pressed against her neck.

The sting from the blade felt familiar—almost like a bad paper cut. A very lethal, very permanent paper cut. Warm blood trickled down her chest. She was an artery away from no return, and all she could do was think to herself, *Is this really it? Is this really my end?*

"Dad?" she wheezed, her voice small and weak. If he was still in there, she had to try.

The grip on her hair tightened, bringing hot tears to her eyes.

"Daddy . . . please."

The hand gripping her head began to shake, and the pressure on the blade subsided—barely, but enough to give her hope.

"Dad, it's me," she cried. "It's Alice. Please don't do this!"

His breathing became ragged and hoarse, and he was now shaking so badly she feared he might cut her throat by accident.

"Daddy, don't—"

"Puh-puh-puh . . . Peanut," he grunted. "RUN!"

The knife fell to the floor with a clang, and she was shoved into the doors with such force that her head smacked the hard pine. She didn't remember falling, or how long she lay on the ground before the dogs started tearing up the doors. She could hear them in the hall, their vicious snarls and the sound of wood splintering as they tried to claw their way through.

Dizzy and disoriented, she attempted to pull herself up. But her vision was blurred. She couldn't see.

"Alice," said a voice. The *other* voice. She slipped and slid back down, frantically casting her hands about for the handle.

"HELP! SOMEBODY PL—"

Hands wrapped around her throat.

Her reaction was pure instinct; she fought with everything she had, her arms and legs thrashing. But the harder she fought, the faster she faded. Her lungs seized, desperate for air, but the pressure only increased. She heard a scream, but it was too far away to make a difference. The dark was already beckoning. It felt good when she finally let her hands fall limply to her sides—when she stopped struggling and simply remembered.

Her last thoughts were of her mom and Molly. The girls. The

love she hoped to take with her. And she saw Colin's face too, clear as day. She clung to it, thankful to have shared those last moments with him, brief as they were. Then the image was gone, and so was she.

Philautia stood before her. Beautiful. Majestic. She *was* Helen of Troy: golden leaf crown, draping white gown, sandals laced to the knee. A face that launched a thousand ships.

Is it really you?

Philautia smiled. *It's how you choose to see me.*

Alice looked around. They were surrounded by a dull gray nothingness. *Where are we?*

There is no name for it. It is simply the place between.

She looked down. She couldn't see the floor. She couldn't see anything other than Philautia—not even her own body. But the fact that she didn't seem to have a throat didn't stop her from feeling it tighten.

I died.

For the moment.

Her nonexistent body relaxed. *I'm going back?*

Yes.

When?

When you've asked the question you've come here to ask.

She didn't need long to decide; she'd been asking this question for weeks. *Why did you choose me?*

Philautia radiated warmth and love. *You are so much more than you allow yourself to believe, Alice. You embrace what you should fear, and fear what you should embrace. You have yet to realize your potential. Your power. But this is not the question you came here to ask.*

More riddles. But something *had* been bugging her—an intrusive thought that had been worming around in her brain since she'd first heard the words spoken.

The deal you made with Hades, for Cithaeron's soul. What was it?

Philautia closed her eyes. A shining tear escaped down her cheek. *You already know the answer to that question, Alice.*

The Huntress was right. There was a clarity in this place Alice didn't understand, but somehow she'd always known.

It's me.

Yes.

How much time do I have?

When the moon turns to blood and Ptah's Fire burns brightest, the hourglass has been turned. You must destroy the last of the demons. They cannot remain.

Ptah's Fire. She could see it, a distant light blazing through the night sky. It was a comet. It was *the* comet.

But how can I do that? One of them just killed me.

That was not a demon. There are those that wage a separate war. They will lose. You must ensure it.

Alice was getting tired. She was ready to leave this place. *What happens to Cithaeron?*

Philautia smiled through tears that now flowed like rivers down her cheeks, glistening like diamonds.

When the terms are met, your soul will belong to Hades and Cithaeron will be free. His debt will be paid.

What if I can't do it?

The power lies with you. The choice is yours.

Destroy the remaining demons, or the deal was off and Cithaeron's soul would be sent back to Hades. Alice might be half-dead in the place with no name, but she knew one thing from the bottom of her frozen heart: she would save him. There was no choice to make.

Thank you.

You thank me, even when I tell you I promised your soul to Hades in exchange for his?

She lifted her invisible shoulders. *I love him.*

In spite of everything, Alice wasn't angry or upset. She was sorry for what happened to Philautia. Sorry for the curse that started it all. She was sorry for a lot of things, but she wasn't sorry that it was her who was chosen. Because she now knew it wasn't Philautia who'd chosen her. It was Cithaeron. She didn't need to ask the question, after all.

Philautia bowed her magnificent head, her tears threatening to engulf them in an ocean of sadness. *He does not know, but he is the reason you are here. His soul's mate. That was the deal. Hades would accept no other.*

Alice had heard enough. Almost. She had one more question. *What happens to you now?*

Philautia's image faded and was replaced by millions of pinpricks of light. They twinkled and swirled like faraway galaxies spinning in perpetuity.

A voice echoed through the infinite space.

I've existed long enough. You were my gift, Alice. Thank you. Forever and always, thank you.

"Clear!"

Zap.

"I've got a pulse."

"Thatta girl. What's her name?"

"Alice."

"Alice? Alice, sweetheart, stay with us. C'mon, you can do it. Stay with us."

chapter 11

Her eyes fluttered open. Moonlight was shining through the window. The air held that stillness that only comes with the dead of night.

She heard a soft noise—a ghost of a breath. With some effort, she lifted her head. He was leaning against the wall by the window, his face obscured by shadow. She attempted to swallow, but her throat was full of fiberglass.

"Colin?" she said, though it came out more like "caw."

He didn't move or answer. She tried again.

"Colin." Better, though she wasn't going to be singing karaoke any time soon.

Still he failed to respond.

She slowly pushed herself up, only then noticing the IV in her arm and the heart monitor attached to her finger. A hospital. She was in a hospital.

"Alice, please lie back down."

It was a rare moment when she was happy to do as she was told. She dropped back down to her elbows and closed her eyes.

"Are you okay?" she croaked.

"Are you serious? Am *I* okay?"

She kept her eyes closed and nodded.

"I don't know what to say. No, I'm not okay. None of this is okay."

She opened her eyes. She could tell from his voice he'd been crying. She hated that it was because of her. Because of this. They had such little time left. Bolle-Marin was here. And the blood moon was four months away.

"You know what's not okay? You all the way over there. Come here." She extended her hand.

"I can't."

She dropped her arm. "You're angry with me?"

"God, no. Believe me, I'd be sleeping in that bed with you if I could. But . . . I literally can't. Hammacher isn't letting anyone near you."

"What?" She craned her head over the side of the bed. Sure enough, Hammacher was curled up on the floor next to it.

"Is she sleeping?"

"Definitely not." He took a step toward the bed. The dog let out a deep, menacing growl. He immediately stepped back.

"Shhhh, girl. Colin's okay." She reached toward the dog.

Hammacher turned her head and licked her hand.

"It doesn't matter," he said. "Barry gave her some sort of command before he left; she won't let anyone near you other than hospital staff. Don't ask me how she knows the difference, but she does."

She let out a gravelly laugh. "That's a little paranoid, isn't it?"

"We're not taking any chances until we know what happened."

Her thoughts went to her dad's face, illuminated by the flames of the fireplace before he moved to attack her. The image would stay with her forever.

"Is he okay?"

"He's going to be fine. Barry called off the dogs before it was too late."

"The dogs? What happened?"

"Schlemmer got a hold of his arm, but there's no permanent damage. Mayron's physician is looking after him. He's currently under lock and key at the Roxlands'."

She sat up, dizzy from the rush. "Lock and key? But you can't. It wasn't him!"

"Hey, shh . . ." He moved toward her.

Hammacher sprung to her feet with a loud snarl and snap of her teeth. He jumped back.

"We know," he said, glancing warily at the dog and keeping his distance. "He doesn't remember anything. In his mind, he went to see you and the dogs attacked him, thinking he was an intruder. But we don't know if the demon's still hiding in his subconscious. We haven't been able to force it out yet. So we're not taking any chances. And that's never . . ."

Alice narrowed her eyes. "What?"

He leaned against the wall again, and Hammacher lowered herself back to the floor.

"Alice, demons are mischievous and selfish creatures. They're only as dangerous as the mind of their host allows. But this was different. If the dogs hadn't broken through in time . . . it could have . . . It almost . . ."

"But it didn't. I'm still here."

A strange noise came from deep in his throat. He sank to the floor, pulling at his hair. The sight was worse than a blade to her throat. She couldn't handle his pain. She wouldn't.

Hammacher's head popped up as she swung her legs off the bed.

"Stay," she ordered, pointing her finger at the ground. The dog whined once, then laid her head back down in a huff.

Alice carefully pulled out the IV in her arm and removed the heart monitor. She didn't need them anymore, of that much she was sure. She lowered her feet to the cold floor, stepped over Hammacher, and made her way to Colin. Kneeling in front of him, she took both of his hands in hers and pressed them to her cheek.

"I'm sorry," he said through a strangled sob. "I'm sorry I—"

"There's nothing to be sorry for." She leaned forward and wrapped her arms around him.

He pulled her into his lap and held her tight. "I almost lost you," he cried into her hair. "Just when I found you, I almost lost you."

She closed her eyes and sank farther into his embrace. "You'll never lose me. No matter what happens, I'm yours, Cithaeron. Forever, I'm yours."

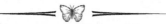

Olivia sat on the floor next to Hammacher, hugging her like a small child. The dog whimpered and slapped a fat tongue across her face.

"Uncle May convinced the hospital to let her in here," Olivia said, wiping dog spit from her chin. "He knows someone on the board or something."

It had been two days since the incident in the parlor. Alice was being released today. As far as the hospital knew, a mentally unstable relative had become confused and attacked her. It was weak as stories went, but thanks to Uncle May there would be no police report. The girls had come to bring her home; they'd had to physically remove Colin from the room to get her ready. He hadn't left since it happened.

Alice turned to Soxie. "Your uncle's home?"

"No. He called from Europe."

"What does he do, anyway?"

"Don't ask," Hadley said.

Soxie shot Hadley a look before answering. "He was military and CIA at one point, but that's all I know." She dug in her bag, extracted a colorful silk scarf, and tied it around Alice's neck.

"CIA?"

"It's a dead end, Alice," Olivia said. "He's Fort Knox."

"Can't you see in his head?"

"Yes, but there's nothing there. Or there's too much. It's weird, but I can't get a solid read. It's like he knows I'm trying too. I stopped because it kind of freaked me out how blank he can make his mind. He's like a monk."

"Fine. I'm good with just demons for now anyway. Is this really necessary, by the way?" She fingered the soft fabric now tied around her neck. "I look like a flight attendant from the sixties."

"Until that cut and the bruises on your throat go away, yes."

She lifted Hadley's hand mirror to study her reflection. The cut on her forehead from banging into the door, which had bled enough to blind her during the attack, had mostly healed already. Though her throat was still tender, she was able to speak—with just a little hoarseness, as if she had been at a loud concert, screaming all night to be heard over the music. Which was good, because that was the story they'd fed her mom. A two-day music festival in Tucson, to be precise. She'd already begun memorizing the set lists, just in case.

"I still can't believe my mom's letting Hammacher stay with us."

"That was all Barry. He can be very charming." Soxie started to brush Alice's hair. For the third time.

"Uh, Sox? That's enough with the hair. But thanks."

Soxie paused mid-brush, then turned to Hadley and Olivia. "Guys, would you mind giving us a few minutes? We'll meet you and Tinsley out front."

Hadley gathered her things, and Olivia clipped a leash to Hammacher's collar. The dog barked and spun in circles, as if they were headed to the moon and not the parking lot. As they were leaving, Hadley gave Alice one of her sweet Hadley winks, and Olivia paused at the doorway. Alice wasn't a mind reader, but she knew what she was thinking.

Me too, she said silently.

Olivia made a weird face. "That's odd. I can't—"

Hammacher pulled her out of sight before she could finish.

Alice watched the door slowly swing shut. Did that mean what she thought it meant?

"It's my fault," Soxie blurted out.

Alice's eyes swiveled to her friend. She was still clutching the brush and staring at it.

"I should have gone with you."

"What? No. No way."

Soxie looked up, her emerald eyes full of fire. "You don't get it. I talked to him before I came to get you. I felt something was wrong. I *knew* it. But then I saw you and Colin, and . . ." She closed her eyes. "I was so pissed. I felt like you were keeping this massive secret from us, and it really threw me."

Alice looked down. "I'm sorry. I should have said something earlier, but I didn't understand it myself."

"Hey, quit trying to hijack my apology."

"You don't owe me an apology. You'd never met my dad; you couldn't have known. If you'd gone with me, you might have ended up hurt too. Or worse."

Soxie sat down on the bed next to her, absently fiddling with the brush. "I've had years to recognize a demon when I see one. I *should* have known."

"It wasn't a demon."

"What? Of course it was."

"I promise you, it wasn't."

"Daniels, what's going on?"

"I don't know yet. But I need to talk to my dad."

"Good luck getting through your boyfriend."

Alice couldn't help but grin like a lovestruck teenager. *Boy-friend.* It was cute in its simplicity. He was so much more, but the thought still made her belly tingle.

She tucked one leg under the other and turned to face Soxie. "Listen, I know he's like a brother to you. Are you okay with this?"

Soxie reached up to finger the white stripe in her hair. "I'm not gonna lie. It's weird. But I've watched him with you these past couple of days. I'm seeing a Colin I've never seen before. And it's good, Ali. It's really good."

"Really? What's different?"

"Love, dumbass."

Alice smiled and wiped a tear from the corner of her eye. "Thanks, Sox. That means a lot to me. You mean a lot to me."

Soxie pulled her close, nearly suffocating her in coconut-scented curls. "C'mon, dumbass," she whispered. "Let's not keep your lesser half waiting."

"Absolutely not."

"Colin, he's still my dad. You have to let me talk to him."

"He might also have a demon hiding inside him. No way. Not until we know it's gone."

She banged her head against the seat. Instead of giving in, he took her hand and pulled it to his lips, keeping it there just long enough to bring heat to her midsection before bringing it back to rest on the center console. His thumb brushed her knuckles as he continued driving in silence, his eyes shaded by mirrored sunglasses.

"Please. Just five minutes. I need to know he's okay."

"Are you ever going to listen to me, or is it always going to be an argument?"

"Two minutes?"

"This isn't a negotiation."

She pulled away, folded her arms, and turned toward the passenger window. Colin laughed.

She scowled. "Is something funny?"

"Sorry. It's the 'cute when angry' thing. You suffer from a very serious case of it."

He reached over to caress her cheek, but she swatted his hand away and leaned farther into the door. *Cute when angry?* What an archaic thing to say. Soul mate or no, how dare he.

"How about angry when I'm angry? What difference does it make if I'm cute?"

"Oh, boy," he mumbled under his breath. Then, with an exaggerated sigh, he checked his blind spot and merged into the exit lane.

She read the sign. "Wait. I thought you were taking me home?"

He ignored her and pressed a button on the steering wheel. Ringing sounded through the car's speakers.

"What's up?" Soxie's voice crackled.

"Change of plans. Head to your place first. Alice wants to pay her dad a visit."

"Barry, we're going home first," she heard Soxie say away from the phone. A dog barked in the background.

"What in the blasted hell, yer always changin' your mind at the last—"

Colin clicked the button and silence resumed.

Alice waited a few seconds before speaking. "Thank you."

Colin remained quiet, intent on the road. She was getting her way, but he was going to make her pay. Well, then—challenge accepted.

She leaned over and let her lips lightly graze his ear. "Thank you," she whispered.

He hit the brakes and veered sharply into a random strip mall parking lot. She lurched back into her seat and then forward as he parked the car with a jolt. The next thing she knew, his sunglasses were on the dash, their seat belts were unbuckled, and his lips were on hers.

Her insides liquified. He kissed her long and deep, staking his claim. Conquering her. Worshipping her. She closed her eyes and let herself fall. Four months or four lifetimes, neither would be long enough, so she'd take what she could get.

When his ardor died down, he placed delicate kisses across her shoulder and along the inside of her arm. He slowly leaned back into his seat, taking her wrist with him, and pressed his lips to it as he looked up at her through dark, hooded eyes.

She could tell her hair was askew and her cheeks were flushed, but for the first time in her life, she felt pretty. Beautiful, even. In his eyes, *she* was Helen of Troy. She pulled his hand to her lips, honoring the man he had become. He'd spent centuries atoning for his sins. Whoever Cithaeron had been millennia earlier, it no longer mattered. He was hers now.

"Happy?" he said, his eyes transitioning back to an elegant blue.

"Yes. I'm happy."

Despite what was coming, she meant it. Right now—at this moment—she was happy.

He held her hand the rest of the way, his thumb tracing slow circles on her knuckles while her locusts and butterflies danced.

chapter 12

"Either I go in with you, or you don't go at all."

Alice prepared herself for another argument. His stubbornness was impressive, but she was learning how to navigate him (and getting pretty good at it too).

"What if Hammacher comes with me?" she asked. "And Schlemmer?" At the sound of her name, Schlemmer's head popped up from her cozy spot by the fire.

Colin sat back, the aged leather of the library sofa squeaking in protest. "Sorry, cutie. No can do."

"I'll be careful. I promise. The dogs saved me before, right?"

"I said no."

"Colin, please. I know I'm right about this."

"No, you're not."

Okay, maybe she wasn't so good at navigating him after all. She sprang to her feet and let out a bratty "argh!" It was pointless, but she hated losing. Colin was predictably unfazed.

Schlemmer, on the other hand, was not. She scrambled to an alert position and barked.

"Shhhh!" Alice snapped. "Be quiet!"

Taking it out on the dog didn't help. The poor thing whined and grunted, then began sneezing uncontrollably.

Colin shook his head. "Schlemmer, girl, it's okay. She didn't mean it."

"What's wrong with her?"

"She gets sneezing fits when she's upset. Ever since she was a puppy."

Alice looked to the heavens in surrender. For a vicious guard dog, this one was ridiculously sensitive.

It took almost five minutes to calm the little diva down. She hopped around the room like a screaming banshee, sneezing and blowing airy mucus all over Mayron's first editions. Alice couldn't help but laugh. Eventually she calmed her down by plopping in front of the fire and inviting her to sit on her lap—all eighty pounds of her. It was a lot of dog but also a lot of love. Schlemmer pressed her head into her shoulder, and Alice's heart melted.

She gave the happy dog another satisfied pat before turning back to Colin.

"What if Barry gives them a command?" she asked, pretending like the idea had just come to her. "Like at the hospital?"

"You're killing me. How many times do I have to tell you no?"

She gently nudged the dog aside, rose to her knees, and shuffled her way over to him. When she reached the couch, she sat on her heels at his feet.

"Don't you trust me?"

"No."

She giggled and laid her head on his leg. "Liar."

"You know, I'm starting to think you might really be a Wayward."

"So now I'm a witch? Thanks, I think."

"No, more like a sorceress. You weave your little magic and somehow always get your way."

She crawled into his lap, curling into him like a cat. "Hmm. A huntress *and* a sorceress. I've had a busy year."

He gripped her waist. "Do you promise? No stupid stunts?"

"Stupid," she deadpanned. "You know, I'm not really a fan of that word. How about a simple 'Be careful'? Same message without the jerk part."

His nostrils flared, but then he appeared to let go of whatever it was he was holding on to. He closed his eyes and leaned his forehead into hers.

"You win. You'll always win," he whispered. "Be careful, please?"

She smiled and planted a soft kiss on his lips.

"I take it back. You are a witch."

"Double, double toil and trouble," she muttered, then playfully nipped his lower lip.

"Is that so?" He lifted her off his lap and pinned her to the couch in one fluid motion.

He was just lowering his mouth to hers when Schlemmer began barking. A car door slammed, followed by an answering bark. The dog hauled ass out the library door, scratching up the wood floor and banging into the doorframe on her way to greet the late arrivals.

Alice was looking forward to continuing their "conversation" later, especially after Colin whispered, "To be continued," in her ear. For now, though, there was more serious business to attend to. They had just managed to right themselves on opposite couches when the girls walked in. The dogs howled their way down the hall, no doubt following Barry to the kitchen for treats.

Hadley took her usual seat by the fire, her phone at the ready in case she got bored. "What's the plan again?" she asked no one in particular.

"Alice wants to talk to her dad," Colin replied curtly.

Olivia flopped on the couch next to Alice and kicked her boots on the table with a bang. "So we'll bring the dogs," she said. "But we should still be careful."

"I think I should go alone," Alice said.

"Yeah, right," Soxie said. "Like that's happening." She dropped onto the opposite couch and let her stiletto heels smack the table with equal force.

Alice winced. Coffee tables in this place didn't stand a chance.

"No—I mean, yes," she stammered. "I'll still take the dogs. I just . . . I think it would be better if I talked to him alone."

"Um . . . that doesn't sound like a good idea."

"Exactly—thank you, Hadley," Colin said. "Alice, he doesn't remember anything. And if there is still a demon hiding in his subconscious, it won't be any help. All you'll be doing is putting yourself at risk."

"But I thought it wasn't a demon."

Colin turned to Soxie slowly, like she was a witness about to perjure herself. "Really. What was it, then?"

"Uh . . ." She looked to Alice for help.

Alice dropped her head in her hand. "I was going to tell you."

"Tell us what?" Hadley asked.

Colin shifted in his seat. "Yes, Alice. Tell us. And please, don't lie to me again."

"I didn't lie to you. I just asked you to trust me."

"Trust you. Maybe I will once you've earned it. Now tell me what's going on."

Her mouth was suddenly dry. She licked her lips to help her get started. "When I died . . . or almost died, I saw the Huntress. I spoke to her."

All three girls spoke at once.

"What the hell?"

"You're just telling us this now?"

"You *spoke* to her?"

Alice looked up. Colin was a human lie detector right now, evaluating every word, breath, and movement. She'd have to tread carefully.

"Yes."

"What did she say?" Olivia asked. The question alone was enough to confirm Alice's earlier suspicion. She could no longer hear her thoughts.

"I'm the last Huntress. The Realm ends with me."

"What?" Hadley exclaimed, hopping up to the arm of her chair.

Soxie kicked her feet off the table.

Olivia just stared at Alice.

Alice turned back to Colin. He was waiting for her to continue. He knew all this—had told her himself. He wanted to know what she wasn't telling him. But then, there was something he hadn't told *her* too.

"What was it, Colin?" she asked him. "What was it that Philautia showed you in her last vision?"

His posture changed as the other three heads in the room turned in his direction.

"It doesn't matter. Things are different now. We adapt and move forward."

So he knew. Not everything. But part of it, at least, he knew. And he was determined to change it. She turned away, convinced now that she was on the right path. He might believe he could save her, but she *knew* she could save him. She forced a smile.

"Speaking of moving forward, once I ash some more demons, we get to go on with our lives."

"Wait, what?" Hadley shook her head. "I thought it almost . . ."

"Well, it wasn't fun, but the only permanent damage seems to be this," Alice said, pointing to her hair. "Nothing a visit to the salon can't fix, right?"

None of them were laughing.

"Alice, you can't be serious. We had to carry you out afterward." Olivia seemed to be attempting to be a voice of reason in a situation that had none.

Colin leaned forward, staring at the floor.

She clasped her hands together to keep them from shaking. "I was given this power for a reason. The Realm is ending. The demons have to end too."

"So that's it?" Hadley asked. "Your hair turns white, and we all live happily ever after?"

"Yes. But the thing is . . ."

"What's the thing, Alice?"

His voice still destroyed her. It was her sacred sound—her *om*. Even when it was demanding and savage. Like now.

"Philautia told me there are . . . others. I don't know who or what they are, but they don't want me ashing demons."

She was met with silence. Their faces showed a mixture of fear, confusion, and, in one case, barely contained anger.

Case in point suddenly stood and walked to the chessboard by the window. "So, let me get this straight," he said, his back to the room. "Not a demon but someone or some*thing* is trying to kill you. And for all we know, it's still in there, with your father."

"Maybe . . . but maybe not. I won't know until I talk to him."

Colin dropped his head and gripped the sides of the table. Then, without another word, he turned and left the room.

Alice watched him go, aching to follow him. To run to him. But instead she sat there like a coward, the weight of secrets she could never tell pushing her into the ground.

"I respect what you're trying to do, Ali, but Tinsley's right," Soxie said. "It sounds too dangerous. You have no idea what's in there."

"But this might be my only opportunity to find out. And what about my dad? It's my fault he's here. How can I help him if I don't even know what we're up against?"

"I get that. But why do you have to do it alone?"

"I told you. It's the only way we'll get answers."

"Lie."

Her head snapped toward Olivia. "I thought you couldn't read me anymore."

"I may not be able to see in your head, but I'm not stupid."

"You can't read her anymore?" Hadley asked Olivia.

"Jesus," Soxie said, "any other surprises you'd like to spring on us, Daniels?"

"Fine! I don't want anyone to get hurt, okay? Whatever it is, it's after me. I can't let you put yourselves in danger."

"And since when do you get to make that decision for us?" Soxie asked, her eyes flaming.

"She doesn't," Colin answered from the doorway. "But I do. The three of you, stay here. Alice, come with me."

She sat up, stunned by his sudden return. He strode across the room and offered her his hand.

"You wanted to see him, right? Let's go."

With one last glance in the girls' direction, she stood and let herself be led out of the room.

He kept his hand closed around hers as they ascended the two flights of stairs to the guest room where they were keeping her dad—"guest room" being a loose term, under the circumstances.

Morgan and Barry were waiting outside the door with Hammacher and Schlemmer. Alice hardly recognized the dogs; they sat like obedient, formidable statues on either side of their master, awaiting his next command.

"How's our guest doing?" Colin asked as they approached.

"Good," Morgan said. "Doc says he'll be just fine, but not sure how much longer we can keep him here."

"I'll take care of it," Colin said.

"Be mindful, Alice," Barry warned. "Ye can't let yer da get too close; the girls here won't stand fer it. Ye'll get a wee warnin', but best ye keep him at a distance to be safe."

She nodded. Then he snapped his fingers, and both dogs immediately lifted their heads to look at him. He pointed at Alice and said one word: "Asset."

They jumped up and proceeded to flank her on either side—her own personal canine bodyguards.

She turned to Colin. "Okay. Wish me luck." She took a step toward the door.

"Not so fast," he said, blocking the entrance.

Hammacher growled.

"Hammacher, no!" Barry commanded.

The dog backed off, and Colin stood his ground.

"Colin, I thought we agreed—"

"WE didn't agree to anything. You asked me to trust you, even after you deliberately lied to me."

"I didn't—"

"Alice, don't. I'm not going to stop you. I'm choosing to trust you, and I'm asking you to trust me."

She placed her hand on his chest. "Of course I trust you."

"Good." He took her hand and kissed it. "Now. Shall we?"

We. She should have known. Well, she hoped he knew what he was doing. With no other choice, she followed him into the room.

———— ✦ ————

It was a bigger guest room than the one she'd stayed in before. There was a sitting area with a wood-burning fireplace, a dining alcove, and even a small bar set in the corner. If this was a temporary prison, it was a gilded one.

"What the hell? Get those things out of here!"

Her dad was sitting in one of the chairs by the fire, a tumbler of scotch in his hand. She'd been so distracted trying to make this meeting happen that she hadn't stopped to prepare herself for what it would be like. Seeing him again after what happened . . . it brought up all kinds of conflicting emotions. But she couldn't afford emotions right now. She needed answers.

"Dad?" she said, slowly walking toward him. Hammacher and Schlemmer stayed glued to her sides.

"Alice, be careful," he said, standing and pointing at the dogs. "Those animals should have been put down!"

Hammacher bared her teeth.

"Dad, it's okay. They won't hurt you as long as you stay calm."

"Calm? No, I won't stay calm. First I'm mauled, and now I'm

in some kind of quarantine?" He turned to Colin. "I want an outside line and I want it now."

She placed her hand on Colin's arm, signaling for him to stay quiet. "Who do you need to call?"

"My goddamn lawyer, that's who. Honey, I don't know who you've gotten mixed up with here, but if those dogs have rabies or some other kind of disease, they've got one hell of a lawsuit on their hands." He lifted the sleeve of his shirt to reveal a bandage on his right arm.

"You're not going to sue anybody, Gavin."

"Alice, you know I hate when you call me that. I'm not your friend; I'm your father. And the hell I'm not."

"Dad . . . just listen to me, please. They're good dogs. See?"

She put her hand next to Hammacher's face. She looked up and whined, confused but eager to please.

"For Christ's sake, Alice, don't be an idiot!"

Both dogs tensed. She could feel the vibration of their growls through the floor.

"They're not rabid, Dad. It's all just a big misunderstanding. I promise. Please let me explain."

She hadn't really planned how she was going to explain this away, but it didn't seem to matter. He shook his head dismissively, swirling his scotch like a first-class passenger on the *Titanic*.

"You're just like your mother. Always making excuses for people who don't deserve it. Well, I guess in this case, dogs." He gave Hammacher the side-eye as he finished his drink.

Part of her couldn't believe this was her father—the man she once thought hung the moon. "Don't you dare bring Mom into this."

He let out a dramatic sigh. "I get it, Alice. I'm a disappointment. I ruined your mother's life. I'm sorry I can't be the person you want me to be. But . . . marriage is hard. One day, you'll understand."

She glanced at Colin, mortified that he was present for this. "I didn't come here to beat the dead divorce horse. I wanted to make sure you're okay. Are you okay?"

He nodded, staring into the flames as if exhausted by life, a sad shell of the man he once was. Maybe one day she would understand. But for now, all she could do was feel sorry for him. Sorry for the disappointment he felt his life had become. She stepped forward.

"Dad, why did you come here?"

He turned to her with a dazed expression. "What?"

"Why did you come here?"

"What do you mean? I came to see you."

"But why?"

He opened his mouth to answer but seemed to second-guess himself. "You know, it's strange. I don't really remember why; I just know that I really wanted to see you. I wanted to see my little girl."

Whatever it was, it was still in there. She could feel it. She could almost see it, watching them silently through his eyes.

"So you were in Fort Collins and just decided to drop everything to come see me?"

He looked down, studying his glass like he'd never seen one before. "I . . . I don't know. Was I? No. I was in Denver. I had a meeting, but then . . ." He stared at the glass. Then he dropped it on the rug and stood there, swaying.

"Dad?"

A sound came out of him that she'd never heard before. It was disturbing and raw. If she weren't staring straight at him, she'd think he was being gutted alive. He clutched his head and clawed at his hair, stumbling back and forth.

"AL . . . Al-ice," he said through clenched teeth.

She immediately stepped forward. "Dad. Dad, what's happening?"

Regardless of his failings, it hurt to see him like this. Colin grabbed her arm to stop her from going to him.

Then something whizzed by her ear, so close she felt the wind on her face as it sailed past. The glass shattered into a thousand pieces on the wall behind her, forcing her to duck to avoid the shards, and the dogs went nuts—not enough to attack but enough to show they meant business. They jumped in front of her, all snapping jaws and foaming mouths, while Colin attempted to push her back toward the door. But she wasn't ready to leave yet. Not when their guest had finally arrived.

She planted her feet and peeked around Colin's shoulder. Gavin was standing a few feet away, his eyes the same yet unrecognizable. He turned his head sideways to look at her.

"The chosen one still lives," he hissed.

Chosen one?

"Reveal yourself," Colin demanded.

"Filthy mortal. You dare challenge a god?"

Colin drew himself to his full height and pushed Alice farther back. The dogs stayed by her side, their hackles raised.

"I see no god before me," he said, taking a small step forward.

"Colin, no," she whispered.

Her dad's face turned to molten rage. "Your day has come and passed, mortal. The age of man will not last."

"Reveal yourself!" Colin roared, his voice so volcanic she didn't recognize it. He took another step, dangerously close to the thing that was her dad. The dogs were on a tight wire, ready to snap.

"Colin, stop," she pleaded.

He either ignored her or was too focused to hear.

"Cithaeron!" she shouted. "Please!"

Gavin's eyes rounded. He glanced at Alice, then back at Colin, his mouth forming into a slow, hair-raising O.

"Can it be? Cithaeron, the prize pet of Hades? He who destroyed the heart of a goddess?"

Colin's body went rigid. He turned to her and mouthed one word. *Run.*

She stared at him, paralyzed. *What?* She couldn't leave him. She couldn't leave her dad. Any second now, the dogs might tear him apart.

Colin turned back around. "Erinyes," he said.

Alice felt ice form in her veins at the sound of the word. *Erinyes.* The Furies.

"YOU DARE SPEAK OUR NAME!" The muscles on her dad's neck stretched taut from the impossible strain. He grabbed a crystal table lamp and hurled it in a fit of manic rage. It missed them both and smashed into the wall, but the shards came even closer to her than the bits of scotch glass had. She teetered for a moment, checking the side of her face to be sure.

"Dammit, Alice, RUN!" Colin shouted.

The dogs were lethal and unglued. She stumbled backward toward the door as Morgan and Barry barged in behind her.

"Get back!" Colin yelled, turning to warn them.

She watched as her dad's body sailed through the air, a long, dark object in his hand. Time slowed; she could almost see the deadly accurate trajectory of the fireplace poker. She threw herself into Colin, pushing him out of harm's way. Then something slammed into her, knocking her to the floor. An ear-piercing howl followed.

She was on her back, her legs pinned under a twitching body. The poker meant for Colin's neck was sunk deep into Hammacher's stomach. Her dad lay on the ground a few feet away, Morgan and Barry holding him down as Schlemmer snarled, just short of ripping his throat open.

She heard a scream in the hall, then Olivia ran through the door and fell to her knees, skidding through the dark puddle already pooling on the floor. She threw herself on top of the dying dog, her cries drowned out by the noise and fray.

Alice felt hands reach under her arms to pull her up, but her body went limp. All she could do was watch as Hammacher used her last breath to lift her head, whimper, and lick Olivia's cheek.

Olivia didn't speak to anyone for two days. She locked herself in one of the guest rooms, refusing both food and visitors, until Colin eventually forced his way in. Alice stood outside the door, listening to him comfort her friend as she sobbed in his arms.

And then there was Schlemmer. As distraught as Olivia was, the dog was inconsolable. After Morgan and Barry secured Alice's father, she howled and sneezed for an hour straight, curled up next to Hammacher's lifeless body. Alice could barely function through her own tears, and seeing Soxie's eyes well up really sent her over the edge. It was an unfathomable loss, and it was all she could do not to drown in her own guilt.

She sat with Colin in the third-floor window seat on that second night, watching the sun set over the Roxland estate, his arms securely wrapped around her. He held her while she cried, assuring her everything would be okay. But everything wasn't okay. Hammacher was dead, and her dad was a captive guest for the foreseeable future.

The bare bones of a plan began to form in her mind as she watched the dusk slowly fade to night. It was a plan that would tear her heart to pieces. But it would save them. It would save him. She laid her head against his chest and closed her eyes.

chapter 13

A horn honked as Alice grabbed a Pop-Tart from the toaster. Schlemmer barked.

"Schlemmer, shhh!" Judy said over her paper.

The dog looked up, wheezed, then sneezed.

"Mooooom . . ."

"Sorry, honey, I forgot. Come here, sweet girl. Mommy's sorry."

Schlemmer slid across the tile at warp speed to get to her "mommy."

Alice laughed to herself. The dog was supposed to be there to protect her, but her true love had been Judy from the start. Barry had asked her mom to take Schlemmer while he trained a new pair of guard dogs. It wasn't a complete lie. Three days after Hammacher was killed, they'd gone to a nearby breeder and purchased two little bundles of black-and-brown fur.

It was Olivia's idea. Soxie thought it was too early, but the look on Barry's face proved her wrong. Tears sprang to his eyes as they all fawned over the pudgy bodies and puppy breath, Hammacher's sacrifice forever memorialized in their innocent, furry faces.

Alice paused before heading out the door, the Pop-Tart hanging from her mouth. Judy was showering the dog's head with kisses.

"Mom, you're making Boop jealous."

Judy glanced toward the kitchen island, where Boop was busy cleaning himself, oblivious to all of them. She turned back to Alice and frowned. "Sweetie, I really don't like the hair. And is that your breakfast?"

Alice rolled her eyes and bent down to give her a kiss on the cheek. "Yes, Judy. Gotta go. Love you."

The horn honked and Schlemmer barked. Again.

"Love you too, Cruella," Judy said. Then to the dog, "Yes, I love YOU too, yes I do . . ."

Alice couldn't help but smile as she opened the door, thankful for another day. Another opportunity to tell her mom she loved her. There was no point worrying about what was coming. Regardless of what Colin was trying to do, it was inevitable. So for now, she'd live for today. She squinted into the morning sun and skipped down the steps.

Hadley was waiting for her with the top down, listening to a song by some nineties boy band. A truck drove by and honked, its occupants hoping to catch the attention of the blond bombshell in the convertible. She ignored them.

Alice tossed her bag in the back seat and hopped in.

"Hey, honey." Hadley checked her rearview mirror before pulling onto the road. She reached her hand out expectantly. "When's your boy getting back?"

Alice snapped the Pop-Tart in half and gave her the bigger piece. "This afternoon. Why, do you miss him?"

"Ha. That'll be the day." Hadley took a generous bite of the pastry. "So, is everything good?"

"As can be expected."

"Have you talked to your dad?"

Alice tilted her head back and looked up at the cloudless sky. "No, but my mom did. She says she hasn't heard him sound that happy in years."

"Well . . . that's good, right?"

"I guess. But let's change the subject. Something a little less—I dunno—real?"

She didn't want to talk about her dad, or Colin's trip abroad. Not yet.

"Okay. How about, we're GRADUATING next week," Hadley said, crumbs flying out of her mouth. "Is that too real for you? We have the whole summer and college to look forward to. Woo-hoo!"

Alice pretended to be excited, even lifted her arms in the air and whooped along with Hadley. But graduation was the last thing on her mind. And she wasn't going to be around for college. She finished off her Pop-Tart and pulled a pair of sunglasses from the glove compartment. She put them on as the wind blew her hair every which way.

Hadley turned off the music. "Hey, wanna raid Soxie's closet for *The Reel*'s graduation party?"

Alice turned to look at her beautiful friend. Her sister. Forever a part of her. She was doing her best to imprint all of their faces in her mind. She had no idea if consciousness would follow her to the next place, but she hoped so. She didn't want to forget anything.

Hadley snapped her fingers in front of her face. "Hey, where are you?"

She sat up. "Sorry, daydreaming. You know how it is."

"Sheesh. He's been gone for four days. You'd think it was a year."

Alice smiled but said nothing. She turned to the window and let her arm trail over the edge, her hand pressed against the wind. The warm breeze felt nice. For several minutes she lost herself in the colorful blur of the world rushing past, lamenting another world already lost.

"Do you miss it?" she eventually heard herself say.

Hadley slowed down to turn into the school parking lot. She pulled into a space facing the Triangle and shut off the engine. "Truth?"

Alice rolled her head to the side to look at her. "No, please lie to me."

Hadley gave her a light shove. "The truth, you twerp, is that I do and I don't."

"Very succinct."

Hadley turned her gaze to the steering wheel, absently tracing her thumb over the car's insignia.

"We haven't spent this much time away in years," she began. "There was a time we were jumping in two, three times a day. And not always hunting demons. Sometimes just flying around playing Conga, or sitting for hours under one of the Huntress's projections, making plans for the future. One time we spent the entire night underwater, surrounded by tropical fish, coral, and even boats moving overhead. It was amazing. It was our home away from home. Our secret, special place. But now . . . I don't know. It feels different."

Alice took off her sunglasses. "Different how?"

"It feels . . . empty. Maybe a little sad."

"It's definitely not empty." The early bell rang, but neither of them made a move to exit the car.

"You know what I mean. Yes, it's full of demons, but I didn't feel *her* there anymore. Did you?"

A few days after Hammacher passed, they decided to do a Realm jump. The second they entered, all three compasses shot forward, splitting into more whirling balls of silver than they could count. It was an invasion. Worse, there were no more black mirrors to send the demons to. The Dark Place was gone. Alice knew what that meant, and to prove it she snuck up behind a demon that was already mimicking a reflection. A man rehearsing a speech in German.

The pain was no less punishing than it had been the first time, but having the knowledge there would *be* pain helped. Once her hand came in contact with the demon, it seemed to recognize her, and it flipped its body backward to grab hold of her with every appendage available. The girls tried to peel it off, but there was no need. It turned to ash within seconds.

She made it back to the studio that day on her own steam, thankful not to be passed around again like a football. She did, however, faint the minute they exited the Backwards Place, and ended up with a thicker strip of white hair—not to mention zero chances of entering the Realm again. When she came to, she learned that Colin had confiscated all three compasses, and would not be returning them. Ever.

"No, I didn't feel her either." Alice shrugged. "She's gone, Hadz."

"But how could she do that? How could she just leave us?"

Alice stared at the Triangle in the distance—all the figures darting back and forth, their lives just beginning. "What do you think it would be like to exist as long as she did?"

"I don't know," Hadley said. "Ask Colin. He's still here. He hasn't abandoned us."

Alice smiled, feeling the familiar tug on her heart at the sound of his name. "That's different. He's been given mortal lives. He's gotten to live and breathe and be. She only existed through her huntresses—pieces of her soul given over centuries. There was a finite amount. There was always going to be an end."

"But why should you have to suffer for it?" Hadley pointed to Alice's chunk of white hair. "Why should you be responsible for cleaning up the mess she made?"

"I don't think it's as simple as that."

Hadley banged her hand on the steering wheel. "Well, I don't care. Colin's right. Screw her, and screw the Realm. We've done enough. If she can't even stick around, why should we?"

"Demons."

"Yes, but the people they infect are already evil. Or semi-evil. Honestly, for all the demons we've sent back, did it ever really make a difference? I mean, look at David."

"Yes, look at him!" Alice said.

"We don't know if that's because of his infection."

"Hadz, c'mon."

Hadley threw her hands up. "Fine, but he's an extreme case."

"Do you think he deserves that? I know he wasn't exactly Gandhi, but maybe one day he would have been a halfway decent person."

Hadley looked at her like she'd just suggested the earth was flat.

"Okay, probably not." Alice sighed. "The point is, we'll never know. There could be more of them like that out there, sticking around and taking bigger roles. Can we really sit back and watch them destroy lives?"

Hadley removed her sunglasses and tossed them in the cup holder. "Since when did you become so altruistic? And for the record, that's not my word of the day." She paused to watch the figures in the distance. "Either way, this whole thing stinks."

Alice agreed with her silence.

"What are we supposed to do?" Hadley continued. "Our compasses are gone. For all we know, Colin destroyed them."

"I might have an idea. But I need your help."

"Of course." Hadley sat up straighter. "What can I do?"

"Colin's taking me camping for the weekend. We get back Sunday afternoon. I need us all together that night."

"Easy enough. We'll do a barbecue at Soxie's or something. But why all the cloak and dagger?"

Alice reached in her bag and extracted the bottle of sleeping pills she'd stolen from Judy's medicine cabinet that morning. She placed them on the dashboard.

Hadley stared at them like they were cyanide. "No . . ."

"It's the only way."

"We've tried before. He's got some way of blocking us. Besides, we still need a compass for a dream hop. And if he finds out we drugged him . . ."

"Don't worry," Alice said. "I'll do it."

"Honey, are you sure?"

"Listen, I know it may not work, but I have to try. And I can't do it alone." Her heart ached at the thought of betraying him, but she'd spent sleepless nights the past two weeks going over every conceivable option, and this was it. The only one that would work.

Hadley unbuckled her seat belt and flung it off of her, letting the metal slap against the door. "Alright. I'll talk to Soxie and Olivia. But they're not going to like it."

Alice leaned over and threw her arms around her. "Love you, Hadz," she whispered, not wanting to miss any remaining opportunities to say it.

Hadley's willowy arms hugged her back. "Love you too, silly."

She got home from school with just enough time to pack and feed the animals, then quickly scribbled a note to her mom:

Schlem and Boop fed. Don't forget the leftovers in the fridge. We may not have service but promise I'll text when I can. Be home Sunday night. Thanks for being the coolest. Love you—Alice

At first, Judy had been anything but cool about her weekend away. Having Colin over for dinner had helped ease her mind, though, and it didn't hurt that he'd brought a friend. Watching her mom and Barry together made her happy. Barry was a good man. Her mom had gone long enough without one.

Boop jumped on the counter and pushed his head into her hand.

"Hey, buddy. Sorry, I have to go, but Schlem will keep you company. Right, girl?"

At the sound of her name, Schlemmer raised her head.

"Some guard dog, huh, Boops?"

He purred.

"I think Mama Judy has spoiled the guard right out of her."

Schlemmer yawned.

Alice felt her butterflies and locusts also yawn as they awakened from their four-day slumber. She grabbed her bag and headed to the front door. When she opened it, Colin was waiting for her with a dimpled smile and a bouquet of wildflowers.

"Hey there, pretty lady," he drawled. He was wearing jeans, a black T-shirt, and a cowboy hat. He tipped the hat with his free hand, and her stomach did a backflip.

"I think you have the wrong house, Cowboy. But come on in before my boyfriend gets here."

He grabbed her around the waist and drew her to him, kissing her hungrily. She held the back of his hat as she sank into his arms and floated away on his kiss, consumed by his need and desire. Living in the moment. Thankful to have it.

When he pulled away, his dark eyes lightened back to their usual sparkling blue.

She gave him a sly smile and leaned forward. "I've missed you," she whispered into his lips.

He groaned, clutched her tight, and kissed her again, pushing them both into the front hall. A second later, they heard a bark and the sound of scrambling paws.

"Damn," he said into her neck.

Schlemmer rounded the corner and skidded to a stop in front of them. She barked once and started bouncing up and down. Colin knelt to give her the proper greeting she deserved, and Alice plucked the hat off his head and placed it on her own.

"Good girl," Colin said, wrestling with the dog. "Have you been taking care of Alice for me?"

"Alice isn't completely helpless, you know."

He glanced up, refusing to take the bait. Instead, he slayed her with one of his killer smiles and held out the bouquet in his hand, now crushed by their hasty embrace. "Sorry about these."

She greedily snatched her gift, brought it to her nose, and inhaled the sweet scent. "You pick these yourself, Cowboy?"

He stood and placed his hands on his hips. "Well, that depends. Would you prefer I'm romantic and cheap, or generous and lazy?"

"Those are my options?"

He pretended to look serious. "Sorry. I don't make the rules."

"Okay. Romantic and cheap. I guess."

"In that case, I definitely did not buy them at the airport."

She laughed, swatting him with said airport bouquet. "I knew it! So much for romance."

He stepped forward and slid the back of his hand down the side of her neck. "Oh, yer gonna get you some romance, pretty lady. Don't you worry none . . ."

She giggled and leaned back, keeping him at arm's length. "Listen, Tombstone, we'd better hit the road before my mom gets home and changes her mind."

He picked up her bag, grabbed the hat off her head, and placed it back on his own. "Well, ma'am, we best get goin' then."

She followed him through the door, thoroughly enjoying the view. "Where exactly are we going, and dare I ask about this new you?"

He turned around. "What, you don't think this is a good look for me?"

He knew full well it was a good look for him.

"Don't get me wrong. Every girl wants to bag a cowboy once in her life. I just didn't think I'd met mine yet."

"Oh, sweetheart, them's fightin' words." He spun her around and threw her over his shoulder like a sack of potatoes.

She started laughing hysterically.

"Think you're pretty funny, don't you?" he said, skipping down the front steps as she bounced and giggled.

A horse whinnied.

She stopped laughing and pushed her hands against his lower back to twist around and see where the noise had come from. Parked across the street was a pickup truck—hitched to a horse trailer.

"Colin," she said soberly. "I've never ridden a horse before."

He set her down by the passenger door and tossed her bag through the open window. Then he placed one hand on either side of her, trapping her. One of his trademark moves.

"Don't worry, I've been riding for centuries. Max and Aggie are pussycats compared to the beasts I've tamed."

She clutched her mangled flowers to her chest. "So modest."

He leaned in slowly, his eyes locked on hers. "And for the record, you've met your cowboy. I am your first, and I'll be your last. You can bet on it."

Her heart melted as he lightly brushed her lips with his.

He was right. She'd bet her soul on it.

chapter 14

The fire crackled and danced, tiny embers glowing red as they disappeared into the night sky. A coyote howled in the distance. The horses let out occasional puffs of air—aware, yet still. Alice stared into the flames as Colin absently stroked her hair, basking in the warmth and aftermath of their lovemaking.

She was no longer a virgin. It was never something she'd been fixated on, like Chloe and Rachel had been. She'd assumed one day she'd meet someone, probably in college, and it would happen. But this, being here with him . . . it was all she'd ever want. She'd already given him her heart and soul. Her body was just the only thing she had left.

"Are you cold?" he asked, planting a kiss on her temple as he pulled the blankets up, burrowing them deeper into a delicious cocoon.

Instead of answering, she snuggled closer, kissing his chest and relishing the heat of his body. Then she settled her head into the crook of his neck and turned to look at the sea of stars above them. Out here, in the middle of nowhere, they were the stuff of dreams. Intense, overwhelming, and almost unreal. Sort of like him.

"Tell me about one of your past lives."

He clutched her tight, rubbing slow circles on her back. "Irrelevant."

"How do you figure?"

"You weren't in any of them. This is the only one that matters."

She couldn't help but smile. As pillow talk went, she doubted more romantic words had ever been spoken. But she was determined to get something out of him. She wanted to know everything he'd done and seen and been. She wanted to drink him in, all sixteen hundred years.

"Well, they aren't irrelevant to me. Please? Tell me a story about a different you. Indulge me."

"No chance I can take a pass?"

She grinned and shook her head.

He trailed his fingers lightly up and down her neck. "Well, let's see. What time period are you interested in?"

She clapped her hands together, excited for this game. He could have been anyone, anywhere, at any time.

"I don't know . . . how about the 1500s? Ooh, were you ever a knight?" She twisted her neck to look at him. The thought of him wielding a sword, all testosterone and courage—it sounded right.

He laughed. "Not even close. It was important I stay under the radar. Less fanfare, more dull and ordinary."

"I don't buy it. Then what were you?"

"I only lived one life in the sixteenth. I was a blacksmith."

She detected something strange in his tone—a reluctance to elaborate, perhaps. But she couldn't help herself. She wanted to know.

"What was it like?"

He rubbed his forehead. "Hard. Life was hard."

"Life's always hard."

He smiled. "I suppose you're right. But if you're thinking it was all turkey legs and jousts, think again. You were lucky if you made it past childhood, and even then it was a struggle. Hunger. Disease. Infections . . . even a simple cut could end up killing you. And the smell . . ." He wrinkled his nose as if the scent of the sixteenth century had just blown through their campsite.

"Granted," he continued, "that's just the way things were. No lifetime was without its challenges. But in that one, only one of my huntresses made it past eighteen. I died at the ripe old age of twenty."

"How did you die?"

"The plague."

Her chest hurt just picturing it. "And your huntresses? How did they die?"

"Two of them died from the plague. The other was murdered."

"Murdered?"

He pulled her closer, his eyes glazing over as the past took a seat on the other side of the fire. "It wasn't easy to justify a role in their lives back then. If my family's trade didn't afford an opportunity to get close, I'd have to get creative about how I communicated with them—how I kept them safe. Sometimes I'd pretend to be a distant cousin, or find a way into the household as a farmhand or servant. But Mary was married off at fourteen, and her husband was a gambler and a drunk. A violent one." He paused. "She was found strangled in her bed. He claimed it was one of the servants. Poor fellow was hanged for it too. We knew it was her husband, but there was no proof. It's not like a forensics team could come in and dissect the crime scene. He got away with murder, and was remarried within a month. New wife, new dowry. I would have killed him myself, but the plague got me first."

"Was he infected? With a demon, I mean . . ."

He reached up to run his fingers through her hair. "You would think so, but no. Just a really bad seed. I knew it from the beginning, and still I failed to protect her."

"It wasn't your fault. You know that, right?"

He kissed the top of her head but said nothing. Even after all this time, the guilt clearly stayed with him.

"Are there any happy memories?"

"I'm making them right now."

She buried her face in his chest. "You know what I mean!"

"Okay, okay. I'll tell you one, but then no more questions about past lives tonight. Deal?"

"Deal."

He thought for a moment. "Have you ever heard of V-J Day?"

"No. What's that?"

"Wow. Doesn't say much for education in this country, does it?"

She bolted up, holding one of the blankets to her chest. "Well, *excuse me*. Some of us haven't been around long enough to know everything about everything."

"You're right, you're right! Forget I said that."

She shot him an annoyed look. "Fine. What was V-J Day?"

He sat up and pulled her against him so they were both facing the fire. He wrapped his arms around her and kissed her shoulder, resting his chin there, before continuing.

"To be fair, it's not exactly a national holiday. At least, I don't think it is. But it was the day Japan surrendered, ending World War II."

Yikes, she probably should know that. Slightly embarrassed, she nodded, encouraging him to continue.

"It was August 14, 1945. I was twelve years old, so I hadn't awakened as Cithaeron yet. We were living in New York with my grandparents when the news hit the wires. People started pouring into the streets. Cars were honking, strangers were hugging each other, crying and laughing. It was remarkable. My little brother, Joey, and I followed a crowd of people into Times Square."

He leaned over and dug his phone out of his bag. He scrolled through his saved images until he found the one he was looking for. "That's when I saw this."

Her eyes lit up as she grabbed the phone. "I've seen this. You were there?"

He nodded, taking the phone back and studying the famous image. "Our dad was in the navy, so every time I saw a sailor I would hold my breath that it might be him. It was the guy snapping photos that seared this one in my memory. When I saw it in my mom's *Life* magazine a week later, I knew I'd witnessed something significant. Not so much the kiss, but the moment in time. Being there—being a part of it."

"Colin, that's amazing."

He tossed the phone aside and wrapped his arms around her again. "It was a good day."

She did the math. "Wait, you could still be alive. I mean, the boy that you were. How long ago did you die?"

"I was in my twenties. Car accident."

Her chest tightened again. "What about your huntresses?"

"I'm the gatekeeper to the Realm. The link between Philautia and them. I like to think they continue their work after I'm gone, but I have no way of knowing."

"Have you ever tried to find them, if your next life overlapped?"

"I haven't had the technological means to do that until this one. And it's not like I always awoke in the same country, or even the same continent. But yes, out of curiosity, I did try to find my last girls."

"And?"

"Margot and Janie are still alive. Cassie passed away in 1984. Cancer."

She gave it a moment before asking. "So did you contact Margot or Janie?"

"I thought about it. But they're in their eighties now. They have families and grandchildren—great-grandchildren. They already did their part. It was more important for me to focus on my new recruits."

"Did you ever . . . Were you ever married? Did you have kids?" She wasn't sure she wanted to know, but couldn't stop herself from asking.

He looked past her. "Besides Philautia, no. I never reproduced again. I don't think it's possible. She wanted me committed to her huntresses. But . . . I was married. Not that many times, considering. But I was."

She cast her eyes down. What could she say? He'd lived on and off for centuries. Of course he'd had relationships. Of course he'd married.

"Hey, look at me."

She hesitated, afraid he would see the jealousy in her eyes.

He lifted her chin. "They were marriages of convenience, Alice. The sister or cousin of one of my girls—whatever made it easier to stay close. I did what I had to do."

"Did you love them?"

"I cared about them. They were good women, most of them. They helped keep the loneliness at bay. But they weren't my priority. It wasn't fair to them, so after a few hundred years I stopped allowing myself to get close to anyone. It made the next life easier."

She turned back toward the fire. The flames were beginning to die down. "And what about your last brother, Joey? Is he still alive?"

He was silent for a few moments. "I did some research a couple years back. He died in Vietnam."

She swiveled her body to face him. The loneliness. The repeated loss. Lifetime after lifetime, waking up with the knowledge and pain. How could he bear it? She placed her hand on his cheek. "I'm so sorry."

His eyes reflected the dying flames behind her. He took her face in his hands. "I'm not. All those lives. All that time. It's brought me here to you. I don't know how, and I don't know why. But I don't care. The past no longer matters; it never did. Not without you."

Her eyes welled with tears.

"I love you, Alice. I've always loved you."

Tears of happiness spilled down her cheeks as he kissed her slowly and they turned their bodies toward one another, making them one again. They made love for the second time under a brilliant starlit sky, her only thoughts of him and this moment in time. This she would take with her to the next place; this she would never forget.

On Sunday morning, after a simple breakfast of bacon and eggs, they got an early start and set out for the trailer. She was feeling a bit more confident on Max, the intimidating black horse Colin had first plopped her on two days before. She'd been nervous then, and the long trek to the campsite had been slow going. But the next morning he'd taken her for another ride, and then another, and now she was actually starting to feel comfortable on horseback.

They took their time on the way back, allowing Max and Aggie to amble along at their chosen speed, which was a lazy walk. It was still early, and the desert had yet to yawn itself awake; the temperature was cool, the insects quiet. They rode in silence, at ease in each other's company. She closed her eyes and leaned her head back. The steady sound of hooves hitting dirt and the creaking of leather saddles was hypnotic. She let her body rock gently back and forth.

"Hey, where are you?"

She smiled, keeping her head facing the sky. "Just enjoying the ride."

He made a clicking sound, and she sensed him maneuvering Aggie forward so he was directly next to her and Max—a pair of carriage horses without the carriage, making their way along the dusty trail. She turned and opened her eyes.

"So we've made a cowgirl out of you after all." He lightly tapped the brim of her hat, a gift pilfered from the Roxlands' tack room.

"Well, I don't know about that. I'm pretty sure Max is doing all the work. Look, no hands!" She dropped the reins and lifted her arms. Max either didn't notice, or didn't care.

"That's it. Next time I'm putting you on Aggie. She won't be as accommodating, so I wouldn't get too used to cruise control if I were you."

She wasn't prepared for him to talk about a next time. Her face fell before she had a chance to stop it.

"Whoa." He reached for Max's reins and pulled both horses to a stop.

She looked down, suddenly nervous.

"Alice. Look at me."

She did.

"What's going on?"

She decided to stick as close to the truth as possible. Lying to him was becoming harder and harder. "I'm just worried. Worried about my dad. About the Realm."

"We've been over this. The Realm is no longer your problem. Or mine."

"But—"

"It's not up for debate. Philautia's gone, and I'm not letting you finish what she never should have started. And I told you I'll take care of your dad. He's perfectly safe right now. And very comfortable, I might add."

She bristled. "Perfectly safe. So long as he's nowhere near me."

He took his hat off and wiped his brow with his forearm. "That's right. And he won't get anywhere near you anytime soon. I'm sorry, but that's the way it has to be."

"But how do you know they can't get a hold of somebody else close to me? My mom, or one of the girls—or even you?"

He placed the hat back on his head. Aggie stomped her hooves and swished her tail. "I think you're safe if you avoid the Realm."

"But you don't know that for sure."

He reached up and caressed her cheek. "I'm not going to let anything happen to you. *That* I know for sure."

She looked down, her eyes on Max's mane. "I know you want to protect me, but what about the people we're supposed to protect? Like David?"

He dropped his hand on his thigh with a slap. Max threw his head up and Aggie skipped sideways. He steered her back with little effort.

"David? You're kidding, right? This is a guy who would sell his mother's soul if the price was right. And as for the rest of these people you're so eager to protect, remember that most of them are just like him. Demons choose them for a reason."

"And you don't think they deserve a second chance? You don't think they're worth saving?"

"I don't care."

She shook her head. She knew arguing with him was futile, but she refused to let him get away with that one. "That's a lie, and you know it."

His eyes darkened. "Alice, you need to understand something. My only priority now is keeping you safe. If that means giving demons freedom to infect as many people as they want, so be it. You're not going back in. That's final."

She turned to face the opposite direction. Max pawed the ground. "At least tell me where my dad is."

"He's with Soxie's parents."

She whipped her head back around. "Her parents? They're alive?" Soxie had never mentioned them once. She was under the impression they had passed away a long time ago. Granted, Soxie wasn't exactly the sharing kind when it came to her personal life, but Alice felt guilty for not knowing more.

"Yes," Colin answered. "They live on her mother's family estate in Spain. We arranged for him to stay with them for a while. Mayron will keep an eye on him."

"What about his work?"

"The Roxlands needed a financial advisor, so it was good timing. He's set up in their guesthouse. Oh, and good news: he's agreed not to sue."

She let that sink in for a moment. Well, good for him. She hoped it made him happy. "But during the trip, was there any sign of . . ." She was hesitant to say their name. "Did anything happen?"

"No. There's been no sign of them since Hammacher died. But I still don't trust they're gone. Until we know for sure, we keep the status quo."

She gripped the horn of the saddle. "What do you think they want?"

"I don't know. Revenge, maybe. I'm the reason Tisiphone ended herself. I'm guessing Megaera and Alecto weren't too happy about that, and if anyone can hold a grudge, it's the Furies."

"It sounded like more than a grudge. It sounded like they're planning something."

"Even if they are, it's no longer our problem. Let the brothers deal with them, if they still exist."

"The brothers?"

He leaned back in his saddle. "You should know this, Alice. The Three Brothers. Who are they?"

She gave him a bored look. "Alvin, Simon, and Theodore."

"Funny."

She rolled her eyes. Apparently school was still in session. "Zeus, Poseidon, and . . . Hades." She hated saying that name out loud; it stuck in her throat like the sharp edge of a chicken bone. "You think they no longer exist?"

"I don't know. I haven't seen any sign of the gods since my time as Cithaeron—not until the Furies showed up in your dad. But if Philautia has given up her existence, who's to say some of the gods haven't as well?"

If only Hades was one of them. She took a deep breath, anxious to change the subject. "I'm sorry I keep pushing. I know you want to keep us safe." She paused, wondering how best to say what she was really feeling. "The truth is, I'm scared."

For a brief moment he seemed almost angry. Then he kicked his far leg over Aggie's neck and, in some kind of rodeo gymnast move, managed to seat himself behind her on Max without ever touching the ground. Aggie quickly sidestepped away to forage in wild grass.

"I told you," he said, wrapping his arms around her, "I'm not going to let anything happen to you. Do you believe me?"

She leaned into him and nodded.

"Then there's nothing to be afraid of. The Furies will never touch you. I promise." He tilted her hat to kiss the side of her neck.

"I'm not scared of the Furies."

He pulled back, an obvious question hanging in the air. In a move that would make her yoga instructor proud, she lifted one leg over Max's neck and twisted around until she was sitting backward. Max remained still, as if he knew she needed to say this.

"I'm scared of disappointing you. What if I don't live up to the person you dreamed of? What if our connection is because of the Realm and the Huntress, and not in spite of it?"

He seized both of her hands and pressed them against his heart. "It's true: you're the mirage I stumbled toward in my dreams for hundreds of years. But that's all it was. A mirage. It didn't exist; it was just an idea. The idea of you. I can't explain it, but when I saw you for the first time, suddenly my dream had a face. Yours. And then I knew. After all this time, it was real. *You* were real."

She held her breath.

"But my dream—she was nothing compared to the living, breathing you. I watched you sit for hours on your rock, wondering what you were thinking, how hard it must be to bear it alone. I've watched you time and again sacrifice your own comfort, even safety, for your mom and dad. For the girls. For me. Never once asking for anything in return. Your strength and resilience amaze me. You make me laugh and you drive me crazy. You challenge me at every turn, and I wouldn't have it any other way. I'm in love with the person you are, Alice. Philautia and the Realm have nothing to do with it."

The corner of her mouth turned up. "So what you're saying is, you were stalking me."

"If you want to get technical . . . sure."

She wrinkled her nose. "Little creepy, don't you think?"

"I think you're pushing your luck."

"Sounds about right."

He patted her hip. "Girl, just wait 'til I get you back to the truck."

"The truck? I don't think so."

"Oh, you'll think again."

"We'll see about that," she said, her butterflies ready to stage a coup. "But first, are you going to show me how to ride this thing backward now?"

He slid an arm around her waist, pulling her close. "Baby, I'm going to show you the world."

It took everything she had to keep it together. She could see it in his eyes. He really believed that. He really believed he was changing the game.

For now, and for what little time they had left, she'd force herself to believe it too. She took his face in her hands. "By the way," she said, her heart simultaneously bursting and breaking. "I love you too."

His eyes clouded dark. "Alice," he said. Then he kissed her with the desperation of a man drowning.

Their hats fell to the ground and a whirlwind of dust spun around them, engulfing them in silent chaos.

chapter 15

They arrived at the Roxland estate around four o'clock. Alice spent the majority of the drive cuddled up to her cowboy, their hands clasped and country music blaring on the radio, wishing for an eternal pause button that didn't exist.

He pulled into the circular drive to drop her off before heading to the stables.

"So, when's this pajama party commence?"

"Hilarious."

He laughed and leaned over her to open the passenger door. "Well, what would *you* call it?"

"It's just a casual girl's night—last one before graduation."

"Any chance I could stay in one of the guest rooms? I promise I'll leave you to your pedicures and pillow fights. So long as you pay me a visit before the sun comes up."

She leaned back. "Pedicures and pillow fights? How do you know we're not drinking beer and playing poker?"

He lifted his hands in the air. "Hey, don't blame me. Blame Hollywood. But if it is poker, just remember Olivia's a ringer. Might as well save some time and give her your wallet."

"Hmph. Who has pillow fights, anyway? Is that even a thing?"

He held her chin and planted a firm kiss on her mouth. "Maybe we should make it one. Just you and me."

She smiled, the vision of the two of them and a pillow fight causing her butterflies to flutter and her locusts to buzz. "You'd lose. I play dirty."

"Is that so?"

"Uh-huh."

"What a coincidence. So do I." He started tickling her, and kept going until she was squealing and squirming like a six-year-old.

"Okay, okay! Uncle! Uncle!"

He stopped, buried his head in her neck, and began placing tender kisses along her collarbone. His hands were beginning to roam when one of the horses neighed and kicked the inside of the trailer.

"Um, I think Max and Aggie have had it with us."

"Fine." He sat back as if offended. "Enough horsing around."

"Wow. How long have you been waiting to use that one?"

He shot her one of his megawatt smiles. "Couple hundred years, give or take."

She laughed in spite of herself. "Okay, old man. I'm going. I'll see you at dinner."

He grabbed her hand and kissed it as a horn honked behind them. When he jumped out to deal with Barry, she found herself staring at the empty seat he left behind, her heart aching for a future she could never have.

She sat on the bed next to him, watching him sleep. Behind closed lids, his eyes darted back and forth. He was dreaming now. She could only hope it was of something good. She ran her finger across his brow, smoothing a line that didn't belong there.

"Alice, it's time."

She wiped away a tear and stood.

Olivia was standing in the doorway. "Are you sure you want to do this?"

Alice glanced at Colin one last time. No, she didn't want to do this. But she was sure she had to.

"Yes, I'm sure. Lead the way."

They walked in silence to a room two doors down. It was a small, square room with no windows. The walls were covered in a thick, dark fabric and the floor was strewn with pillows and overlapping rugs. Candles illuminated the space in a soft, dim glow. Movement above caught her eye. The entire ceiling was covered in mirrors, reflecting the flickering light.

"What is this place?"

Soxie and Hadley were lounging in the center of the room, waiting. Olivia took a seat on the floor next to them, and Alice did the same.

"Meditation room," Soxie said, lighting a stick of incense.

"You meditate?"

"Sometimes, but mainly we use it for dream hops. And I want to go on record that this is a bad idea."

"Yeah, Alice. What's your plan?" Hadley asked. "I still can't believe we're doing this."

"I still can't believe he didn't notice you dump that stuff in his drink." Soxie snorted. "Sorry, Daniels, but you'd make a horrible spy."

"She's right," Olivia agreed. "I could have sworn he noticed."

Alice hugged a pillow to her chest. "Well, excuse me. I guess I missed the class at school on how to roofie someone properly."

"He's going to kill us," Hadley whispered.

"Can we please just get this over with?" Alice said.

Soxie crossed her legs and leaned back. "I don't know what you expect to do without a compass."

Alice looked around the room, searching for clues. "Tell me how a normal dream hop would go."

"We place a piece of the dreamer's DNA in a compass, then focus on each other in that." Soxie pointed at the mirror above them.

"It takes a lot of concentration, and we don't always get in. We tried three times before we made it into yours."

"DNA? What did you use for mine?"

As she asked the question, she recalled the moment in her bathroom when she could have sworn she felt a tap on her shoulder. She put her hand up. "Never mind. I think I know. That scared the crap out of me, by the way. Couldn't you just have waited until I was gone and grabbed it from my brush or something?"

"Sorry. We needed to make sure it was yours and not your mom's. Oh, did anyone think to get—"

"Yep. Got it," Olivia said, holding up a few strands of short, dark blond hair. She placed them in Alice's hand. "How do you want to do this?"

Alice gripped the hairs she couldn't even feel. "You said he has a way of blocking you. How?"

"His subconscious has built some kind of protection against it. The only time we tried, we found ourselves trapped in an endless maze. We never even got close to his dream story."

"Dream story?"

"Whatever he was dreaming about that night. We didn't see any of it, just spent hours wandering in his maze until he decided to wake up," Olivia explained. "The worst part was, he knew we were there. We were so nervous we hid from him in the Realm for an entire day."

"Wait . . . Has Colin never been in the Realm?"

"Nope," Soxie replied. "She only allowed her huntresses in. Well, and demons, but not on purpose."

"You're kidding me. All this time, he's never been inside?" Alice didn't want to believe it. It seemed so cruel.

"Sad, right?" Hadley said, flopping onto her stomach. "In the beginning we'd be really excited about our Realm jumps and couldn't wait to tell him about it. But after a while, we got the feeling he was just humoring us. Then it felt mean to keep throwing it in his face."

"I keep forgetting how little you know, Daniels," Soxie said. "It's weird."

"Thanks. That's super helpful."

"Easy, killer." Soxie patted her knee. "So now that you know, what're you thinking?"

She looked up. Her reflection stared back at her, daring her to try. She turned back to Soxie.

"How much do you think Colin weighs?"

It turned out that six-plus feet of sinewy muscle weighed more than they thought. It took all four of them to lift his unconscious body and transfer him to the meditation room. After a few complaints about half-baked plans and pulled hamstrings, they had him situated in the middle of the room.

"Okay, he's here. Now what?" Soxie asked.

Alice looked from Colin to the ceiling and back. "The compass uses a tiny bit of DNA. If we have the mother lode, and we really focus, maybe we can jump in without it."

"That's your plan?"

She closed her eyes. "Yes, that's my plan. I'm open to better ones if anyone would like to chime in."

"Worth a shot I guess," Hadley said. "But what about his maze?"

"I'm thinking maybe since he's drugged, it'll be harder for him to keep us out."

"Hmm . . . that might work." Olivia nodded slowly.

Soxie blew out a short whistle. "Geez, Daniels. Remind me never to get on your bad side. You're like Lex Luthor."

"Really, Sox? Like I don't feel awful enough as it is?"

"Sorry. You're right. That was low."

Alice put her face in her hands. "I can't believe I'm doing this to him."

"Honey, you don't have to go through with it. We can lug him back into the guest room and he'll never be the wiser."

She peeled her hands off her face. "Thanks, Hadz. But I've been over this and over this. It's the only way."

"The only way for what?" Olivia demanded. "You still haven't told us why you want to do this."

"I'm hoping to find where he hid the compasses."

"What? Alice, when we get in there"—Olivia pointed to Colin's prone body—"IF we get in there, we're going to be hitching a ride in his dream. We might be able to control some of it, but remember, his subconscious is the main driver. He'd have to literally be dreaming about where he hid those compasses—the actual place, not something concocted in his mind. Do you get what I'm saying? That's like looking for a needle in a stack of needles."

"I know."

"Then how do you expect to find out?"

"We're going to ask him."

"Just breathe and focus," Soxie said, her eyes making contact with Alice's in the mirror. They were lying on their backs, two on either side of Colin's inert form, using his body like a pillow. Red, black, blond, and brown hair surrounded their faces like puddles of silk, shining in the flickering light. They held hands, creating a linked circle over their sleeping subject. A thin ribbon of incense smoke floated above them, the scent of sandalwood filling the air.

"Breathe in . . ."

"Breathe out . . ."

Soxie's husky voice blanketed Alice's ears with its soothing repetition. She focused on the images in the glass.

"Breathe in . . ."

"Breathe out . . ."

Her vision began to tunnel, darkness encroaching from the sides. She let her mind go, little by little, with every exhale.

"Breathe in . . ."

"Breathe out . . ."

Their breaths slowly synchronized. It was getting hard to tell them apart; it was like they were breathing as one.

"Breathe in . . ."

Her eyes were closed.

"Breathe."

She tried to inhale but couldn't. Normally she would panic, but she didn't feel short of breath. It was an odd sensation. She was there; she could feel the floor beneath her, the hands clasped in hers. Yet nothing was happening. Not even the rise and fall of her own chest. She felt . . . suspended. An image captured in a Polaroid. A static version of herself. It didn't feel right. But it didn't feel wrong. It was nothing. It was between.

She heard a loud puff of air, followed by a familiar giggle. Her eyes shot open. She was looking at a blinding night sky. Millions of twinkling stars, neon-bright nebula clouds, and planets with spinning rings she could almost touch. It was an artist's rendition of the universe, only she was inside it.

She heard the familiar laughter again and turned toward the noise. There, in front of a cozy campfire, was Colin, his arms around her, both of them staring into the flames. She watched him whisper in her ear and heard another soft laugh come out of her own mouth. It was like watching a surreal Super 8 movie of herself. She looked so happy. They looked so happy.

"Whoa," someone whispered.

Olivia, Soxie, and Hadley were sitting next to her, equally mesmerized by the world around them. It was their campsite, on steroids. Magnificent night sky aside, the ground glistened like a geode and the giant red rock formations that should have been painting the horizon surrounded them instead. They were in a canyon of dizzying light, color, and moving shadows. It reminded her of the Realm.

Their stargazing was interrupted by the thundering sound of hooves. They turned just in time to see a large black horse barreling toward them. The ground rippled and shimmered from the vibration. Dream Max was at least three times bigger than real Max, and he leapt over them as if they were nothing more than pesky desert tumbleweeds.

"Jesus!" Soxie whispered.

They watched as Max launched himself through the campfire, its flames now blue and raging, licking the stars above.

Colin's laughter echoed around them as he whispered sweet nothings in dream Alice's ear, planting tender kisses down her neck.

It was her, but it was a flawless, stunningly beautiful version of her. She had never, ever looked in the mirror and seen that Alice before. She stared, transfixed by the sight. "That . . . that's me?"

"Who else would it be?" Olivia asked.

"But I'm . . . It doesn't look like me."

"What do you mean?" Hadley asked. "It looks exactly like you, silly."

Perfect Alice began laughing as she struggled to escape Colin's tickling grasp. A pillow appeared in her hand, and she playfully swatted him. He ducked and produced another pillow. Feathers began floating from the sky, coating the sparkling ground like snow. Max made another thundering pass, leaping through the tall flames and dispersing puffs of white into the starlit night.

Alice shook her head. "Hadley, are you blind?"

"Honey, I think you're the one that's blind."

"Guys, we don't have time for this," Soxie sang under her breath.

It stopped snowing feathers. Colin and Alice were now covered in blankets, locked in a lover's embrace.

"Um . . ." Alice tore her eyes from the scene. It felt like she was invading her own privacy, strange as that was. She turned to Olivia. "What do we do now?"

"Well, we bypassed the maze, and he hasn't noticed we're here yet. We need to confront him, but be prepared for this entire dream story to change when we do."

She turned back to the happy couple. The fire had died down from a raging blue inferno to twinkling yellow-and-red embers. Colin and dream Alice lay tangled in each other's arms, blissfully content and in love. She hated to interrupt this beautiful dream. It was hers too.

"Alice, are you ready?" Olivia whispered.

She nodded and began walking toward them. But after two steps her hair blew sideways as a strong wind almost knocked her over, and Max landed with an ear-cracking bang right in front of her, blocking the path forward.

He pawed the ground, his beach ball–sized hooves threatening to flatten her with one strike. She stepped back.

"Guys . . . what's going on?"

"It's his subconscious," Olivia explained. "It knows we don't belong here."

Another Max appeared next to the first, this one equally as pissed.

"Okay," she said, continuing to back away. "Now what?"

"We made it this far, so the drugs must be working. I think we can get through; we just need to distract these manifestations."

A third Max materialized, this one expelling angry blue flames with every snort.

"Hadley and I got this," Soxie said. "You guys do your thing."

Alice didn't even have a chance to ask. One second Soxie was standing next to her, and the next she was sitting astride the first Max, her head barely reaching the bottom of his silky black mane. With an ear-piercing neigh that sent a shock wave through the surrounding dreamscape, he rose onto his hind legs and shot forward into the night. The other two were right on his heels, Hadley clinging to fire-breathing Max. Laughter echoed off the red rocks as her blond hair left residual streaks in the air behind them.

"Hurry, we don't have much time," urged Olivia.

Still reeling from the "manifestations," Alice turned back toward the campfire. She and Colin were still lying in each other's arms, their smiles and laughter breaking her heart all over again.

She stepped forward, unimpeded this time. "Colin," she said. She intended to speak normally, but her voice carried as if it were being broadcast in a packed football stadium. His head shot up and her gasp coincided with Olivia's.

It wasn't Colin. It was Cithaeron.

And just like that, his dream story changed. There was no warning—no gradual fade to black or telling musical score. One moment she was at their campsite, and the next she was standing in a different kind of desert.

It stretched on for miles—cracked and white—with not a plant, insect, or living thing as far as the eye could see. The baked earth reflected the sun in a blinding way. She squinted to see as a warm wind blew through her hair.

"My love," said Cithaeron. He was there, his dark eyes worshipping her, his face familiar yet foreign. It was Colin. It was Cithaeron. It was every incarnation he'd ever been, morphed into this unimaginable vision before her. She closed her eyes as his lips found hers; the sensation was nothing short of mind-bending. His love engulfed them in a whirlwind of air and light.

"Where have you been?" he asked.

The wind around them swirled, kicking up dust and enveloping them in a silent cyclone of white.

She opened her eyes. "I'm here now."

He kissed her again and their bodies began to float, the swirling air lifting them toward the expansive blue above.

"Alice . . . Aliiiice . . ."

What did Olivia want? Why was she yelling?

Colin caressed her cheek, his blue eyes shining in the morning light. She felt movement beneath her and realized they were seated on Max, loping across the golden desert, Colin's lips on hers, their bodies moving to the rhythm of the horse's stride. She closed her eyes. Lost. Happy.

"Alice!"

Cithaeron ran his hand through her hair, studying the long white stripe that now interrupted the brown. His dark eyes, intent and piercing, reflected the glowing embers of the dying fire. "I love you, Alice. I've always loved you."

She felt tears spill down her cheeks, so grateful to be reliving this moment. He was telling her he loved her for the first time. Again.

"Alice!"

Her body jolted.

Colin smiled and stepped forward, trapping her against the ballet bar. "I guess I'm going to have to try harder this time."

They were in the dance studio. She remembered this. It was real once. But not anymore.

"Alice," Olivia said. "We're running out of time." She was standing with Soxie and Hadley by the piano.

Colin lowered his head to kiss her. It took all her strength to stay focused and not float away again. She pushed against him.

"Colin."

He said nothing, just continued to honor her with his eyes, running a hand through her hair.

"COLIN. Where did you hide the compasses?"

His hand froze. "Alice?" he said, his voice uneven.

She looked to Olivia, who just shook her head. She tried again. "Colin. Where. Are. The. Compasses."

He pulled back, his eyes dark and stormy. "Alice? What are you doing?"

She had him now. She was sure of it. "I'm sorry, but you have to tell me where you hid those compasses."

"Where I hid . . ." He paused to look around him, noticing the girls for the first time. "How did you—"

She placed her palm on his cheek. "Please, Colin. Just tell me."

"No, you're not doing this," he said as he stumbled backward. "No, dammit, *no*!"

They were back at the campsite, but it was cold and lonely. No fire was lit. No horses galloping in circles, or couples making love. Even the stars had disappeared.

Cithaeron stood tall and threatening, anger clinging to him like a poisonous vapor. She heard a sound to her right. Colin was digging a hole next to a large, brown boulder. She could see the campsite behind him, the fire lit once again, her sleeping form nestled in front of it. He had brought them here. He'd had the compasses with him the whole time, had waited for her to fall asleep so he could bury them and be done with it.

She turned back to the formidable figure in front of her, tears of anguish and rage in his eyes. He reached down to touch her hair. She was lying flat on her back, the sound of organ music whispering in her ear. *Sleep now*, it said. *Sleep forever.* She saw Olivia's face. Then Soxie's and Hadley's. They were looking down at her, their faces ashen and somber. She floated above herself, already knowing what she would see yet unable to look away.

Her body lay still in a satin-lined casket, every hair on her head white as snow.

And then she screamed.

chapter 16

"What the . . ." Soxie gasped for air.

All four of them bolted upright the second they were pushed out of the dream. Colin remained unconscious, his jaw clenched and his eyeballs moving rapidly back and forth.

"Oh my god," Hadley said. "That was . . . I don't know what that was."

Alice rested her forehead on her knees, willing herself not to get sick. She felt a hand on her shoulder.

"You okay?" Olivia asked.

She nodded, unable to formulate words just yet.

"I can't believe it worked," Soxie said.

"Do you think he'll remember?" Hadley asked.

"Let's hope not," Soxie replied. "But that last bit, what the hell was that?"

"A nightmare, maybe?" Hadley ventured.

"No," Olivia said.

Alice lifted her head. Olivia was looking directly at her.

"Alice knows exactly what that was."

She hugged her knees close. "It could just be a nightmare."

The doubt on Olivia's face was glaring. "Alice, your plan worked better than you expected."

"What do you mean?"

"While you were being tossed around by his subconscious, I could hear his thoughts. And they were loud and clear at the end. That wasn't his vision. It was *hers*."

"O, what are you talking about?" Soxie demanded.

"Olivia, don't," Alice pleaded.

"I'm sorry, but they have a right to know what we just helped you do."

Hadley looked from Olivia to Alice. "What *did* we help you do?"

"It doesn't matter. We know where the compasses are now. We can clear the Realm."

"And then what?" Olivia asked.

"It's the way it has to be." Alice looked away.

"Wait a second," Soxie said, unfolding herself from the floor. "Are you telling me Snow White in the casket is real?"

Alice looked at Colin, wishing she could crawl back into his dream. But Olivia was right. It wasn't fair to them. She'd asked for their help, deliberately not telling them the whole truth. They deserved to know.

"Yes. It's the last vision Philautia shared with Colin."

"Alice . . ." Hadley whispered.

Soxie stood over her, her arms crossed. "So that's why he took the compasses away. How long have you known?"

"The Huntress told me when I died. But I only knew the when. I didn't know the . . . how. Until now."

"So you were going to let us help you clear the Realm, knowing that every demon you ash brings you closer to that coffin."

"Sox—"

"No, Alice. We're not going to let you do this." She kicked a cushion across the room and pointed to Colin. "And the minute he wakes up, I'm telling him everything."

"Soxie, please. You can't."

"The hell I can't. As far as I'm concerned, he can dig those compasses up and drop them in the middle of the fucking ocean."

Alice jumped up and grabbed her by the shoulders. "Sox, listen to me. I have to do this. You don't understand."

"What don't I understand? That you plan to martyr yourself? And for what? A bunch of asshole humans and a bitch of a Huntress who just up and disappears?"

Soxie was livid, and a little bit frightening. Alice had never seen her so undone. She turned to Olivia and Hadley for help, but both of them remained silent, Olivia's eyes cast down and Hadley's swimming with tears.

"Sox," she said quietly. "I don't have a choice."

"Bullshit."

"A deal was made."

Olivia's head popped up. "What deal?"

Alice sank back to the floor next to Colin. She felt like she could pass out next to him and sleep for a lifetime.

"What deal?" Soxie repeated.

Hadley sniffed, waiting.

"Did you guys ever wonder what Philautia promised Hades in exchange for Cithaeron's soul?"

The three of them stared at her. She couldn't bring herself to say it, so she just glanced at her reflection in the mirror above.

"What?" Hadley said. "How is that possible?"

Olivia looked almost homicidal. "You? No. That can't be right. There's no way. Unless . . ." She turned to look at Colin.

"Unless what?" Soxie snapped.

"Unless I turned out to be his soul mate," Alice said. "It was the only trade Hades would make."

"No," Hadley squeaked.

Olivia just kept staring at Colin, shaking her head in denial.

"Son of a bitch." Soxie sank to the floor. "I take it he doesn't know."

Alice gripped her arm. "No, and I need you to promise me he never will. Please. He can never know."

"And if you don't go through with it?"

She placed her hand on Colin's chest, his breathing deep and steady. She hoped he and dream Alice were lying together again, happy under his extraordinary night sky.

"Either way, Hades is getting a soul. It might as well be mine."

They left shortly before dawn.

Even with the trailer still hitched to the truck, it took over an hour to load the horses and tack. The barn phone rang right before they were leaving, but Soxie instructed them not to answer. It was probably Morgan, she said, and the less he knew, the better. He didn't work for her; he worked for her uncle. And when it came to taking sides, Uncle May always took Colin's. With thousands of years of practice, a man can manipulate anyone. Even an ex-military/CIA operative.

Soxie flipped the visor down as the morning sun blasted her. Alice watched her, so comfortable and confident behind the wheel of the heavy-duty truck.

"Thank you for doing this," she said. She was answered with uncomfortable silence. Not wanting to push her luck, she turned her head and stared out the window, barely registering the passing scenery.

"Just so we're clear," Soxie said, "we're helping you retrieve the compasses. We're not—"

"I know."

The rest was better left unsaid.

No one spoke for miles, each lost in their own thoughts. Alice closed her eyes and pictured Colin's sleeping face. They'd managed to return him to the guest room; she prayed he was still fast asleep and would remember nothing. But she had a sinking feeling he would remember everything—the depth of her betrayal most of all.

"Is this the turnoff?" Soxie asked.

Alice opened her eyes and saw the familiar Shell station where Colin had kissed the inside of her wrist before hopping out to fill the tank. She nodded, and they continued on.

After an hour of deserted road, she could stomach the silence no longer.

"Guys—enough, okay? I'm still here. I'm not dead yet."

She heard an intake of breath from the back seat. Soxie remained quiet. Alice looked over her shoulder at Olivia and Hadley; they refused to make eye contact.

"So now it's the silent treatment?"

Soxie slowly brought the truck to a stop in the middle of the road. Not that it mattered, out here. She stepped on the parking brake and let the engine idle.

"What do you want us to say?"

"I don't know."

"Well, neither do we."

Alice looked down. "Fair enough."

Soxie released the brake and continued driving. A moment later, she offered Alice her hand. They stayed like that, their hands clasped, the rest of the way. It was better than words. It was sisterhood.

The trail was easy to spot from the road. An accomplished equestrian, Soxie took the lead on Aggie. Alice followed on Max, and Olivia and Hadley brought up the rear, riding double on a Belgian draft horse named Oscar.

Despite starting out at a good clip, they took a wrong turn and were forced to double back. Twice. By the time they found the campsite, the sun was directly above them and tempers were high.

"We didn't bring a shovel? Are you kidding?" Hadley shouted into the desert.

"I'm sorry! I just didn't think of it," Alice said, lifting the hair off the back of her neck. She kicked at the charred wood of the campfire, as if it were to blame for their current predicament.

Soxie ordered Alice and Olivia to start digging (somehow) while she and Hadley took the horses to get water. After pointing them in the direction of the creek, Alice squatted and rested her hands on her thighs. She felt the top of her head already burning. She hadn't even thought to bring hats. Colin was right. She was stupid sometimes.

"We can use this." Olivia held up a shovel.

Alice sprang to her feet. "Where did you get that?"

"He must've left it. Maybe he planned to dig them up the next time you guys came back."

Next time. Again, those words—the same as a searing hot knife to the chest.

"Well then, guess we better start digging."

Olivia's face fell. "Alice. I know you think you need to do this, but maybe there's another way. At least give us some time to come up with another plan."

Time. There wasn't time. Time to find another way. Time to say goodbye. Her eyes stung, the dam holding back her pain weakening with every moment they stood here. There was no other way. There was no more time. Certainly no time to sit and talk about it here, with no shelter under a sweltering sun.

She snatched the shovel from Olivia's hand and walked to the brown boulder, sitting just where they'd left it in Colin's dream. She started digging, the blade slicing through dry earth like butter. Olivia knelt beside her, using a large, flat rock to clear away more dirt. Soon, metal clanged on something hard.

She tossed the shovel aside, and the two of them used their hands to pry up a long, metal box. They were both filthy and drenched in sweat, but neither one could help but smile when they secured their prize.

Alice moved to lift the lid, but Olivia grabbed the entire box, jumped up, and backed away.

"Olivia . . . what are you doing?"

She hugged the box to her chest. "Just tell me one thing. If the tables were turned, would you let him do this for you?"

"Of course not. But this is the way it is. A deal's a deal."

"A deal you had nothing to do with."

Alice wiped the sweat from her brow. "So? It doesn't change anything. I still have to clear the Realm, and I have less than four months to do it. Then everyone will be safe. And Colin will be free. I don't expect you to help me. I'll do it on my own if I have to."

Olivia threw the box on the ground between them. Loose items clanked inside.

"Don't you dare play the lone hero. What do you think we're doing out here? You think we like traipsing into the middle of the desert in hundred-degree heat? How can you even say that?"

"I just don't—"

"NO. I get that you think this is a solo mission, but what you keep forgetting is that we're connected. When you die, a part of us dies too. Think about what it would feel like if I died right now. Or Soxie. Or Hadley."

Alice opened her mouth, then shut it. She let herself imagine what it would be like if she lost one of them. The pain was overwhelming. There was no simple answer here. She sank to her knees and looked to the sky.

"I don't know what to do!"

"Then maybe you should start trusting us for a change. Start realizing that good or bad, we're in this together."

Alice met her friend's eyes. She was right, of course. She always was.

"I'm sorry. I thought it would be better this way."

"You thought wrong."

She rose and dusted herself off. The dirt dispersed in little clouds, but the shame would take longer.

"So I guess I'm still stuck with you guys."

Olivia took her by the shoulders and pressed her forehead to hers. "Forever, you dope."

The metal box was locked, and rather than smashing it with a rock, Olivia suggested they wait for Soxie and Hadley.

"Why? It's not like either of them has a key."

"You'll see."

And see she did. Upon their return, Olivia handed the box to Hadley. She took one look at it, dug in her boot, and extracted a small, oblong tool. She plopped herself on the ground and, with some impressive maneuvering, made quick work of the lock. She opened the lid with a satisfied smile.

Alice gaped. "Where did you learn to do that?"

"My dad."

"I thought he owned a car dealership?"

"He does," Hadley said. "But he used to work for his dad, and well, Grandpa Frank sort of dealt in car . . . parts."

"What's that supposed to mean?"

Hadley rolled her eyes. "Haven't you ever heard of a chop shop? They stole cars and sold them for parts."

Alice just stared at her. As if Soxie's black-ops uncle wasn't enough, now she learns Hadley comes from a family of car thieves? She wondered what secrets Olivia was hiding.

"Guys, it's coming up on noon. He's definitely awake by now."

Alice looked up at the midday sun. Soxie was right; they needed to hurry. She turned back to Hadley.

"Well, since you popped the lock, you wanna do the honors?"

Hadley lifted the thick velvet sheath protecting the contents of the box and opened the flap. They each held their breath, hoping dream Cithaeron hadn't led them astray. One of the horses shook its head, rattling the reins. Otherwise, the desert was silent.

Hadley let the bag's contents slide onto the ground, and they all breathed sighs of relief. The compacts were there. But also . . .

"Is that what I think it is?" Soxie asked.

They all leaned away from the item in question, its leather handle impressively preserved, its long, straight blade covered in silk wrapping.

"It can't be . . ." Alice tentatively reached for the dagger.

Just as her fingers were about to touch the handle, Max let out a loud neigh.

They all looked up. The horses were agitated, their heads pointed in the direction of the distant highway. A second later, they heard it.

"Crap," Soxie said. "I guess he remembered."

Alice stood and whirled around. There in the distance, she could just make out a trail of dust as a lone dirt bike cut a path straight to them, sunlight glinting off metal parts. There was no hoping it was a random teenager out for a joyride. It was him; she could feel it. His anger seemed to have already reached her, traveling ahead and breaking the sound barrier.

She was scared. It seemed illogical that she would be frightened of the person she loved most in the world, but there it was. She'd lied to him, drugged him, and invaded his dreams. She'd completely violated his trust, and there was no telling how he'd react.

Hadley scrambled to her feet. "What do we do? There are only three compasses; Alice's isn't here." She held the silver compacts in her hand.

Alice grabbed the velvet bag and shook it; the dirt bike's engine was getting louder with every second. "What would it look like outside of the compact?"

Olivia shook the metal box and dropped it on the ground next to the dagger. "Just a piece of jagged obsidian. I don't understand. It should be here."

"Can't we jump in with yours?"

"We can, but you can't."

"What?"

"A direct Realm jump only works for the owner of the compass. I—I'm sorry, Alice. I don't know what to do."

"Guys . . ." Hadley backed away from the oncoming bike.

The horses were flat-eared and spooked. He was closing in, and fast. Alice could make out his familiar shape now, his face hidden behind a dark helmet. If he got hold of the compasses again, he would destroy them. They were her only hope of clearing the Realm. She had to protect them.

"Go. Now. Get to the Realm!"

"Alice, we're not leaving you!" Soxie shouted as she struggled to calm the horses. Max reared up, freeing himself from her hold on his reins, and took off at a fierce gallop.

"Please, just go! He'll destroy them if you don't!"

One last surge of the engine brought rider and bike to a sudden stop a few yards away, the wind carrying its cloud of dust in their direction. Alice heard the sound of more retreating hooves as Aggie and Oscar made their escape.

The engine died. She coughed, her eyes burning, as she squinted through the dust. A dark shape made its way toward her. She heard another cough behind her.

"Go!" she yelled.

Seconds later, the dust settled, and she and Colin were alone at their campsite.

She stared at her reflection in his visor. He was five feet away, but it felt like miles—miles from the intimacy they'd shared in this very same place. Her irritated eyes teared. She blinked and wiped her face with the back of her hand, grit tearing at her skin like sandpaper.

A minute passed. Then two. The desert hushed. The sun screamed. Yet still they stood—lovers turned adversaries, meeting on the battlefield for the first time.

A raven cawed in the distance. Alice turned toward the noise, swaying. Goose bumps rose on her arms and she licked her dry lips, tasting the desert. Her vision blackened. If only her canteen hadn't galloped away with the horses. She dropped to her knees and dipped her head below her heart. She couldn't pass out now. Not when the battle was about to begin.

The helmet dropped on the ground beside her. Within seconds, a bottle of water appeared next to it. With shaky hands she grabbed it, twisted off the cap, and drank. Water spilled down the sides of her mouth. When the bottle was empty, she tossed it aside and sat back, wiping the moisture from her face and neck.

"Thank you," she said to the ground.

His boots crunched in the dirt as he walked away. She was expecting him to yell or scream. She was ready for it. But the silence was killing her. When she finally looked up, she found him sitting on the brown boulder, watching her.

"I guess you found what you came for."

She glanced at the discarded box and dagger. "Colin, please. I realize you must hate me right now, but you have to know . . . I had my reasons."

His shoulders shook with silent laughter. "Hate you? No, Alice. I don't hate you. I wish I could, because then maybe I wouldn't have to do what I'm about to do. What your actions are forcing me to do."

She slowly rose to her feet, the threat ringing in her ears.

He turned his head toward the horses grazing in the distance. "Tell me. Which part did you find most difficult? Drugging me, or pretending to love me to get close enough? I must say, it was a stroke of genius. I've never, in my dozens of lifetimes, had one of my huntresses break into my dreams." He moved his gaze back to her. "I guess Philautia really did save the best for last."

He might as well have taken that thousands-year-old dagger and pierced her right through the heart. She wanted to speak—no, scream,

scream at the top of her lungs that he was wrong, that she did love him, more than anything in this godforsaken universe. Even when her soul was reaped by Hades, she would love him still. She wanted him to know that, but the words wouldn't come.

He laughed out loud this time. A cold, callous laugh. "What's the matter? Boop got your tongue?"

Her breaths turned shallow. This wasn't a fight she could win. She had a chance against anger and rage. She never expected indifference.

He stood so fast she stumbled backward, losing her balance and landing with a hard thump on her rear end, her wrist painfully banging the metal box.

His eyes darkened. "You're scared of me."

No. *Yes.*

He stepped forward and knelt in front of her.

"I know you saw the Huntress's last vision in my dream. Make no mistake, Alice. You are not ending up in that coffin. I will do whatever it takes to prevent that from happening."

He reached into the pocket of his jacket. She stared at him, fear and love overwhelming her senses with their opposition. He caressed her cheek and slowly leaned in.

"I'm sorry," he whispered. Then he pressed his lips to hers.

The familiar sensation of love and wanting was interrupted by the feeling of a needle sinking into her arm.

A cry erupted from deep in her throat.

He grabbed the back of her neck and pressed his face to hers. "Shhh . . . baby, it's okay. You're safe. I won't let anything happen to you. I promise."

Her eyelids were already heavy, and she could feel her head lolling to the side; his embrace was the only thing keeping her from falling over. She heard a distant thumping, like the whomp-whomp of a helicopter. But it made no sense. Nothing made sense anymore. She was slipping into the abyss, and there was no stopping it. She flailed her arms about in one last surge of panic.

Her hand brushed the soft leather of the dagger's handle. Without thinking, she closed her fist around it. She had the brief sensation of searing heat followed by the feeling of her body being slingshot through a long, narrow tube. She would have thrown up, but the darkness got her first.

chapter 17

Her face was smashed against something cold and hard, and her arm was pinned beneath her. It took three tries before she managed to flop onto her back. When she opened her eyes, she was staring at a ceiling of floating glass. She was back in the Realm.

She struggled to sit up, her arm still numb, and felt something scrape the mirror beneath her. Her hand was still clutching the dagger. She dropped it like it was on fire. It made a clanging sound that echoed through the empty corridor.

She stared at it, the silk wrapping uncoiled and hanging loosely from its base. It didn't look like much: dull and brown, with a straight blade that narrowed at the point. She expected the dagger of a goddess to be more goddess-like. Covered in jewels, or glowing like a radon stick. But this—this seemed so ordinary.

She slowly ran a finger along the smooth leather. How had Cithaeron kept it safe all this time?

She carefully picked it up. It wasn't particularly heavy or light; it was just an old knife. Its blade could even use some sharpening. But it was the dagger Tisiphone had used to slit her throat—the one Philautia had used to create the Realm. It meant something that Alice had it now, and that it had brought her here. *This* was her compass.

She gripped the handle tight and gave it a decisive order.

"Find ballet studio mirror."

Nothing happened. She tried again.

"Find hidden map."

Again, nothing. No levitating off her hand or spinning into a ball of silver light. She even placed it flat on her palm and tried to spin it like a real compass. Instead of pointing the way, it just wobbled until she almost dropped it. It may have brought her to the Realm, but otherwise, the thing was useless.

With no better plan, she began walking, sluggishly dragging herself from mirror to mirror. She did her best to stay quiet, too weak to even think about ashing a demon. She felt like each of her legs weighed a ton. She had to get out of here. She had no idea what Colin had injected her with, but she was thirsty and tired. So tired.

After hours of stumbling through mirrored hallway after mirrored hallway, she came to the harsh conclusion that she wasn't getting anywhere. In all likelihood, she was walking in three-dimensional circles. She dropped to the floor, spent and exhausted, staring blankly into an endless maze of color and light.

It was all starting to feel hopeless. Her destiny, her fate. And where were all these demons she was supposed to be ashing? Two weeks ago the place had been teeming with them. Now she was completely and utterly alone. Trapped. Philautia was gone. The Realm was dying. And she was racing against an arbitrary clock set by a god who counted his souls like a child counts marbles. That's what she felt like right now: A toy for collecting and discarding. A pawn in some weird game between gods and men. And she was giving up everything to play. Her life. Her love. Her soul. Even in her feeble state, she wanted to pound her fists and scream.

Why not? There was no one here to listen anyway.

She screamed as loud and long as her breath would allow. Then she inhaled, and screamed again. Her throat began to burn as her vocal cords turned raw, yet still she screamed, the sound bouncing from mirror to mirror, creating a cacophony of otherworldly noise.

She no longer cared if a demon heard her. Let it come. Let them all come. Maybe she could ash them all at once and be done with it. What did it matter anymore? Regardless of what she did, she was still hurting everyone she loved. If she lived. If she died. There was no door that led to happily ever after. So screw it. For now, it felt good to scream. So she screamed.

Eventually her screams turned to nothing but loud exhales of air. She strained and strained, but her throat was finished. She fell forward and stared at the mirror beneath her—another worthless piece of glass that refused to reflect her image. She hated these mirrors. She hated this place. As beautiful and impossible as it was, it never should have been. Damn the Furies. Damn the Huntress. Damn them all. In a moment of violent madness, she took the dagger still gripped in her hand and stabbed the silver floor.

The glass neither shattered nor cracked. The knife, her hand, then her arm sank straight through, taking the rest of her body with them. She didn't even have time to scream—not that she had a voice left to do that with.

It was hard to understand what was happening. It was like falling into a puddle that was dry on the other side. Alice somersaulted and her back made contact with something hard before bouncing off and hitting the ground. Chafing dishes full of food rained down around her, one of them nearly falling on top of her as it crashed to the floor.

She heard voices and clambered to her feet, taking quick stock of her surroundings. The room was small and appeared to be used for food prep or serving. She glanced at the mirror she'd fallen through, then at her empty hand. Where was the dagger? Alarmed, she sank to her knees and shoved chafing dishes aside until she spotted it lying in a puddle of stew. She reached into the muck and grabbed the handle. Nothing happened. She switched hands. Still nothing.

Someone shrieked behind her.

She shot back to her feet and spun around. A short, stout woman was standing in the doorway, staring at her with big eyes. A tirade of words spilled from her mouth. It wasn't Spanish. Maybe Portuguese? Alice lifted her hands in surrender.

"English? Do you speak English?" she tried to say. But her ravaged throat prevented it.

It didn't matter anyway, because the woman was fixated on the dagger. She turned and yelled something that sounded like a call for help. A male voice answered. Then another, followed by pounding feet.

This was bad; she had to get out of here.

There was a set of swinging doors to her left. Alice burst through them and into a dining room. A table was set for a large party, one she hoped had not yet arrived. She darted around it and through the door on the opposite side. She didn't think; she just kept running in whichever direction felt right. Mainly, away from the loud voices behind her. At the end of a long hall, she rounded a corner and slammed into a large wooden door.

She wasted precious seconds fiddling with the handle before flinging it open. She was rewarded with cool darkness and charged into the night.

The steps were a surprise. She fell down them and landed flat on her face in damp grass. The wind knocked out of her, she clawed and slithered her way forward, her fingers gripping the wet sod to pull herself up.

"*Menina! Pare!*"

She gave her eyes a second to adjust, then took off at a hard sprint. Dogs barked and lights flooded the drive. What sounded like a gunshot rang through the night. In a panic she leapt off the road into the trees, running faster and harder than she would have thought possible. She tripped over roots and was slapped in the face by errant branches, but she pushed on, slowing only when she was sure no one was in pursuit.

She was grateful for the night's cover. And it was *dark*. There were no streetlights; there was no city glow to lead the way. Nothing but trees and undergrowth and the barest sliver of moonlight.

She stumbled her way through the dense woods, praying there weren't predators lurking about—animal, human, or other. She heard running water and let her ears lead the way, her mouth so dry she could barely swallow. When she found the stream, she splashed in up to her waist, scooping handfuls of water down her throat. She didn't care if it was safe to drink.

After drinking her fill, she crawled her way up the opposite bank. She was too tired to stand up and keep going. She was done. She curled up in a ball next to a mossy tree, the dagger securely pressed against her chest, and fell fast asleep.

His strong, confident arms wrapped around her. She snuggled closer as he placed soft kisses on the back of her neck.

"The past no longer matters; it never did," he whispered. "Not without you."

She twisted around to look at him, his passionate gaze reducing her limbs to jelly. She ran her hand across his cheek, leaning in to give him a gentle kiss.

He grinned into her lips. Something growled.

She turned toward the noise. Hammacher was at the end of her bed, her fangs bared. Boop sat beside her and hissed.

"Shhh!" she said, worried they would scare Colin away. She needed him here. She needed him to know she loved him. Boop hissed again, then sneezed.

"Boops, stop it!"

"Shhh . . . it's okay, baby," Colin whispered again. "I won't let anything happen to you. I promise."

This time she wasn't surprised when the needle pierced her skin. She was just sad. So sad. She began crying uncontrollably. Harder than she'd ever cried in her life. She sobbed and sobbed, her body convulsing with every wail.

He held her tight, kissing the side of her head and rocking back and forth.

"Everything will be alright. Just tell me where you are, Peanut."

A pit formed in her stomach. She pulled away to find her dad smiling at her. She slammed her eyes shut, willing herself to wake up.

"Wait! Alice, don't wake up yet!"

She opened her eyes.

"Alice, it's me. Tell us where you are." Her dad said it, but with Olivia's voice.

She shook her head, dazed. Hammacher barked.

"Honey, it's us," Hadley said. She was sitting on the floor of Alice's bedroom, cradling a purring Boop in her arms.

Alice sat up and looked around. Soxie was leaning against the window, smoking. It felt wrong, but for some reason, it looked normal.

"Since when do you smoke?" she asked.

"It's your dream," Soxie replied, pausing to exhale a perfectly round ring of smoke. "You put the cigarette in my hand; I might as well enjoy it."

"Alice, quick—tell us where you are," Olivia said. Hammacher and Boop were gone. The bedroom was gone. The four of them were now standing by the tree where Alice was sleeping.

"Where the hell is this?" Soxie asked, turning in circles.

"I have no idea. The house I was dumped in was full of people speaking Portuguese. I think."

Hadley leaned down to look at sleeping Alice. "You don't look so good."

"Trust me, I feel worse."

"How did you get here?"

"The dagger. I think it's my compass, only I can't figure out how to get back in."

"Alice!" Colin's voice called from somewhere in the trees. The sound of a dirt bike filled the night.

"We can't control this much longer," Soxie said. "Find a way to call us when you wake up."

"But—"

"Dammit, Alice," Colin said. His black visor was pulled down, and a shiny hypodermic needle glinted in his hand.

She closed her eyes, willing the nightmare to end.

It wasn't quite dawn when she awoke. She followed the stream to a winding road flanked by trees. She had two choices: up or down. She chose down, hoping it led to a nice touristy town.

She had no money. No identification. And her phone was gone—either in the desert, the Realm, or the chafing dish she'd landed on. She was also covered in mud and cuts, and her hair was so natty she could barely get a hand through it. She needed help.

It was at least an hour before she spotted the beginnings of civilization: a gas station. She tore off the bottom of her T-shirt, wrapped the blade of the dagger in it, and tucked the bundle carefully into the back of her jeans. Then she waited across the road until she saw someone who looked safe to approach: a chic young woman in a red Fiat.

"Excuse me, do you speak English?" she asked once she was close enough to be heard.

The woman took one look at her and jumped, bringing her hand to her heart. "*Menina, oh meu Deus*! My poor dear. What eez these that happened to you?"

Oh, thank God.

She was in Brazil. On the outskirts of a town called Lençóis, nine hundred miles north of Rio. It took a few tries, but she was finally able to reach the US. She didn't know Soxie's number by heart. She didn't know anyone's number by heart, other than her own. And her mom's.

"Mom?"

"Alice! Oh my god, sweetheart. We've been out of our minds. Where are you?" Judy was crying.

"I'm really sorry, Mom. I can't explain right now, but I promise I'm okay. I don't know how long this connection will last, and I need a favor."

"What do you mean you can't explain? Alice Marie Daniels, you tell me where you are right this second"—(white noise)—"mean it."

"Mom"—(strange beeping)—"Mom? Can you hear me? Just listen to me please. Get a hold of Soxie. Tell her Lençóis, north of Rio. She'll know what it means. L-E-N-C—"

"What are you talking about? What do you mean *Rio*? As in *Brazil*?"

"Yes. It's a long story and—"

"Colin, what the hell is going on? What is my daughter doing in *South America*?"

Alice's heart stopped. She heard muffled arguing as the phone changed hands and waited several seconds before getting up the nerve to speak again. "Mom? Mom—"

"Alice."

His voice broke her. Tears began streaming down her face.

"Are you okay?"

She wanted to answer. She wanted to say, *No. No, I'm not okay. I love you and I will never see you again, so no. I am forever and irrevocably not okay.* Instead, she gripped the old, grimy phone and covered the bottom to mask her sobs.

"Alice. I'm sorry . . ." His voice cracked. "I don't know what I was thinking. Please forgive me. Please . . . I can't . . ."

The line went dead.

She slowly hung up the phone, then sank to the floor of the dingy gas station, crying as hard as she had in her dream. Harder.

Someone eventually pulled her up and deposited her in a vehicle. It may have been the red Fiat, but she wasn't sure and didn't really care.

chapter 18

She spent the rest of the day and night in the quaint town of Lençóis. The woman in the Fiat, Ana, brought her to her family home. Alice was welcomed and doted on as if she was a member of the family. Ana's mother was particularly concerned with how skinny she was and demanded that she eat, then eat some more.

They were so kind. So good. These were the people they needed to protect. They may not be ideal hosts for demons, but they could still suffer at the hands of someone who was.

As much as she wanted to, she didn't dare call home again. Instead, she sent her mom an email on Ana's laptop.

I'm sorry for making you worry. Just know that I'm okay and I'll be home as soon as I can. I love you, Alice

She wished it could be more, but Colin already knew too much.

After emailing the girls, she spent a nail-biting two hours peering through the window of Ana's house and wondering who would show up first, them or him.

It was them. And not a minute too soon. After saying goodbye to her hosts, they walked onto the cobblestone street just as two black SUVs rounded the corner. The behemoths were so out of place they might as well have had signs on the side that said MAYRON's GOON SQUAD.

They took off running.

Lençóis was a colorful little town, full of charm. And lots of pedestrian streets too narrow for monster vehicles. They ditched the goon brigade and within minutes found a small café bathroom with a mirror.

Once safe inside the Realm, they all sat down to rest.

"The map's still working?" Alice asked.

Soxie nodded. "For now. We used it to get to Vegas and here, so let's hope it stays open."

"Vegas? Why Vegas?"

"We needed a room with a mirrored ceiling for your dream hop."

Alice pictured them falling through the ceiling onto a hotel bed in Vegas, only to learn their next stop was Brazil. They'd gone through a lot to find her.

"Thank you for finding me. How did you know I got away?"

"Colin called me from May's helicopter," Soxie explained. "He thought you were with us."

Helicopter. So she wasn't hallucinating. His access to resources was starting to make her nervous. Really nervous.

"Tell us what happened after we left the campsite," Olivia said.

She couldn't bear to walk them through the worst of it, so she stuck to the part that mattered. The dagger.

"I'm still not sure how it brought me here, but I think it opens all mirrors."

"How?"

"Here, watch." She knelt next to a large mirror and stuck the pointy end through, bracing herself to avoid falling in. As soon as the tip penetrated the glass, they were given a full view of what was on the other side.

The three of them crouched down for a better look.

It was a crowded restaurant, patrons going about the business of eating and drinking while waiters scurried back and forth. Alice withdrew the knife, and the restaurant scene disappeared.

"I didn't even know it did that," she admitted. "I fell through before I had a chance to see what I was falling into."

"Pretty useful tool to have," Soxie pointed out.

"How useful is it when I can't get it to work when I need it most?"

"Maybe it did work."

She turned to Olivia. "How do you figure? I promise I could have used it when that woman was screaming at me in Portuguese."

"Maybe it was protecting you. What if it knew you weren't safe here alone?"

"Then why did it bring me here in the first place?"

"Because you were in more danger where you were."

Alice stared at her, her stomach churning with anxious butter-flies. "He wouldn't have hurt me."

"No, he just stuck a needle in your arm and planned to hold you against your will," Soxie spat. "We saw it in your dream, Ali. Don't try to defend him."

"How is that any worse than what I did to him?"

"She has a point."

Soxie whipped her head around, her curls bouncing. "Seriously, Hadley? You of all people, taking his side?"

"I'm not taking sides! I'm just saying it's not so black and white."

"Then what—"

"You're right!" Alice said. "But so is Hadley. I can't defend him, but he's not the only one in the wrong here. Either way, it doesn't matter. All that matters is that we move forward."

Soxie pulled her hands down her face. "Fine. Whatever. How do we do that?"

Alice looked at Olivia. "Any ideas? I was here for hours the other day and never came across one demon. Where are they?"

"There were plenty when we came through to get you," Hadley said, looking around the empty hall. "Our compasses went nuts; it was tough just getting to the map."

Alice stared at the silver compass in Hadley's hand, which was refusing to levitate and spin. "I don't get it. Are they staying away because of me? How do they know I'm here?"

Soxie slowly rose to her feet, her green eyes fixed on a point over Alice's shoulder. "Maybe something else knows you're here."

The look on her face said it all. *Something else* was in the corridor with them. Alice turned around.

Two figures were standing in the middle of the hall, silent and watchful, like crows on a barnyard fence. But they weren't the hideous creatures Colin had described; in fact, there was a certain grotesque beauty to their appearance. Their skin was smooth and flawless, as if carved straight from alabaster, and paper-thin wings floated behind them like fluttering kites. Hundreds, maybe thousands, of iridescent serpents writhed and hissed on their heads, creating the illusion of silky locks blowing in the wind. They wore identical robes of black, and their translucent arms were adorned with golden snakes that coiled in repeated, ominous loops. They stood so still Alice would have thought they were mere effigies of themselves, if it weren't for the moving hair and eyes, black as pitch, that were regarding her with pure hostility.

The girls immediately closed ranks until the four of them stood in a line on the oversized restaurant mirror, facing down the wrath of the Furies.

One of *them* laughed. At least, it might have been a laugh. Their presence was madness in itself; it created a feeling of confusion and paralyzing fear. Alice gripped the handle of the dagger until her knuckles turned white.

"THE WEAPON OF A GODDESS IN THE HANDS OF A MORTAL. MAY IT DESTROY YOU AS IT DESTROYED OUR SISTER."

It came out like a warped gramophone playing in surround sound. She couldn't tell which one had spoken. Neither of their mouths had moved.

Soxie grabbed her arm. "Alice, what are you doing?"

She looked at the knife in her hand, now turned toward her. Even as she understood what was happening, she pulled against Soxie's grasp, willing the dagger into her own chest. It was as if there were two sides to her brain—one controlling motor function while the other watched helplessly, powerless to stop it.

Soxie's face turned purple as she struggled to stop Alice from stabbing herself in the heart. Hadley and Olivia jumped in, and it took all three of them to wrench the dreadful thing from Alice's hand. They watched as it fell, pointed end first, and sank right through floor, reopening the restaurant scene below and taking them all with it.

Their arrival in the crowded restaurant was something for the history books. The mirror they fell through was high on the wall, tilted to reflect the dining room below. Two round banquettes were positioned beneath it. Unfortunately for all involved, it was the height of the dinner rush.

Alice felt her feet hit something soft before she was catapulted forward. Glasses and place settings went flying when she hit the table and slid off the other side. At least this time she didn't land in steaming hot food, but she left plenty of wine-soiled linen in her wake. She fell in a heap on the floor next to Soxie, banged up, bruised, and already sick of falling through mirrors.

A collective intake of breath brought with it a moment of stillness. Diners sat frozen, their forks in midair and their drinks still tipped toward their mouths.

Moments later, pandemonium.

Chairs scraped on mosaic tiles and plates crashed to the floor as people leapt to their feet. Thanks to four years of language electives,

Alice was able to make out some of the words being hurled at them. *Filles. Mon dieu. Merde.*

She rushed to her feet and helped Soxie up as the chef and two waiters began berating them in heavily accented French. A man with a bent cigarette in his mouth gestured maniacally to the mirror above him, and the woman next to him sat motionless, her pretty white dress covered in red wine.

Alice plugged her ears for a moment of sanity and noticed Olivia and Hadley pulling themselves off the floor in front of the other banquette. They were in bad shape. Millions of mirrors in the Realm, and she picks another one hanging over food. Poor Hadley looked to have face-dived into a casserole. They made eye contact as a lump of potato slid down her exquisitely dainty nose. Alice couldn't help it. She started to laugh.

It began as a small giggle, but the more she took in the absurdity of their situation, the funnier it became. And her laughter was contagious. It took only a few seconds before Hadley cracked a smile, even less before they were all doubled over in hysterics. It was the kind of laughter that brings tears to your eyes and makes it hard to breathe. The kind that only gets funnier the longer you laugh.

Sadly, no one else was amused.

They spent the rest of the night in a *commissariat*, doing their best to convince the French authorities they were not vandals, burglars, or terrorists. The Lyon police questioned everyone present at the time of the "disturbance," but none could agree on where the American girls came from. They were just suddenly there, smashing up tables and interrupting what should have been a lovely evening.

It was a sticky situation, in more ways than one. None of them could present a passport or a suitable explanation for their presence in France. Worse, their belongings—including the dagger and compasses—were all seized.

With no other option, Soxie called her uncle May.

Apparently, Mayron "knew people" in Europe. Someone showed

up from Interpol within the hour, convincing Alice that good ol' Uncle May was more than ex-military and CIA. In her mind, he was basically James Bond.

While no charges were filed, they were slapped with a significant fine. It took a few hours, but eventually they were taken to a nearby airstrip, where, before boarding the private jet that awaited them, they were told in no uncertain terms that they should cross Lyon off their list of French cities to visit again, then handed their compasses. Not the dagger. They tried to plead the case for antique relic, but the gendarmes were having none of it. Impounded it would remain, for the time being.

Once they were in the air, relief washed over them.

"I don't know what to be more thankful for," Soxie said, pouring them each a glass of champagne. "That we escaped the Furies, or the French."

They all looked at each other, then burst out laughing again. And God, it felt good to laugh, Alice thought. To forget for a moment what they were up against. What she had already lost. To just let a point in time be full of laughter and friends. This moment would help get her through the dark times.

And the dark times were coming. They all knew it. But for now, they laughed.

"Our main priority right now is to understand what the Furies were doing in the Realm." Olivia tapped the table in front of her. "Anybody got any theories?"

"Pretty sure they were there to stop me from ashing demons," Alice said. "Oh, and apparently to kill me. Same difference, I guess?"

Hadley threw a pretzel at her. "It's not a joke, Alice."

"Do you see me laughing?"

"Listen," said Olivia. "I think we should stay out of the Realm until we figure out what's going on."

"You know I can't do that. I have to clear it."

"But why now?" Soxie asked. "Demons have been roaming it for centuries. What's the difference?"

"I don't know. I didn't broker the deal. I'm just the payment. And if I don't come through, the deal's off. I can't let that happen."

"Even after what he did to you, you're still willing to go through with it?"

"I love him, Sox. I have to save him."

Soxie seemed to deflate in front of her. "Okay. We get it. But you learned all this from the Huntress before she disappeared. What if she wasn't being truthful? How do you even know it was her?"

Alice appreciated the straw grab. She'd already been down this road herself, trying in vain to come up with another explanation. Maybe it was a dream, or a vision created by her dying brain. But in the depths of her soul, she knew it was real.

"I promise you, it was her. And I promise she was telling the truth. I can't prove it. I just know."

Soxie just nodded and turned to look out the window next to her. No one said anything for several minutes. Other than the occasional bump from mild turbulence, the cabin was quiet.

Hadley was the first to break the silence. "So what happens now?"

They all looked at Alice. Before she allowed them to go any further, there was something she needed to say.

"I know it's not fair for me to ask for your help."

Olivia opened her mouth to protest, but Alice signaled for her to stop.

"Please, let me finish. I need you to know I'm not choosing him over you. Yes, regardless of what's happened, I'll always love him. But there's a reason I can destroy demons. I can't ignore that. And if the Furies are trying to stop me, it's even more important that we don't let them. This is bigger than me and Cithaeron. Bigger than all of us. Something's changed. You all feel it. I know you do."

Before anyone had a chance to argue, the intercom dinged. "Ms.

Roxland, this is Captain Jacobs in the cockpit. We're beginning our initial descent into the New York area. We should be landing at Teterboro within the half hour. Mr. Roxland has been in touch with passport control, and your escort will be waiting on the tarmac to take you to the hotel."

Soxie looked at Alice and held her eyes for a beat before pressing the button on the intercom. "Thanks, Captain. Did my uncle say who he sent to meet us?"

"Yes, I believe Mr. Colin Tinsley has already arrived. If there's anything else I can help you with today, please let me know. Lucy, please prepare the cabin for arrival."

Alice's stomach dropped, and not because they were losing altitude. "Sox, we can't . . ."

Soxie's expression was grave. "Ali, if we do this, we're on our own. Colin has spent the past five years gaining my uncle's trust. They're allies. Mayron won't help us run."

"I understand."

All four of them sat frozen, the question of which direction their lives were about to take hanging over their heads like comic strip balloons.

Soxie pressed the intercom again. "Change of plans, Captain. Any chance we can land at JFK?"

"I'll have to check with air traffic control. One moment, please."

Alice clasped her hands in front of her mouth, saying a silent prayer that the skies over New York were clear.

The captain's voice burst through the speakers faster than expected.

"Ms. Roxland, we have clearance to land at JFK's private jet terminal. We should touch down in approximately twenty minutes. Shall I inform Mr. Tinsley?"

"No, thank you, Captain."

Alice let her hands drop. She wasn't sure she'd have the strength to leave him again, and the four of them disappearing through the plane's bathroom mirror would be an international incident.

The jet banked slightly to the left. Lucy, the lone flight attendant, appeared to ensure their seat belts were fastened for landing. When she finished, Soxie, Olivia, and Hadley exchanged looks.

"Alright, Daniels." Soxie threw up her hands. "You win. Let's go ash some d-bags and save the world."

His funeral service was held on a warm Saturday in October. The small Lutheran church was packed with family and friends. Remington Carver and Aaron Tapper stood next to each other, their heads bowed and their hands folded in front of them—the epitome of respect and decorum.

Alice noticed other familiar faces. Her first period teacher, Mr. Stein. Ed LaPorte, the lacrosse coach. Kelly, the girl she'd shared a water-soaked laugh with once upon a time.

There were many others, people she recognized but had never gotten the chance to know. It was nice to see them here. To know his life, albeit short, had touched so many.

A closed casket sat next to the altar, but it was common knowledge it was empty. His car had been found abandoned on a remote dirt road, far from even the outskirts of civilization. The desert, while scenic and beautiful, could be a dangerous and lethal place. After six weeks, the search was called off. Cause of death: likely exposure. Remains: unrecovered.

Alice stared at the empty coffin, mourning what once was. The man he'd been before. Before he'd almost destroyed her. Before she'd destroyed him.

The pastor began his sermon.

"Let us pray."

part
three

chapter 19

Alice studied her reflection. Her mom was right; she was Cruella de Vil. Her hair was white on one side, brown on the other, as if she'd turned sideways and dipped half her head into a vat of bleach. In the beginning they'd tried coloring it—not so much for vanity's sake but because she'd started to stick out like a sore thumb. Unfortunately, no matter how long they left the dye in, her hair refused to take color.

Hadley had suggested they just dye the rest white, but since a full head of white hair equaled Alice in a coffin they'd ignored the suggestion and Soxie had bought her a wig instead.

They were officially on the lam. The use of credit cards was out of the question, and the last time Soxie withdrew cash they'd had one of Colin's goons tailing them within a couple of hours. It was only through sheer luck that they'd evaded capture. Colin was operating with the full force of Mayron's arsenal, and their only means for survival involved criminal activity, and staying mobile.

So they kept moving—never sleeping more than one or two nights in the same place, stealing cars when needed (thanks to Hadley's unusual talents), and breaking into empty houses and motel rooms. They left anonymous IOUs and recorded the address of each victim when possible. None of them liked it, but they all agreed there was no other way.

It would be easier if Alice could jump directly into the Realm; evading the goons would be a cakewalk then. However, the dagger was still in the custody of the Lyon police, and even if she did have it, she couldn't use it—not unless she wanted some quality time with Megaera and Alecto.

Since landing at JFK two months earlier, she'd set foot in the Realm exactly one time. They'd entered through a mirror at an airport hotel. Similar to the previous time, there had been no demons on site, just the Furies. They hadn't seen them, but they'd *sensed* them. After experiencing that maddening feeling once, there was no mistaking it the second time. Not keen on another chat, they'd immediately exited through the hotel mirror, and spent the next two days deliberating whether this mission wasn't more of a mission impossible.

Alice was the only one who could ash a demon, yet her very presence made them all but invisible, not to mention summoned two very scary goddesses who wanted her dead. So how was she supposed to clear the Realm?

The Backwards Place. It was Olivia who suggested it. The Furies didn't seem to know about it, so Alice was safe there if she didn't cross over. The girls were still able to move freely in the Realm without triggering any immortal alarms, and as long as Alice wasn't present, there were plenty of demons to play with.

They first tried bringing one into the Backwards Place, but they couldn't get it to enter the mirror with them. A week of brainstorming, arguing, and much trial and error ensued, until finally they discovered a loophole for ashing demons the Furies had missed.

His name was David.

"Hey, Pepé Le Pew, quit preening. I need to take a whiz."

She cringed. *Think of the devil . . .*

"One minute," she called.

"Fine, then, I'll just piss on the carpet."

Ignoring the urge to yell something obscene, she turned around and flung the door open. He was leaning against the wall with his usual cat-that-ate-the-canary look on his face. If he weren't the worst human ever, she would be able to admit she'd once thought he was handsome. But he might as well have snake hair and bat wings like the Furies. All she saw was a monster.

He pushed past her, smacking her on the behind as he went, then paused to give her a once-over.

"Hmm. You're looking a little soft, skunk. Maybe lay off the fries for a while." He then turned to do his business, not caring in the least that she was still in the room.

She wanted so badly to punch him in the head. Instead, she gritted her teeth, marched out, and slammed the door shut behind her.

"Where are we again?" she asked the room.

Hadley was sitting by the window, her head buried in a magazine, and Soxie was on the bed filing her nails.

"North Dakota," Hadley said.

"South," Soxie countered, blowing on a nail.

Hadley stretched her arms above her head. "Okay. South Dakota. Why?"

Alice pointed her thumb behind her. "Just wondering if I'll get the electric chair when I murder him."

"Ha. Get in line."

Alice flopped down on the bed and covered her face with a cheap foam pillow. She screamed into it. No one bothered to ask if she was okay. They were all screaming into pillows these days, ever since David joined their little gang. She yanked it off her face and stared blankly at the depressing popcorn ceiling.

"Can we please, please splurge for a bigger room tomorrow? Or break into one?"

"*We* can't break into anything," Hadley pointed out. "And it's not as easy as it looks, by the way."

"We're down to our last hundred bucks as it is," Soxie said, picking up the remote to turn off the old television. "We have to do a Realm jump for provisions."

Alice sat up. "What, tonight? No!"

Hadley tossed her magazine aside. "Sorry, honey. You're babysitting."

Alice shoved the pillow back over her face and screamed into it again. Maybe she could succeed in smothering herself with it. She heard the toilet flush and the bathroom door open.

"What's for dinner, witches?" David snatched the pillow from her and sat down on the bed, shoving her aside to make room for himself. Then he leaned over to grab the remote from Soxie and propped the pillow behind his head.

"For the millionth time," Alice said. "We. Are. Not. Witches."

He grabbed a beer off the nightstand and cracked it open. "Whatever, like I give a shit," he mumbled, his focus now on the television.

Alice turned to Soxie. "Can't one of you stay?"

"Sorry, babe. You know we need all hands on deck for these."

Her head drooped. "I know. Wishful thinking, I guess."

The bathroom door opened again, and Olivia entered the room.

"How'd it go?" Hadley asked, standing up to put on her jacket.

"Fine."

"Any news?"

"Not really. Though there's another fun item in *The Reel* about us."

"Do we even want to know?" Soxie asked.

"Just another conspiracy theory. This time we killed David and we're using his organs for some kind of satanic ritual."

David snorted. "Tapper and Carver are tools."

Alice ignored him. "Any emails?"

Olivia reached into her jacket for the latest printouts. She handed two pages to Hadley, one to Soxie, and one to David. David glanced at his briefly, crumpled it, and threw it at the waste bin in the corner, missing by two feet. Hadley folded hers and stuck them in her pocket. Alice knew she would find some privacy later to read them. Soxie opened hers and scanned it, then quickly followed David's lead and tossed it in the trash. At least hers made it in the bin.

They had agreed to one online log-in a week, far from their physical location. Olivia was the messenger, visiting random cities via the Realm to send and receive emails on their behalf.

"Anything for me?" Alice asked.

Olivia handed her a printout. "Just your mom."

Alice read it immediately.

Hi, honey. I'm staying at the Roxlands' for a while. I couldn't sit alone in that house for another second, waiting to hear from you. Boop is fine. We're all fine. But I'm tired of this, Alice. I'm tired of begging you to tell me where you are. I'm tired of talking to the police. Your father and Molly are out of their minds. Rachel and Chloe keep calling, asking for updates I can't give them. If you're in danger, then you have to let me help you. If you've done something wrong or if you're in trouble, we'll get through it. Whatever it is, you're my daughter and I love you. Please come home. Mom

She finished reading and quietly folded the paper in half. She'd done everything she could to assure Judy she was okay. Every email Olivia sent on her behalf was a different version of "I'm sorry," "I can't tell you why," "Please trust me," and "Don't worry." What else could she say? That she was on a mission to fulfill the terms of a two-thousand-year-old deal? That her hair was turning white but not to worry, she'd be dead before it mattered? There was nothing she could say. Nothing Judy was going to accept. So she stuck with simply "alive and well, and hope to be home soon." The least she could do was give her hope. Even if she'd lost her own weeks ago.

She hated communicating through email, but as much as she would love to hear her mom's voice again, their mobiles were long gone, and landlines were too easy to trace. For all intents and purposes, they were off the grid. These weekly updates were their only real connection to the world, outside of what they could learn on the news. And since David usually bogarted the remote, that wasn't much.

"You guys ready?" Soxie stood up and pulled her hair into a ponytail. She was wearing a sweatshirt, yoga pants, and sneakers. Seeing her in such casual clothing had been a shock at first, but comfort and function were all that mattered now.

She pulled out her compass. "We'll be back as soon as we can. Sun-up, at the latest."

"Hey, forgetting something?" David said, snapping his fingers and reaching his hand out.

Soxie dug in her bag and threw the last of their money on the bed next to him.

"Thanks, Red." He stuffed the bills in his pocket. "And don't forget, I want a Rolex this time."

"This isn't a shopping spree," Hadley growled. "Cash and essentials only. We're not stealing you a watch."

He finished his beer, crushed the can, and threw it at the waste bin, missing again. It clanged off the TV stand, splattering remnants of his backwash against the wall. He smiled. "Then you can find another demon magnet."

The four of them looked at each other. They'd done this dance already. Soxie's jaw jutted out.

"Fine. We'll get you a Rolex. Anything else?"

"Nope, that's good for now. Thanks, sweet cheeks." He reached for another beer.

Alice cringed. *Worst. Human. Ever.*

The girls disappeared into the bathroom, and within seconds she was alone with David—her least favorite place in the world to be. She looked down at the folded piece of paper.

"Aw, what's wrong? No more love notes from your boyfriend?"

She turned around. He was giving her an exaggerated pout, turning his fist at the corner of his eye.

"Why do you always have to be such a jerk?"

"God, Alice." He let out a loud belch. "You're so BORING."

Staying calm and keeping her cool was really the only way to handle David. But sometimes . . . sometimes he just made it too hard.

"Grr-ARGH!" She stomped her feet and stormed outside, slamming the door as hard as she could behind her. David just laughed and yelled another "boring!" through the door before changing the channel and forgetting all about her.

She took a moment to rein herself in. There was no point blowing her top; he would still be there tomorrow. And the next day. And the next.

She looked over the second-story railing at the sad, empty parking lot. This wasn't how she wanted to spend her last few months. But nothing knew evil like evil. And David was their necessary evil.

When they found him he'd been in horrible shape—far worse than the rumor mill had implied. Originally believing he was suffering from a drug addiction, his parents had forced him into rehab. His condition had quickly deteriorated, however, and they'd moved him to a hospital. It was there that the girls had managed to test their theory, luring a demon to a mirror in his room. Until that point he had been unresponsive, and close to skin and bones. But after a good dose of demon, he was right as rain. Turned out it was his version of methadone. "Methademon," Soxie called it. It was stupid, but it stuck.

Alice gripped the railing, watching the cars and semis pass on the nearby interstate. The piece of paper still in her hand crinkled against the rusted iron. She was happy to hear from her mom—to know she was okay, all things considered. But she wished there had been another email waiting in her inbox.

There was no reason to believe there would be. She'd never responded to the only one he'd sent, the night they'd left him waiting on the tarmac at Teterboro. There was no point trying to explain herself. What was done was done. Or would be soon. She had written one note, though, which Olivia currently had in her possession, not to be given to him unless . . . Well. Unless. It was short and to the point.

Colin,

I did what I had to do. Promise me you'll make the most out of this life. You're free. Be happy.

Alice

She'd considered adding, "I'll love you forever," but decided the message didn't translate on paper. It felt basic and trite. Besides, more was just more. It would be easier for him this way.

She reached into her back pocket where she kept the worn print-out of his email. She'd read it so many times she could recite it by heart. But seeing the words on the page made her feel closer to him somehow. He had typed them. He had sent them to her through space and time. She could see him at his laptop, his face illuminated by the screen, the words reflected in his blue eyes with every angry and pleading keystroke.

Alice,

Why? I told you I would protect you. You don't owe Philautia anything. You don't owe anyone anything. This is insanity, what you're doing. It's stupid. I know you hate that word, but maybe that's the only way to get through to you.

I'm sorry for what I did. I panicked. I plan to spend the rest of my life making it up to you. But you need to stop this and come back. Right now. I need to know you're okay.

I'm asking you to trust me again. I know I don't deserve it, but I promise I'll listen. Just tell me what's going on. We'll figure it out together.

You don't have to love me. You don't even have to like me.
But please, Alice. I'm begging you. Come back to me.

Colin

Her heart ached every time she read those words, but her eyes no longer filled with tears. She'd cried enough. Now she just felt like an empty vessel, destroying evil one demon at a time, inching her way toward Hades and his Underworld. She wished there was a way to speed things up. She wanted the girls to get on with their lives. They should have been able to attend their own graduation—gone on a senior trip, enjoyed their last summer before college. Instead, they were stuck with her and David, living off fast food and squatting in crappy motel rooms. The sooner the end came, the better. Besides, she had something she'd like to say to Hades when she finally met him.

Go to hell.

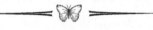

"How long has it been?"

"Relax, skunk. Two minutes longer than the last time you asked. Now quit annoying me."

"Gee, my mistake. I thought maybe you'd want to get some use out of your fancy new watch."

He looked down to admire his latest acquisition. "Eh, I would have preferred a newer one, but this will do. For now."

She closed her eyes and counted to ten. They were in the dressing room of a musty secondhand shop somewhere in Omaha, waiting for the girls to get back with David's latest dose. The store looked like it had been closed for some time—no alarm system or purveyors to speak of, one of their easier B&Es.

David was bouncing up and down on the balls of his feet. As antsy as Alice was, she could tell he was even more so. More than one or two days without, and things got bad. For everyone. She hoped they might eventually find a cure for his ailment, but so far it seemed methademon was the only thing keeping him alive. He had to know there was an end game, but he never brought it up. The next fix was all he cared about.

"Question. You're toasting all these demons I bring you, but what about the ones infecting other people? How do you get them?"

"You writing a book?"

"Relax. Just making conversation. I know it's not your strong suit, but try to play along."

She had to admire his meanness. It was so consistent. She leaned against the wall and sighed.

"If you really want to know, we don't. But the theory is they get bored and reenter the Realm to find someone more interesting."

"Man, you guys are clueless."

"Thanks."

He gazed at her in the mirror's reflection. "Mine never would have left."

"Really. Because you're such the expert on demon behavior."

He shrugged. "I'm just saying it was happy in me. The only reason I'm here is because the rush from each new one packs a huge punch." He jumped back and forth and stretched his neck like a prizefighter in the ring.

"David, you do realize it was controlling you. You're fine with that?"

He laughed. "It wasn't controlling me. It *was* me. I don't expect you to understand. It's a symbiotic relationship. We belonged together."

"So romantic."

"You know what? It kind of is."

"Gross."

He rolled his eyes. "You're such a miserable little witch. You make me want to vomit."

She took in their cramped surroundings. "Please don't. I am curious, though. What *does* it feel like?"

He stopped bouncing. "It feels . . . powerful. Omnipotent."

"Omnipotent," she repeated. Coming from him, it sounded deranged.

"Yes. Like nothing is out of my reach. Not even the world."

The dressing room walls started to close in. It never occurred to her that David might have his own agenda in this surreal beat-the-clock game they were playing. Perhaps they needed to keep a closer eye on him. But time was running out. Her hair was still only half-white, and the lunar eclipse was in three and a half weeks. She couldn't help but think they were doing something wrong. They were falling too far behind.

"Finally," David said when Olivia suddenly appeared.

She made eye contact with Alice. "You ready?"

Alice nodded. Olivia took her hand and flipped open her compass, instantly bringing them to the Backwards Place. David was now the only person being reflected in the small space. Olivia disappeared into the Realm to alert the others.

The hardest part was getting the demon to the right mirror. But once it saw David on the other side, they had it. No demon to date had ever turned away.

Alice braced herself, watching him for the telltale sign of infection.

He was never more still and quiet than in these moments. It was her favorite part, watching him keep his fat mouth shut for five seconds. But then she had to witness a full-body spasm and the look of pure, black-eyed bliss he wore as he threw his head back and took the demon in.

She moved next to him and waited. It took about thirty seconds for him to get his required fix.

When his eyes turned back to their light jade green, she waved a hand through his body. She felt a surge of electricity as the demon became aware of her presence and clawed its way into the Backwards Place to get to her.

Although she'd done this a hundred times now, it was no less painful, and there was always a split second when she thought her heart might stop beating. But then the demon would turn to ash, and she would go on living another day—exhausted and drained, and one chunk of white hair closer to the end.

David, veins popping out of his neck and forehead, sprang into the air with a raucous "WOO-HOO!" Meanwhile, it took both Soxie and Hadley to keep Alice standing. She didn't pass out anymore, but she needed at least an hour-long nap after each ashing before she was able to function again.

They brought Alice back and the tiny dressing room got even smaller, their five bodies squished together like canned peaches. Hadley helped her to an old couch in the front of the shop while Soxie and Olivia tended to David. He was so amped after each dose that it took constant vigilance to keep him from doing anything stupid. But thankfully Alice didn't need to worry about that; all she needed to do was sleep. Sleep, and dream of better times. Moments spent in her love's arms under a beautiful canopy of stars.

She rested her head on his shoulder, looking out over the Roxland estate from their favorite window seat. The sun began to sink behind the mountains, and the light faded to that dreamlike quality. Twilight, but not quite.

She inhaled—breathing in his masculine scent, intoxicated by it, always yearning for more.

He kissed her temple. "Hey, where are you?"

She smiled. "Oh, just enjoying the view."

"But where are you?"

She turned to look at him. "What do you mean? I'm right here."

He gazed down at her, his blue eyes darkening. "Do you still trust me?"

"I want to."

"Then tell me where you are."

She placed a hand on his cheek. She hated when the veil lifted—when he said the thing that gave it all away. When her dream turned lucid. But her subconscious always found its way to this guilty place. Colin demanding to know where she was, she unable to tell him.

"You don't have to tell him. But you do need to tell us."

Everything went sideways at once, as if her dream had turned a page and plunked her in a different narrative. The window seat was gone. She was alone on the musty couch of the secondhand shop.

"What's happening? Who said that?"

A hand landed on her shoulder. She turned to see an unfamiliar woman sitting next to her, a kind look on her weathered face. Despite the woman's frail appearance, the grip on her shoulder was tight.

"Alice, where is this place?"

She knew something was wrong, but she couldn't stop herself from envisioning the WELCOME TO OMAHA sign they'd passed on the freeway, her dream story depositing her and the strange woman in the car.

The woman smiled as the car pulled into the parking lot of Luletta's Consignment Shop.

"We're sorry about this, sugar."

"What's going on? Who are you?"

A different woman with bifocals and long gray hair patted her on the cheek. "Don't you worry, dear. Everything's going to be alright. You just rest some more."

This was bad. She didn't understand why, though. Part of her felt a strange camaraderie with these women—like they were related, or on the same team. But another part of her was sounding the alarm to abandon ship, and fast. She squeezed her eyes shut and focused, hard. *Wake up, Alice. Wake up!*

"Shhh . . . plenty of time to wake up later," Colin said, kissing her cheek and pulling her close. She was back on the window seat, safe in his arms. The only place she really wanted to be. She knew she should fight it, but she needed this. Just for a little bit longer.

She closed her eyes and dug deeper into his embrace.

"Wake up, sleepyhead."

Her eyes popped open. Sun was streaming in through the broken blinds of the consignment shop, dust motes swirling in the crooked beams of light. She sat up so fast she nearly fell off the couch.

"What time is it? How long was I asleep?"

Hadley looked at her watch. "It's just after six. We figured you should get a full night's rest for once. You looked like you could use it."

Her heart started pounding. She jumped up, dizzy as the blood rushed from her head. "We have to go. Now."

"Why? What happened?"

"I think I just had a visit from Margot and Janie." She grabbed her bag off the floor, then paused as she realized how quiet it was. "Where is everybody?"

"We're meeting them at the diner down the street . . . What are you talking about? Who are Margot and Janie?"

She grabbed Hadley's hand, pulling her toward the back exit. "Colin's huntresses from his past life, and it looks like their compasses still work. I'll explain on the road."

Hadley followed without further inquiry. If three months on the run had taught them anything, it was to trust when one of them said it was time to actually run.

Alice cracked the back door open an inch and peeked through, assaulted by the scent of a nearby dumpster. She could see part of the rusted Lincoln they'd stolen the day before, parked right where they left it. She scanned the rest of the lot. All was quiet except for the sound of morning birdcalls. The coast was clear.

They made a dash for the car and jumped in. Hadley brought

the old beast back to life, and bald tires were spinning on asphalt in no time. Alice turned to look at the dilapidated building as it receded behind them. No goons in sight. She let out the breath she was holding, but she wouldn't be able to relax until they were out of Omaha. Or even Nebraska.

Two blocks down, they pulled up in front of a diner. She leaned over and hit the horn. Through the dirty window, Soxie's red head turned to look at them. Alice motioned that they needed to go, then caught Hadley staring at her.

"What?"

"Nothing."

But it was too late; she saw the eye movement toward her hairline. She flipped open the visor to check her reflection in the cracked mirror. There was a fresh streak of white near the top of her left temple—the side that until now had remained brown.

"Oh, well. At least it's starting to even out. David may even approve. What do you think?"

She fluffed her hair and flipped it back, adding a silly duck face.

Hadley frowned. "Why do you have to pretend everything's a joke? It's not helping."

Alice snapped the visor shut and looked back at the diner. Olivia and Soxie were just emerging. "You're right. I'm sorry. It's just easier."

"We're gonna find another way, Alice. You believe that, don't you?"

She reached up to clasp the hand now resting on her shoulder. She didn't want to lie, so she said nothing. Then she realized David was still inside the diner. As Soxie and Olivia climbed into the car, she leaned over and hit the horn again. Finally, he walked out, but instead of booking it to the car he turned his head to the sky, stretching his tall frame and basking in the morning sun.

"David," she shouted, "we have to go!"

He ignored her. With a groan, she pushed the door open and hoisted herself out of the car. After flipping the hood of her sweatshirt up, she jogged over and grabbed him by the elbow.

"Don't touch," he sang, snatching his arm away.

"David, please. We need to get out of here."

"Yeah, yeah. Don't get your panties in a bunch."

He strolled toward the car, giving her a hard smack on the bottom as he passed her. She clenched her fists and looked down. God, she hated this man.

She started to follow him but ran into him instead.

He turned around. "And another thing. Enough of this one-or-two-demons-a-day crap. I want more."

The demand took her by surprise. "More? I—I don't know if I can."

"Oh, I think you can."

She closed her eyes. There was no point debating it. He would get his way; he always did. It wasn't going to be easy, but it made sense. They were running out of time. For once, David was the voice of reason.

She opened her eyes. "Fine."

He smiled, then cocked his head to the side. He pushed her hood back, grabbed a handful of hair, and yanked.

"Ow!"

"Nice," he whispered.

"Do you mind?" she said, slapping his hand away.

The car horn blared.

"Guys, c'mon!" Hadley yelled.

David clapped his hands together with glee and called shotgun before racing to the car.

Alice followed him, absently rubbing her head. She may have joked that he'd approve, but she couldn't shake the feeling that something else was going on. David was many things—annoying, narcissistic, obnoxious, and rude. But never unpredictable.

Until now.

chapter 20

Two weeks later, Alice had destroyed more demons than she had in the previous two months combined. After a heated debate, she'd convinced the girls to bring back two demons instead of one. It was a success. Instead of fighting over him, the demons merged, as if they'd agreed this human was worth sharing. It was still painful, but David was right: she could handle it.

Before long they were luring three or four at a time, four to five times a day. Her hair was now mostly white, with only one thick strip of brown left. And she was tired. All the time. But they were making progress.

She stared out the window of the vacant cabin they'd found in the Northwoods of Wisconsin after leaving Omaha. They'd driven for ten hours straight that day, stopping only for bathroom breaks and gas; for all she knew, Colin had missed them by mere minutes. He could have been tearing the old consignment shop apart when she was arguing with David two blocks away.

They'd escaped, but Margot and Janie would try again. If she was stronger, they wouldn't have a chance. But demon destroying had taken its toll. Boop could probably break into her dreams if he wanted to.

To be safe, she was limiting her sleep to half-hour increments. So far it was working, but she was a walking zombie.

She yawned as she watched the sun glisten off the clear black lake. In the distance, a boat bobbed on the water as a lone fisherman cast out his line. She struggled to stay awake, her eyelids growing heavy.

She heard the girls in the kitchen discussing tonight's supply run. Although no one was saying it, they all knew it would be the last. Her job was almost done. The blood moon was in ten days.

Ten days. At the rate they were going, she would have a full head of white hair by then. Whether that would mean all demons were accounted for, she had no idea. But at least her part of the bargain would be fulfilled, according to the Huntress's vision. And Colin would be free.

If only she could say goodbye. It didn't seem like too much to ask. Hadn't she given up enough? Hadn't she given up everything? It was so unfair. If the universe had a suggestion box, she'd have set it on fire by now.

She spotted an eagle as it floated above the lake, its wings catching on the warm wind. She wished she could trade places with it. Feel the air lift her up and up. Above the worries and fears, the pain and the hurt. Simply float away.

"Alice!"

She woke with a jolt, lifting her head off her hands and blinking three or four times. "I'm awake. I'm awake."

"Here, you'd better have some more coffee." Soxie took her hand and wrapped it around a warm mug. She sat on the love seat and ran her hand over Alice's hair. "How're you doing?"

"I'm good," Alice lied.

"Listen, I think we should slow down for a few days. And before you say anything, just hear me out."

Alice was about to disagree but held it in.

"David won't know the difference. And the truth is, we're having a hard time finding them. The Realm is quiet. You're doing it, Ali. But you need a break."

Her green eyes shimmered. Alice took a mental picture of her face, thinking back to the first time she saw her.

Soxie leaned back. "What?"

Alice reached up to finger a piece of curly red hair. "I was just remembering that first time I saw you in David's bedroom. Standing there in one of your thousand-dollar outfits, laser focused and ready to vanquish a demon. You were like this fiery warrior queen. I remember thinking later, *What's her story?*"

"What do you want to know?"

Of course Alice still had questions. The parents, for one. The uncle. The money. But that was all just smoke and mirrors. There wasn't anything she needed to know that she didn't already know. She dropped her hand and clasped Soxie's tightly.

"I want to know that you're going to live a long, happy life, Sharon Roxland. We've been crushing demons for months, but I think you might have some of your own. Those are the ones I'd like to see destroyed."

"Alice . . ."

"Hey." She shoved Soxie lightly in the shoulder. "It's gonna be okay. It really is."

Soxie closed her eyes and shook her head, her thick curls swishing back and forth. "I'm just asking you not to give up yet."

Alice hugged the steaming mug to her chest. "I'm not giving up. I'm giving in. There's a difference."

"Bullshit!"

Alice jumped, spilling hot coffee on her lap.

Soxie stood and walked a few paces before turning around. "There's no difference. Giving in. Giving up. Same. Fucking. Thing."

Olivia and Hadley poked their heads out of the kitchen.

"Sox—"

"No, don't Sox me. You don't get to call me that. Only my friends call me that, and you're no friend of mine, Alice Daniels. My friends don't just give in. They fight. They . . . they . . ."

And then something really awful happened. Soxie burst into tears. Full, body-racking sobs. Alice watched with wide eyes as her friend's strong, confident body crumpled to the floor.

Olivia and Hadley exchanged looks, as if each was waiting for the other to do something.

Alice sat still, listening to Soxie's awful wails. She'd known this day was coming. They were starting to fall apart. But what could she say? Thank you for helping me die? Because that's what they were doing. As hard as this was for her, at least she'd have the benefit of not living through it. Her job was the easy one. Talk about unfair.

She set her mug on the windowsill and stood. Soxie was on her knees, her arms wrapped around her waist. Alice walked over and knelt down in front of her.

"Sharon."

Soxie placed her hands on the rug. She took a few deep breaths and wiped her face on the back of her arm.

"You're wrong," Alice said. "I am your friend. And I'm doing what has to be done. For you, and Olivia, and Hadley. For my mom and dad. For Ana and her mom in Lençóis. For Colin. Even for that dirtbag in the other room." She motioned to the den, where the ever-present sounds of channel surfing could be heard.

"Okay, maybe not so much *him* . . . but for what he might have been. In a parallel universe."

Soxie's shoulders moved as she stifled a laugh.

"But I'm no hero. Not like you guys." She turned to look at Olivia and Hadley. "You're the ones making this possible. I never would have made it this far without you. And if I had to do it all over again . . . if I had the choice to be born as someone else, to never know you? Not a snowball's chance in Phoenix I'd take it."

Soxie laughed out loud, then sniffed and leaned back on her heels. "Don't call me Sharon ever again."

"Deal."

Olivia and Hadley knelt down on the floor next to them. Without another word, the four of them linked hands. Alice made eye contact with each of them, the love in her heart tamping down the pain. Her sisters, her beautiful, warrior sisters.

Thank you, Philautia, for choosing them. Wherever you are.

"We'll try to make this one quick," Soxie said as she pulled her hair into a ponytail. "It looked like that place down the road might have pool tables if David gets restless."

Alice laughed. "Perfect. I can't wait to watch some local clean the table with him. I hope it's a girl. Speaking of the capital D-bag, any special requests?"

"No," Olivia said. "Which is kind of odd. Makes me nervous."

"He's probably just too amped on methademon." Alice snorted. "The way he describes it, nothing beats it. Even a solid gold Rolex."

"Well, I don't like it. Just keep an eye on him."

"I live for it."

Hadley pulled her in for a quick hug. "We'll be back soon," she whispered.

Alice hugged Olivia and Soxie goodbye, then watched as the three of them disappeared into the bedroom mirror. She looked at her own reflection, wondering if they ever lingered in the Backwards Place, watching her. She waved at her reflection just in case.

She glanced at her watch. Five fifteen. She could probably get in a half-hour nap before David began pestering her about dinner. She shuffled over to the bed and set the old windup alarm for thirty minutes.

"David, I'm taking a quick nap," she called.

"I'll alert the media," he called back.

She flipped him the bird through the wall. Sometimes it was the little things that brought the most joy. She smiled and let her head fall on the pillow.

Her eyes popped open at the sound of the harsh jangling bells. She blinked and studied the clock's face. Five forty-six. *That was fast.*

She sat up and rubbed her eyes. She could hear the sounds of a soccer game coming from the den. At least David was still occupied. She stretched her arms above her head, yawning. Coffee. She needed more coffee.

After making her way to the kitchen, she poured herself a big cup and stood sipping it black, looking out the window above the sink. The fishing boat was gone, and so was the eagle. The lake was glassy still, a giant mirror to the sky above. The sun still hung above the horizon too. It didn't set until late this time of year. It would be a pretty spectacle when it did, but she missed her desert sunsets.

She'd never wanted to move to Arizona, but it had become the seat of her happiest memories—transformed from ugly and brown to golden and resplendent. It was her home, and she missed it.

She missed her mom and Boop too. According to the latest emails, they were doing well, still living at the Roxlands'. At least her mom wasn't alone. And Boop—well, she didn't need to worry about him. He probably had the entire household eating out of the pad of his paw. But it was time to face the undeniable truth. She wasn't going to get to say goodbye to them either. Or to Aunt Molly. Her dad. Her oldest friends, Chloe and Rachel. Deep down she'd known this when they went off the grid, but she'd never let it sink in until now.

She found some stationery in an old desk and sat for an hour, scribbling every thought and feeling she had for each intended recipient, until her hand cramped. She thanked them. Made them promise to choose happiness. Said she'd always be with them. She'd always love them. And she hoped one day they'd forgive her.

She couldn't bring herself to write notes to the girls, though. They deserved those words face-to-face.

She finished stuffing the letters into envelopes and hid them in the inner pocket of Olivia's backpack. Then she poured herself another cup of sludge and went to check on David.

She found him fast asleep, snoring on the checkered recliner.

"David." She reached for the remote to turn down the television. He grunted.

She kicked the chair.

"DAVID!"

"Relax, Hades," he said, his eyes closed, his head lolling to the side. "It's under control."

She dropped her mug on the hardwood floor and it cracked in two, splashing brown muck everywhere. She jumped back as David awoke with a start.

"Who's that? What's going on?" he said, looking briefly confused before awareness dawned and he noticed her staring. He curled his lip in disgust. "What do you want?"

She felt unbalanced, as if the old cabin had just been knocked off its foundation. "Wh- what were you dreaming about?"

He snatched the remote from her hand. "Not you, thank God. That would be a nightmare." He started to flip through channels, but when she didn't move, he seemed to lose what little patience he had. "WHAT?"

"Um . . . I . . ."

He turned back to the television, dismissing her with a flick of his wrist. "Weirdo."

She stood there, trying to convince herself it meant nothing. David didn't know or care about what they were doing, beyond providing him with a steady dose of methademon. Sure, he'd probably overheard them mention Hades once or twice, but he'd never even batted an eye. Couldn't a dream just be a dream?

Maybe. But maybe not. Either way, she wasn't about to take any chances this close to the finish line. She walked over to the couch and flopped onto it with an exaggerated sigh.

"What's your problem?" he mumbled.

"I dunno. Stir-crazy, I guess. I could use a little fun."

"You and fun? Your picture is next to 'dull' in the dictionary."

"You may be right, but yours is still next to 'asshole.'"

He nodded and pushed out his bottom lip. "I'll give you that one."

She put her hands behind her head and stared at the ceiling.

"Okay, I'll bite. What does dull Alice consider fun?"

She slowly grinned, keeping her eyes on the old wooden beams.

It was only ten thirty and they'd already been kicked out of three bars in the sleepy little town. One because they couldn't produce IDs, but the other two were solely due to Alice. She was channeling all her anger and despair to create what she believed was the female version of David. A rotten, despicable human being who cared only for herself. She pretended to get drunk. She insulted people. Laughed at them. She even tried hustling. When she lost, she snapped the pool stick in half and threw her drink in the man's face.

It was horrible, like she was on autopilot, letting the ghosts of all the demons she'd ashed run the show for a while. But David ate it up. The more awful she was, the more entertained he became. Soon, they were a team. A drunken, bar brawl–causing Bonnie and Clyde.

They stumbled in the dark toward the only bar still open.

He threw his arm around her. "I am loving this side of you, skunk!"

She tried not to cringe. *Be Bonnie. Be Bonnie.*

"Yeah, well, I still hate you and your stupid face."

"Yes! See, doesn't it feel good to be bad? To just say what you feel? I hate all this politically correct crap these days. The world and everyone in it is so fake. He's going to change all that."

Her pulse quickened. She wriggled away and continued stumble-walking ahead. "Where's this bar anyway? Where are all the people? This town sucks."

She kicked over a garbage can, spilling trash onto the sidewalk. An empty beer bottle rolled to a stop in front of her. She picked it up and hurled it down the middle of the street. The sound of smashing glass echoed against closed storefronts. "Sucktown, USA!"

David started slow clapping behind her.

She turned around. "What's with you?"

He stopped and casually leaned against a parked car. "I know this is all an act, but I'm really enjoying it. You have potential, Alice. I think he might be wrong about you."

"He who? What are you talking about?"

He looked to the night sky as if seeking celestial guidance. "Fine, we can keep playing your bad-Alice game. But let me just say, when you asked that guy if he was what the cat dragged in . . . girl after my own heart. I don't even care that you were pretending. It was hot." A wolfish grin appeared on his face.

Oh, no. She wanted to bond with him, but not *bond* with him. She stood up straight. "For your information, that wasn't even mine. I read it in a book once."

He slapped his thigh. "Even better! You're a plagiarist! Why not steal someone else's line? If the shoe fits, take it! Don't you see? You can shine for real—not because you're following the plastic rules of a plastic world, but because you're following your base instincts. You might think you were acting, but I think you've been acting for eighteen years. Tonight you let the real Alice through. And she was magnificent." He took a step forward.

She stepped back. No more pretending. "I don't care about your psychotic version of utopia. Is Hades trying to change the terms of the deal?"

Her frankness seemed to catch him off guard, but he recovered quickly. "Please. He's not selling used cars. He's changing the world. He's a god, Alice. Older than your Christian god. Older than recorded history. He doesn't have to make deals."

The cards were on the table now. She just had no idea how to play them.

"How . . . how do you know all this?"

He took another step forward. "The Furies might control the demons, but where do you think they came from? Who do you think *created* them? Do you really think I've learned nothing after being infected as many times as I have?"

In two steps he closed the distance between them, plucked the straight black wig off her head, and dropped it to the ground. Her world was turning upside down and all she could do was stand there, hyperventilating, as he ran his fingers through her stark, mostly white hair.

"You don't have to hide anymore. He wants you tending the Realm, but I think I can persuade him to keep you here for a while. He's not immune to my charms, and I have a feeling you aren't either." He leaned down and pressed his lips to hers.

Omigod, omigod, omigod. What was happening? David was kissing her. DAVID. A strangulated yelp escaped from deep in her throat, and she pushed against his chest with all her might. He stumbled back and she slapped him hard in the face. Before he could recover, she slapped him again.

"That's my girl," he sneered, then grabbed her by the neck and crushed his lips back to hers.

She was going to be sick.

Tears streamed down her cheeks as she tried to push him away. But as she'd grown weaker, he'd only grown stronger. His kiss was ruthless and repulsive. Foul. She wanted nothing more than to escape out of her own skin. To strip it off like an old dress and burn it. This was worse than ashing a demon. This was becoming one.

She closed her eyes to wish it all away. And then she was screaming.

She was on the ground screaming and David was on top of her, blood pouring down the side of his face. His mouth moved, but no sound came out. Then his eyes rolled back and he collapsed onto the pavement next to her, red still oozing from a gash on his head.

She crawled backward, her hands and feet slipping on the gravelly asphalt. Her back slammed into the curb and she sat in the gutter, dazed and wheezing.

David lay unmoving, rivulets of blood slowly trickling down the street. A lone figure stood over him, its body silhouetted against the light from the streetlamp. It raised its leg and nudged the inert form with the toe of a high-heeled boot.

"Shoot, I didn't mean to kill him. Oh, well."

Alice gasped, and Molly lifted her head.

"Hiya, sweetie," she said, dropping the bottle she was holding. It clanged loudly on the road as it bounced twice and then slowly rolled away, swallowed by quiet darkness.

chapter 21

"Aunt Molly?"

Molly's head turned toward the sound of an oncoming car. "We have to go." She wobbled, her heel catching on the uneven cement. "Damn. I just bought these."

Alice stared at her, then at the dark shape lying in the road. The headlights from the oncoming vehicle were seconds away from casting it in a finite, murderous light. But she didn't want to leave; she wanted to wait and see what happened. To see if there was any hope left for him, or for her. She felt like a computer about to crash—the blue screen of death before everything is lost.

"Sweetie. It's okay." Molly extended her hand. "But I need you to move. Now."

Alice snapped out of her trance and took Molly's hand. They ran for a block in shadow before ducking into an alley. A second later, she heard the screech of tires and shouting. David had been discovered.

They stood flat against a crumbling wall as Alice tried to put her fractured mind back together. *Molly killed David. David is dead. Molly . . .* She turned to look at her aunt's pretty profile. What was she doing here? Then she heard a familiar voice.

"Alice!"

Her body floated off the wall. She could feel the desperation in his voice. It reverberated through the sun-warmed bricks of the town, calling her home. Colin was here. He'd found her. She didn't know how and she didn't care.

She was halfway down the alley, ready to call out his name, when a hand clamped over her mouth.

She heard a strange sound behind her—like nails on a chalkboard, but deeper and amplified. Then she was being pulled back. At first it was Molly, but then it wasn't. Something else had her. It was all around her, within her, yanking her from the gut and dragging her down. Down, down, down.

If a human being could survive a black hole, this had to be what it felt like. Her body imploded in on itself over and over until she was a microscopic pinpoint of nothingness. She *was*, then she *wasn't*, then she *was* again.

She tried waving her hand in front of her face. She could see it, but only in blurry increments, like someone had taken half the frames out of a reel of film.

She looked around. She was in a long hallway, similar to the Realm except that the mirrors were not reflecting each other. There was no dance of color and light, just impossibly black glass set within each different-shaped frame. A dark energy hung in the air like a dense fog. She could feel it trying to seep into her eyes and ears. Her nose and mouth. The very pores of her skin. Evil. Pure and unfiltered.

Her mind was already unraveling. She had to get out of this place; she was sure it would drive her insane. She started to run, but she couldn't tell if she was moving or if the hall itself was moving. There were no elevator shafts, no tunnels leading left or right. Just a nightmare of evil and darkness that stretched on and on.

How long had she been here? It felt like months. Years. She was losing her grip on reality. There was no more reality. There was only confusion. She gripped the sides of her head and screamed. It echoed around her, getting louder and louder, until she thought her eardrums would burst. She closed her eyes and curled into a ball, her only defense left.

Then she felt something deep in her gut, pulling again. This time upwards. She was floating, up and up. She was the eagle on the lake, drafting on a warm wind. She kept her eyes shut and focused on another set of eyes. Light blue, and clouding dark. Smoldering with desire. Brimming with love. Pure and unfiltered.

She heard a familiar ding. There was something solid beneath her now. And behind her. Even in front of her. She was crammed into a tiny box. A tiny, smelly box. The box rattled and shook.

Ding.

"Ladies and gentlemen, this is your captain speaking. We're gonna try and get above some of this bumpy air. I've gone ahead and turned on that fasten seat belt sign. If you could please stay seated with your seat belts fastened, we'll try to get you out of this as soon as possible. Flight attendants, take your jump seats."

Alice opened her eyes as someone knocked on the flimsy folding door.

"Alice? Sweetie, are you in there? It's Aunt Molly."

She pushed off the floor, and a piece of errant toilet paper stuck to her hand. *Yuck.* She grabbed the tiny sink and pulled herself up.

Molly knocked again. "Alice?"

"I'm here. Just give me a minute."

She leaned against the wall, breathing in through her nose and out through her mouth. The plane dipped and tilted, launching her sideways. She almost fell in the toilet.

"Honey, you need to take your seat. It's not safe in there."

"I said give me a minute!"

She had just taken a trip from the Northwoods of Wisconsin to thirty thousand feet over who knows where, with a fun little stopover in hell. And Molly had booked it. She could damn well give her a minute.

"Okay, but please hurry. Seat 2A."

Alice closed her eyes and braced herself as she was bounced around the cramped bathroom. Turbulence used to freak her out, but this was nothing compared to what she'd just been through. Bring it on, Captain.

She scrubbed her hands raw and splashed water on her face as her body swayed back and forth. She gave her reflection a cursory glance, turned away, then paused and looked again.

It wasn't her sunken cheeks or puffy eyes that caught her attention. It was her white, white hair. She leaned forward, lifting pieces of it to be sure. The brown streak was gone. Whatever that place was, it had sealed her fate. All that remained now was a funeral and a coffin.

She exited the bathroom as the plane took a nasty pocket of wind shear. Her body was flung forward, and she landed on seat 13B's lap.

"Miss!" a flight attendant snapped. "You need to take your seat, now!"

"I know, I know. I'm going."

She apologized to 13B and, ignoring the judgment from her fellow passengers, pinballed her way down the aisle.

She'd never flown first-class before. Seat 2A was less a seat and more of a roomy pod. She saw Molly peek around the corner from her jump seat and motion for her to sit.

She fell into the seat as another bump splashed wine past the rim of nearby glasses. The plane was tossed around for another fifteen minutes before leveling out. She kept her eyes closed the whole time, gripping her armrests and trying to make sense of the insensible. But it was pointless. Molly was the only one with the answers now, and with the next ding of the seat belt sign, it would appear she'd have to wait until after beverage service.

She fiddled with the control panel until her chair slid into a flat position. And wasn't this nice—a fluffy down blanket, just for her. She settled in for a nice long sleep. It didn't matter if Margot and Janie dream-hopped her. The only explanation for Molly and Colin showing up in Wisconsin was them. They must have successfully broken in during her half-hour nap. She'd been so tired she didn't even remember, though she wasn't all that surprised. It was only a matter of time. But now she had no idea where she was, other than on an airplane in mid-flight. Should narrow it down to a few thousand possibilities. Good luck with that, ladies.

She closed her eyes, and she slept. A deep and much-needed sleep. Only this time she dreamt of nothing. Nothing at all.

Molly nudged her awake as they were beginning their descent into Paris, according to the announcement.

She pressed Alice's passport into her hand, along with a bottle of water. "How are you feeling? You slept seven hours straight. Are you hungry?" Without waiting for an answer, she placed a plastic-wrapped cheese croissant on Alice's lap. "We'll get something more after we land. I'll meet you right outside of border control. Just tell them you're on vacation, returning Monday. You're staying at the Hôtel de Vendôme with me. And don't worry about Colin. I've been following him for days; he got lucky, but I got to you first. Everything's going to be okay."

Alice just stared at her and nodded, even though she didn't fully understand what she was hearing. Her head felt thick and her mouth was dry.

Molly moved on to prepare the cabin for arrival, and Alice transformed her bed back into a chair. She gulped down the water and devoured the cheese croissant in four big bites.

Her body replenished, she spent the next thirty minutes falling down rabbit holes. Molly. Colin. The Dark Place. A deal with the devil. David.

David. She thought of his blank eyes as he collapsed on top of her. The rancid feeling of his lips on hers. She wasn't sorry he was dead. She was sorry for what he had become. What he'd never had the chance to be. Maybe in death he'd find salvation. She hoped so. She really did.

But David was more than what they'd originally thought. More than a demon magnet. He'd known things he shouldn't possibly know. He'd been communicating with Hades—or perhaps "communing" was the more appropriate word. He'd spoken of him with the reverence of a devoted worshipper. A sycophant. A soldier.

She sat up straight. Soldier . . . that hit uncomfortably close to home. Hadn't he basically been trying to recruit her? *You have potential, Alice.* Potential for what? She dug her nails into the armrest.

The age of man will not last.

It was so long ago that the Furies had cast their warning. But she'd never made sense of it until now.

Hades was building an army. And she may have just spent the past few months helping him do it.

———— 🦋 ————

She scanned the crowded arrivals terminal, gripping her passport so tight it curled into a tube. Molly flagged her down, holding a sign above her head that read "Mademoiselle Alice."

Alice beelined toward her, shoulder-checking people along the way. When she reached Molly and her ridiculous sign, she snatched it and tore it in half. Then she punched her square in the face.

She'd never punched someone before. It hurt. A lot.

"Son of a . . ." she hissed, flicking her hand to rid her knuckles of the sting.

A small crowd gathered, and within seconds airport security showed up. She was really batting a thousand with French law enforcement. Someone pressed a cloth to Molly's nose, but she waved them off as someone else pulled her to her feet.

"*Merci. Ça va.*"

"*Madame, êtes-vous sûr?*"

"*Oui, oui,*" she said, leaning her head back to stop the bleeding. She waved them off again.

Alice received a minor tongue-lashing from the guard but kept her eyes on Molly the whole time. When the bystanders got bored and security took their leave, she folded her arms in front of her and waited.

Molly patted her nose gingerly and sniffed. "I guess I deserved that."

"Who are you?"

"Alice, sweetheart, you know who I am."

"Who were you before? I want to hear you say it."

Molly slowly bent down to retrieve her bag off the floor. She dug inside, produced a pair of oversize sunglasses, and placed them carefully on her face, then linked her arm through Alice's and headed for the doors. Alice tried to pull away.

"Don't worry," Molly said, tucking her back into her side. "I'll tell you everything. Promise. But first I need a drink."

She smiled and walked them through the automatic doors to the curb outside, where they were greeted by a bright Parisian sun.

Paris. The City of Lights. Alice watched it fly by from her taxi window, wishing she had time to see it. Really see it. But there would be no strolling along the Seine or visits to the Louvre. This car ride was it.

When they got to the hotel, Molly steered them straight to the restaurant, where they sat in a quiet window booth. She ordered a bottle of wine and poured two glasses.

Alice pushed hers away. "No thanks, Tisiphone."

Molly coughed, spilling wine down her chin. She dabbed at it with a linen napkin. "Tisiphone? Alice sweetie, Tisiphone's been gone for centuries. What on earth would make you think I'm one of the Furies?"

"But . . . then. I don't understand. Who are you?"

Molly reached across the table to pat her cheek. "When you were five years old, I bought you a parakeet. Do you remember?"

"What?"

"You called it a parakeetie, and named her Keetie for short." She leaned back and took a sip of wine, as if settling in for a nice, cozy chat.

Alice fought the urge to scream. It was typical Molly to switch gears like that; she never did bother reading her audience. She talked when she wanted about what she wanted, and if the listener wasn't following? Well, too bad for them. Unfortunately, Alice wasn't following.

"What are you talking about?" she managed, barely.

"You were so excited," Molly continued, oblivious to the tension. "You'd been asking Judy for one ever since we took you to the bird house at the zoo. A green one, you said. So she didn't get lost in the sky."

Before Alice had a chance to get angry, a birdcage flashed in her mind's eye. It was shiny and ornate, with gold bars that reflected sunlight as it rocked gently in the warm summer breeze. But it was empty. Where was the bird?

"I remember a birdcage . . ." she said, half to herself—and then, "Wait. Did Keetie talk?"

"Hello, Alice."

"Huh?"

Molly took another sip and smiled. "That's what you were going to teach her to say. Hello, Alice."

Alice moved her gaze to the window. She could almost see the little bird, perched on the sill, staring at her through the glass. She blinked. "Did something happen? Did Keetie escape?"

"Yes and no. You set her free."

"Why would I do that?" she snapped, uncomfortable with where this story was going.

Molly twirled the stem of her glass back and forth. "You were sleepwalking. Did you know you used to do that? You came to my room in the middle of the night—I was between jobs, living with your parents—and you told me that Keetie needed to see the world. You loved her cage—the golden swirls and crystals—but you said it was still a cage, and Keetie was too special to live the rest of her life in a cage, no matter how pretty it was."

"Hang on. You let me release a domestic bird into the wild? Do you know how many cats were in our neighborhood?" Alice was mortified. The implication that she was a bird murderer—or at the very least a bird neglecter—was enough to steer her off course. For a moment, anyway.

"You're missing the point," Molly said.

"There's a point?"

"The point"—Molly looked straight into her eyes—"is that even at five years old, you understood the concept of loving something enough to set it free."

Alice pressed her forehead into her hands, miles past her wit's end. "Molly, please. What does this have to do with anything?"

"I'm trying to tell you. That's when I got the job with the airline. That's when I decided it was best if I stayed away as much as possible. You saw too much. I was keeping an eye on you, but I was never supposed to care for you. I was never supposed to love you."

"Never supposed to love me?"

Molly reached across the table and took her hand. "Honey, I do love you. I tried not to, believe me. But I was naive. It was fascinating watching you grow up, seeing you become this strong, independent woman. Taking care of your mom and putting up with me. The smile on your face every time I showed up—it broke my heart."

Alice ignored the lump in her throat. "Why?"

Molly sat back, drained her glass, and poured herself another. Instead of drinking it, she stared at it, her eyes lost in the ruby-red depths.

"Molly Wilkins—your real aunt—took her own life when she

was nineteen years old. Her soul left this world one year before you were born. That's when I stepped in."

Alice swallowed, unable to speak.

"She made her choice, and so did I. I may have been a queen, but I was still a prisoner. I was still Keetie in her golden cage. This was my chance for freedom. It was my chance to see the world. So I took it."

She looked at Alice as a thick tear rolled down her cheek. "I'm so sorry, honey. I'm so very sorry."

Alice felt the wrongness of Molly's words like they were being fed to her with a barbed wire spoon. She grabbed the glass of wine she'd pushed away and gulped it down, red wine sloshing down her chin. When she slammed it back on the table, the flimsy stem snapped in two.

She shoved the broken glass aside and wiped her mouth with the back of her hand. "I'll ask you one more time. Who. Are. You."

Molly wiped the moisture from her rosy cheeks. "I'm usually referred to as Kore, but I prefer my given name. Persephone."

Alice waited for the punch line. It didn't come.

"You," she said with a forceful snort. "Queen of The Underworld. Sovereign of an entire world. You MUST be joking."

Molly lifted her glass. "It's a hell of a lot easier than working economy to Reno, I'll tell you that much."

Alice burst out laughing. The universe was mocking her. Persephone, the abducted wife of Hades, was sitting across from her, tucking into her second glass of Côtes du Rhône. She laughed, if only to stop herself from screaming. Because it wasn't funny. Not really. A goddess possessed the body of her dead aunt. An aunt she never knew. The sister Judy didn't even know was gone. That wasn't funny. That was tragic.

Her laughter died away, and she placed her hands flat on the table. "Why are you here?"

"He sent me to claim your soul."

"What?"

Molly's eyes teared. "I wasn't going to do it. You need to know that. I couldn't."

Alice said nothing. It was time for the truth.

Molly went on. "You have to understand, The Underworld is a strange and confusing place. Not necessarily bad; it just depends on the soul. But it's still a prison, and I don't want that for you. I don't know what happens in your heaven, or even if there is one. But if so, I know in my heart that is where your soul belongs. At peace and free."

Alice suddenly felt like she was sinking in quicksand. "But . . . what about Cithaeron? The deal with Philautia?" She grabbed Molly's hand. "Persephone, you have to take me. Please. You can't let him have Cithaeron again. You can't!"

Molly shook her head. "Oh, sweetie. Hades was never going to let him go."

chapter 22

She couldn't see through the tears. Everything she'd done, every-thing she'd sacrificed, was for nothing. She lay sobbing on the bed in their hotel room, Molly attempting to comfort her by rubbing circles on her back.

"Honey, shhh . . ."

Alice shoved her away. "Why didn't you let me go to him? I have to find him. I have to see him!"

"I'm sorry, sweetie, but it's not safe."

Alice sniffled and wiped the snot from her nose. She didn't care whether it was safe or not. Spotting the phone by the bed, she made a grab for it, but Molly got to it first and yanked the cord from the wall.

"You can't see him," she said, hugging the phone to her chest.

Alice glared at her. Who did this *goddess* think she was? She wasn't her aunt, that was for sure. She didn't owe her anything. "Just try and stop me," she spat before jumping up and heading for the door.

Molly leapt in front of her with the spryness of a jungle cat. "Honey, listen to me," she said quickly. "I was protecting you. I was protecting you both."

Alice took a step back, more from surprise than fear. "From what?"

"Each other."

She laughed. "You've been lying to me my whole life. Why should I believe you now?"

Molly sank against the door. "I never lied to you."

"Lie."

"I said I was a goddess. I never said I was perfect. But I'm telling you to trust me on this. The Furies haven't stopped looking for you, and they have ways of finding you outside the Realm."

"Do you think I care about the Furies anymore?"

"You should. You've been destroying their only means of punishing mankind. It's all they have left."

Alice's thoughts went back to that day in front of the fireplace—the haunted look in her dad's eyes. "Explain."

Molly's energy faded in an instant. She plunked the phone—still clutched in one hand—on the table by the door and headed straight for the minibar.

She was just pulling a half-bottle of wine from the fridge when Alice marched over and took it from her.

"Explain," she repeated.

Molly eyed the bottle longingly, then dropped her head like a child and shuffled over to the couch. She fell onto it with a sigh and proceeded to fiddle with a stray cushion thread. "The Furies were part of The Underworld," she eventually began. "When they weren't punishing the living, they were punishing the damned. Cithaeron's soul was one of the damned."

Alice sat on the bed and hugged the bottle close, its coldness no match for her own.

"Hades only provided the means," Molly continued. "The Furies were responsible for the execution. But Cithaeron surprised us all. The Furies never had to lift a finger. He created his own nightmare."

"What do you mean?"

"His soul punished itself. The damned don't do that. But he did.

And the more he suffered, the stronger his soul became. That kind of strength is unheard of. He quickly became one of Hades's most prized possessions."

"Then why did he release him?"

"You have to remember that Hades is a god. Two thousand years is nothing. He can afford to play the long game."

"The long game?"

Molly's eyes dropped to the bottle still clutched in Alice's arms. "Sweetie, I could really use a drink."

"Fine. Here." She tossed the bottle on the couch. Molly grabbed it, twisted off the screw top, and took a hurried and generous swig.

"Why do you drink so much?" Alice asked. It was off topic, but she couldn't resist. Alcohol seemed like such a *human* crutch.

Molly closed her eyes. "It makes it harder for him to get in my head."

"Who, Hades?"

"Yes. And the longer I go without claiming your soul, the harder he tries." She lifted the bottle and took another drink.

"But what about the legend? Aren't you, like, bound to him because of some pomegranate seeds or something?"

Molly stifled a laugh. "It's a little more complicated than that. Your myths got a lot of things right, but they got a lot wrong too."

"Then tell me what's wrong. Why does Hades want my soul?"

Molly met her eyes. "It's not just your soul, Alice. He wants your world."

"What do you mean, my world?"

"Where do you think we've been for the past twenty-five hundred years? Do you think the gods just decided one day to up and leave?"

Alice felt rage start to brew again. Every answer only brought more questions.

"I have no idea what you're talking about."

"The comet, Alice. Ptah's Fire. It changed everything. It took you—it took mankind—away from us."

"How? Why?"

Molly took yet another drink and shook her head. "We don't know. Ptah was the Egyptian god of creation, but the comet is his in name only. He didn't create it. We're not sure who did, or where it came from. It contains a power older than the gods—maybe even the universe."

Alice rubbed her head. Egyptian gods? Did that mean *they* were real too? It made sense, in a way. Clearly the Greek gods of legend were anything but; it stood to reason the same would go for the gods of ancient Egypt. But they were getting too far off track. She didn't have time to keep tearing away more layers.

"Okay, so the comet's back." She lifted her hands. "What does that have to do with me and the Realm?"

"Philautia was the daughter of a Fury," Molly explained. "She was connected to The Underworld. When she created the Realm, she created a bridge between our worlds. Mine was already dying. It had been five hundred years since Ptah's Fire split us apart. This link was another chance. The only chance."

"Dying? How do immortals die?"

Molly shrugged. "Boredom."

"C'mon . . . dying of boredom? Give me a break."

"Imagine everything you enjoy about your life suddenly taken away from you. Whatever it is. Food. Dancing. Laughter. Love. All of it. Gone. And you're left with nothing but the memories of what used to be. Forever."

Alice wasn't sure if she'd call that boring. More like sad. Or just plain meaningless.

"And you're right," Molly went on. "Immortals don't die. Death means rebirth. Your soul continues. We don't have that luxury. The only choice we have is to exist, or not. We need purpose. Mankind was our purpose."

"Then why are the Furies trying to hurt us? If the gods love us so much, then doesn't it defeat the point?"

"I said *purpose*, I didn't say love. Does a cat love the mouse he tortures? No. But he's sad when it's gone."

A glacial breeze swept through the room. Or at least it felt like it.

"After the War of the Titans, the Three Brothers drew lots. Zeus got lord of the sky and earth, Poseidon the sea, and Hades, well, you know what he got. But with the Realm, he can have more. He can have it all."

Alice stared at her. "But not without me. He can't have the Realm without me."

"Smart girl."

Molly's tone was resigned. She spoke as if she'd known all along it would come to this—that one day she'd have no choice but to transfer the weight of humanity to someone else's shoulders. A huntress's. The very last.

Without realizing it, Alice stood and walked to the window. She needed time to think—to take everything in and plan her next move. But for all her planning, she wasn't any closer to saving Colin, let alone the world. If anything, she'd made things worse.

Just then a tour bus drove right by the hotel, rattling the window and startling her. Its top deck was filled with tourists, most of them snapping photos that would probably be posted online before the bus made its way past the Place Vendôme. It made her wonder what their vacation would look like in a different world.

One ruled by an indifferent god.

A god with an army of demons.

She watched as the bus rounded the corner and disappeared. Then she turned back to Molly.

"He's been using me. The demons . . . they were his all along. I haven't been destroying them, have I?"

"No. You've been sending them to the Hall of Demons."

Alice felt a jolt of something familiar and dark, and gasped. "Hall of Demons?"

"The entry point between the Realm and The Underworld. You were just there."

"How . . . how could you send me there?"

"I'm sorry, honey," Molly said. "We needed a quick exit. It was my only option."

She would have preferred Guantanamo. "Then why was it empty? Look at my hair. I've been sending them back!"

"It wasn't empty. He's been hiding them from the Furies. Those demons have been gathering information for centuries. Once he takes control of the Realm, he'll use them to identify his first flock of followers—humans receptive to his vision who will carry out his plans. The Furies may have thought they were using him, but it was the other way around. With Hades, it always is."

Alice sat back down on the bed. "So all this time, Philautia was fighting a losing battle."

"She did her best. Once she realized the Realm was compromised, she gave up her soul to save it. Some of the worst crimes against humanity were committed by infected humans. If it weren't for her huntresses, this world would be a very different place."

Alice could only imagine. She fell back on the bed and stared at the ceiling. "At least it's over."

"It's not over."

She popped back up. "What do you mean? I thought he needed my soul."

"When Ptah's Fire burns brightest, Alice. He still has the comet. It was powerful enough to break our worlds apart, and if he has to, he'll use it to break universal law and take your soul by force. It's a brief window, but it's enough. It's his fail-safe. You're the last huntress, and the Realm is connected to you. Once it's gone, our link to your world is gone. He's not about to let that happen."

Alice's eyes started to sting. The blood moon was just a few days away. Had she ever had a chance? Had any of them?

She fell to the floor on her knees. "Please, Persephone. I—"

Someone banged on the door, putting both of them on immediate alert.

"Alice, I know you're in there. Open the door. Now."

It was Colin. He was here! She leapt to her feet. "Colin!"

Somehow Molly made it to the door before she did. The difference this time was that Alice was prepared to run right through her.

"Get. Out. Of. My. Way."

There was worry in Molly's eyes, but she stood her ground. "Alice, no. You can't open this door. The Furies are still looking for you. They have an agenda and they won't quit. If there's a demon hiding inside him, it's over. Do you hear me? They will kill you both."

The door handle rattled. "Alice. Open this door, or I swear I will break it down."

Her eyes met Molly's. It was the span of a second, but the truth was there. She saw it. She couldn't put him at risk. Even if Hades still governed his soul, she had to give him a chance at a normal life. A normal, happy life.

She covered her mouth as tears filled her eyes, nodding that she understood. Molly picked up the phone, walked to the nightstand, and plugged it back into the wall.

"*Sécurité. Oui. Depeche-toi, s'il vous plaît.*"

Colin banged again. Unlike the flimsy motel room doors from their days on the run, this one was solid and reinforced. Nothing short of a battering ram was getting through. Molly had thought ahead.

"Alice!" he yelled.

The fear in his voice was more than she could bear. She sank to her knees and pressed her forehead against the door. "I'm sorry," she said quietly. "I'm so sorry."

"Alice? Alice, baby, please. Just open the door." He was following the sound of her voice. "I need to know you're okay."

He was level with her now. An inch of wood was all that stood between them. An inch of wood, and an eternity of loss and pain.

"I can't."

"Yes, you can. I spoke to the girls. I know why you're doing this. I know what Philautia told you. But you're wrong. You're wrong if you think sacrificing yourself will save me. Because the only thing that will do is kill me."

Tears poured down her face as she clawed at the door, his words annihilating her. She couldn't breathe through the pain.

"Alice, please." His hand slapped the door.

She placed her palm against the wood, imagining his mirroring it on the other side. They would never be this close again.

She struggled to get the words out. "Goodbye, Cithaeron."

He was silent for a beat. Then a strange sound seemed to come from his gut—from the core of his being. "Don't. Don't you dare, Alice. You open this door. You open it NOW!" He was up again, pounding and banging with everything he had.

She stood and backed away, her body shaking from tears that refused to stop. She heard a crack as the wood splintered.

"I won't let you do this, Alice! You have no right! I do not give my permission, do you hear me? Do you understand!? I won't—"

"Monsieur! Arrêtez-vous!"

A furious struggle took place on the other side as hotel security tried to take him down. She ran to the bathroom, locked the door, and turned the shower on full blast to drown out the noise. She stepped in and let the cold water beat down on her—the colder, the better; anything to numb the pain.

She leaned against the wall and let her body slide to the floor. She stared at the white marble tile, picturing the charred lump of flesh that must be her heart. Whatever beats it had left were wasted. It was beyond saving, and so was she.

There was only one thing left to do. Trust and let go.

So she did.

At some point she was pulled out of the shower. She vaguely heard the sound of her own teeth chattering, but she felt nothing.

Time went by and she slipped in and out of consciousness, awareness diminishing bit by bit. She could see Molly's face—her mouth moving, her eyes pleading. A silent movie playing before her. She watched it with quiet disinterest, wondering if there was a remote nearby. Where was David when you needed him?

Somebody was crying. She was so sick of that sound. She'd cried and cried, but nothing had changed. Nothing was ever going to change. She was lying on her deathbed, her hair white as snow and a moon the color of blood glowing through the window. Someone take her soul already. Persephone. The grim reaper. The devil himself. She didn't care where it ended up. She didn't care, period.

She waited patiently for the darkness. But it didn't come.

Instead she found herself floating over a clear, glassy lake, a cool wind lifting her from within. It was quiet and peaceful up here. Beautiful. The sky was a painting of color and light—deep red, purple, and orange reflected in the still water below. She felt herself smile and her green wings caught a strong updraft, launching her higher.

"Keetie!" she heard someone yell from far below.

It was strange; the voice was familiar. It pulled at the distant recesses of her memory.

"Keetie!" the voice cried again.

It bothered her. Something about it made her flap her wings harder.

"Keetie . . . come back. Please, come back . . ."

It was difficult to ignore, this voice. It cut her deep, slicing through her very being and pulling her in. Without realizing it, she was flying toward it, nose-diving at alarming speeds to reach it before it was too late.

She landed on the windowsill of an isolated dwelling—a simple white structure with four walls and four windows, surrounded by miles of cracked, scorched earth in every direction. The single room was empty, save for a little girl sitting in the center, cross-legged, on a reflective floor. She was staring at her image in the mirrored glass.

"Mirror, mirror, in the floor. Tell me, tell us, where's the door?"

Alice craned her neck to see and realized the little girl was right. There was no door. What a strange room. She placed her hands on the windowsill and looked down.

What happened to her wings? And when did she grow legs?

She looked back up to find the little girl standing on the other side of the glass, staring at her.

Five-year-old Alice regarded her with slitted eyes. "Mirror, mirror, in the flesh."

Alice held her breath, waiting for the next verse. Tiny palms slammed into the window.

"I don't like you," said little Alice.

"Why not?"

"Because you don't love me."

"Why would you say that?"

She banged on the glass. "You left me here! You flew away and left me here all alone!"

"I'm sorry! I didn't know!"

"You knew. Giving in. Giving up. Same. Fucking. Thing."

She whirled around. Soxie stood just behind her, her curly hair blowing in the wind and stiletto heels stabbing the black earth.

"What's the question?" she asked.

"What?"

"What's the question?" Olivia repeated.

"What's the question?" Hadley repeated.

"What's the question?" little Alice repeated.

Alice slowly turned in a circle, four pairs of eyes trained on her with veiled contempt.

"I don't know anymore!"

"Alice, baby. Yes, you do." She turned back to the window. Cithaeron stood on the other side, his eyes clouded dark. He placed his palm flat against the surface. She lifted hers to meet it. All that stood between them was a thin pane of brittle glass. A sliver of hope.

She raised her eyes. Soxie, Olivia, and Hadley stood behind him, the four of them waiting outside the tiny house she was now standing inside. She heard a soft giggle. She turned to see little Alice, seated in the corner, Keetie perched on her shoulder.

"Hello, Alice," Keetie said.

Little Alice giggled again. "I'm glad you came back. We missed you."

"I missed you too," Alice said.

"But it's time for us to go. Do you know the answer yet?"

"I thought it was a question."

Little Alice rolled her eyes. "Same thing."

"Why did I give up?"

"NO!" she yelled.

Keetie squawked and flapped her wings.

Colin tapped on the glass. "Don't you dare, Alice. Don't you dare."

Her heart swelled as she looked into his eyes. As she looked into Soxie's, Olivia's, and Hadley's. As she looked into her own.

"Why I'll never give up," she said. And meant it with everything she was.

Little Alice smiled and nodded toward the door now set in the wall.

Alice reached for the knob.

"Alice."

She turned toward the unearthly voice. Philautia's aura filled the room, a thousand pinpricks of light shimmering around her. They moved and changed and finally combined to form the vision of a white-robed Trojan princess. A face that could launch a thousand ships. But this wasn't Helen of Troy. Philautia hadn't brought down an empire. She'd created one.

The weapon used, however, was the same for both.

Love.

And that was the answer. It was always the answer.

Philautia smiled, and Alice opened the door.

chapter 23

"God is our refuge and strength. He dwells in His city, does marvelous things, and says, 'Be still and know that I am God.'"

Alice listened to the priest's words with a fresh perspective. Hades may be a god, but it didn't make him *the* God. Greek gods. Egyptian gods. Norse gods. Who was to say they hadn't all existed at some point? Maybe they'd all had their shot, like the dinosaurs had had theirs. But now it was someone else's turn.

She looked down at her body in the casket, white hair blending with white satin. It was odd to see it without her soul. She'd read once about a doctor in the early 1900s who believed when a person died, they lost twenty-one grams of weight. Was that what she was right now? Twenty-one grams of Alice, hiding in the Backwards Place? It was an interesting thought.

Molly let out a soft wail. It was sort of convincing, if you didn't know her. The girls were in the front row, their heads down, at least one of them trying not to laugh. As funerals went, this was the least attended and least sad Alice had ever seen.

Her dad approached the coffin, his face drawn and ashen. Unlike the rest of them, he truly looked the part. The guilt she felt as she took in his disheveled appearance was crushing. The only saving grace was that he would likely forget—lose time, like David once had. If only she could forget seeing him like this. It would haunt her until her last day. And contrary to what the occasion might suggest, that was not today.

The large mirror on the opposite wall afforded her access to most of the room and its few mourners. Anything not reflected was a direct entrance to the Realm, which it was important she avoid. So she stayed close to her coffin and waited.

Gavin's eyes were glassy and red. She studied his face, for the first time seeing it through a different lens. He was distraught, there was no question about that. But she detected something new. A sense of purpose. Self-worth, maybe. She'd been so focused on his betrayal that she'd never stopped to wonder why he'd done it.

He'd been young when she was born. Only a year or two older than she was now. Maybe she was wrong to judge him so harshly. The truth was, Judy hadn't been happy for a long time either. Long before the affair. Gavin might have gone about it the wrong way, but in the end, getting divorced had been right for both of them.

Tears streamed down his face as he stared into her dead one. He braced himself against the coffin. A tear dripped onto her black silk dress.

And then it began.

His pupils expanded, bleeding into his eyes like a runny Rorschach painting. His neck muscles strained and his lips curled.

That was her cue. She pulled herself through his body, inviting whatever was hiding inside him into the Backwards Place.

The Furies accepted her invitation.

When they appeared before her, they were more remarkable than she remembered. The confusion on their alabaster faces was almost poetic. It made what she was about to do that much harder.

Black eyes settled on her soul. They could see it, and in that moment, they knew. If she could have said sorry, she would have.

Instead, she rejoined her body.

It was a bizarre sensation, settling back into her own skin. Like being frozen, then thawing out in record time. Millions of tiny sparks spread through inert muscles, coaxing them back to life. Capillaries expanded and contracted. Brain synapses fired and lungs filled with air. Then her heart started beating, fluttering like mad before finding its rhythm once again.

A lot happened that day. Alice came back from the dead, and two infernal goddesses ceased to be. Three seconds after Gavin's body fell to the ground, Soxie pressed a button that released the heavy mirror from the wall and sent it crashing to the ground, where it landed in an explosion of shattered glass.

The Backwards Place was more than just an antechamber to the Realm. Going there was entering a mirror. Becoming a reflection. And should that mirror cease to be, any reflections still stuck inside would cease to be as well.

To be safe, Alice, Hadley, Soxie, and Olivia carefully bagged up all the fragments and set them ablaze in the funeral home's crematorium.

That night, they sat on the balcony of their hotel, observing the tiny streak of light that was Bolle-Marin as it passed by at a distance of ninety million miles—a hair's breadth in galactic terms. It would be visible to the naked eye for several more months, yet never closer than it was now.

"Twenty-five hundred years," Hadley said as she stared at the night sky. "Can you imagine? What do you think the world will be like when it comes back?"

"I don't know. But I know what we need to stop it from becoming."

"Don't worry, Alice. We will. It won't be for nothing."

Alice closed her eyes as the pain in her chest threatened to rip her in two.

The Huntress's vision had come to pass. Thanks to Persephone,

Alice had "died" on the day of the blood moon, when Ptah's Fire burned brightest. The girls had helped gather the ingredients, but Persephone had been responsible for the recipe. A potion—something used to cheat death in her time. Ground-up puffer fish, and a few other things Alice didn't want to know about. A dangerous gambit, but their only chance.

If anyone had bothered to look closely, they would have noticed three strange pieces of black glass clutched in Alice's almost-dead hands—the contents of the remaining compasses. They were the link that allowed her soul to remain tethered to her body but hidden in the Backwards Place. Safe from Hades and his two-thousand-year-old fail-safe.

Her dad was none the wiser, and with Barry's help her mom was still in the dark.

Unfortunately, so was Colin. When she was in her little room with no door, making the choice to live or die, he was making the choice to save her.

He tried to enter the Realm.

The heart monitor beeped steadily, mocking her broken heart. She held his hand, gripping it tight. She wasn't sad. She was angry. Angry at him for being so stupid.

"That's right," she said out loud. "Stupid. Stupid, stupid, stupid!"

She noticed a nurse pause at the doorway but spared her only a glance before settling her gaze back on the stupid love of her life. She willed him to wake up, if only to scream at him. She didn't have a leg to stand on, though. Not really. He'd only done the very thing she'd tried to do—sacrifice himself to save her. They weren't sure what he'd expected to do if he actually made it into the Realm, but it didn't matter. He'd known better and attempted it anyway. The desperate act of a desperate man.

She closed her eyes and laid her head on his chest. She prayed for his life. And if she couldn't have that, she prayed for his soul—that it might find its way to freedom and peace. At a soft knock at the door, she lifted her head.

"It's been two hours," Hadley said. "We should go."

Alice nodded, stood, and leaned over to press her lips gently to his forehead.

"Come back to me," she whispered.

They had a plan. Sort of. But first they needed to make a little stop.

"There's got to be a mirror we can enter," Soxie said, biting her nails, as she stared out the window.

They were on the high-speed TGV train from Paris to Lyon, barreling through the French countryside at two hundred miles an hour. With the freedom to use Uncle May's credit card again, Soxie had reserved the entire car. They needed the privacy.

"But probably not in the evidence room," Olivia pointed out. "Hadley, do you think you can get us in there?"

She let out a puff of air. "I don't know. Depends on the lock, and how much time I have. If it's key coded, forget it. Uncle May really can't help?"

"He's done everything he can," said Soxie. "They aren't budging."

"You guys, there's no way I'm not coming with you."

"Daniels, our only out is a direct Realm jump. You'll be a sitting duck if we get caught."

"Not if Molly comes with us."

Soxie turned toward the front of their car. Molly was lying in a reclined seat with a face mask on, her headphones full blast, and a glass of wine clutched in her hand.

"Uh . . . not sure that's a good idea," Hadley said as Molly drained half the glass.

"Listen, I know she can be a little—"

"Alcoholic?" Olivia interrupted.

"Scattered," Alice finished. "But think about it. She could have claimed my soul ages ago, and she didn't. Not to mention, she's still a goddess. If we're breaking into a police station, it might be a good idea to have one of those with us, right?"

Soxie sighed. "I suppose . . ."

"Worst-case scenario, she can get me out through the Hall of Demons."

"Yeah, but didn't you say that was basically hell?" Hadley asked.

"Oh, it's definitely hell. But we need more bodies to run interference. This isn't up for debate. We're coming with you."

"Gosh, Daniels. You're so bossy now. Death has changed you."

"Funny." Alice threw her half-eaten bread roll at Soxie.

They continued discussing different methods of entry. As Olivia and Soxie argued whether disguises were necessary, Alice's thoughts drifted to why they were doing this. Of course they needed the dagger—but would it be enough?

Philautia's premonition had technically come to pass, and the window for Hades to take her soul by force had closed. But the Realm still existed, which meant the last huntress did as well. She may have cheated death once, but she wasn't immortal. Death would find her again.

That didn't mean Hades was simply going to wait for nature to take its course. He still needed her soul to take over the Realm. If Persephone refused to claim it, she was under no illusion he would fail to find another way. He wanted their world. He wanted dominion over the living, and he played the long game. This brief intermission they found themselves in meant nothing. He would never stop.

There was one obvious solution. Take the grand prize out of the equation: sever the link, destroy the Realm. Whether there was a way to do this without destroying Alice in the process remained to be seen. Time would tell. But time was a luxury Colin could no longer afford.

The prognosis was bleak. He had suffered severe brain damage and was currently on life support. According to Barry, his parents had arrived in Paris shortly after this crew boarded the train to Lyon, and the doctors had told them to begin making preparations.

It was the equivalent of a cosmic slap in the face. She had cheated death, but at what price? He was dying. It was a foregone conclusion. And a part of her would die with him.

She'd spent the last few months believing she would go first. This was so much worse.

She stood. "Guys, I'll be right back."

Alice made her way to the front of the car, her body swaying with the steady motion of the train. She took the seat opposite Molly and heard the tinny sound of jazz music coming from her airline headphones.

Before disturbing her, she turned to look at the picturesque landscape rushing past, imagining what it would be like to see it under different circumstances. To see it through his blue and cloudy dark eyes. Would he have taken her to places he'd lived once upon a time? Shown her the ruins of an old English castle he'd worked in, a battlefield he'd fought in? Would he have taken her to Times Square and kissed her in that same iconic spot?

Baby, I'm going to show you the world.

She closed her eyes, thinking of those last happy moments they'd shared together. God, it hurt. She wondered if the pain would ever stop. He wasn't just her soul mate. He was her reason. And that kind of loss didn't fade; it would stay with her.

If she survived this, she'd have to learn to live with it. But for now, she needed to stop torturing herself with what might have been.

She opened her eyes to nudge Molly's leg and was surprised to find her sitting up, watching her.

"You know, I was in love once too," she said with a wistful smile.

Alice felt her hackles rise. The comparison seemed far from fair. "Love? He literally forced you to be his wife."

"Forever's a long time." Molly turned her gaze to the window. "Hate can easily turn to love; it's practically inevitable."

"I don't know what to say to that."

Molly stared, unseeing, at the passing scenery. "Hades is . . . complicated. Moody. Occasionally hostile. But there were moments when he needed me. When I was all that mattered. And I guess . . . I guess for me, that was enough."

"Then why did you want to leave?"

Molly took an uneven breath. "He loved me. I know he did. He even gave me some of his souls, to prove I was his partner. That we ruled together. But the lure of mankind was too much. The possibility of finally outshining his brothers . . . those wounds ran deeper than his love for me. Somewhere along the way, I lost him."

"Is that why you're really helping me? To punish him?"

"I suppose that's part of it."

"What's the other part?"

Molly carefully traced the rim of her glass with her index finger. "I don't know who he is anymore. His obsession with this world is all that's left. He's never been evil, but now he's using evil to further his agenda. And that's what worries me."

"Worries you? It scares the crap out of me."

"That's good, Bunny. Because it should." Molly finished her wine.

Alice leaned back and closed her eyes, pulling her hair away from her face. "Great. So glad we had this talk."

"I just think you should know what we're dealing with." Molly paused, and the deep whir of the train filled the silence. "And I'm sorry about Cithaeron."

Alice kept her eyes closed. She didn't want to see the pity in Persephone's eyes. "How do I save him? How do I free his soul?"

"You can't. It belongs to Hades."

"No!" she yelled, jumping to her feet.

"Alice?" Soxie called.

Alice knocked the glass out of Molly's hand; it shattered against the wall. "I'm sorry you fell in love with a psychopathic god. I'm sorry you've wasted the past eighteen years drinking yourself stupid to forget him. But if you want to help me, you need to start owning your share of responsibility in this. You've known what he was planning since the beginning. Did you even try to stop it?"

The other girls quickly made their way to the front of the car; she felt their comforting presence just behind her.

Molly gripped the armrests of her seat. "Alice, sweetheart, I did stop it. I didn't claim your soul."

"You might have changed your mind after you got here, but he had a reason to send you. A reason to trust you. What was it? And if you say love, I will throw you off this train."

Molly stared at her, unblinking. "I suppose it's because he didn't have a choice."

"Why didn't he have a choice?" Olivia asked.

Molly kept her eyes on Alice. "Because you're one of mine."

"One of your what?" Hadley whispered.

"Souls," Alice answered. "And he didn't send you here to claim me. He sent you here to bring me back."

chapter 24

They arrived in Lyon shortly before 5:00 p.m. and checked into a hotel to establish a base of operations. They agreed that going in after midnight, when the station might be staffed with a skeleton crew, made the most sense.

Olivia and Soxie were in the Realm, searching for a viable mirror to enter through the map, and Hadley was helping Persephone whip up another potion. Something she'd suggested they have on hand. Alice knew she should be helping, but no one objected when she said she needed some time alone.

She meandered along the river, past a crowded square, and into the winding stone streets of Lyon. Ornate, medieval buildings sat nestled on a hill overlooking the oldest part of town, the slope of which was littered with steepled cathedrals and stone walkways. In the gray-and-yellow light of the gloaming, it was peaceful. Divine, almost.

Her random path led her to a small chapel, hidden away on a narrow street. Candles were burning, yet its altar and pews were empty. At dinnertime, it seemed, wayward worshippers were left to pray unattended.

She knelt in a pew near the back, placed her hands in prayer, and bowed her head. She'd never been very pious, but when she was little,

Judy would tuck her in and together they would recite the Bedtime Prayer. She mouthed the words now, the faintest whisper of sound coming from her lips:

Now I lay me down to sleep,
I pray the Lord my soul to keep.
If I should die before I wake,
I pray the Lord my soul to take.

"My soul to take." It was strange to consider the meaning of those words, knowing what she knew now. She was of the old world. The world of the ancients. Long, long ago, her soul had inhabited a different body. She wondered who she'd been—what kind of life she'd led. If she'd been good or bad. Or perhaps, like most, somewhere in between.

Before Philautia's deal was made, Hades had begun searching for her father's equal. He'd known it was only a matter of time before she would need help with the souls of his damned—the demons he'd allowed the Furies to release. And as a demi-goddess, her connection to her humanity would ensure she asked for one soul, and one soul alone: Cithaeron's.

Hades was happy to oblige. Of course she could have her father's soul. For a price. It was a decision Philautia did not come to lightly, but the chance to redeem Cithaeron while also protecting her precious mankind was too good to pass up. A soul mate for a soul mate. It would be the ultimate sacrifice for all the wrong he had committed in life, and perhaps bring him true salvation in the end. So she agreed.

She had no way of knowing the game was fixed. Hades had no intention of letting Cithaeron simply "find" a soul mate. No. He couldn't afford to take that chance. He needed to ensure it happened when Ptah's Fire returned, when the opportunity to take the Realm was all but guaranteed. And he needed that soul to become a huntress—the last huntress. So he added a condition to their otherwise straightforward deal.

Should the soul mate ever be found, Philautia must give up her existence and surrender the Realm along with it. Hades knew she would agree; there was virtually no downside. If Cithaeron ever actually found his soul mate—and it was common knowledge that soul mates were rare—then she would gladly give up her existence. The mate would be armed with the last of her soul, and thus the power to clear the Realm. Once she died, the Realm would die too. Either way, mankind would be safe.

The deal was made. All that remained was choosing a soul. But there was a problem. Hades brought thousands of souls to Cithaeron, and he rejected them all.

Distraught, Hades entreated Persephone for help. Perhaps the soul they sought lay not within his flock, but hers?

It worked. Cithaeron's soul made its choice immediately. Alice was the chosen one in more ways than one.

By binding them, Persephone and Hades created their key to the Realm. They need only wait until the timing was right. It was a two-thousand-year-old game of chess, and checkmate was the first move.

Alice closed her eyes. She didn't know the secrets of the universe. She didn't know if heaven or hell existed, or what journey souls of this world embarked on when leaving it. But she was here. And she was still Alice. Until her heart stopped beating, that's who she would be. It didn't matter who she'd been before, or where she ended up. What she did now, in this life, was all that mattered.

And as far as she was concerned, the deal was off. Hades wasn't getting that soul.

Their suite was buzzing with activity by the time she returned. Soxie and Olivia were back, poring over architectural blueprints, while Hadley and Molly were still hard at work in one of the bedrooms.

Alice peeked over Olivia's shoulder. "How'd you get those?"

"Take a wild guess."

She looked at Soxie and shook her head. "Never mind. How's it looking?"

Soxie snapped the gum she was chewing. "Well, the mirror we marked is here." She pointed to a restroom on the basement level. "It's a straight shot to the evidence room. The door locks aren't key coded, but there's always at least one desk guard on duty."

"So what do we do?"

"That would be Persephone's department," Olivia said. "And I can't read her, so I have no idea what she's up to in there."

Alice turned toward the closed bedroom door. "Can't you see through Hadley?"

"She doesn't have a clue either. She's been playing messenger all day through the map. So far she's been to Costa Rica and Peru, I think."

"By herself? Is that safe?"

"Trust me, our supermodel can take care of herself," said Soxie. "Papa Caldwell taught her more than just how to pick a lock and hotwire a car."

Alice fell into a nearby chair. "When this is all over, remind me to build monuments in your honors. You guys could rule the world."

Soxie took a breath, deflating the giant bubble she'd just blown. "You're probably right. But let's save it first."

Alice grinned and reached her hand out as Soxie walked by, slapping her a casual side five. They were a team again—only this time one of their members wasn't on a suicide mission.

The bedroom door opened. Hadley walked out, stretching her tall frame. "I'm gonna grab some coffee. Anyone want some?"

"What have you guys been doing in there?" Soxie asked.

Hadley stifled a yawn. "I honestly can't tell you. She's cooking up something, with like strange insect and lizard parts."

"Ew. I hope she doesn't expect us to drink it."

"I don't think it's meant for *us*, but . . ." She looked at Alice.

Alice's face fell. "Really? The death potion wasn't enough?"

Before Hadley could answer, Molly appeared in the doorway. "Alice, sweetie. Can you come in here for a minute?"

Alice leaned her head back and looked to the ceiling for answers. None forthcoming, she slapped her hands on the armrests and jumped to her feet. "Sure, why not."

She followed Molly into the room and closed the door behind her. Looking around, she expected to see a bubbling cauldron, or beakers full of smoking liquid. But it was just Aunt Molly, Queen of The Underworld, dressed in stylish athleisure wear and seated cross-legged on the bed.

Alice leaned against the door, unsure of how to act around her now. She thought back to the times Molly would breeze into town without warning, bearing exotic gifts and even more exotic stories.

When Alice was younger, she would hang on to her aunt's every word, enthralled by her carefree lifestyle. She'd wanted to be her when she grew up, free to travel the world and experience all the wonders it had to offer. As she got older, she started to see some of the cracks in the facade. The selfishness and the drinking. The forgetfulness. But none of this took away from her aunt's charm—her unique Molly-ness. She was who she was: unapologetic and living the life of her choosing. In that regard, Alice still wanted to be her when she grew up. If she got that chance.

Molly cocked her head to the side. "What're you thinking about, Bunny?"

"Still with the Bunny?"

"Sorry. It's just that look on your face. It reminded me of when you were little. When you would hop on my lap to hear my latest tale, your big brown eyes always seeing more than you let on."

Alice crossed her arms and looked down. "Listen. I know this is late, but I'm sorry for hitting you."

"Oh, please. I've taken worse from overhead bins and elbows."

Alice laughed out loud. "This is so crazy."

"What is?"

She threw her hands in the air and gestured to nothing in particular. "You. Me. All of this. I mean, I get it. You're an ancient goddess, and my soul belongs to you."

"Belonged. Past tense, Alice. You're free."

Alice walked to the bed, kneeled next to Molly, and grabbed both her hands. "But don't you see? It doesn't matter. It doesn't matter if you can't set him free too. Otherwise, you might as well take me back now."

"Oh, honey. It's not that simple."

"Of course not. I don't even remember what that word means. But we can try, right? I can't live the rest of this life knowing I didn't do everything I could to save him. I don't care what happens to me, as long as he's free."

Molly cupped her cheek. "I'm sorry. I'm sorry about all of this."

"I'm not. I'll never be sorry he chose me, that you brought us together. You may have had ulterior motives, but it doesn't change what I feel."

She paused, considering her next words.

"I am sorry my aunt Molly died. I know she was sick, and I guess I was never supposed to know her. But it still makes me sad. Mostly for my mom. But here's the thing. When I think back on the past eighteen years, I can't imagine my life without you in it. So you may be this powerful, ancient goddess. You may be Queen of The Underworld, keeper of my soul. But to me, you'll always be Aunt Molly."

Molly's pretty cheeks blushed pink. She pulled Alice into a fierce hug.

"Love you, Bunny," she whispered.

"Love you too, Moll."

Molly's potion of lizard and insect guts wasn't a potion at all. It was a powder, and thankfully it wasn't meant for any of them, including Alice.

"What's it do, Perse?" Soxie asked as she lifted silver domes, inspecting the latest room service delivery.

"You don't want to know. I'm hoping we don't have to use it. It's nasty stuff."

"You . . . you're not going to kill anybody, are you?" Olivia asked, dropping her grilled cheese back on her plate.

"No, sweetie. Don't be ridiculous."

"Well, to be fair, you did kill David."

Molly shot Soxie a disapproving look. "That's different. First, it was an accident. I only meant to knock him out. Second, I was protecting Alice, so it doesn't count. And third, he was already gone, so that doubly doesn't count."

"Is 'doubly' a word?" Hadley asked the room. "And what do you mean, he was already gone?"

"He'd already given his soul to Hades. Nothing was ever going to change that."

They all looked at each other.

"I'm not sorry he's gone," Alice said. "I'm just sorry it had to end that way for him."

Molly patted her on the knee. "Don't be. Nobody forced him; the choice was his to make."

Olivia raised her hand, as if they were in class. "I have a question. If our worlds split, how are you here? How were you able to send Alice's soul, or take David's?"

The question seemed to surprise Molly. "The comet, of course."

"I don't follow."

"For the past two thousand years, only demons could pass through the Realm. Remember what they are; they may be desperate, tortured souls, but they were once human. Their link to mankind enabled them to cross over when immortals couldn't. But Ptah's Fire changes things."

"How?" Olivia asked.

"Think of our worlds as two tectonic plates, floating in space. As the comet draws near, our dimensions move closer together. The closer the comet, the stronger the connection. But once it passes, that connection will fade again. That's why Hades wants her." Molly lifted her wine glass toward Alice. "With control of the Realm, not only can he keep the bridge open, he can use it."

Alice looked up. "So what happens to you if we manage to destroy it?"

Molly smiled. "I've loved being human and living this life— seeing the progress mankind has made, up close and personal. But now I understand why you were taken from us."

"Do tell," Soxie said.

"We were holding you back. If we were still around, I guarantee you wouldn't be flying around in airplanes, visiting the moon, or talking on those." She pointed to Hadley's iPhone. "Mankind needed independence to thrive. To make mistakes, and learn from them. We would only have hindered that. We don't belong here."

"So that's it? You just leave, and Molly dies?" Alice demanded, her voice betraying her emotions.

"Yes, honey. Molly's time has passed. One thing I've learned in my thousands of years in existence is that the universe does not like to be manipulated. It has ways of sorting itself out."

"Maybe there's a way for us to save you too," Alice suggested.

"There's nothing to save. Whatever happens to me and my world, being here was a gift. It's enough." Molly drained the remainder of her glass and leaned back, closing her eyes.

"Besides, forever's just too damn long."

"I like her," Soxie said as the four of them made their way through the Realm, Olivia's compass leading the way. "At first I thought she was a little nutty, but she's grown on me."

"I feel bad for her," Hadley said. "Married to the devil, and now her world is dying. And she doesn't even seem to care."

Olivia hopped onto a side wall. "Hadz, Hades isn't the devil."

"How do you know? Have you ever met the devil?"

"No, but I've met David. Close enough."

"Ha. Good point," Hadley agreed.

"Plus, Hades didn't just get bad souls. He got all of them. He was the only game in town back then. Oh, sorry, Alice."

"Why? It's not like I remember any of it. The Underworld, I mean."

"Thank Zeus for that," said Soxie. "But can you blame Persephone for not caring? What do you do with forever? It sounds exhausting."

They all agreed in silence. The fountain of youth sounded good in theory—you'd have more time—but what good was more when you had it all? An eternity's worth. Soxie was right. It did sound exhausting.

Alice dropped into an elevator shaft behind Hadley. Despite the gravity of their situation, the familiar rush of shifting gravity made her smile. It was good to be back.

She leapt into the air and allowed her body to float for a moment in suspension before turning and landing gracefully on a square mirror. She paused for a moment to take it all in—the miracle that was the Realm. If they succeeded, this could be her last visit.

She understood now why Persephone had tried to keep her away, safe and sound in Colorado. But the truth was, she felt robbed. Robbed of five years in the Realm with the girls. Five years with Colin.

Pain squeezed her heart, and a loud clap of thunder slammed through the corridor.

"What was that?" Soxie yelled.

A flash of light momentarily blinded them.

"I don't understand." Olivia frowned. "Who's projecting this?"

It was a virtual rainstorm. Thousands of mirrors each displaying a tiny piece of the grander design: a dark and stormy sky.

Alice had seen her fair share of summer rainstorms in Fort Collins. When she was eleven years old, it had rained on and off for a week straight, starting the day her first cat, Amos, died. Even though she'd been old enough to know better, she'd been convinced her sadness was the cause.

She closed her eyes and thought of happier times. Hot chocolate with Judy on a cold Christmas day. Laughter with the girls under a Polynesian sun. Riding through the desert with her cowboy, his dimpled smile shaded by the brim of his hat. Memories that made her heart swell and the ache subside.

Someone let out a long, slow whistle.

She opened her eyes. They were in the desert, a pink-and-orange sunset glowing on the horizon. Geometric rock formations, Joshua trees, and saguaro cacti littered the landscape; the comforting ebb and flow of cicada song filled the air.

"Beautiful," Hadley whispered, trailing her fingertips over a nearby mirror.

Alice turned in a slow circle. She could almost feel the waning heat from the setting sun, and the faint breeze as a tumbleweed somersaulted past them from mirror to mirror, on and on.

Olivia stepped in front of her. "It's you."

She could only shrug in response.

"How are you doing this?" Soxie asked, kneeling to place her palm flat on the surface of a mirror that displayed dusty red earth.

"I'm not sure. I think it's connected to my mood. Or what I'm thinking about . . . or both?"

"Quick, think of something else."

"Like what?"

"Doesn't matter," Soxie said. "Anything."

She blew out a breath, closed her eyes, and searched for another memory—a happy one. Their family trip to New York City when she was ten popped into her head. She remembered being excited by the noise and the lights. The energy. She had stared out the taxi window, craning her neck to see the tops of buildings, amazed by the number of people on the sidewalk and their harried pace.

A horn blared.

"Holy shit!"

Alice opened her eyes in time to hit the deck with the rest of them.

"Wow," Hadley said as she picked herself up off the mirrored floor. Or as it now projected, Thirty-Fourth Street.

Thirty-Fourth Street and Fifth Avenue, to be exact. The Empire State Building loomed over them, blocking out the sky, as taxis and delivery trucks barreled by on either side of them. The traffic noise was deafening, increasing in volume with the hum only millions of people can make.

Olivia covered her ears. "Can you stop it?"

Alice squeezed her eyes shut and thought of the lake in Wisconsin. How peaceful and quiet it was, the sky and trees reflected in its calm surface. The traffic din faded.

"Much better," Soxie said. "Pretty."

When Alice opened her eyes, the glassy lake was just as she remembered. She'd even managed to include her fisherman on his little silver boat, bobbing in the distance.

"Pretty crazy, right?" she said.

"Crazy?" Olivia repeated. "I think you're missing the bigger picture."

"Figures, but luckily you never do. Well?" Alice prompted.

"Don't you see?"

Soxie tapped her designer shoe. "Okay, genius, quit milking it and just tell us."

"Fine. Alice, if you can do this, it means Philautia left you more than just the last of her soul. She's given you the powers of the Realm." Olivia made an exaggerated sweep with her arm.

"Powers of the Realm? As in, plural? I wouldn't go that far."

"I would." Hadley hopped from mirror to mirror along the lake's surface. "Look at me. I'm walking on water!"

"Calm down, Jesus." Soxie rolled her eyes. Then, to Alice, she said, "She's right, though. None of us could ever do this."

Olivia nodded. "We need the dagger. It's the only missing piece."

The lake scene slowly dissolved, and the usual dim and colorful light of the Realm returned.

"Well then," Alice said, "let's go get it."

<hr />

The girls landed with a collective thud in front of the police station mirror, Olivia's compass hovering to display the reflection on the other side. It was a typical public restroom mirror, set over two metal sinks. They could see five wooden bathroom stalls, all of which were closed.

"Let's wait a couple minutes," Olivia said. "Make sure those are empty."

Alice glanced at her watch. Despite their virtual trip to the desert and New York City, they were still on schedule, and Molly should already be in place. A toilet flushed.

"Ugh. Not empty," Soxie said with a frown.

A petite woman backed out of a stall, lugging a mop and cleaning bucket with her. She opened the next stall door and propped it open with the bucket before turning around to face the mirror. She washed her hands and started humming a tune while fixing her hair.

"Doesn't look like she's in a hurry," Soxie continued. "How much time do we have?"

"Six minutes."

"Guys, I still don't know what kind of lock we're dealing with, and you can bet it has an alarm."

"None of that's gonna matter if she doesn't leave soon."

They watched as the woman checked her profile, then folded

her body over the sink until her face was inches from the glass. She then proceeded to pop a pimple on her chin. They all leaned back.

"This is so wrong."

"We don't have time for this," Soxie said. "Who wants the honors? Not it."

"Not it!" Hadley and Olivia said in unison.

Alice sighed. "What's happening?"

"You're going first, Daniels."

Her shoulders slumped. "Sounds about right."

It was times like these she felt a little excluded—not so much as an outsider, but as the latecomer who still didn't know the rules and got the short end of the stick because of it. But the past was the past, and there was no changing it now. She'd gladly trade her dignity to be part of their squad for as long as the universe would allow.

Right now, that meant stepping through a mirror and giving this poor woman the scare of a lifetime. She only hoped she didn't have a preexisting heart condition.

After a couple quick stretches to limber up—which the girls clearly found comical—she took a deep breath and crawled through. She immediately swung her legs around and leapt off the counter, prepared to do whatever she could to stop the woman from screaming and alerting the entire station. But she didn't scream. Instead she simply looked up, dropped her phone, and fainted. Alice caught her before her body hit the floor.

Soxie's curly head popped through the glass. "Nice work!"

They pulled the tiny woman into a bathroom stall and propped her against the back wall. Alice did her best to arrange her comfortably. She was going to wake up on the floor next to a toilet, but at least it was the one she'd just cleaned.

When she exited the stall, Olivia was already peeking into the hall.

"How many?" Hadley asked.

"It looks like just the one. Time?"

"One minute."

A loud crash sounded above them, shaking the walls. Fluorescent lights flickered, and a ceiling tile fell to the floor.

"She's early!"

Olivia slammed the door shut and pressed her ear against it. A few seconds later, she turned to Hadley.

"He's on his way upstairs. You ready?"

Hadley nodded as an alarm started blaring. Olivia cracked open the door again and peered out.

"All clear. Go!"

She threw it open and Hadley darted through, the rest of them right on her heels. She sprinted across the hall and slid to her knees at a white metal gate. The hall lights dimmed to an emergency red. She shoved a tiny flashlight in her mouth and got to work on the lock. Bits of plaster fell from the wall.

"It sounds like a bomb went off up there!" Soxie yelled, ducking to avoid sparks from an overloaded bulb.

Olivia looked toward the stairwell, squinting. "Maybe something went wrong."

"No, I think it's okay," Alice said. "She'll be here." It was strange, but she could almost feel her immortal presence in the building. Persephone would come through; she had to.

"I'm in!" Hadley lifted the latch on the outer gate, yanked it open, ran past the empty check-in desk, and fell back on her knees by the inner door, where she deftly began working the more complicated lock.

The door to the ladies' room opened behind them. The cleaning lady wandered out in a daze. She held her head and stared at the emergency lights.

"Alice, stay here. O, let's go." Soxie and Olivia began leading the woman down the hall, struggling to keep her upright. The sound of people shouting had them nearly carrying her up the stairs in their urgency.

When they were out of sight, Alice started bouncing up and

down like David on methademon, anxious to be waiting with no occupation. One minute went by. Then two. Hadley made a frustrated noise with every failed attempt to get the door open.

At four minutes, Alice was ready to abort. It was taking too long.

"Hadz, I think we better—"

"Got it!" she yelled. She turned the handle and flung the door open.

A harsh beeping sound commenced, and a panel on the wall flashed red.

"What's that mean?" Alice asked.

Hadley pulled her inside and shut the door behind them. "It means they already know we're here. We have to hurry."

It was a long, narrow room with row upon row of ceiling-high shelving stacked with various items in clear plastic bags. Knives, guns, brass knuckles, even swords . . . loads of weapons, tagged and bagged, some piled on top of each other. It was overwhelming to look at, let alone sort through. How were they ever going to find it?

Hadley was already digging through the nearest pile when Alice heard male voices in the hall. She quickly grabbed a stepladder and shoved it up against the door. Then she turned around to scan the room again. No mirrors. If they didn't find the dagger, she was trapped. Focus restored, she followed Hadley's lead and got to work.

Mounds of evidence quickly piled up on the floor. They were two madwomen, haphazardly searching for a dagger in a dagger stack. The labels were all in French, and half of them were just numbers and letters.

Hadley groaned and shoved an entire shelf full of items to the floor. "This is impossible!"

She was right; it was impossible for them to find it in time. So Alice would need *it* to find *her*.

"Hadley, quick, give me your hand."

Hadley didn't hesitate. "Now what?"

"Ask your compass to find the dagger."

Hadley's eyes darted to the door as someone banged on it. "They don't work outside the Realm."

"Please, just do it!"

Hadley pulled the shiny disc from her pocket. "Find dagger!"

It remained motionless in her hand. Alice willed the thing to life as the banging got louder and the stepladder began to buckle.

Hadley's eyes were round. "Alice, I can't leave you here!"

"You have to. We can't both get arrested!"

"No!" Hadley shouted. Then, before Alice could object, she forced the compass into her hand—and something exploded from a shelf in the corner, dispersing bags of evidence in every direction and heading toward them like a bullet.

"Look out!" Alice screamed.

The dagger shot toward them, the door burst open, and they both hit the floor, covering their heads.

"Oooh," sang a nasally voice.

Alice looked up. Molly was leaning in the doorway, her hand splayed in front of her face, the dagger poking straight through it. She studied it for a moment before grabbing the handle with her other hand and yanking it out. Blood flowed freely from the wound, yet her expression was one of curiosity, not pain.

"Interesting," she said. "Mortals often equate injury with suffering. This"—she paused to flex her bleeding hand—"is nothing. Mankind's weakness never ceases to amaze me."

Alice felt her pulse begin to race. On the floor at Molly's feet were two police officers, their eyes glassy and faces covered in a thin sheen of powder. What was she doing?

"Persephone?"

Molly's head snapped in her direction. Her eyes were like ancient tar pits, and when she smiled Alice no longer recognized the woman she'd loved her entire life. Whatever humanity she'd possessed was gone.

"You've done well," she said, flipping the dagger upside down. "But it's time to come home."

Home. If that meant what she thought it meant, they may have already lost. Fine. Alice had been prepared for that. But there was no way she was letting Persephone take them both. She reached behind her and pressed the compass into Hadley's hand.

"No, Alice . . ."

She twisted around and grabbed her by the shoulders. "Hadley, I'm begging you, go. You have to—"

She stopped as the breath was suddenly ripped from her lungs. She looked down. The tip of the dagger was protruding just below her sternum, slicing through her chest as easily as it had sliced through Molly's hand. She blinked twice to be sure. And then she felt herself falling.

As the evidence room turned sideways, her last thought was how weird it was that she felt nothing. Nothing at all. Even when Hadley screamed.

chapter 25

This had to be it. How many times could a person die? A dagger had cut a hole straight through her chest. That kind of thing usually sealed the deal. So why was she thinking about being dead? Why was she thinking, period?

She opened her eyes. It was dark and cold, and wickedness smothered her like a thick blanket.

She was back in the Hall of Demons. But this time, she was not alone.

He stood directly in front of her, his steel-gray eyes regarding her curiously. Something about them—something about *him*—was familiar.

The answer is we.

"That night—my dream," she said. "It was you."

"Yours was carefully chosen. I leave nothing to chance."

"No. Cithaeron chose me."

A slithering reptile of a sigh escaped from his mouth. "An illusion. A choice with no choice. Every soul in my world would choose the same."

Every soul in my world. Suddenly, she understood.

"I never belonged to you. You gifted me to Persephone, but I was never yours to give."

His face was difficult to identify. It kept changing, cycling through a myriad of freakish masks. He was trying to scare her, but her fear had been used up.

"It's why you can't claim me. Why Persephone never could."

"My beloved has lost her way, and for that she will suffer. Your soul would have given itself to her, had she but asked. She tended it for centuries. Do you think it did not recognize her? It is of little consequence. You presume I did not account for infinite variables in this game, when I myself created it. You will give your soul to me. That is how this ends."

"Free Cithaeron."

She might have imagined it, but for a fraction of a second—a tiny, infinitesimal fraction of a second—he looked almost sad.

"You mistake the meaning of my words. You are not here to barter. You are not here to choose. You are here to give me your soul. Do it now, or you will suffer in ways you cannot begin to comprehend."

She had no doubt he would make good on that promise. But she had a promise to keep too. To never give up. If she went down, she was going down fighting.

"I have a better idea. Why don't you just go to hell instead."

His eyes turned black, then his body split into a hundred screeching crows that surrounded her in a whirlwind of flapping wings and razor-sharp claws. She felt herself get shredded to bits, and the pain was beyond anything she'd ever endured, including while ashing a demon.

She screamed in agony. It went on and on; the torture was relentless.

It was impossible to think of anything but the pain. *Please, please make it stop*, her mind begged. *Please let death take me.* But it didn't stop. And death could not take her, because she was hidden from death. Would be kept prisoner in the Hall of Demons until she relinquished her soul. And her tormentor had all the time in the world.

Persephone awoke on a thin cot in a tiny cell. Her head was pounding, and her body felt like one big bruise. She attempted to sit up but cried out when she put pressure on her right hand.

It was covered in a thick bandage, and blood was seeping through both sides. She stared at it, searching her memory for some kind of clue.

She carefully pushed herself up and leaned against the cement wall. An old box fan sat just outside the bars, blowing stale air her way. What was the last thing she remembered? Leaving the hotel shortly after midnight, driving the old truck Hadley stole. Parking near the police station and waiting for the designated time to create a distraction. She saw the iPhone timer in her mind's eye—three minutes, thirty-two seconds to go. But then . . .

She closed her eyes, and felt him. His essence. His residue. *Hades.* He had broken through. Despite her efforts to confuse him, he had finally gotten to her. She had hoped she'd be able to block him a little while longer. At least until it was over. When the Realm was destroyed, and Alice's soul was free.

Alice's soul . . . her gem. Her salvation.

She'd known it was special from the start. It was one of thousands he'd gifted her, but this one had shone like a diamond among coals. Even the most enlightened souls needed guidance to keep from getting stuck in perpetual loops of guilt or regret. But this one had been different. Its reality was full of fear and hope.

Fear was reserved for the damned; hope was reserved for the *living*.

It was the most peculiar eternity she had ever seen in a soul, and she'd treasured it, sometimes at the expense of others in her flock. She'd once asked Hades where it came from, and why there were not more like it. She'd been rewarded with unparalleled malice, followed by decades of sulking and silence. She'd learned her lesson, and never asked again.

She'd had every intention of ruling this new world by his side. He was her moon and stars. She would do anything for him. And a soul was just a soul, after all. They had millions.

It was a perfect plan. He was brilliant—far more brilliant than his brothers gave him credit for. He deserved more. More than to be banished to The Underworld and ignored for thousands of years by the one whose love and approval he sought above all others. This was his chance to prove his worth and break free. This was *their* chance.

Then Alice was born.

Persephone was not prepared. She herself had placed the soul in Judy's womb, yet there was no rational explanation for her reaction when that soul became Alice. It was as if her immortal heart took on the properties of her mortal one, and not the other way around. The moment she laid eyes on her, she was lost. There was no going back.

She still loved him, regardless of what he had become. But when the time came to make a choice, it was the easiest she ever made. Love, or purpose.

Hades was one. Alice was both.

What has he done?

Hadley couldn't stop trembling as she gripped the leather handle of the dagger. It wasn't fear that shook her; it was fury. They had been betrayed. Persephone had betrayed them, and Alice had died right in front of her. Those last moments continued to play on repeat in her head. The evil look on Molly's face. The dagger popping through Alice's chest. Her confused smile as she toppled to the floor like a rag doll.

How could it have ended this way? It wasn't fair. Alice didn't deserve this. Not after everything she'd sacrificed. After everything they'd done.

With a flick of her wrist she flipped the dagger; she caught the flat end of the blade, then sent it hurtling across the hotel room suite. It landed right where she wanted: embedded in a chair by the window. If only Molly were sitting in it.

She pulled her knees up and started rocking back and forth, wondering how she was supposed to go on living with this gaping hole in her heart. She knew Soxie and Olivia were suffering too—but they hadn't been there. They didn't have to see the resigned look in Alice's eyes as she disintegrated into nothing—ashed, like a demon. All that was left was the dagger Persephone had tricked them into retrieving.

And what had she done? She'd screamed, like a coward. Grandpa Frank was probably rolling over in his grave.

If only she'd killed her. She was right there; she could have taken the dagger and stabbed Molly in the throat. Instead she'd panicked and jumped back into the Realm. Now Molly was safe in some Lyon holding cell, and the rest of them were left to wonder what it had all been for.

She stared at the dagger sticking out of the chair. At least she hadn't left it behind. At least she'd done that one thing right. She wanted nothing to do with the cursed thing, but if they still had any chance of stopping Hades, it might be their only hope.

Olivia lay on the bed staring at the ceiling, listening to her friend's thoughts in the other room. Hadley was wrong; she *was* there. She was seeing the same horrible images as they played over and over in Hadley's head. She closed her eyes and placed her hand over her chest; watching that knife go through Alice tore a hole in her heart too.

How had they so misjudged Persephone? If only she'd been able to read her. She hated her gift; as far as she was concerned, it was a curse. But she'd accepted it, and tried to use it responsibly. Now it had let her down when she needed it most.

Her black clothing and harsh makeup were her armor. It kept people at a distance, where she needed them. Besides the girls and

Colin, animals were the only companions she could bear. Now Alice was gone, and Colin was dying. Hadley and Soxie were all she had left.

But something wasn't adding up. Why would Persephone save Alice, only to take her in the end? It didn't make sense. They'd used the Realm to escape the police station. It still existed, and as far as they could tell, Hades wasn't controlling it. Yet. What was he waiting for?

She grabbed a pillow, shoved it over her face, and screamed into it. They needed answers. If there was still a way to stop him, they had to keep trying.

I'm sorry, Alice—It's my fault—I put the compass in your hand—I'm so sorry—I'm so sorry—I'm so sorry—I'm so sorry . . .

Hadley. Olivia took a deep breath, unfolded herself from the bed, and joined her friend in the other room. She found her curled into herself on the couch.

Olivia didn't want to cry anymore. Alice deserved more than their tears; she deserved their action. But as she wrapped her arms around Hadley's wailing form, the tears came back all the same.

Soxie signaled the bartender, motioning toward her empty martini glass.

She couldn't sit in that godforsaken suite another minute. The crying. The goddamned crying. She couldn't do it anymore. She couldn't cry anymore, and she couldn't listen to them cry anymore either. She didn't know what to do, so here she was—smoking her first cigarette in years, and hopefully getting drunk enough to stop feeling.

If only her parents could see her now. They'd probably assume she was riding an oxy high and send her right back to rehab. Hypocrites. Where did they think she got the pills in the first place? And did they even once bother to ask why? Maybe if they weren't so closed-minded and sheltered, things would have turned out differently. But the truth was, she was better off with May. And once she'd found the girls, she hadn't needed the damn pills anymore. Or her parents.

But Alice. She needed her. They all did. That little wisp of a thing had gotten under their skin right from the start. How were they going to live without her?

Soxie took a pull on her cigarette as her leg bounced up and down. She wondered what else could distract her from the pain. Because this sucked. It wasn't supposed to end this way. They'd already fixed it. Philautia's premonition was intact. So what was it all for?

"*Mademoiselle*," the bartender announced with a flourish as he replaced her empty glass with a fresh, chilled martini.

She grabbed it and gulped half of it so fast that vodka dribbled down her chin. She set it down and wiped her face with the back of her hand, only then bothering to say, "*Merci*."

He gave her a sympathetic smile before moving down the bar.

She closed her eyes for a moment as the liquor warmed her chest, hoping it might find a way to plug the hole that now resided there. It hurt. Damn, did it hurt. But Hadley and Olivia, they were hurting too. She needed to be strong for them.

She took one last drag on her cigarette, then stubbed it out in the ashtray. She watched as the red embers turned to ash. Alice wasn't perfect. She was naive and idealistic. Stubborn, even. But she didn't do anything half-assed. When she loved, she was all in. After everything she had been through, they'd asked her to keep fighting. Now it was their turn.

Alice lay still on a floor of cold, black mirrors. Her body was broken, and her spirit wasn't far behind. It was a miracle she'd lasted this long. His torture was inventive and absolute. The crows were just the opening act. She had been consumed by angry red flames, the skin melting off her body like hot wax. Torn limb from limb by vicious, doglike creatures with rows of shark teeth and needles for fur. Stung by thousands of scorpions that covered her in a nightmarish coat of red pinchers and curling tails. She had been drowned, blinded, deafened, and eaten alive. She had become misery incarnate.

Between each new and improved brand of torture, she was granted a brief intermission. Her body would be put back together, good as new, awaiting one of two things: submission or pain.

Give me your soul.

No.

Pain.

Give me your soul.

No.

More pain.

Give me your soul.

No.

More pain.

She wasn't going to last much longer. She knew that now, even as she readied herself for the next horrible wave. Her body was technically intact, but her mind's capacity for suffering was waning.

It didn't matter if she'd been here for hours, days, or years. He was immortal. This would be her forever. She wished she was strong enough to endure. After all, wasn't the fate of the human race at stake? But she might as well face it; for all her posturing, she was never going to save the world. All she could hope to do was save one man. And she'd failed him too.

She raised a trembling hand toward the dark glass, picturing his face one last time. She'd only known him as Colin. But she had loved him in every form, even when she was still a captive soul, centuries away from being reborn. She didn't care that Persephone and Hades had bound them, had manipulated the outcome. The why and the how didn't matter.

Love was love.

As her fingertips met the cold glass, an image of him appeared—wavy and distorted at first, but soon clear as day. She was projecting a random montage of moments. So few, but what heartbreakingly beautiful moments. His arms wrapped around her on the window seat as the sun dipped below the mountains. Driving down the highway with her head on his shoulder, lulled by soft music and softer kisses. A cowboy hat, a crushed bouquet of wildflowers, and the promise of love. Moments Hades and his torture could never take away. He might eventually win the day, but these memories were hers. She felt herself smile as she focused on the images in the glass.

Give me your soul.

No.

And she endured.

chapter 26

Persephone paced her cell, her hand and her head throbbing. She needed to get out of here. The police were demanding answers she couldn't give. Who were her accomplices, and how did they escape? What did they steal from the evidence room? And was a form of anthrax used in the attack? They were referring to the Gorgon powder, of course. Hades had used it on at least six people. The paralysis would have worn off by now, but those poor men and women would be in a world of hurt for a few days. She was in a lot of trouble.

She was relieved the girls had escaped but concerned that she had yet to hear from them. It's not like she was going to call them; she'd seen enough crime dramas on television to know those conversations were monitored. But with each minute that passed, she was becoming more agitated. Where were they?

Other than the proper legal channels, her only way out was a one-way ticket. Sending Alice to the Hall of Demons before had carried little risk; Hades would never have touched her before the blood moon. But now all bets were off. If either of them returned to the Hall, there was no coming back.

She continued pacing, sticky with sweat and in desperate need of a shower. As prison cells went, this one didn't seem all that bad. There was no natural light but it was private and clean, with only a mild scent of disinfectant. It was hot, though. Hot and humid—a truly awful combination.

She lifted the hair off her neck and turned toward the fan. A figure stood behind it, watching her.

Despite being a goddess, and immortal, she responded like any normal human being would have: she nearly jumped out of her joggers.

"Goodness, you scared me!" she squealed, breathless and slightly embarrassed. "Who are you?"

The man said nothing. He wasn't attractive in the traditional sense, but he was definitely striking. Judy would call him tall, dark, and mysterious. As if adhering to those clichéd guidelines, he wore a long black coat over a black suit. His hands were in his pockets and his eyes were trained on her.

She placed her hands on her hips to steady herself. "How long have you been standing there?"

Instead of answering, he motioned to someone over his shoulder. She stood back as a police officer turned the corner and opened the cell door. He walked in and ordered her to lift her hands.

She looked from one man to the other as steel handcuffs were slapped on her wrists. "What's going on?"

Again she received no response; she was simply led out of the cell and handed over to the man in black. He took her roughly by the elbow and marched her straight through two lockup gates and out the front door. No questions. No paperwork. Just silent nods from the guards as they buzzed them through.

A black SUV pulled up as they exited the building. A man in the passenger seat jumped out and opened the back door. Her captor proceeded to pull her toward the vehicle, but she dug in her heels.

"Wait. I don't go anywhere until you tell me who you are and what's going on."

"You're not in a position to be making demands, Molly. So if I were you, I would get in the car and stay quiet." His voice was deeper than she expected. Pleasant, yet menacing.

Whoever he was, he had at least gotten her out of that stifling cell. And it wasn't like she had other options. She might as well go along. For now.

She climbed into the car. As he reached over to buckle her seat belt, his head brushed her chin. She caught the scent of soap and sandalwood. It made her sit up straight—and wonder why she was noticing the way he smelled.

He shut the door and walked around to join her in the back seat. A second later, they were on the move.

"Where are we going?"

He said nothing—just continued facing forward like she wasn't there. His profile was sharp angles with an aquiline nose. He reminded her a little of Achilles. He had that angry, reluctant-hero look about him.

"Hello?" She looked at the men in the front seat. "Can someone please tell me what is going on?"

They also ignored her.

She turned back to the man beside her. "I asked you a question."

"And I told you to be quiet."

The curtness of his reply hit a nerve; the goddess in her fumed. She might be at a disadvantage right now, but he was still a mortal. How dare he.

"I dislike your tone," she said sharply. "You would be wise to change it."

The driver coughed, and her mystery man looked shocked. *Good.*

When he spoke next, his body was a master class in stillness. "My niece would like a word with you, but circumstances have made it difficult for her to remain in Lyon. We will meet her in Paris."

"Your niece? Oh, you must be Uncle May!" She practically yelled this into the driver's ear as she leaned forward.

This time, the man in the front passenger seat coughed.

"I prefer Mayron, if you don't mind."

Relief in the form of strong air-conditioning—and the knowledge that this man was *not* an enemy—washed over her. She felt her body relax into the plush leather seat.

"Mayron," she said with ease. "You have no idea how happy I am to see you. The girls are in Paris?"

He waited a beat before responding. "You're . . . happy to see me. I don't understand."

"I've just been so worried." Then, lifting her cuffed hands, she added, "Do you mind if we take these off now? They're a little uncomfortable."

He opened his mouth to say something, hesitated, then turned to the window before saying, "Molly, I've gone to a great deal of trouble to get you out. I don't think you understand the severity of your situation."

She shook her head, confused. "Didn't Soxie tell you who I am?"

"The woman who murdered her friend? Yes. She told me."

Her human heart almost stopped beating, and it was difficult for her words to catch up to her racing thoughts. "What? Someone was killed? Why would he . . . Who was it? Olivia? Hadley? It doesn't make—is Alice okay? She's okay, right? Please, Mayron. Please, you have to tell me!"

He leaned back to get a good look at her. "Am I to understand you don't know? I would assume this is an act, but I happen to be very good at separating truth from lies."

"What don't I know?" she whispered.

He averted his gaze, apparently preferring the window to her pleading stare. "According to Sharon, Alice is dead. By your hand. There is no evidence to support this, but there is CCTV footage of you taking down six armed police officers, and I'm told you manufactured the chemical agent responsible. I have a few colleagues who will be interested in speaking with you after Paris."

Persephone felt bile rise in the back of her throat. His words were poisonous and cruel. Alice dead? No. No, it wasn't possible. "Alice can't be dead!" she blurted out.

"My niece believes she is. Sharon possesses talents I have yet to understand, but lying to me is not one of them. Whether she is mistaken or not, I advise you to cooperate, or . . ."

He kept talking, but she was no longer listening. It couldn't be true. She *refused* for it to be true. Why would Hades kill Alice if he didn't yet have governance over her soul? Whatever crimes he'd committed in Molly's body were premeditated. He would never make that mistake. Which meant only one thing.

". . . courtesy of answering my question."

She turned her head in a daze. "I'm sorry, what?"

His hand curled into a fist. "If you are FSB or Mossad, I will know soon enough. But it would be in your best interest to tell me now."

She had no idea what he was talking about, and she didn't have time to find out.

"Listen, May—sorry, Mayron—I need you to give Soxie a message. It wasn't me. It was Hades, and Alice isn't dead, she's in the Hall of Demons. And I'm going after her."

She noticed the men in front exchanging looks.

"Tell her . . . tell her there's a good chance I won't make it back. But I'll do everything I can to save her. Will you do that? Tell me you understand."

He glanced up front, shifting uncomfortably in his seat. She leaned forward and grabbed his face with her cuffed hands. She didn't have time for him to make up his mind about her.

"Mayron, what do you see? Truth or lies?" She gave him a moment to read her face, knowing full well what he would see.

Her eyes pricked as she realized what Alice must be going through. If she failed, she needed the girls to know. If she couldn't save her, she needed them to keep trying.

"Please. Tell me you'll pass on this message. I'm begging you."

He barely nodded, as if agreeing in spite of himself. It was odd, but she trusted him. He was a man of his word, and she'd known so few.

Without thinking, she pressed her mouth to his. His lips were warm and firm. She closed her eyes and allowed herself five glorious seconds of . . . What was it? Passion? Lust? There was definitely desire. It was so raw. So carnal. So mortal. It may well have been the finest moment she'd ever spent in Molly Wilkins's body.

She pulled away and smiled. "Thank you," she breathed out.

The look on his face plucked at her heartstrings. But Alice needed her; it was time to go. She tore open the gateway and disappeared, leaving the handcuffs behind to fall in a jangle of metal on Mayron's lap.

For an immortal with all the time in the world, Hades seemed to be losing his patience. Alice was holding on; the images she was projecting were giving her strength. There was no limit to the creativity of his torture, but he seemed to be getting bored. During a longer than usual respite, he broke his demonic fourth wall. The god behind the curtain emerged, albeit briefly.

This is tiresome. Why do you not submit? Your soul will not thank you for resisting. It will not reward you in the end. It will simply claim its spot in my kingdom, and you will have suffered for nothing.

It doesn't belong in your kingdom. And neither does Cithaeron. Not anymore.

You ask for what I cannot give. Cithaeron's soul will always return to me.

Free him, and let's find out.

As usual, she had gone too far. This time it was thousands of locusts, blanketing her in a black swarm of biblical proportions. She was being devoured from the inside out and outside in. The pain, excruciating. But . . . locusts?

She did her best to close her mind to the pain and concentrate on her other locusts. The ones that danced with her butterflies. The ones that had recognized her soul's mate long before she had. Hades had made a mistake. Locusts had become a symbol of her comfort and her joy. How could they hurt her?

She closed her eyes and felt the pain begin to fade as thousands of insect bodies took flight, lifting off her body in droves. She imagined the winged creatures morphing into magnificent monarch butterflies, their movement synchronized as they flapped around her in a protective tornado of wind and color.

She heard a deep rumbling sound as the energy in the hall itself began to vibrate. When she opened her eyes, she was assaulted by light streaming in through each barren frame. Millions of her monarchs were floating in the glass all around them—moving images portrayed against fields of green and blue. A vision of heaven, projected on the walls of hell. And she was making it happen. She had taken his power and used it against him.

A soul-shattering scream erupted from her captor, freezing her insides and lifting her off the mirrored floor. When she was slammed back down, she felt her back break. She lost her hold on her projection, and the hall was once again bathed in dim and menacing light. Her beautiful butterflies were gone, replaced with rageful darkness.

She felt something clamp around her neck and lift her slack body into the air. He held her at arm's length, his gray eyes slitted and his face sneering.

GIVE. ME. YOUR. SOUL.

He was done with the inventive torture games. This was hands-on and personal. Intimate. She felt her eyes begin to pop out of their sockets as he squeezed, but she managed a weak laugh.

Get your own.

It was the ultimate rebuke. For all the souls he possessed, there was one he could never have. His own.

His eyes turned black, pure hatred emanating from the depths of his being. The pressure on her neck increased, then her broken body sailed through the air, thrown savagely into a mirror that shattered from the impact.

Black glass fell around her, disintegrating into dust. Too preoccupied to notice, he descended on her like a hawk on its prey, his hands turning into bladelike talons. Alice braced herself for the next assault.

Hades, no!

The hall seemed to turn on its axis, his shock creating an imbalance that set everything off-kilter. Alice felt her body flop and roll with the turn. She landed in a pretzeled heap, her view of the current exchange now sideways.

Kore. You've returned.

Yes.

Come to me.

He was no longer the cold, calculating thing that was about to rip her apart. He looked like a man coming home after a long journey.

Persephone slowly moved toward him. She was still in Molly's body, but in this place, she was also a goddess. The image flickered, like an old projector running choppy reels of film.

Hades, my love.

The closer she got to him, the less Molly shone through. Soon it was just Persephone, kneeling before him in supplication.

She was exactly as legend described—a lovely and youthful maiden. The epitome of classic beauty. It was easy to see why he wanted her. But there was something false in her appearance. The perfection felt wrong.

You seek my forgiveness.

No.

With his attention elsewhere, Alice felt her body begin to knit itself back together. She pulled herself off the floor and crouched next to the wall. Her first instinct was to run—but to where? And besides, something important was happening. Something she needed to see.

I seek your mercy.

Persephone's words were not taken well. His anger began to build again; Alice could feel it in the walls around her, pulsing like a beating heart. His face looked almost pained. Human, even.

Mercy? Have I not given you a kingdom? My souls? Yet still you forsake me. And now you ask for mercy. You test me, Kore. My patience wears thin.

I will not claim this soul for you. It is over.

He laughed. A normal, patronizing, utterly human laugh.

You cannot claim that which was never yours. Now I bore of your insolence. Go and await my command. You have failed me, my heart, but do not fear. This soul will give itself to me. It is all but done.

For the first time, Persephone's angelic form turned toward Alice. "Sweetie, do you trust me?" She sounded like Molly.

The question startled Alice. Did she trust her? She wanted to. Even though she couldn't technically claim her soul, she'd never tried. And how many times had she saved her? From David? The Furies? Even death? But in the end, it really came down to one thing. The question and the answer.

"Yes, Persephone. I trust you."

"Smart girl."

Molly reached a hand toward her. Alice took it, and gave Persephone her soul.

Hades's godliness seemed to shrink before their eyes, reducing his imposing figure to nothing more than a shocked little man. Alice was forgotten. His focus was on Persephone. He flinched when she spoke.

I asked for your mercy. Will you now ask for mine?

Give me that soul.

His voice shook with rage. The power had shifted. He had been outwitted at his own game.

Will you torture me for eternity? Your heart, your queen?

He didn't hesitate.

I will unleash the wrath of the gods upon you, Kore. Do not make me do this. Give it to me.

Persephone bowed her head. Alice could feel her pain seeping into the air around them.

So be it.

Then Molly turned to her and smiled.

"Goodbye, Bunny."

In the blink of an eye, she was gone—and with her, the Realm.

chapter 27

Alice launched off the floor of the evidence room as if breaking through the surface of water, her lungs gasping for air with a loud, squealing wheeze. Sunlight poured through narrow slats set high in the walls, creating crisscross patterns through the musty air. Her chest heaved as she fought to catch her breath. She crawled onto all fours and slowly stood, amazed that her body was still working. Amazed to be alive.

She looked around at the empty shelves. What she'd left in disarray was now an evidence room with no evidence. Hopefully that meant she was in a police station with no police. Either way, she needed to get out. She needed to find the girls. She needed to get back to Colin before it was too late.

Both the inner and outer doors of the evidence room were open, and the check-in desk was empty. She turned into the hall, and did her best to look unhurried and calm in case she came across anyone. When she reached the stairs, she heard voices and movement above. She jogged up with the air of someone who belonged.

On the first floor she caught a whiff of fresh paint and heard the distant sound of a power saw. The hall off the lobby was split in half, one side hidden by a plastic tarp. Two men in hard hats burst through the plastic and spared her a casual nod as they strode past. She walked past the tarp and through a temporary lobby where dozens of people were going about their business, none of them the least bit interested in the girl with the white hair.

Outside the building, the sun was warm and inviting. She lifted her face to the sky and closed her eyes. She'd survived. She was free. But victory was bittersweet.

There would be time later to sift through it all—to let the reality of Persephone's sacrifice sink in. For now, she needed to get to Paris.

"Alice? Alice Daniels?"

She turned toward the voice, lifting her hand to shade her eyes from the sun. A black SUV was parked a few yards away. Leaning against it was an impeccably dressed man with dark hair and darker sunglasses. The coloring was different, but the resemblance was there. She smiled.

"Uncle May."

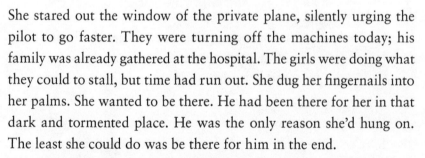

She stared out the window of the private plane, silently urging the pilot to go faster. They were turning off the machines today; his family was already gathered at the hospital. The girls were doing what they could to stall, but time had run out. She dug her fingernails into her palms. She wanted to be there. He had been there for her in that dark and tormented place. He was the only reason she'd hung on. The least she could do was be there for him in the end.

May sat down across from her and motioned to the heaping tray of food behind him. "You should eat something."

"Maybe later." It had been two days since she'd disappeared, but other than water, she didn't trust she could keep anything down.

"I understand you've been through something traumatic." He lifted his hand. "Don't worry, I won't ask you to elaborate. But I wonder if . . ."

"What is it?"

He leaned forward. "Your aunt Molly. I take it she found you?"

Alice considered him for a moment—this mysterious man who, under normal circumstances, she might be wary of. But normal no longer applied to her. All that mattered was that he somehow knew Molly. She wasn't surprised. Curious, maybe. But not surprised. For better or worse, he was part of this now. He deserved answers too.

"Yes, she found me. She saved me."

"And where is she now?"

Olivia was right. This man was impossible to read. Though his eyes were penetrating, his face held no expression. He could be angry, sad, happy, or anxious—there was no way of knowing. He just *was*, and it was slightly unnerving. It made her wonder what Persephone had made of him—what had happened between them. Maybe one day she'd ask. Right now, though, answering the simple truth was all she had energy for.

"I'm sorry, Mayron. She's gone."

His gaze moved to the window. "Gone," he repeated. "And I presume she will not be returning."

"No."

He nodded once, then stood and buttoned his jacket. It was formal and curt, as if he was ending a meeting that should never have taken place.

"We'll be landing soon," he said, no longer meeting her gaze. "Please, eat something. You'll need your strength." He pressed his hand to her shoulder before retreating to a seat at the back of the plane.

———— ✿ ————

Soxie was waiting for her at the hospital entrance, a cigarette dangling from her right hand.

"So you do smoke."

"Back off. My best friend died."

"Again?"

"Yeah, she's getting to be a real pain in the ass that way." She took a long drag and said through the inhale, "Last one. Promise."

"Good." Alice watched her exhale, then extinguish the cigarette in a sand ashtray by the door.

Their eyes met, and they tiredly wrapped their arms around each other. It was an embrace of relief. She was alive, but there was no occasion to celebrate. Not now. Maybe never.

Soxie gripped her shoulders and pulled back. "Alice, listen to me. I'm going to tell you something, and I need you to stay calm."

She felt her legs almost give out. "I'm too late."

Soxie licked her lips and swallowed. She seemed to be trying to find the right words, but there were no words. Not anymore.

Something deep inside Alice snapped. It shocked her, because she thought she was prepared. She thought she was ready to say goodbye. But in that moment, nothing could stop reality from crashing down on her like a rogue wave. He was gone. He was really gone.

She had no idea when she started running. Suddenly, she just was. Through automatic doors, through corridors that smelled of iodine and disinfectant, and up empty concrete stairwells. Soxie yelled for her to stop, but she didn't. She couldn't.

She burst through a door on his floor, slipped on the tile as she turned, and slid painfully onto her side. Olivia and Hadley were standing at the end of the hall; their heads swiveled in her direction.

She picked herself up and kept running, but it felt like she was moving through water. The hall got longer the harder she ran. Then she was on the ground, clawing at the floor and screaming. She could see the door to his room—could see his mom and dad as they poked their faces into the hall. But someone was pulling her back. Hands were gripping her legs, dragging her away. Away from him.

She felt the familiar sting of a needle in her arm, and her body was flipped over and pressed to the floor. Tears ran down her face as she stared at the ceiling, a prisoner in a cage of bodies. Why were they doing this? She just needed to see him! She needed to say goodbye. One last time . . .

Her eyes were already closing when a cold hand caressed her forehead. She forced them open.

Colin was leaning over the side of a wheelchair, looking down at her.

"Hello, Alice," he said with a smile. "How wonderful it is to see you again." And for the briefest of moments, his blue eyes turned a cold, icy gray.

chapter 28

Hades examined his reflection in the mirror. It was a shame the Realm was gone. He would have preferred to be on the other side of this glass, with unfettered access to every corner of the globe and every mortal that passed in front of a mirror. To have entered this world in his own form . . . oh, the things he could have done.

Instead, he was forced to make do with this pathetic human vessel. It was confining and limiting. Degrading, at times. And learning all of modern man's ridiculous customs was an exercise in godly patience. How had Persephone adapted so quickly?

Persephone. It pained him to think of her. Her betrayal would be a thorn in his side for eternity. He had given her everything. Chosen her, above all others, to rule beside him. He'd even loved her once. She'd been his rose in the desert—his island at sea. She'd made The Underworld home, for a time. The novelty of her may have worn off, but her loyalty was what had sustained them. Or so he'd thought.

He supposed he was partly to blame. He'd sent her here; he'd created the opportunity for her to lose her way. She was not strong enough to ignore the temptation of mortality. She tended her souls with empathy, not sympathy. This alone was the reason he'd gifted her the stolen soul. It was the only way to ensure it remained viable, the only way to ensure it would choose her in the end.

And he was right. It did choose her. He just never counted on *her* not choosing *him*. Somewhere in the deep recesses of his being, it hurt. For her to give up her existence, like so many of their fellow gods—he never thought it possible. For all he knew, he was the only one left. Even the Furies, those vile, wretched things, were gone.

Someone was knocking on the door. "Colin, are you okay? It's time for dinner."

He closed his eyes. The mother and father. The architects of this human body. They were becoming a nuisance. He might have to kill them, eventually. But right now he needed them to navigate this strange, new world.

"Thank you, Mother. Dinner sounds lovely. I will emerge shortly."

"O . . . Okay. See you in a bit."

He turned back to his reflection. It was a decent face and body. Nothing compared to the beauty of Adonis, but it would do. It was healthy and strong, and possessed attributes that were pleasing to other mortals. Cithaeron had taken good care of it.

Poor Cithaeron. Doomed to the misery of his own making. His soul was back where it belonged, living in a nightmare of guilt and shame. It would spend eternity in an endless loop, trying and failing to save its other half. If only it knew she saved herself in the end.

That blasted soul. That insufferable human girl. It all came down to her. *Alice.* She'd ruined everything. She turned his love against him, and rendered his demons useless. In one fell swoop, his carefully cultivated crop of cacodemons were transformed into nothing more than detestable butterflies. Two thousand years of knowledge and power, gone in an instant. How did she do it? The Hall of Demons was his creation, not Philautia's.

There was only one conclusion. Philautia knew. She knew, and had somehow armed the girl with the power to stop him. Was he doomed to be consistently betrayed? If she had not already blinked out of existence, he would do it for her. But Alice. Alice still existed.

And she was the reason he was here. Cithaeron's soul was his last remaining link to this world. When it came time to reap it, he made a decision that startled even him. For the first time in thousands of years, he left his kingdom unattended. That was how important she had become to him.

When Colin's mother prattled on about some mundane mortal dilemma, the only thing that stopped him from cutting out her tongue was imagining what he'd do to Alice when he found her. He'd revel in her suffering—to actually smell her flesh burning rather than creating the feeling in her mind.

But too much time had passed since she'd slipped through his fingers at the hospital, and the world had become a much bigger place since he'd last been there. Left unchecked, mankind had spawned at an alarming rate. He'd never seen so many mortals, and from what he was told, there were billions more. *Billions*. Finding her was going to be more difficult than he'd thought.

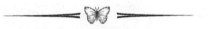

Dinner that evening was its own form of torture. Hades considered the possibility of adding a meal with Colin's parents to his plans for Alice, but even he was not that cruel. He laughed at his own humanlike wit.

"What's so funny?"

He took another bite of semi-edible food. "Oh, nothing, Father. Just enjoying this wonderful nourishment."

"Colin, please. Don't talk with your mouth full."

He quickly set his knife down, lest he accidentally shove it through Mother's ear. He slowly chewed the rest of the unpalatable substance and swallowed.

"Sincere apologies," he said with his brightest smile, one he'd practiced earlier in the mirror.

He noticed the female exchanging looks with the male. She did this quite often. He found it irritating and disrespectful. Did he really need both of them? Perhaps he should kill the mother now.

"We want to talk to you about something," the mother said.

He leaned back and crossed his arms over his chest, mimicking the posture of the father. "I would enjoy talking about something, Mother. Please, proceed."

She glanced across the table before continuing. "Do you remember your friend David? He was on the lacrosse team with you at Remington."

He perked up. David, his demon gatherer. He had forgotten about him. After the connection was severed, he'd lost interest. The bulk of his army had already been returned; he'd had more than enough information and power for his invasion. The mortal had become obsolete.

"What do you know of David?"

"Well, there was an accident. Actually, no. That's not the right word. Incident, maybe? It was awful. His poor mother."

"And what was the nature of this incident?"

She looked to the father, who cleared his throat and continued for her, "Your friend was hurt in some kind of attack. He's alive, but not doing well. He's on life support and . . . well, his parents have decided to take him off."

Hades frowned. David's soul was technically promised to him, but he wasn't sure he still wanted it. The human had been predictable and boring. He doubted his soul was much of a prize. But he might as well claim it while he was here.

"I understand. Where might I find it? Er . . . him?"

The mother grabbed his hand. "Oh, sweetheart, will you really go see him? I know his parents are struggling with this decision, and if they see you, maybe it will change their mind."

"Change their mind? Why would I want to do that?"

She sat back. "Because you're living proof that prayers can be answered—that miracles happen. When I think about what we almost did . . . Oh, Colin, will you ever forgive us?"

Tears began rolling down her ruddy cheeks. Hades cringed; it was a pathetic display of human emotion.

The father shifted in his chair. "Son, I don't know if David's got a chance, but your mother here believes the Martins should talk to you before they go through with this. We were wrong to give up hope. Maybe they are too."

Ah, now he understood. They believed hope was the same as worship and sacrifice—that their son's recovery was due to divine intervention. In that sense, they weren't wrong; a god had intervened. Yet still they insisted on giving credit to "hope and prayers." How much these humans had to learn.

"Very well. I shall go." He had no intention of doing what they asked, but an interesting thought occurred to him. If he could take over David's body as well, the possibilities were limitless. Perhaps he still had a shot at this world after all.

He was led to something called an intensive care unit. A woman with swollen eyes greeted them outside David's room.

He barely listened as the mortals exchanged words.

We're so sorry, Kathy.

Thank you for coming, Maureen.

If there's anything we can do . . .

Really appreciate it, Bill.

What do the doctors say?

Well, as you know . . .

It went on for ages. He had no choice but to interrupt.

"I wish to see David now."

Kathy paused, glancing at Colin's mother. Perhaps this infuriating habit was a female thing.

"Would this not be suitable? I mean only to pay my last respects. I am told you intend to terminate the body soon."

The three of them collectively gasped. He had said something wrong.

Rather than attempt to remedy his mistake, he simply stayed silent. The concept of embarrassment had always baffled him; it was such a mortal emotion. Yet all three humans displayed dreadful examples of such embarrassment, making the whole scene quite comical.

After a silly explanation about the residual effects of something called amnesia, Kathy was led away like a child and he was at last sent into David's room alone.

He could not have asked for a more perfect outcome.

The second he entered, he could tell the soul had already detached from the body. It was still tethered, but it was lingering. The complicated machinery surrounding the deathbed was succeeding only in trapping it here. Keeping the body alive and preventing the soul from moving on was pointless and wasteful. In time, he'd put a stop to such senseless rituals.

He clasped his hands behind his back and moved toward the bed. The room was full of annoying sounds—whirring, beeping, whooshing. He leaned forward, mesmerized by the movement of the chest as air was pumped into the body, mimicking the breath of life.

He could feel David's soul searching for him, ready to fulfill its commitment. Prize though it was not, reaping it was the only way to test his theory. He closed his eyes and reached into his immortal being to claim that which had been promised to him.

"Hades."

His eyes popped open. *Alice.*

What a delicious surprise. If he hadn't been focusing on David, he would have sensed her sooner. A smile crept onto his face, and he slowly turned around.

She stood just inside the doorway, her hands clenched at her sides.

"I have missed you, Alice. I grew weary searching for you."

"You don't belong here. And you don't deserve that body."

She was a sad little thing, visibly trembling. He leaned against David's bed, making a show of inspecting Colin's body.

"You are right. I do not deserve this body. It is less, while I am more. But do not worry. I will make far better use of it than Cithaeron ever did."

Her face paled, and the pain he saw there warmed his immortal heart.

"Did you take him? Did you take his soul?"

He laughed. "You ridiculous child. Of course I did. It belongs to me. I do not forfeit my most precious toys."

"And Persephone? Was she just another of your precious toys?"

He stepped forward. "Be careful, little one. Your suffering will be immense, but I am quite capable of prolonging it for years. Decades. You will be begging for death, and should you continue to test me I will ensure it does not come for a long, long time."

Her dull eyes shone with fear, but she continued to stand her ground. It was both impressive and aggravating.

"This isn't your Hall of Demons. You have no power here."

He shook his head, disappointed by her naivety. "Perhaps not yet. But it is typical you would underestimate me. You have no respect for immortality. It knows no bounds. You will suffer, and then you will die. That is how this always ends."

Her eyelids fluttered. She took an uneven breath, no doubt preparing to insult him once again. But then—

"Do you still want my soul?"

He snapped to attention, her question more astonishing than her courage. He slowly stood to Colin's full height. "You would willingly give it to me, after all that has passed?"

"Maybe. On one condition."

He took a step toward her, ready to wrap his bare hands around her tiny throat. "Condition?" he spat.

"Tell me where it came from, and you can have it."

This stopped him short. Clever, clever girl. For his own protection, he had never spoken of it. At this point, he was probably safe. But 2,500-year-old habits die hard. He stalled.

"It is of little importance. In the end, all souls belong to the universe."

A strange sort of stilted, piglet sound came out of her nose. "Nice try. But try again."

He could not help himself. One giant step forward and the back of his hand struck the side of her face, sending her body careening into the wall.

He stared down at her cowering form. "Do you think you experienced pain in the Hall of Demons? That was nothing compared to what you will endure here. You—"

He was interrupted by a loud, sustained noise, followed by a series of staccato beeps. He turned around. David was standing directly behind him, a flimsy, paperlike gown hanging loosely from his skeletal frame.

"The mortal is right, Hades. You do not belong here."

Colin's heart began to beat erratically.

"Is it really you?" Hades whispered.

"Yes, brother. It is me."

His eyes welled with tears. Thousands of years of silence. Thousands of years believing he was forgotten. Discarded. "Why? Why did you abandon me?"

Zeus stepped forward. "I did not abandon you, brother. You abandoned yourself. By failing to accept your destiny, you abandoned us all. Now our world is dying. Olympus is gone. The seas have turned to sand. Soon there will be nothing left but a barren and lifeless wasteland. Even I cannot stop it."

"Then rule this world with me! It is ripe for change. With you by my side, there is nothing we cannot conquer!"

Zeus placed a hand on his shoulder. "You reach for the stars without leaving the ground. You harness energy you do not understand. The power of Ptah's Fire does not come without a price. It is a dangerous game you've played, brother. I am sorry, but you have lost."

"Please, my king—I beg you," Hades pleaded, even as Colin's legs buckled beneath him. Mortal tears flowed freely down his face as he realized what he had done. For it was not once he used Ptah's Fire, but twice. The second time was to rule mankind, but the first was to steal a soul. An *original* soul. Such a prize had felt worth the risk. It held the basic code to creation and could have provided answers for them all. Instead he'd used it for his own gain, and it would seem that Ptah's Fire did not approve.

He was the reason his world was dying.

Osiris had vowed revenge. Twenty-five hundred years later, he was finally getting it.

Hades fell to his knees. Zeus was right; the game was lost. For all his power, he had been bested by an Egyptian god who no longer existed. In the end, neither of them had won. But the universe was having a good laugh at their expense.

He felt the sting of a scorpion on the back of his neck and wondered how he could have been so blind. But it was too late; the darkness was already approaching. He fell to the ground and drifted away.

"What a dick."

"Yeah, but didn't you feel a little bad for him too?"

Alice pressed the ice pack to her face and held her tongue. She'd let Soxie and Hadley hash this one out on their own.

"Um, that's a hard no, Hadz," Soxie said.

"Sorry, that came out wrong. I meant, what made him that way? From what I've read, he wasn't supposed to be evil. Not in the true sense of the word."

Soxie snorted. "I guess he missed that Wikipedia entry."

"Ha ha. I'm just saying. I know we had help, but if a powerful god like Hades folded that quickly, what does that say about what we're dealing with now? Should we be more nervous?"

No one responded. Hadley had a point, but it was a little premature to start hypothesizing about something none of them could even begin to understand. Besides, they weren't finished dealing with the current threat.

Alice turned to look at the unconscious body lying in the back seat. It was hard not to see Colin lying there. It was hard to admit he was gone. She'd cried for days after Paris. The girls had known the minute he awoke that it wasn't him. Soxie had tried to warn her, but it had happened the way it happened. And part of her had died that day.

That part of her would always be dead. But the rest of her would go on living. She owed that to him and the girls. She owed it to Persephone.

"Jesus, it's dark out here. Are the brights on?"

Hadley felt around the steering wheel. "I thought . . . Oh, here we go." The deserted road was bathed in a stronger beam of light.

"I thought you knew everything about cars," Soxie said.

"Give me a break. Grandpa Frank never dealt in Escalades, and my dad hardly ever has them on the lot. If he finds out it's missing, I'm screwed."

"Relax. We'll have it back before dawn. Just try not to run us off the road."

"Do you want to drive?" Hadley asked.

"Guys, c'mon. Keep it down," Olivia said. "Let's just get there. I don't want him waking up before . . . well, before."

Hadley glanced behind her. "Is that a possibility?"

"I don't think so. I gave him enough to tranq a horse. But, you know. He is a god."

They had spent the past few weeks in hiding. Mayron had sent her mom and Barry to Spain to stay with the Roxlands, and he'd promised to have eyes on Olivia's parents. Hadley had told him not to bother with hers—said her dad and brother could take care of themselves, and if they found out they were being watched, it wouldn't end well. Alice wasn't sure if she was protecting them, Mayron, or herself.

It was brutal, the waiting. Wondering where Hades might cause harm. Wishing she could warn Colin's parents. Anyone who came within twenty feet of him.

They'd all started to wonder if this was the new normal. And then she'd had a dream that wasn't a dream but a vision. A message from a god. The king of the gods.

"Slow down," Olivia said. "I think the turnoff is up here."

Hadley peered into the darkness and brought the vehicle to a crawl. "How did you even know this was here?"

"It's protected land," Olivia said. "I drove here with my dad when I was twelve, when he was working for the state. I remember thinking that it felt like being on another planet."

Alice agreed. They were now bouncing along an uneven dirt road, barely visible even in the Escalade's high beams. Tall tufts of dry weeds grew down the middle. It was clear no vehicle had traversed this road in some time. Possibly since Olivia and her dad.

Twenty minutes later, they hit asphalt.

"Did we make a wrong turn?"

"No, this is perfect," Olivia said. "It's an abandoned highway. They stopped paving it when they discovered some rare plant or something. We're as far out as we're gonna get. Hadley, pull over wherever it looks good."

They were all quiet as Hadley slowed down and put the car in park. The reality of what they were about to do was sinking in. Could they even do it? They had to. They had no choice.

Alice had no choice. It was her responsibility, and it should be her that did it. She looked down at the worn relic in her hand. The dagger that started it all. The dagger that would end it all. She took a deep breath and opened the door.

chapter 29

The Remington Reel—Thursday, December 12th
Moving On

Well, Sharks, this is it. Our final Reel. It's been an honor serving the Remington community these past four years. We hope you've found our online publication useful, informative, and entertaining.

And now, a crap poem:

With the holidays here,
Parties beckon with eggnog and beer.
But before we sign off,
A few last items to bring you cheer.

David Martin has made a full recovery. As most of you know, he was part of that group that went missing last summer. He suffered a nasty blow to the head, but our sources say he's back to his handsome, charming self. Good as new. Maybe even better. But as for what he and his Wayward gal pals were up to, it's anybody's guess. This reporter received nothing but the runaround from local law enforcement. So what was it? Were they on the run from a drug cartel? Knocking off Shell stations on old Route 66? Or were they just sowing their wild oats before adulting turns real? Whatever it was, we're glad they're home safe and sound, if still a college semester behind.

Speaking of the Waywards, we hear a little wedding is taking place on the Roxland estate this Saturday. It seems the chauffeur has found true love at last. Eat your heart out, Downton Abbey. Barold William McGregor, we wish you and your bride years of happiness and joy.

And finally, don't forget to sign our virtual yearbook. You'll want this perpetual link to your teenage years so that ten, twenty, thirty years from now you can look back on how young and dumb we were (but damn were we good-looking).

Thanks again for letting us document the highs and the lows, and everything in between. Go, Sharks. Onwards and upwards!

Your friends,
Remington & Aaron

This final installment of The Reel is dedicated to the memory of former lacrosse captain and Remington graduate Colin Tinsley. We hope you're hitching a ride with Bolle-Marin, waving good-bye as you head back out into the great unknown. Farewell and Godspeed, brother. Godspeed.

Alice sat alone on the window seat, her long silk bridesmaid dress pooling beneath her, her strappy shoes kicked to the floor. It was only five, but the sun was well on its way to setting and the party downstairs was just getting started. She could hear Barry's brother Hamish starting in on the bagpipes again. She smiled as she heard the band trying to compete. Nobody cared. There were a lot of happy, smiling faces down there, ready to let loose. And that was good; some of them had been through a lot these past few weeks. It was time to celebrate.

She heard a soft meow. She turned to see Boop sitting on the floor next to her shoes, watching her.

"Hey, buddy." She patted the cushion next to her.

He lifted his paw and began to clean himself.

She chuckled and looked back out the window. If he joined her, it had to be his idea. Cats.

She loved this view. The pink-and-orange sky, the dusty brown hills. She still couldn't believe she lived here. At least until next fall. She and the girls were deferring college for a year, maybe to do some traveling. Although in less than a year she'd already been to South America, Europe, and most of the Midwest. She might just stay put for a while.

She heard a high-pitched laugh break through the noise from below. Chloe. She and Rachel had flown in from Colorado for the wedding, and she was already a big hit here. Hadley was ready to adopt her, and Olivia couldn't stop reading her bubbly thoughts. She was just that girl. Adorable and carefree. It was impossible not to fall in love with her.

As for Rachel, there had been a little tension between her and Soxie at first. They were just very similar creatures: hard edges and suspicious minds, but big hearts. All it had taken was Rachel mentioning she'd kill for Soxie's hair, however, and the next thing Alice knew she'd been knee-deep in her closet, trying on shoes.

She felt a thump as Boop landed next to her.

"Oh, so nice of you to join me."

He purred, pushing his head into her hand.

"Someone thinks he's lord of the manor, doesn't he?"

He purred louder and nipped her arm.

She laughed and petted his shiny black fur to avoid further punishment, then turned back toward the window as the light began to fade, absently stroking his vibrating coat. She was thrilled for her mom; she and Barry finding each other was the best thing to come out of all this. Even her dad had come out on top—still working for the Roxlands and, from what she heard, doing a bang-up job. Go figure.

Life went on. Against all odds, she was still here. White hair and all. A genetic defect, they were calling it. She didn't mind. Every time she looked in the mirror, it was a reminder of what they'd managed to do. Hades may have had other plans for those demons, but in cop parlance, at least they got them off the streets. Had they saved mankind? Hardly. Immortal was immortal. The dagger may have sent Hades back to The Underworld, but she didn't trust that big brother could keep him in line forever.

The door was open now. The Realm was gone, but Zeus had used her to create another. This one didn't need mirrors; it was a straight line of sight. Through her. Through Soxie, Olivia, and Hadley. Even Janie and Margot, retired though they may be. Part of Philautia's soul still existed in all of them. She was the link; she always had been. And now, so were they.

"Hey, thought we'd find you here."

She smiled and turned around to greet her friends. Her sisters. They were all wearing a different color of the same dress: Alice's was white, Soxie's was green, Hadley's was blue, and Olivia's, of course, was black. Judy had wanted them all in the wedding, including Molly. Right up until the last minute, she'd had a yellow dress steamed and hanging in the wardrobe. Molly's phone was disconnected, her landlord hadn't heard from her in weeks, and she'd been terminated from the airline, and still Judy refused to believe she wouldn't turn up.

One day she would have to face the truth, and Alice would be there for her when she grieved. She'd be grieving for two different people, but that was okay. Both would be forever loved.

Alice pulled her knees up to make room. Boop gave her a dirty look, then jumped down and sauntered off, annoyed by the intrusion. Hadley and Olivia climbed over her to lean against the window, and Soxie flopped down in Boop's now-vacant spot.

"You okay, Daniels?"

"Yeah. Just needed a minute."

They all turned toward the other end of the hall as raucous laughter traveled up the stairs.

"I don't blame you," Hadley said with a giggle. "It's getting pretty nuts down there. Barry's family can party."

"I'm sure Chloe and Rachel will give them a run for their money."

"FYI, Chloe is crushing hard on Barry's nephew Niall. Poor guy doesn't stand a chance, does he?"

Soxie slapped Olivia's arm. "Can you leave her head alone for five minutes?"

"Ow. Not possible. It's like background music. It's always there, but kind of nice at the same time. I just pay attention when it gets good."

Alice made a show of putting her face in her hands. "Poor Chloe."

"Well," Olivia said, "there was one other thing."

She looked up. All three of her friends were staring at her.

"She's worried about you, Alice. Now that your mom is remarried, she and Rachel want you to move back to Colorado. We . . . we understand if that would be easier for you."

Was this some kind of test? Or did they just want to get slapped?

Fine, then. She smacked each of their legs like she was whaling on a drum set. They all yelled different versions of "Ouch!" and "What the hell!"

"I came back from the dead *three times*," Alice snapped. "Who do you think I came back for? They're my friends, but you're my family."

Olivia rubbed her leg. "Fine. We're family. Just—everybody stop hitting me."

The four of them looked at each other and laughed. Seconds later the band started playing "Moon River," and they linked hands.

"I love this song. And I love you guys." Hadley leaned her head against the window. The sun was just setting behind her, casting them all in a dreamlike light.

"Me too."

"Me three."

"Four," Alice added with a smile, then closed her eyes. They held hands through the entire song. As broken as her heart would always be, she couldn't argue that she wasn't blessed. She was here, and so were they. And life would go on.

the gift

Two and a half weeks later, Alice found herself alone in the Roxland mansion for the first time. Barry and Judy were on their honeymoon, the wedding guests had taken their leave, and the staff was off for the holiday. May was off doing whatever it was May did, and Soxie was on her morning ride. It was New Year's Eve.

With a satisfied yawn, Alice slowly padded down the stairs to the kitchen. As she turned the corner, she was greeted by the sound of scrambling paws. The so-called guard dogs hopped and howled. Fred and Ginger, the "puppies," were even bigger than Schlemmer now.

"Guys, c'mon. I know you've been fed." At the sound of her voice, all three plopped down on their haunches and cocked their heads to the side.

"No way. I'm not falling for it!"

Ginger barked, Fred whined, and Schlemmer sneezed. She threw her hands up. "Fine."

They started spinning and barking, all clacking paws and wiggling behinds. She shook her head as they followed her to the pantry. They sure knew a sucker when they sniffed one.

She made each of them sit and shake before giving them their organic something-or-other milk bones, then shuffled over to the kitchen island to pour herself some liquid morning. Soxie had brewed a full pot, bless her heart.

It had been an exhausting Christmas—the wedding, the house-guests, the holiday parties. It had been nice to have everyone under one roof, but less nice answering questions about their disappearance. Mayron had helped with the police, but their friends and family had needed more.

In the end, they'd settled on "wrong place, wrong time"—a crime witnessed and four girls forced to go into hiding. Now that the situation was resolved, did they want to talk about it? No, not yet. One day, perhaps. But please forgive them if that day never came.

She made her way to the library, her favorite place in the house. It was cozy and quiet. She settled onto the leather couch and plopped her slippered feet on the table. Sipping her coffee, she stared at the mirror above the fireplace. It was hard to believe the Realm was gone. That nothing existed on the other side of that glass but a brick wall and a hidden safe. A safe that held no money or stock certificates. No bars of gold or precious gems. Just an old, tarnished knife.

Protect it, he'd told her. *Do not let it fall into the wrong hands.*

Wrong hands? And who would those belong to? He hadn't given an answer, just a vision of a hospital room, a god masquerading as a man, and the question that would help bring his brother to his knees. None of them had thought it would work. But it had. If it weren't for Zeus, there was no telling where they'd be right now. But, as she was quickly learning, in the game of gods and men, no good deed went unpunished.

The dagger. Her soul. Maybe neither belonged in this world, but for now, that was where they would remain. She missed the Realm, but she had the girls. That was enough.

As for Cithaeron . . . she tried not to think about him too much. It wasn't fair, but she had to compartmentalize. Her survival depended on it.

She reached her hand toward the mirror, picturing his face. The surface rippled and an image appeared. He was smiling at her, tipping the brim of his hat.

The Realm was gone, but her power to manipulate mirrors remained. It probably meant something. Something significant. But until Olivia figured it out, Alice would pretend it was for this. A way to keep him with her. A reminder that somehow, some way, she would find him again.

David pulled into the circular drive, his palms damp with sweat. He hadn't been this nervous in . . . well, he couldn't remember how long.

How was she going to react? He still didn't know how to process everything himself. All he remembered was waking up in the hospital and being told he was lucky to be alive. He had been in a coma no one thought he would survive. The doctors were stumped. It was a miracle.

It had taken some time and physical therapy, but he'd gained some weight and was walking again. Every day he was building back his strength. Becoming himself again.

He had wanted to come sooner. It was hard to stay away, but when he'd looked in the mirror, all he saw was the horrible human being he had been. What if that was all she still saw too?

He reached up and felt his cheek where she'd once slapped him. He'd known then he was falling for her. Hell, as much as he'd tried not to show it, he'd already been in love with her. And kissing her . . . kissing her was everything. It was coming home.

Would she ever let him kiss her again? Or would she take one look at him and slam the door in his face? He closed his eyes and took a deep breath. He had waited long enough. He was here. He had to try.

He exhaled, grabbed her gift off the passenger seat, and stepped out of the car.

She was just pouring her second cup of coffee when the doorbell rang. The dogs jumped up from their sunny spots by the window and went berserk, flying out of the kitchen toward the front of the house.

She looked at the clock on the microwave. 8:45 a.m. on a Sunday? Whoever it was would have to come back later. She wasn't answering the Roxlands' door in a robe and flannel pajamas.

She decided to wait in the kitchen until they were gone. She topped off her coffee and took another sip before a thought occurred to her: *How did they get past the front gate?* She should have received a call to buzz them in.

She set down her mug and ran to the nearest security panel in the butler's pantry. She scanned the small boxes, found the front-entrance camera, and tapped to enlarge. Whoever he was, he was still there, sitting on the steps with his back to the door. She minimized, searched the other boxes, and enlarged the one trained on the driveway. She couldn't make out the person, but she knew that car. She definitely knew that car.

She slowly leaned back. What was he doing here? Was he hoping for another fix of methademon? Or to gloat that he survived when Colin didn't? Or worse . . . could Hades have found his way back somehow? Was that him outside, ready to murder her the minute she opened the door? She stared at the images on the screen, panic building in her chest. Why was he just sitting there?

She whistled quietly for the dogs.

"Schlem? Ginger?"

She was answered with silence.

She looked back at the security panel; he hadn't moved. Her eyes hovered over the intercom button. She steeled herself and pressed it.

"You have exactly thirty seconds to leave before I call the police."

His head snapped up and turned toward the door. "Alice?"

"I mean it, David. Leave. Now."

Suddenly, he was up and standing, his hands pressed against the door. She jumped back.

"Alice, please. Let me talk to you."

She maximized the front-entrance view again. Something was . . . wrong. But that wasn't her problem. He, thankfully, was no longer her problem.

"I'm not interested in anything you have to say. Now please, leave."

He pushed off the door and looked up, searching for the security camera. He found it a second later.

"You told me to come back to you."

She stopped breathing, staring at his face on the screen. Her hand slid off the intercom and fell limply to her side. A slight dizziness came over her, as if her mind and body had just been sent adrift, sailing away on a soft ocean breeze. She closed her eyes, not daring to hope.

"Baby, it's me."

Flutter.

Her eyes popped open, and she covered her mouth as a sob escaped. Before she knew it, she was floating through the kitchen. Down the hall. Past the three dogs who were sitting like statues, staring at the front door. She watched her hand reach for the handle and pull it open.

He was just turning around from picking something up. He froze as their eyes met.

She stood in the entryway, her hand gripping the solid wood door for support. She blinked back tears as a dog whined behind her.

"Cithaeron?"

His green eyes clouded dark. He stepped forward, a bouquet of wildflowers clasped in his hand.

"What, you don't think this is a good look for me?"

She laughed as tears streamed down her face. "You pick those flowers yourself, Cowboy?"

"Damn. I knew you were going to ask me that. What's the right answer again?"

She stared into his eyes. Green. Blue. Cloudy. Dark. They could be bright yellow, for all she cared. It didn't matter—it had never mattered—because they were his.

"It's really you. You're here."

He took her hand and pressed it to his heart, drawing her close. "I came back to ask you something."

"Yes."

He grinned and shook his head. "Can you let me ask you first?"

"Okay."

He traced his finger down the side of her face. "Alice Marie Daniels, will you marry me?"

She sniffed, her smile so wide it hurt. "David Martin and Alice Daniels. *The Reel* would have had a field day."

His eyebrow lifted. "Is that my yes?"

She stepped into his arms. "It was always your yes."

He'd kissed her before, and he'd kiss her again. But this kiss was different. It was passion, hurt, love, and betrayal. Lies, truths, fear, and desire. It was all the good and bad—everything that made up a life—wrapped into one long, divinely perfect kiss.

It was forgiveness, and a new beginning.

She pulled away, tears still rolling down her face and salting her lips. "I've missed you."

He groaned, lifted her in his arms, and carried her across the threshold, pressing his mouth back to hers. Excited dogs twirled around them, howling their approval, while on the doorstep another bouquet of wildflowers lay forgotten, crushed by love.

about the author

L enore Borja grew up in Phoenix, Arizona, and attended Arizona State University before moving to New York City to study acting at the American Academy of Dramatic Arts. After a brief career as an actress, she spent several years working in executive search and human resources in New York and San Francisco. She now resides in Fort Collins, Colorado, with her husband and a bossy feline named Maximus. When she's not writing, she enjoys adventure travel and anything that gets the heart racing, whether it's hiking, running, or getting lost in a good book.

Author photo © EJimmyD

selected titles from sparkpress

SparkPress is an independent boutique publisher delivering high-quality, entertaining, and engaging content that enhances readers' lives, with a special focus on female-driven work. www.gosparkpress.com

Caley Cross and the Hadeon Drop, J. S. Rosen, $16.95, 978-1-68463-053-0. When thirteen-year-old Caley Cross, an orphan with a dark power, is guided by a jumpsuit-wearing mole into another world—Erinath—she finds a place deeply rooted in nature where the people have animal-like powers and she is a Crown Princess—but she soon learns that the most powerful evil being in *any* world is waiting for her there.

Eye of Zeus: Legends of Olympus Book 1, Alane Adams. $12.95, 978-1-68463-028-8. Finding out she's the daughter of Zeus is not what a foster kid like Phoebe Katz expected to hear from a talking statue of Athena. But when her beloved social worker is kidnapped, Phoebe and her two friends must travel back to ancient Greece and rescue him before she accidentally destroys Olympus.

The Medusa Quest: The Legends of Olympus, Book 2, Alane Adams, $12.95, 978-1-68463-075-2. Phoebe Katz is back on a new mission to save Olympus—this time to undo the fallout from her last visit, which changed the outcomes of several important myths, including the trials of Hercules and her brother Perseus's quest to slay Medusa. Can Phoebe collect the items she needs to stop Olympus from crumbling?

The Goddess Twins: A Novel, Yodassa Williams. $16.95, 978-1-68463-032-5. Days before their eighteenth birthday, Arden and Aurora's mother goes missing and they discover they belong to a family of Caribbean deities. Can these goddess twins uncover their evil grandfather's plot in time to save their mother, themselves, and the free world?

Above the Star: The 8th Island Trilogy, Book 1, Alexis Chute. $16.95, 978-1-943006-56-4. *Above the Star* is an epic fantasy adventure experienced through the eyes of three unlikely heroes transported to a new world: senior citizen Archie; his daughter-in-law, Tessa; and his fourteen-year-old granddaughter, Ella. In this otherworldly realm, all interests are at war, all love is unrequited, and everyone is left to unravel the truth of who they really are.

Below the Moon: The 8th Island Trilogy, Book 2, Alexis Marie Chute. $16.95, 978-1-68463-004-2. Cancer has left Ella mute, but not powerless. When she finds herself in a parallel dimension, she must paint to communicate, fight alongside fearsome warrior-creatures, and—along with her mom, Tessa, and grandpa Archie—overcome the Wellsley family's past in order to ensure a future for everyone.

acknowledgments

First and foremost, thank you, reader, for picking up this book. I hope you enjoyed getting to know Alice as much as I enjoyed bringing her to life. The opportunity to share her journey with you is a gift I will forever cherish, so thank you, again, from the bottom of my heart!

Writing can be a solitary endeavor, but without the support of my family and friends, it would be impossible. To my first draft readers, Tina Abrahamson, Tara Botwick, Ethan Duff, Lauralyn Duff, Melissa Gabriel, Sara Giller, Jillian Karner, Amanda Kost, Mandy O'Connell, Melissa Powers-Depauw, and Suzannah Silva: You were handed a whopping 160,000-word manuscript, and I cannot express how thankful I am for your time, input, and encouragement.

I'm equally thankful to those of you who came on board at drafts two, three, four, and beyond. To Dawn Cook, Turney Duff, Janet Fitzgerald, Adelaide Hogan, Anna Belle Holly, Lauren Kondi, Paige Patterson-Duff, Keith and Brooke Savitz, Dan and Darci Storms, Michele Stocknoff, Jocelyn Strutt, Leona Thacker, Andrew Walker, Alida Wittevrongel, and Dawn Wyllie: Thank you for indulging me. Your participation and support kept me going!

Additional thanks to Patrick and Nikl Burke, Lola Duff, Vivian Fong, Angela Terry, Jennifer and Julia Wanner, and my Golden Girls, for your much-needed advice and insight. High fives and hugs all around!

While I'm grateful to so many people for their friendship and unwavering support, I'd like to give a special shout-out to those individuals who helped get me over the finish line.

To Turney Duff, who provided one heck of an amazing blurb. Thank you for your support. I'm so grateful to have you in my corner!

To Andrew Walker, who encouraged me to write long before I knew I was a writer. It took me a while, but I finally listened. Thank you for being that pushy voice in my head that never quite went away.

To Krissa Lagos, for your keen eye and editing superpowers. You took my manuscript to the next level. Thank you for your expert guidance. I feel lucky to have worked with you!

To Brooke Warner, Shannon Green, and the team at SparkPress: Thank you for your professionalism, expertise, industry knowledge, and one stunning cover. I've known I was in good hands from the start, and I cannot imagine a better home for *The Last Huntress*. Thank you for helping me bring this story to life!

And finally, to my supportive, patient, kind, loving, talented, charismatic, and all-around amazing husband: Ethan, you are my rock. There's no way I could have done this without you. Thank you for believing in me even when I didn't (and sometimes still don't). Like Colin is to Alice, you are my reason.